War of Silence

By Eren Viau

I would like to thank everyone who is reading this book. Xai's story is means more than the world to me. When I say this story is more than 20 years in the making I do mean it. Xai is my original imaginary friend and her story is what got into creative writing.

I would also like to thank my team who have been with me the entire time:

Gg, Michelle, Sami, and Autumn.

My parents who have always supported my crazy dreams:

Diana, Elric, Tracy, and Tracy

And finally the person who helped create part of the world and some of the characters:

Ashley (who created Lux and Jackdaw)

Thank every one of you.

Trigger Warning:

Before reading War of Silence please be wary that this book contains:

~ Profanity

~ Violent language

~ Past suicide attempts

~ Enslavement of people

~Genocide

~Violence against Women and Children

~Bigotry and Racism

Please keep this in mind while reading this is a work of fiction, please read at your own pace and discretion.

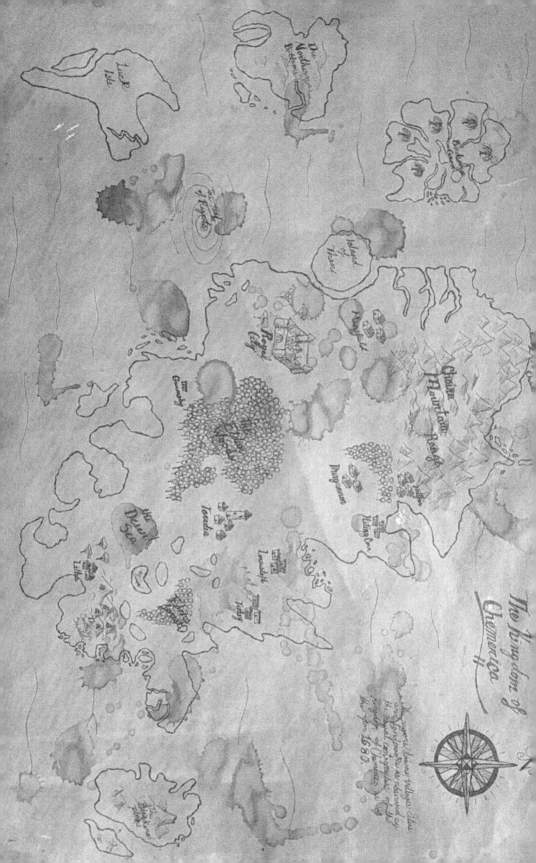

Table of Contents

In the ancient texts, history states three original clans were made by the decree of the gods from which all other races were born. Each of these original clans stood as a symbol of characteristics the gods cherished. The vampires were known for their strength and courage in their long lives, letting nothing deter them from whatever path they chose. The daemons stood for loyalty and honesty, once gaining a daemon's trust they would lay down their lives for those they cared for. Last was the humans, the shortest living of the original races, who were respected for their compassion and determination. Eventually, the other races branched off of them, either by mixing or giving up the night for the sun and mutating. Centuries later the Council of the Originals was formed and with the help of a generous King and Queen the continent was at peace, each of the races and clans coexisting. The races are each broken down by their characteristics and the gods who made them, the earth-bound Terra races, the moon-bound Lunar races, and the sun-bound Solar races. These were only titles that corresponded with where and when the races were the most powerful. But this was all ancient history, at least the coexisting peacefully part.

Chapter One: The Mage

"Get her, she is one of those things." The large man in armor ran down the crowded path in the market. "The one is the green cloak. She is a Lunar!" He shouted as loud as he could. The woman dancing through the crowd with a drawn hood was not concerned with the guard plowing through the people behind her, chasing her with purpose. When the crowd tapered off she stopped abruptly and spun around making the man trip over himself and collide with the dirt.

"Excuse me sir, as amusing as this chase has been, how do you know you have a reason to pursue me in such a manner?" The woman asked politely. Her purple upturned eyes stared at him cruelly, pupils all but slit. Her thoughts clouded with how easy it was to taunt the town guard.

"Just look at you, you aren't even hiding yourself." The guard growled out lifting himself from the ground. She didn't even flinch at the words considering how often she heard them. She did not hide her heritage. "Your eyes are like a cat's, your hair is two-toned, and you have spots on your skin. I bet if I ripped that hood from your head you would have animal ears instead of the ears or a person." Such rhetoric was common in recent generations, that any of the Lunar races were less than. This poor man was only digging his own metaphoric grave. She had promised not to kill today but the filth from his mouth was going to make it harder. Patience was never a virtue the woman was able to harness, neither was composure.

"Sir I never once hid I was a Lunar but I asked if you had a reason to pursue me. The last I heard it was not a crime to be a Lunar walking in the daylight." The man was not taking the

13

hint of a dangerous aura around the woman, only the innocent act she put on. "Even though it is not a crime I know the type you serve, let me rephrase. how do you know that I do not have a solar companion or handler? Or is someone of Terra descent waiting for me outside the market? I am only running some errands." The woman had to hold back a gag as her stomach turned at the words. The thought of someone trying to tame her was abhorrent, to try and take her freedom and bend her to their will. This was not like the times of old when it was a privilege and a sought-after honor to have someone ask to be a handler of a daemon.

"Then take off your cloak, your top only reaches your ribs so I should be easily able to tell if you have been collared. Show me your mark and you can be on your way." The smirk breaking across the guard's face made the woman's skin crawl. This was becoming less of her heritage and more about her sex. This man was planning on using his position to take advantage if he hadn't been planning that from the beginning.

"Sir I am not comfortable disrobing for you and that is not something you should be asking a lady to do. Once again it is not a crime for a specific race to be walking the market in the daylight. I need not show you anything without a valid reason and your racism is not a valid reason."

"If you would rather I can take you back to the post and make you take it all off to inspect you." The man stepped forward making the woman step back, he was too comfortable with those words, this was not the first woman he had taken advantage of that was no doubt in her mind. She was curious if his type was scared Lunars or any woman he could trick into thinking she had done something wrong.

"Well aren't you a pervert, how many times have you played this trick? How many women have you scared for your pleasure?" The innocent act allowed for a bit of venom without breaking character. "I believe we are done here, Sir." The woman began to talk away slower than she normally would.

"With a mouth like that, I am going to have to bring you in. Disrespecting a guard is at least a night in a cell." He grabbed for the woman and tried to force her to stop and look once more into his bloated and red face. The grip made her stop, not out of strength but out of how uncomfortable the physical touch made her. It took only moments for her to turn around and grab his wrist, using his own pressure points against him to force him to release his grip.

"I think you misheard me, I said we are done here." The innocent act completely dropped. Only a predator stood before the man but his vanity and pure audacity made him think he was still the dangerous creature in the walkway. "Normally I would say you may kiss my tail but you would take that as an actual invitation." Finally, the self-indulgent smirk left his face and was replaced by a frustrated sneer. Walking back from him without taking her eyes off the offensive man was easy enough for someone like her.

"Come here, woman." He lunged again, clunky in his armor making him slower than a normal man. His age and apparently weight are not helping him be as nimble as a normal guard should be. It brought unplanned joy to kick him back to the ground before he could make contact with her skin again. A bubble of laughter escaped her throat only frustrating the man who laid on his back in the dirt once again at her hands. "Damn bitch." He growled trying to get back up much like an overturned turtle.

"How about this fat man, if you can catch me then I will go quietly with you." She said looking down at him in more ways than one.

"Why you...?" He spat as he stood up, trying to lung at her again, only for the woman to dance out of his range.

"Why me? That is a very good question." She laughed, and the part she played completely fell away so that even her attacker could notice. Provoking the man was the easiest of entertainment. She took off down the dirt path, weaving back and forth down alleys and main streets, making sure to keep the guard in view the entire time. The thought of him not knowing what was happening did not sit well in the part of her mind that did not want to see all-day dwellers as complete idiots. Skillfully she went down a maze of alleyways, leading to a dead end in the middle of the town, completely devoid of all other life. By the time the man 'backed' her into the alley, he was dripping in sweat and breathing like a dying boar.

"Got you now bitch." He gasped. The woman almost felt bad for the state of the man physically if not for what she already knew about him.

"You caught me did you?" The man sneered but puffed his chest as if he was proud of himself. That was until he stepped into a laid hole in the ground. "Or have I caught you?" The woman broke out into laughter looking at the struggling man, she almost doubled over in her laughter. Safely out of his reach, she walked out of the alley and back through the labyrinth of alleyways. Only when she made it back to the main road leading back to the market did the man start screaming loud, enough to finish her errands that she actually did need and then go back home. Today was not just about trapping some asshole for her. She had an inkling that others would not feel nearly as much joy in her trap as she did, giggles still randomly coming out of her lips. The well-laid plan had gone off without a hitch and it should be the easiest of escapes into the crowd. Of course, that was when fate decided to take matters into its own hands. The man who had been contained within the ground was not a Royal Guard but the men walking down the main street of the market were. Rearranging her cloak the woman tried to make herself smaller than she was, trying to keep her obvious features hidden.

"Dear lady, could you come here please." One of the guards with the royal symbol on his armor called out to the woman. She had been close to getting into the crowd without being noticed.

"Yes sir?" She kept her head down and was submissive to the new man. Walking over to him carefully trying to seem as dainty as possible. Only moments later did the town guard that needed to be stripped of his armor and publicly shamed come rushing out of the alley mouth, he looked around wildly while talking to a few of the town's guards and a Royal Guard. He was making it obvious that he was looking for the woman that the Royal Guard with her obscured. She knew there was no way that she would be able to act as though it was an accidentally found hole if she was confronted. Maybe they would listen to her about the abuse of power and self-defense if they were not bigots. This situation stunk of fate, how else would this Royal Guard in particular pull her out of the people working around at the market entrance?

"Sorry to stop you but do you know what happened with that town guard who was calling for help in the alleyways?" He asked gently, obviously thinking the woman was scared of him.

"No sir I do not but I know that guard has many enemies in town, he has been taking advantage of the woman in town and trying to assault them. He went into the alley with another cloaked woman. It looked like he had pushed past me to chase her. I am sorry I don't remember her cloak color or anything else." The woman lied smoothly. She began to pray to each of the gods that the gentle guard would believe her and let her go before the pig could make her out. Her actions were without a doubt punishable by the law, with or without bigotry, even without a good cause she at minimum had assaulted a town guard with physical violence. Within the moment the fat guard was looking around the Royal Guards' side, not being as tall as the man, that was the moment she knew she was caught.

"There you are, you Lunar bitch." He spat pushing the other guard out of the way to grab the front of the woman's cloak. "Did you think you would get away with trapping me in that hole?" There was no point for the woman to run and she knew it. She was on her way to her own one-person cell, though in this town it would be easy enough to get out of, she would be on her way home by nightfall. Deciding to not go silently to the woman she stood up tall looking over the town guard with her cold purple eyes, the change made the Royal Guard flinch back.

"I would release me before you lose that hand, pervert. But if I am to be taken away for you falling into a hole in an alley because you were chasing me to try to assault me then I will make sure I am put in a cage for a real reason." The woman hissed. "I would watch yourself next time you decide to try to take advantage of another woman in this town, I am not the only daemon willing to protect the people here." The Royal Guard sighed pulling the town guard off her.

"I am sorry ma'am but you will have to come with us. Though we will be taking care of this man as well." He said looking sympathetic to the woman. He passed the stunned town guard to the Royal Guard with him but pulled out his shackles. "Unfortunately he is charging you with assault. We will plead you are released for protecting the town's women, with you being of daemonic descent it should help you."

"As long as he is getting removed for the harm he has caused." He nodded and gestured for the woman to turn. "You are much nicer than most of these small-town guards, less of a bigot as well. It is a definite change." The man grabbed the chains connecting the shackles cautiously pulling them to make sure they were secure. "I know the drill I will follow you to the cell. I will be much more favorable as long as you do not put your hands on me." She smirked as the no longer guard seemed surprised as he got shackled with more force than I did. There had been about a fifty percent chance of the woman's plans ending with her in a cell and she knew that, though she had hoped it would end with her slipping out, damn Royal Guards. Fang had warned the woman that the Royal Guard had been patrolling through the towns surrounding the Royal City, they would be livid when they realized that the Royal Guard caught up with the woman on such an easy trip into town. She was already working on escape plans from the local cells, it would be easy enough for a full-blooded daemon like herself. Those plans were put on hold when she realized that they were not putting her in a cell but a barred carriage, they had come looking for some sort of dangerous criminal. Three hours in the mobile cage later and she was dragged out to see the bottom of the castle, the jail where they keep the most wanted criminals, and dangerous vampires and daemons. The entrance to the jail was underneath the southern castle wall, right above the sheer cliff facing down to beautiful fields that would make an easy escape if she knew for a fact the jail wasn't enchanted against the strongest of races. One of the guards at the door roughly pulled the woman through the door earning a hiss as she stumbled, her boots catching the door lip.

"Don't be so rough, can't you see I am fragile?" She spat.

"Shut up, you have no power in these walls, Lunar." One of the guards snapped, shoving her forward. She almost tripped again but was able to regain her footing quickly with her natural grace.

"That was rude, I am a lady. Where is the guard from earlier? He didn't confuse fear for anger and try to mask it with a show of power." She smirked, the growl behind proving she hit him in the ego. She wasn't surprised when she got pushed again down a hallway lined with thick stone cells. They brought her to the far back of the jail, the magic in the air made her shiver as they reached the maximum security area, the area they kept the Lunars they were concerned about. The spells were set into the stones to drain both physical and magic abilities, it left anyone as weak as a fatigued human. The feeling of being so disconnected from her power or more importantly her shifted form was disconcerting and unbalancing. Eventually, they pushed her into a cell, letting her hit the back wall of the stone box, but there was a small mercy of them removing her shackles since the spells made her fairly harmless. "Bye-bye boys try not to miss little old me too much." She cooed as the men stepped from the cell, slamming the iron door shut. She watched them walk away without another word leaving her in silence, the only sounds being the bugs that start to sing below in the fields when dusk hits in the spring that she could hear through the singular small window that let in the fresh air. At least the Royalty wasn't cruel enough to leave their captives in stagnant air. A snicker came through the air, from the cell next door, finding amusement in the sarcasm that came from their new neighbor. Looking over the daemon noticed the barred window into the cell next door, there sat an older woman, runes tattooed into her skin, over her face, and down into what was covered by ratty cloth. The runes covering her face gave away her specialty, she was a time mage, one of a few born every few centuries. Looking up in the dimming light the woman had eyes like the night sky, no white just black from corner to corner, it was like looking into the void itself. The old woman beckoned the daemoness closer to the iron bars separating them.

"You are the one child." She spoke without hesitation.

"I am what?" The daemoness asked, her eyes wide in concern. When a time mage calls on you it is the voice of fate calling for you.

"You are the one to restore what is right. You can start the restoration of the original clans. Listen to me well child, you are the key to the start, and your partner holds the gateway. You need one pure-blooded human and one pure-blooded vampire by your side with the same destiny to help you but you are the one. You are the savior of this world child. Only you can call the hero, the weapon to save us all back to our world. You have to call for the weapon of the gods. You will find your human to the south, heated by the desert, and your vampire to the north, frozen in the mountains. You must hurry, child, your destiny is calling." With those words, the old woman crumbled into dust and blew through her own window. A sigh left the woman as she looked around, not knowing if the mage was dead or not but she was gone. A time mage never lies, they only help those who need a push forward on fate. Fang was never going to believe their accomplice, but their lives were only going to get more interesting than roughing up corrupt town guards and saving Lunars where they could. A jailbreak was in order and the time mage said she had to hurry so there had to be a way before the night was over. The sun was barely over the horizon so there was time. As the sun sank below the horizon and the moon began to rise the woman's skin began feeling too tight. Being separated from any part of her other form was excruciating, even her ears were that of a human instead of a feline, and the lack of a tail made her equilibrium non-existent. She had grown up having to be seen like this and she had sworn to herself as she escaped her gilded cage to not let herself stay disconnected too long. Her accomplice was probably worried themselves sick at this point. She watched the moon get higher in the sky as she played each and every lecture she would gain upon her return. The feeling of the moonlight on her skin made her calmer, even with the feeling of wrongness in her body the nearly full moon was like a sedative on the pain. Her contemplative staring into the night sky did not mask the sound of two sets of distinct footsteps walking down the hallway of cells.

"The guards were right brother, she is breathtaking. She is completely awe-inspiring, look at her coloring, her stature." She looked away from the window and into the poorly lit corridor. The two men were younger than her, which was easy enough to tell by their mannerisms, they must not live too hard of lives with that kind of tone standing next to someone like herself. Other than that they were wrapped completely in cloaks, their hoods pulled as far down as they could to obscure their faces from her. From their movement, it appeared the smaller one was the one who had spoken in such a light cheerful voice. If not for his size his voice alone would have made her think he was a child. It reminded her of a child's voice of the past, one from long-ago memories.

"Daemoness, what is your name?" The larger man stepped forward, bringing more attention to himself. His voice is deep and familiar as well. It was like it was pulling her into memories that no longer existed for her.

"That depends boy, are you going to tell me who in the tail you are?" She replied with an arched eyebrow. She no longer had the patience to deal with self-absorbed men today, she was tired and in pain. Instead of any ounce of fear or frustration at her tone both men laughed, one deep and the other like a child's.

"She is just like her brother." The child-like one spoke with audible glee. "It must be her; listen to her voice, her tone, her sass. It has to be her." He beamed like he had discovered his long-lost toy, something or someone he had looked for a lifetime to find. The woman was incredibly confused at what his musings had to do with her. Neither seemed to be willing to explain whatever they were talking about.

"Now it is even fairer, you are talking about me like I am a creature on display. Who are you?" She sighed, leaning against the far wall, arms crossed as she eyed them with boredom.

"Fair point as always daemoness, we forgot our manners. We are two of the three Princes of Chemerica. Now you are?" These men were clever, she would have to give them that. The woman had not seen the Princes since she was a child, it had been seventeen years since she had run from the Royal City. She wished they would take their cloaks so she could see them. If they were the Princes or even from the castle it would explain why they sounded familiar even though it had been almost two decades

"If you are the Princes you should know my name then." She hissed, not trusting her voice.

"Xai, one of the last pure-blooded daemons in the world. The definition of freedom and wild spirit." The taller one whispered.

"And I would like to keep my freedom if you don't mind. Were you looking for me? Was that why I was brought here for a simple fight with a town guard in a town three hours away from here? Why the Royal Guard was sniffing around bringing out the mobile cell?"

"You are Xai." The smaller one beamed. "I told you to look for someone with her coloring." It was strange to think that these were two of the set of three she had known as children. "What subspecies are you?"

"If you are two of three you should know that, or am I so forgettable? It was long enough but not a full life that I have been free."

"She is a feline, white variant of a leopard." The large one spoke with fake fondness.

"I missed your hair, it's as beautiful as I remember." The shorter one breathed. It was always a comment around the palace when she was younger, her hair was the topic of envy. It grew as black as volcanic glass down to her chin then it became as stark white as the snow she prefers to run through.

"I would say thank you but I do not wish for the praises of you or your people, solar. They are meaningless words." she sighed leaning back towards the window. Years of distance did not remove the pain of deep betrayal.

"Brother." The larger man sighed. "Let us leave, for now, she is here with us again and does not wish for our company any longer this evening." She could hear one of them, the smaller by the gait, walk away from the cell. The larger was waiting until he was out of earshot for whatever he wished to discuss. "Xai, I have a question or two for you if you will hear me out."

"You have no right to call my name Princeling." She hissed, not taking her eyes off the moon through her window.

"What do you have against us Xai?" That got a reaction from the woman, more violent than the Prince was expecting. She spun on a point and was suddenly at the barred door, she knew better than to reach out for him but her teeth were bared in a warning.

"You are either incredibly stupid or incredibly brave to ask me such a foolish question boy." She growled with as much venom as she could. "Your kind have stolen our land, our culture, our families. Your people sell mine into slavery like livestock and treat Lunars who are your ancestors like dirt beneath them. You and your brothers personally betrayed me on top of that." Her voice was low and as cold as ice as she forced the words out. "Did you need any more clarification, Your Highness?" She made the title sound like an insult.

"What did we do to betray you? Why do you hate the Royal family so much?" Though for him it was actual confusion for her it was the last straw.

"Get out of my sight." She hissed. "I would rather be executed than continue this conversation or any conversation with you."

"Xai, I can only apologize so much for people outside the city. I am sorry my people are ignorant assholes. But you have no reason to take it out on my brother and me. We never did anything to betray you.?" He turned and walked out with a calm step, seemingly unbothered by her words. The daemoness on the other hand was fuming. They had all betrayed her and they couldn't have the decency to remember. Now that she knew they were aware of her presence she had to escape as soon as she possibly could, she knew it would be a fight without her strength. She walked back and focused out the window to actively plan when she saw a figure in the field below. The hooded figure was just standing there below her, they seemed to glow in the moonlight. After a moment they made a movement, a wave, clear enough indicating to move backward to anyone watching. Once she moved back to the door in confusion the entire wall gave way to her cell, and the cells around her were all empty cells. Once the dust and rubble cleared she walked towards the new hole noticing the stone debris making a path to the safety of the field below and the forest beyond. Her powers rushing back to her with the spell disturbed was almost enough to bring her to her knees as she stood on the edge of freedom. She was cautious about her escape but not enough to look at a gift like that and decline. By the time she made it to the field, the figure had vanished completely, with no sign of who they were or their ever being in the field below the castle. There was also a lack of investigation into the falling wall and the one escaping prisoner but the daemoness was not going to see when that would start so using the powers the gods gave her she ran, ran into the woods, she ran through the night with only her thoughts to keep her company. Too much had happened in only a few short hours, the time mage gave her prophecy, how was a self-made orphan supposed to save the people? Restore the original order? She was just one person, one daemon who could barely protect people in a town she was passing by. But that was the drawback to the daemon clan wasn't it, she thought, so much physical power but the inability to deny helping. It was in their blood, to protect those who can not protect themselves. Thinking of her people cowering, starving, and dying was enough to make her know she would have to at least try. She knew no real king would let this happen, especially at the voices of the Council. But for the damage done, he would have to be removed, either peacefully or by force. The time mage said this would be a prophecy filled by those of the original purebloods and here she stood one of the last pureblood daemons in the world. Even if she was not the one sent on the mission she would be involved with the prophecy at some point. Then there was the visit from the Princes that used to be hers. How did they play into this, would they truly stand in her way? They used to love the Lunar races, would they stand idly

26

by if their father was killing her kind outside the walls? Did they even know? Or did they grow to be naive and unobservant? It had been too long for her to know for certain. Her thoughts were still a mess when she sniffed out the clearing she had been sharing for the last few weeks.

"You got caught didn't you?" A resigned voice sighed as Xai broke through the treeline at the same time as the moon dipped towards the horizon. She turned to see the other daemoness sitting on a stump. Her eyes glowed gold in the dimming night light like all other wolves. In the daytime, her eyes were like liquid silver but they always glowed golden in the reflecting light. They were the kind of eyes that could see through anyone, including her best friend who had been missing since the afternoon.

"That depends, Fang my dear," Xai smirked, walking closer to the other daemon. With the grace of an overtired toddler, the feline dropped to lay in the grass, letting her hood finally fall back from where it had been pinned to hide her pointed ears.

"Depends on what Spot?" She sighed again watching her counterpart.

"It depends on your definition of being caught." The feline smirked, closing her eyes. She was guessing which lecture she would get tonight.

"Xai, that is not funny. You are not a child anymore. What if you couldn't escape?" The wolf, Lux, was always the more cautious of the two of them. Maybe it was the fact she was almost two years older than the feline and that mattered when she had found the dual-haired woman when they were kids, now it went from being a mother hen to being the overly worried companion.

"Before you get further into this lecture listen. I didn't break myself out, someone else did." She spoke quietly. "And that wasn't the only thing weird about today." And so she talked, talked until the sun came up. She told her friend everything from the town to the prophecy. Even seeing the Princes was mentioned.

"Did you not grow up around the castle before you ran? You never explained what happened to make you hate them so much."

"We were one of the only pureblood families left. The royal family used us as lap pets to keep in cages instead of the warriors that we are. I refuse to live in captivity especially when I have seen the tragedy that is beyond the walls.

"But what if they had handlers and were happy? You were only eleven when you ran?" Her voice held the same dreamy quality it always did when the canine talked about handlers, it was the one romanticized idea she dreamed about.

"If they were happy my mother would not have helped me escape all those years ago Lux. She didn't want me to live like that as much as I did not want to live like that."

"You are right, you would never be able to live like that. You are one to live freely, sleep under the stars, to experience the front line of battle. If you were to ever have a handler they would have to be the same; the free, stubborn, fierce, loyal, thickheaded, protective, and untameable spirit that you have Xai.

"I never want a handler, but if you had one they would have to be; loyal, level-headed, energetic, compassionate, and humorous. They would also need to be strong-willed to match you."

28

"Thank you, Xai. And I know how you feel about handlers and I understand your mother's sacrifice. But I just don't understand. Now, do you think we should start your prophecy later today? I know we don't necessarily need sleep but we do need to get ready to take a real adventure."

"We? Are you joining me?"

"Of course I am. I am not letting you do this without me, otherwise, you would get yourself arrested and not get anything done. So where are we going first?" The wolf smirked knowing she had won a fight before it started.

"The old mage said the vampire is up north and the human is south, so we should go north first before we get snowed out for the season. The vampire colony I know of is up near the peak of Mount Chaira."

"So northeast from where we are now?"

"In simple terms, yes."

"And what about after spot?"

"The old mage turned into dust before giving clear directions so I have no idea where the human villages in the south are."

"What a convenient time to die. Either way, let us get some rest and we can go to town later today and out to the north in the morning." She said watching her counterpart yawn. Both women curled together in the grass, each knowing their lives would never be the same.

Chapter Two: Jackdaw and Truen

"Xai, come on and move, we have to go." A man's voice roared, his familiar voice laced with panic. He screamed for her to open her eyes, sounding more frantic as the seconds drew on. When she opened her eyes she realized she and the dark figure crouched next to her were surrounded by walls of fire. "Come on Xai, I am not leaving you here. I am not going to leave you to die. You have to get up please, I am begging you." The voice was so familiar to her and so close to tears but she could not see who the shadow person was. She tried to get up as he instructed but as she did a sharp pain went through her side, and she fell back to the ground. Looking down to her own horror she saw she was completely split open from shoulder to hip, bleeding out profusely.

"I can't, I can't get up. Just leave me and go, save yourself. Please just leave me here." She cried out, she could not let him risk himself, whoever he was. Her eyes burned with smoke and tears but the shadow man would not leave her. "Go save yourself." She pleaded again.

"No, I will not leave you, understand me Xai I will never leave you behind." With that, the man picked her up from the ground as gently as possible. The pain ripped through her as he adjusted her in his arms and she screamed in agony. He was strong enough to carry her with ease which was lucky for her and her injuries. As fast as he possibly could he ran through the ring of fire that surrounded them. She could not believe the shadow would run through the inferno with her securely in his arms, she couldn't even feel the intensity of her wounds.

"Why wouldn't you leave me?" She demanded through gritted teeth once he stopped running, she was hoping they made it to safety if he was no longer at full sprint. He set her

30

carefully on the ground to look once more at her wound as she spoke at him, she couldn't even tell if he was listening to her at this point. "Why do you always insist on being with me? Saving me? Protecting me? I am a daemon, your daemon. I am disposable in this relationship. Is it for the extended life I can provide you? Is it for the power that comes with being a handler? Just tell me please because you are making no sense."

"Xai you should know me better than that by now." The shadow sighed, his voice resigned. "It has never been about the power, the near immortality, or anything else that people get from becoming a handler. It never has and it never will be any of those reasons Xai. It has always been more important than that." He caressed her face with one hand as he tried applying pressure with the other. Her blood was a highlight on his shadowy body.

"Then why?"

"Because I love you Xai, always have and always will."

She woke up in complete shock, she had never had a dream like that before that she could remember. It was so clear and vivid, that she even felt the pain from her wound so distinctly that she had to look down to see if there was blood. Laying back down into the grass her thoughts were racing. Who was the shadow man? What in the tail was that dream even about? Love and handlers were two things she did not believe in, she knew of their existence and that both could do a person good or destroy them entirely, she had seen it, but not ideals that were possible in her own life. But that dream seemed almost premonition-like and that was something she could not ignore after the run-in with the time mage the day before. By the look of the sun absent from the sky, hours had passed since they had curled up, and the moon itself was high

31

in the sky. They needed the rest and she knew that but it put her on edge. Lux was still sleeping peacefully next to her, fully shifted into her lupin form, whatever she was dreaming about was putting a smile on her face. There was a part of the feline who was jealous of her companion for being so free in her shifting. Xai had grown up to use her shifted form only when necessary so the daemons of the castle didn't take up too much room. A shifted daemon was a large creature, as a child Xai alone who was not the largest daemon came up to her grown father's waist in shift, now she could easily reach a grown man's chest at her shoulder, and Lux herself was quite a bit larger than her feline counterpart.

Yet here she was sleeping so peacefully. Xai hated to wake her companion but she knew they had to leave. They had to gather supplies for the journey ahead and get out of the range where the castle was looking for her. Not that the shops would be open until a little after sunrise but she could not sleep any longer. Xai looked down at the sleeping form beside her and knew that once the sun rose and they went into town Lux would have to be the speaking face of the duo. The purple eyes alone were a clear sign of her pure blood, and recently that was dangerous for herself and those around her. It was a strange concept: the markers of the purebloods being the eyes. A pure-blooded vampire had eyes like rubies, a bright and spellbinding red, unlike the browns or yellows of all vampires born and turned. Pure-blooded humans got an emerald green eyeshade that rivaled a clearing in the spring. The daemons got an otherworldly amethyst that became the color of loyalty. Deciding that her compilations on the unfairness of those of pure blood could not hide their distinction Xai decided to wander, she had seen a rock formation only a few yards from their current clearing and decided to sit on the edge. It was close enough to hear what was happening and protect the sleeping daemoness but far enough away not to disturb her sleep with the others' musings.

Sitting alone on the small cliff face in the night air was comforting. The moon being almost full helped as well. That was the other difference she thought, the fact that all the Lunar races drew more power from the moon instead of the sun like the solar races. Such a stupid thing to find superior, especially since the solar races were descendants of the Lunar races as a whole. Xai for the life of her could not wrap her head around the hatred that had been suffocating the Lunar races for the last few generations or where it had even begun. No one could pin down the source of the shift either, no historian or text had answers and Xai had been looking ever since she fled the castle and saw the horrors beyond the walls.

Soft and careful steps caught her attention, approaching from the path instead of the woods. They were cautious and acted as though they did not know if she was dangerous as they approached the stranger in the night. There were two, one strong and one with a limp so caution was needed, anyone could be dangerous this time of night especially while you tried to protect someone. Sound enough their heartbeats were clear enough to hear, coming closer and closer. The daemoness threw up her hood before they could break the treeline.

"A beautiful woman such as yourself should not be alone in the night like this, let alone on a cliff. Someone must be worried about you." A deep familiar male called out into the cool air., causing shivers to run across her skin. There was no way that voice could be here. She left that voice a few hours of a journey away, back in the castle city.

"It is bold of you to assume that I am alone and or that I am incapable of taking care of myself." She spoke calmly, continuing to watch the forest below her.

"It is beautiful here isn't it." The voice of the second male spoke melodically. "The moon should be full soon should it not?"

"In the next few days, it should be full." The first spoke again, his voice grating on her nerves. It had to be them but there was no way they could be here. It made no sense for it to be true and yet without even looking it had to be. The Princes whom she had just seen hours prior were a half days ride away at a minimum.

"You are not wrong about that." She agreed, they were too close to her hidden companion for her to attack them without cause. They stayed silent as the moon dipped below the skyline and the sky changed colors, not in peace but in a truce. By the time the sun started to rise the sound of their heartbeats vanished without the sounds of retreating footsteps. Spinning around she saw they were gone, not even a scent to follow to suggest they had ever actually been there at all. Was it a hallucination? A cry to simpler times when she knew those heartbeats and steps with an accuracy that often impressed those around her. A sense of emptiness filled her like it hadn't in years, a hole inside her she tried to bury deep where the promises of the past lay broken and sharp even a lifetime later. Standing from her search she shook her head, clearing those thoughts that begged to drag her down from her mind. Slowly she walked back to the clearing to see her lupine awake and alert.

"Hey Spot, you're up early." Lux stretched her large body, her tongue hanging from the side of her mouth. The inherent magic in daemon blood allows her thoughts to be heard aloud within the shifted form. A gift from the gods themselves to the daemons so we could communicate with those around us no matter the form we have to take.

34

"I couldn't sleep, I went to the cliffside." She replied with a sigh.

"How much sleep have you been getting lately Xai?" Her voice filled with concern.

"A few hours a night, I get enough Fang don't worry." This was not the first time Lux had expressed her concern about the feline's ability to take care of herself above the minimum needed for survival. "I am fine, but now that you are awake we need to get into town and get some supplies so we can get moving. I know we require rations to restock our first aid pouches. If we are going to get hunted we need to be prepared.

"Why won't you talk to me about the things that bother you?" She asked with frustration.

"There is nothing to talk about. I have only ever slept a few hours at a time, you know this. You also know it is not wise to ignore the prophecy of a time mage, that is a death sentence and I would rather get going knowing the castle is hunting me personally."

"Something happened, I know you are leaving something out Xai, you are poised as if there is a threat and you were not like that when we went to sleep. Something happened while I was asleep."

"Lux please drop it and get ready, I want to leave in five. If you are not ready I will leave you here and go alone." She did not want to talk about whatever happened this morning, she didn't even know if it was real or a figment of her imagination. Seeing the Princes and being at the castle made memories resurface and now nothing was certain. Those were the Prince's voices on the cliff, that was Daw's limp. She had thought she left all this behind her as a child and used these years to heal from the betrayal that threatened to kill her back then. Gathering all their belongings kept her body busy as Lux shifted and put her clothing back on. Her open tunic and her pants were on by the time Xai had put their packs in the center of the clearing. Her timber-patterned hair was up in her signature ponytail and her boots ready to be laced.

"Are you ready to talk to me?" She asked again without looking up with her pale eyes.

"Are you ready to leave?" The other responded as she pulled her pack on expectantly.

"Fine but I will get answers out of you eventually. Someone needs to know what is going on in that trap of a mind of yours."

"Never again if I can help it. Let us make this an in-and-out type of endeavor." The short journey into the town was not in silence as Lux continued to complain that Xai refused to let anyone in further than Lux herself was. Xai never answered, only walking in silence and smirking every time her companion began to think of new creative complaints and insults about her inability to share her thoughts and fears with anyone. She cursed a past she barely had an idea of that scared her friend into silence and mistrust of those who were living.

"I will get the food and the first aid, the stalls are near each other. I know you have gotten some new blades commissioned, go check on those and I will meet you in the town center in a bit." Lux sighed, obviously feeling better after her rants, as they breached the town limits. Shaking her head with a smile, Xai walked off towards the blacksmith from whom she was supposed to pick up her commission from yesterday. Xai had been looking forward to her new blades for days, a set of silver blades perfectly balanced for throwing and a set of steel and iron curved daggers. They were going to be engraved with runes to allow her to not lose them in a fight or damage the blades as long as she took care of them. It had been a present to herself for living another year, not that Lux knew that she had left her birthday in the castle with her past no matter how those who found her tried over the years to pry the information out of her and celebrate the life she ran from. Eventually, they gave up but Xai would get herself something like she would have for the one person in the world she should have been able to celebrate with.

"How in the blood-soaked hell are you here still?" shouted an incredibly drunken voice, the entire curse being a slurred mess. Turning to where the voice came from only made her come face to face with the red-faced stumbling form of the disgraced town guard from the day before.

"I could ask the same question of you but I would like to know how you can be so incredibly tankard this early in the morning. Dear gods man, have you no self-restraint." She hissed, trying not to gag as his stretch became overwhelming as he staggered across the cobblestone street. "I am not even surprised you were released by your companions but have you not stopped drinking since?" The man lunged, grabbing her wrist with his sticky hands. His touch made her skin crawl but his drunken strength was too much for her to get away from without causing a scene. "Let me go before I break every bone in your arm. I was released by the Royal guard and you have no reason to lay your hands on me. You did not yesterday and you most certainly have no right today." She wrenched her arm from his grip causing him to lose his balance, falling to his ass on the street. Using the distraction she strode quickly into the blacksmith's shop a few buildings further down. Thinking she was safe she let out a sigh of relief causing the blacksmith to raise an eyebrow.

"You okay girl?" his voice was impossibly low.

"I am fine, just having an issue with a drunkard outside is all. How did my order come out?" She changed topics quickly. The man let it drop and walked back behind his counter pulling out the leather he had the blades folded into for safekeeping. They were absolutely beautiful and perfectly balanced and the details engraved were stunning. "Thank you, these are perfect." She smiled again putting the daggers on the belt looped around her waist, the knives slid perfectly into the pouch nestled on her thigh above her pants.

"Of course, and be careful out there. Come back if that drunkard keeps harassing you." He nodded before going back to the fire behind the counter. She knew she wouldn't but the offer for protection was sweet, not many would offer protection to a daemon willingly when they were the symbol of protection. Quickly and silently she left the warm building and back into the fresh air of the market outskirts. She was barely a step away from the door when hands reached for her again, this time she was able to dodge the strong smell of alcohol and rot since it had been waiting and stewing by the blacksmith's door warning her the guard was still prowling around.

"Come on girl, I think we should get to know each other. If you come with me silently I can drop yesterday's charges against you." He slurred, his anger mellowed into an even more disgusting lust.

"Not even if you were the last living creature on this planet. What makes you think trying to assault someone and trying to throw your nonexistent power around would make any woman want you? You do not scare me, and I will not bend to your wishes. If you make another attempt to touch me I will make good on my earlier words except I may not break your arm but your jaw." The coldness of her voice seemed to be enough to sober the man back up a bit and back into the rage of being humiliated and rejected. His power had no sway on her and he hated it.

"Then I will watch you burn myself." At least he didn't consider trying to force her to bind to him, she thought as she maneuvered out of his path again by dancing into a side street.

"Is there a problem here sir?" A voice called from the main street. Another man stood there as stiff as a board. A few others with hoods drawn stood behind him but there were no markers of who they were on their clothing.

"This Lunar is refusing to come with me." The guard huffed at them.

"Then please sir let us handle this. We will give her the public discipline she deserves and then hand her back to you." Deserves, she thought, how could she deserve anything like that from what the guard said?

"And who are you?" The drunkard asked.

"We are part of the Solar Liberation Army. We are on a mission to put all Lunars in their rightful place and make sure nothing threatens solar supremacy." The mouthpiece recited like it was not one of the vilest things the daemoness had ever heard. But there he was standing proud like he was doing the good work of the people.

"Then, by all means, drop her off at the guard tower when you're done. I will take her from there." The drunk nodded at the average-looking blonde man like he was asking to borrow a tool. The moment the guard walked away the walking god complex turned his black eyes to me, and a wall of fire spread around us cutting off the outside from whatever was about to happen. It was to stop her from running or someone else trying to help her, to cut her off from any way of escape.

Clever tactic though it did give away a spellcaster or an enslaved mage within thor group of four.

"So much fanfare for one Lunar? I am starting to think this town believes I am special." She sighed removing her cloak and tossing it to the ground behind her so it would not get in the way of the inevitable. As soon as the fabric touched the stone though it was reduced to ash. "Neat trick. Though now you owe me a new cloak." Sighing again she looked up at the man who was taking himself far too seriously. He was stretching and rolling his shoulders as if trying to intimidate the daemoness who could not care in the slightest. This man had no chance of winning no matter his bloodline, even all at once Xai had no doubt she could walk away from this fight even if it would be difficult on her own.

"You won't live to buy another daemon." He spits. "That I can promise you."

"You have a lot of confidence in yourself for a man who has terrible form. I could knock you over easily if this was a training spar. My money is not on you winning magic users or not on your side. But if you would like to dance with me you can." She sighed again remembering the days learning to spar with the Royal Knights, her teacher would have an aneurysm with her challengers' form.

"Yes, young one let's dance shall we?" He nodded lunging forward with such a predictable opening move that the daemoness just stepped out of his way.

"First of all who are you calling young one and second you are being too predictable. Try something like this." She said jabbing him in the ribs quickly causing him to stumble back. "Now just because I am giving you pointers does not mean I will go easy on you. Though you need to learn more before challenging someone like me."She sighed, not expecting to give

40

lessons today. "The real challenge will be once I pull out my claws, let us see if you can dodge them." The man laughed, obviously losing any fear he had gained with the fairly quick beating he had received. She knew something was wrong, and she quickly found she was unable to shift even her hands, much like in the cells she was cut off from her animalistic side. "A much more interesting trick."

"Not me darling but him back there." He stood pointing to the shortest hooded figure, one would think it was a child. We have a pixie with the ability to nullify any racial ability including shifts."

"I have heard that some pixies are born with that ability. Unfortunately for you a daemon's strength is not magic nor is my training so your exploitation of that child means you can go ahead and kiss my tail."

"You are not going to try to plead your innocence, are you? Or make me think you are more than your bloodline traits." He laughed.

"No, but if I need to be crude for you to understand me, how about 'cram it with walnuts ugly', get out of my way." She retorted, losing the little bit of patience she had. This was taking far too long and Lux was bound to be looking for her by now which would put her in danger as well.

"Cram it with walnuts?" He looked surprised lunging again.

"I try not to cuss in front of children." She said with a shrug. "I do have some morals even though you think I am some sort of monster." Without a second thought, she struck again throwing him off balance much as she did before.

"I would back away from her." Spoke in a voice with so much venom it sounded lethal. Xai and the man looked up to see a blade to the throat of one of the hooded figures, the others on the ground already. Xai would have been impressed if the new voice wasn't the same as the one earlier that very morning. His hood was up but the hunter emblem on his sleeve was clear as day.

"Step away from them, bounty hunter." The blonde screamed.

"Then step away from here and have the firewall drop." He spoke calmly and with a voice that promised death if his orders were not followed.

"You are a traitor to your people." The blonde shouted as the fire receded. The moment the flames were gone the hooded figure slammed the hilt of his dagger into the other's temple making them drop like a corpse to the ground.

"My turn." Xai huffed under her breath, she made quick work of the blonde who had his back turned to her in shock at the other's actions. "Are you expecting me to thank you for your assistance?"

"Not really, I know better." He smirked, taking the hooded cloak with unneeded dramatics. "Just so you know I am not an actual bounty hunter." The man stood tall beside her with a grin on his face. His iridescent hair was back in a braid, his warm brown eyes full of amusement, his entire being a slap in the face. He looked exactly as she thought he would when he was grown.

"Why are you here?" She hissed.

"No need for that dear heart, we have much to discuss but here is not where we talk. My brother should be collecting your partner."

"You leave her alone."

"I mean no harm, not now not ever, but do you think they would only go after the one daemoness in town?" She wanted to believe him but she knew she couldn't but she needed to get to Lux and make sure she was safe. "He should bring her to the northern path out of town." The tall man gestured walking quickly in that direction. Though she growled at him she followed knowing that her companion most likely had no knowledge of these men and would follow the youngest out of town. Unfortunately, she was correct in her assumption, and at the edge of town stood a much smaller man with curly blonde hair and the same mischievous green eyes as the man in step with her. Another growl ripped from her throat only to be met with a returned growl from her friend who stood between the blonde and the daemoness. The look of surprise that came across both of their faces made all four of them stop in their tracks.

"Lux it is okay, I know she means me no harm. If they went through the same thing we did she must think she is protecting you. You said she was your sister of course she would be concerned about the strange man next to you after an ambush." Xai was taken aback slightly at the obvious denial of their relationship. She could tell that he had some sort of long-term plan he was already putting into place, as the mastermind, he had always been.

"Lux, why are you protecting him?" The feline asked with ice in her voice. She looked them both up and down looking for damages and changes to either of the two standing before her. Nothing was noticeably out of place but there was a power shift in the air around them, in the way she was standing by him. Helping a daemon in a fight would get protection but something so simple would not make a daemon put themselves between the stranger and s pack bond. Noticing no injuries but some blood her eyes zeroed in on the marking on the forearm of the blonde.

"Xai it is not what you think." The lupin's eyes widened as she saw what her companion saw.

"You have only a moment to explain." Lux could see the walls riding quickly. "And do not lie to me." The daemoness' voice was cold, not angry but as if talking to a stranger she had no care for.

"I took him as my handler while he was protecting me in town. I needed the power and my entire being was calling for him, you have to understand Xai I didn't plan it." She rushed out as fast as she could. "I felt like I had to do it, I felt the call in my blood."

"Were you coerced or was it consensual?" Xai asked calmly if not coldly.

"Consensual. Completely consensual I promise." Lux whined looking down. "Please don't think less of me."

"I do not think less of you, I know how much you have always wanted a handler Lux, but this is goodbye. Take care of yourself, but I can't be around handlers like this, and I can not let them jeopardize the tasks I have been given." Xai sighed, dropping her pack from her back at the raven's feet, and began to walk past them all before any of them could comprehend what she had said. Her heart began to break before she was too far along as she began to hear the screams of her would-be sister but she could no longer travel with her. The bonds daemons make were part of their beings, to sever one as deep

44

as what was between the two daemons was physically excruciating for the both of them. Breaking ties was the only option if the wolf had bound herself to the family that took everything from her, that kept taking everything from her. She would have to make this journey on her own, fight on her own, and live on her own.

"Xai don't do this." His voice made her falter, to stop in her path as it always had. He was out of breath but the raven had caught up to her, he had to have been the first to gain his senses as always. "Please don't do this to yourself or to her."

"I can not trust you or your brother so I can not trust her any longer. She will never be her own self ever again, always her and your brother. Two halves of a whole being." She spoke quietly.

"She doesn't know who we are, she had no idea who Jackdaw was when they bounded. She didn't mean to upset you and as I told you we have not betrayed you. I don't know how to prove that to you Xai."

"Your family, no you have taken everything from me, you stole everything from me Truen."

"I have no idea what you are talking about Xai, I swear to you. But the mage told us it was time and I can not move forward without you, I couldn't then and I won't now. You have always been my future Xai and until we figure out together what happened and you trust me again I will not stop trying. You need us and we need you, everything is relying on this Xai."

"Xai." The smaller blonde walked over with a hardened look in his eyes. "I do not know what happened between you and my brother but this does not have to destroy Lux in the process, you are better than that. Now I know I am the soft-spoken brother and always have been but you need to do what is right for everyone. We are coming with you. You are going to tolerate my brother and me joining you. Hopefully, we can regain your trust but you will not hurt my Lux. Go tell her to join us and we will meet you back here with everything." He was correct, in her memory, she could never remember Jackdaw being cross with anyone or raising his voice. Hissing she complied to walk back to the other daemoness who was crying into the dirt of the path.

"Come on Lux, get your ass off the dirt, we have a mission to get on with." Xai sighed. The wolf looked up in surprise, not expecting the leopard to come back. "We have a lot to talk about with this and it will take me time to trust you with this but we can figure it out. We need each other, at least you and I do. We are sisters and this shouldn't break our bond." Lux scrambled off the ground and slammed her body into the smaller female, arms wrapped around her in a hug that would break a weaker body.

"I promise I will not break your trust." She whined.

"None of us will break her trust." Truen smiled, having walked back to check on the women. "I am not sure which one of us needs her the most."

"That would be you brother." His brother calls back. "Can we hurry, please? I either need to sit or keep moving."

"Fine but if we are traveling together there will be rules." Xai sighed, grabbing the pack she had left with Lux and moving forward again.

"That is fair, we will adhere to your rules as we gain your trust." Jackdaw smiled calmly as Lux walked instinctually over to him.

"Do not touch me is the biggest one, any of you," Xai spoke with agitation, staring daggers at the raven male.

"Well, you just made my brother's life harder." The blonde smirked at his flushed brother, the back of his neck still blushing with the rest of him.

"Why would that be an issue?" Lux asked almost innocently.

"For the same reason, I wish to touch you, dear." He smiled, causing her to cough out a laugh. It was livelier than Xai had seen her companion in years. She knew the draw Lux was feeling, the pull to a specific soul. A daemon's mate called to the daemon with an unfathomable pull. It was something she herself had been suppressing since coming to age knowing exactly where her mate was. A mate she had refused to seek out but not strong enough to refuse. And yet here she would be standing beside him as her sister in all but blood got to enjoy such a connection while she had to focus on keeping everyone alive. And somehow this journey was just getting started.

Chapter Three: Handler

"Please tell me you can sense them trialing us," Truen whispered, he was becoming tenser and tenser as the days progressed. The group that had been trailing them wasn't doing so with any sort of skill that would come from someone who had hunted before. It wasn't hard to tell, even if he was a stranger, that he had never been hunted like an animal before, like a fugitive.

"Yes Truen, I am well aware we are being followed and we have been since we left town days ago. I can hear them." She sighed much more relaxed walking along the path, Lux, and Jackdaw a few steps ahead. "Leave them for now, I want to know why they are following us and they are more likely to let their guard down the longer they assume they are unnoticed."

"How are you so calm with this?" He asked under his breath.

"Do you think this is the first time we have been followed? Lux and I are daemons and until recently neither of us had a handler. We have had multiple people over the years trying to steal us away for various things. Not to mention we are both women as well which makes the chances of someone trying to traffic us even higher and the reasons vaster."

"That is horrifying. How have you lived like this all this time?" He asked in complete horror.

"It was better than what I had with you at the end. I couldn't stay there any longer. The danger out here was worth staying in one piece" Xai shrugged.

"Are we going to talk about that?"

48

"Not if you would like to keep the peace. We will have to eventually, I know we will have to but right now I am trying to deal with the fact your brother is bound to my best friend without dealing with the mess you made." She sighed, the further she could bury the memories the easier it was to ignore the connection that had come back to the forefront of her mind, the connection that was formed many years ago. "Though we will need to make camp soon so not only you and your brother can rest but so I can attempt to get information from our devoted claque."

"I will go with you." He blurted out.

"One Solars shouldn't be out at night." She bit back, tone low enough that the happy couple could not sense the change in the thinly veiled calm atmosphere. "And two I do not trust your kind of help Princeling."

"I have done nothing to make you not trust me Xai, let me help you." He pleaded, trying to reach for her arm. He should have known she wouldn't let him touch her as he had in the past. The daemoness dodged his hand making him grab air as she walked over to their companions. Truen had no understanding of why she treated him this way, he had done nothing wrong to her in their lives, and yet one day she was gone and the daemon he knew was now lost to him. The raven-haired man was silent as they found a spot off the path to set up their meager camp. It was enough to keep the two spellcasters warm in the cooling night air, the daemons themselves were built for this. By the time the sun had set and the moon had risen the world somehow seemed safer, no it was just in the little bubble they found themselves in together.

"Jackdaw, watch your brother, Lux watch the Solars. I am going to go see if our devotees are loose-lipped tonight." The feline stood from her spot on the far side of the fire.

"He will do what he wants Xai, have you not learned that by now." Jackdaw grinned from his place lounging against the large wolf, knowing his words went deeper than they appeared on the surface. "Anyways you two should learn to work together since we will be side by side for a long time to come."

"Lux do something about your pet's mouth." Xai sighed knowing that unfortunately, he was right, Truen would do what he thought was best. Lux just sighed, wrapping herself around the blonde and pretending to be asleep. "I don't have time for this, I will be back in a bit, don't get into trouble while I am away." Xai sighed again in frustration as she turned to leave the group.

"And I will be coming with you. And before you try and protest against it again know that you can not stop me so you will either have to harm me which we both know you won't do, ignore me, or give up and let me help you." His voice had an air of finality. He knew he had won against her.

"If you get in my way you will learn how capable I am of harming you." She hissed, turning her back to him and walking into the shadows of the forest. Luckily the man knew how to walk silently and how to follow the spotted daemoness in the night. The camp of followers had set up not too terribly far down the path behind them. They barely hid their scent or their camp, they were either trying to be found or incredibly bad at hunting. It wasn't hard to keep downwind and in the shadows to spy on the group of three; a man, a woman, and a young boy. The boy was a young little thing, reminding the daemoness of the children she used to watch that belonged to the workers in the castle, innocent with big eyes. The parents gave her the impression of sleazy rodents, both having overly angular features that put her on edge and a coldness in their eyes that gave the impression that they would even sell their child for some gold. They seemed too entirely comfortable and

50

oblivious to be seasoned hunters. It hit her suddenly with the gear laid out by the tents. "They are not hunters." She whispered

"Then why are they following us? They have not tried to make contact with us." His voice in a hushed tone was confused.

"That is because they are traffickers. They steal people and they are teaching their child. Look over at their gear and you will see cuffs and spell runes to magic people away." The man stiffened as his eyes zeroed in. It was the exact example she had given him earlier that day that shocked him to his core.

"But why are they here? Traffickers don't go after claimed daemons and you are traveling with two men, they don't have enough people to try and take you from us. You are not traveling alone."

"I have no idea, they are also of Lunar descent, are we at the point where Lunars are hunting Lunars and selling them into slavery." Her voice was part of the wind, her mind a million thoughts in a second. This was new and dangerous.

"Hey, dad?" The voice of the child pulled the attention of everyone to the young boy. "I still don't get why we are going after a daemon. I thought you said daemons were dangerous and you said she was pure. You and mom always said we had to protect the pure." The little boy seemed entirely confused and torn. "Won't their handler be mad at us?" He had to only be eight or so and he looked like this was cracking the foundation of where his world stood.

"That is easy enough son, times are changing, and to survive you have to adapt. The old ways are dying." The father spoke without an ounce of trepidation. This did not weigh on his conscience at all. If it helps the pure feeling is not the

51

marked wolf it's the feline walking around, she is the one we are after. She is still dangerous but not very observant. That daemoness somehow got quite a bounty on her head. That power she showed in that last town was incredible. I am not going to lie."

"Your father is right son that woman has the power to give us back the life we had and protect it. There are people who want to pay good money for her. With that kind of power those who want her can wipe the rest of the wild daemon population out of existence and put collars on all those animals that they want. The rest of us will be safe with them gone."

"But I thought the daemons protected us? What if the scary-looking man is with her, her handler?"

"He doesn't look strong enough to handle her kind of power, much less put her back in her proper place." The father scoffed. "We could easily overpower him, kill him if he won't give her up willingly." Truen stiffened again by her side in the shadows, the anger rolling off him was almost palpable. Muttering something not even she could hear him spit on the ground, most likely a spell that would not end well for the traffickers.

"But won't that kill her?" The little boy asked with fear in his eyes. This child would never make a living as a trafficker, he had too much compassion in him.

"Don't worry about that kid, we have our ways of stealing claimed daemons right from the marks. Though if I kill him I am tempted to take her for myself. Maybe you can have the wolf and keep the set." The man sneered. The boy watched the older man in thinly concealed horror. The daemon had heard enough, she grabbed the spellcaster's arm before he could blow their cover and pulled him back to their camp where their companions were waiting for them. Both were too angry to speak on the walk back, so angry they did not notice her hand still pulling him along. By the time they made it back to their fire, the daemoness sat back down, Truen pacing back and forth behind her. Jackdaw had been brushing through Lux's fur when they returned but now both of them were watching the returning members carefully. They watched and waited until both had calmed down enough to explain what had happened.

"I am assuming that went poorly?" Jackdaw spoke calmly and slowly not to startle or set off any already flaring tempers.

"Not as entertaining as I would have hoped though it did confirm certain fears that I had about them."

"Do you want me to bring them up to speed? I am still getting fed information." Truen looked down at her from where he stopped pacing.

"Eavesdropping spell?" She asked.

"I thought it would be a good idea since I didn't know how much longer I could stand there without setting fire to their camp." He shrugged, rolling her eyes she gestured for him to continue. Turning to the others, Truen stepped in between Xai and them as if to protect her from the words. "They are after Xai, they are a team of traffickers, and not for her sunny disposition and friendly demeanor." His attempt to lighten the mood got a snicker from the wolf and a pebble thrown at the back of his head from the feline.

"Keep up your jokes spellcaster and see what happens. I happen to be a delight." Xai hissed.

"They plan to either keep her for their benefit or sell her to some sort of seller who wants to use her to enslave all the daemons they can and execute any they can not force into a collar. The parents are currently talking about the hunters and traffickers that had been summoned to the town you tore up by the buyer. You seemed to put on a show of power for all those who now see you as not only a weapon but a payout. They are bitching about all of those who saw the damage and backed out because they were scared of what you would do to them or what the buyer would do if they could get their hands on you." That town hadn't even been a real show of power in Xai's defense.

"Xai what are we going to do?" Lux asked, obviously shaken by traffickers being so close and an apparent bounty being put on her friend's head. "We have to do something right?"

"What would you like me to do?" Xai sighed. This wasn't the first time she had a bounty and she knew that. She probably had multiple across the kingdom if she thought about it. "Would you like me to surrender myself? Or would you like me to right now go before a literal army of people who see me as a way to get rich? Would either of those options bring you peace? Because I don't think I would come back from either especially to finish the quest we decided to embark on as a group, the journey given to me." She knew her friend never had to deal with the bigotry or the fear. She tended to look less like a daemon and more like a nondescript Lunar or even a Terra so in a town she never got the stares or things thrown. She passed as one of them and never got a second glance from those who hated others based on appearance alone. She tended to stay in the woods around towns and then deal with the public of small towns that looked down on them. She never got a bounty for any reason or had to be on the run for trying to survive. It was an ignorance that Xai was jealous of but on this journey, she would have to lose to make it to the other side.

"No, that is not what I am suggesting and you know it. I don't want you to sacrifice yourself but even with being an assigned assassin class you need help." Xai growled at the wolf, she wasn't supposed to mention her classification. Truen spun around to look at Xai with surprise and pride in his wide eyes.

"I am sorry you are assigned what?" Jackdaw spat out looking at the spotted woman with wide eyes. Truen seemed to stop breathing at the news.

"When daemons are a certain age they can get classified if they want." Lux began explaining, looking Xai in the eyes as she did, she was not afraid of her friend. "It shows us what demographic we fit into. There are five of them."

"Pet, Protector, Warrior, Weapon, Assassin. It depends on genetic makeup, strength, instinct, and how concentrated the purpose of the line is in your blood." Truen swallowed reciting what her father had told them as her sister and she had gotten closer to the age of classification. "There is also lower, higher, and elite of each class."

"Exactly, I got classified as a higher protector." Lux continued with old jealousy in her voice. "I am lower than Xai by a lot but she is also pure blood."

"What level did you get Xai?" Truen all but pleaded.

"She got elite." Lux supplied before Xai could tell them it was none of their business.

"Not many have ever met an elite assassin class before," Jackdaw spoke with awe.

"They are the hardest class to handle, not even a master of any variety can force that classification to submit." Truen continued.

"Which is why it is even more imperative that no one tries to get their hands on me. Even those in my classification can be forced but not through brute strength, magic, or torture. There is a way to break everyone, to force submission. If anyone finds mine then a lot of people are in danger. We are the master weapons no matter if we are of pure blood or not. Only the gods can stop that kind of massacre because that is what it would be. Only another elite assassin can match the power but it doesn't mean forced or enraged that they would win."

"It would take a special handler to help you tap into that power and boost it at that," Lux spoke calmly looking away from her friend and into the fire, she knew this was not what her friend wanted to hear but it was true. She saw the connection between her friend and her handler's brother, she could almost feel it when they were around each other. "To tap into the potential that you on your own can't. That kind of power would be unstoppable. We wouldn't have to worry about traffickers or bounties or whatever else they throw at us while we complete the Time Mages' tasks."

"I pity any fool who thinks they can bond with me, a force as wild and untamable as nature itself is how we are described. No one is worthy of that kind of power or trust even if I did not loathe the idea of handlers." She was being purposely obtuse as she glared daggers into Truen's hopeful eyes.

"Xai please, you know we can not let your power fall into the wrong hands, you said it yourself in sadistic hands even someone as stubborn and powerful as you can fall. A truly matched bond also can not be broken or stolen by stealer runes and spells." Lux pleaded, eyes still staring into the fire.

"Even if I agreed it would take a long time to get someone ready to receive that amount of power if they were not already capable and those who are as few and far between as elite assassins are. To find a handler that I would accept would be some sort of miracle and that is a slim chance even with all this extra influence in play." Xai knew what she was suggesting but it was not happening. She would never consider the raven-haired male as a suitable anything.

"You would need someone strong, correct? Someone who is strong of heart, mind, and physical body? Pure and noble intentions maybe? Unbendable, unshakable, devoted to you and your ideals? Would it be beneficial for them to have stronger abilities of their own, correct, and knowledge?" Jackdaw caught on to what his daemoness was suggesting. The devious glint in his eyes did not escape Xai's notice at all. She knew what they wanted. She had known it was inevitable from the time she was young but it did not mean she was not going to fight it. Her wants had changed since she was an innocent child thinking about fated bonds and handler marks. "If that is all I think we have the perfect candidate right here." He finished looking at his brother who was still staring mesmerized at the daemoness before him.

"I know what you are thinking, this is less clever than past plans and the answer is no. I refuse." That seemed to pull Truen back out of his trance, only to glare at his brother.

"Don't push brother." He spoke coldly, catching Xai's attention.

"Xai why won't you take Truen as your handler?" He continued as if no one had said anything. He leaned further into Lux's side who had finally tensed up not expecting her partner to ask outright. She knew that such bluntness would get backlash, even his own brother told him not to push but he did anyway. She knew he had a plan but maybe this time his calculations would break instead of working out for the better.

"You don't know what you are asking." The daemoness looked into those mischievous green eyes that always seemed to be ten steps ahead of fate itself. "The answer is no." The words came out in a hiss.

"But I want to know what the answer is, why?" He knew he was poking and prodding at open wounds.

"Because boy first off as I said earlier we have no time to train him and I doubt he is ready as of right now. Second, if he is not strong enough he will die being overwhelmed by my natural power and I will not have that blood on my hands. And lastly, I would never let one of you be my handler." Words are chosen carefully to be truthful but purposely misleading. The Princes knew exactly what she meant with that last remark but Lux was left thinking the issue was them being of a Solar race.

"Well, then kitty kat I offer you this" his eyes hardened. She knew the nickname was said as a slight but memories came flying to the forefront of when it was a playful tease. He knew what he was doing and she knew he would always get what he wanted. "A five-minute round with my brother. You win and I drop the topic for good, he wins and you put your stubborn pride away."

"You are evil." Truen shook his head.

"This is why I hate anyone who can manipulate time." Xai sighed knowing even if not tonight she would lose this fight, not that she would go down quietly.

"It would be easier if you stopped fighting against the path set in front of us," Jackdaw smirked knowing he had won against both of them. Fate would correct what had been tampered with.

"Wow, you are good." Lux hummed. "Spots just go with it."

"Spots?" Truen choked out, laughter taking him by surprise. The laughter didn't last long as Xai stood and backhanded his chest taking whatever breath he had in retaliation. She had no doubt he would have a hand-shaped bruise forming soon.

"Like you are one to talk fangs." The feline hissed back, her tail swishing in agitation at everything happening.

"Fangs?" Cooed Jackdaw.

"Don't you dare," Lux growled.

"Don't worry dear I will come up with a better nickname for you than fangs, something special." He laughed, turning and nuzzling his face into her side.

"He is completely evil." Truen groaned as he recovered his breath.

"What is the target Jackdaw? I want to get this over with." Xai sighed, trying to will her tail into being still.

"You want evil? Your target is getting my brother's tunic off of him." Jackdaw smirked, his face still pillowed in fur.

"Off of him?" Xai groaned. How was this man twenty-five years old and not fifteen and pulling off inappropriate pranks?

"Yes off him, and since you are so partial to my abilities as a time caster I will set the match for you."

"I have been meaning to ask, what exactly does a time caster do? I know it is a branch of spellcaster but you never seem to use your abilities as Truen does." Lux asked in curiosity.

"I manipulate time. Much like my brother's rune casting, I was given a set specialty. I can speed up time, rewind time, add time to someone's life, and see just a bit into the future, amongst other things. Very close to something a Time Mage might be able to do but nothing nearly as strong and much more localized." Jackdaw explained simply, that it's why he always seemed steps ahead of everyone else. He had the tactical mind and the advantage of literal time on his side.

"Evil little shit with a smart little package." Truen snorted.

"You got to be kidding about his tunic." Xai groaned not wanting to do this.

"I could make the mark on his trousers," Jackdaw said in the most innocent voice he could muster.

"Be glad he is on our side." Truen looked back at Xai completely resigned.

"Truen what is your specialty?" Lux asked, her mind somewhere completely different.

"I am an elemental rune caster. All six elemental runes are on my body and they let me manipulate them with more accuracy and ease than my natural magic. Since I am a rune caster I have a few others as well but they are not things I can manipulate at will more so they are singular spells."

"Are we done with the spellcaster lesson? I want to get this ass beating over with." Xai asked, backing up, and stretching some of her limbs.

"Begin now." Jackdaw nodded, setting the daemoness against his brother. Truen didn't even start with any of his spells, instead as she leaped at him he dodged, forcing her away from the campfire and closer to the tree line. From the viewpoint of the witnesses, it was a deadly dance of dodging and well-placed spells. A small cyclone to move the trajectory, an ice wall to stop claws, and a layer of electricity above the grass to force the daemon into the tree limbs. It didn't take long for her to slip his view and drop from above, knocking him flat on his back, and dispelling all of his elements in his shock. Before he even got his breath back again she straddled his hip and grabbed the front of his tunic, locking him to the ground in shock. "So close dear scary daemoness but time is up." Came Jackdaws' amused voice from where they left the campsite.

"Those two are terrifying." Lux shuddered.

"You can get off my brother now, I don't want to be witnessing anything you two might get caught up in after sparring." Xai looked down at Truen who was breathing as hard as she was, his face completely flushed. The excitement and familiarity of sparring with him were shattered as the bet and what she lost came back to light. This wasn't a match for the fun of it or to see if they were still as in sync as they had once been. This had been a match with her past for her freedom and she lost. She let go of his tunic and shot up off him, leaving the raven by himself in the dirt. He sighed and picked himself back up, sparring with her had been more than he remembered.

"Xai, I am sorry. I know we had a deal but we don't have to do this." Truen called after her, he didn't follow her back towards the campsite but he knew she heard him. He knew the pain this would cause if they didn't do this for the right reasons. Spinning around in frustration and hurt, Xai stepped back up to him and almost spit in his face.

"Do not pretend you know what this is like for me, do not pity me, and do not pretend. You know nothing of who I am now after you left me in pieces." She hissed. "You don't know everything I will lose with this."

"Then why did you make the bet?" He tried, reaching out towards her without thinking only to get shoved away.

"To survive." She spat. "I know that it'll get forced one way or another. Just because it is the snake I know doesn't mean I want to be bitten again." Her entire self was filled with pain and fear.

"A deal is a deal Xai." Jackdaw's voice brought them back again. Turning Xai saw Jackdaw and Lux standing behind her, watching everything unfold, making sure she didn't run and Truen didn't fold.

"Fine, then it's time to put your collar on me." Only those who knew her now could hear the fear and resignation in her voice, as though instead of gaining she truly thought she was losing everything.

"I don't want to collar you, I don't want to tame you, I don't want to control you." Truen pleaded. "I just want to protect you, in any way I can."

"Protect me my ass, all you want is the power. With this, I am just a piece of property." She growled. Instead of yelling back or backing up Truen stepped into her space and grabbed her chin, forcing her to look at him and nothing else but him.

"Do not ever call yourself property ever again." He growled in a way that sent a shiver through everyone present. "I will not stand to hear you or anyone else ever degrade you again. Not now, not ever." He was suddenly the Prince she thought he would grow into.

"If not for power or claim then why?" Her voice was smaller than anyone had ever heard it before.

"Because a very long time ago an old Time Mage pulled me aside and told me that the daemoness with black and white hair, spots on her skin, and amethyst eyes that look like liquid magic was my past, present, and future. She would be my life and my destiny. It would be my job to protect her and care for her as she changed the world. Forever I would be intertwined with her until the moment I took my last breath with her. I tend to not question Time Mages."

"I wonder if that is the same Time Mage Xai met?" Lux asked, breaking the spell.

"You will have to tell me about your time with her." Jackdaw sighed.

"I can tell you while they go have their moment. This seems to have been a long time coming and we shouldn't intrude." Lux looked at Xai and nodded, pulling Jackdaw away.

"Let us find somewhere a bit more private." Truen smiled gently, letting go of her face, giving her the space she needed as he began walking into the darkness, the moon his only guiding light. Luckily it only seemed to take moments of walking in a daze for him to lead her into another clearing, this one full of moon flowers in bloom. "This seems appropriate." He sighed,

63

turning back to the silent daemoness. "I will gladly accept all you are willing to give me. We don't have to do anything now if you don't want to, no matter what my brother says."

"You know our lives have been leading to this Truen. You have felt the pull, same as me. Time Mage or not we were always bound to each other. But if we do this handler and daemon are all we can be, I trust you enough to know I can incapacitate you without killing you if you try to use me. I don't trust you anymore and we are not the same people we were when we were kids. You were always strong enough for my power but I am no longer strong enough to accept you again."

"We will figure that out Xai, you promised we would talk about that. But I was not lying when I said I would accept whatever you are willing to give me. I have a healthy fear of you and your power but that girl I used to know is not the woman standing before me. I want to know who you are now." His eyes never left hers.

"Fine but you are going back to training in the morning. You are rusty on how to fight with me and this will be more than we ever trained before. I didn't go easy on you back then and I will not now."

"I am ready for whatever you want to throw at me." He grinned with confidence.

"You are going to regret that." She smirked back, calmer than she was earlier.

"I am a lot better than I was when I was eight, seventeen years is a long time. I think I will surprise you."

"We will see but you are right, seventeen years is a long time to change, I am no longer the eleven-year-old who went easy on you. Now if you don't mind I would like to get this over with."

"I have one question about this." He finally looked down away from her, a flush once again rising on his face.

"Spit it out Truen." She sighed.

"Can we do this traditionally? That was our plan when we were kids and I still hoped." He was embarrassed to bring their overly romanticized childhood fantasies into this.

"I don't see why not." She smiled softly knowing he couldn't see since he was still intently looking at the flowers surrounding them. Pulling out one of the knives from its pouch she removed her cloak, setting it on the ground beside her. A chill ran over the exposed skin of her back. "Give me your arm." She reached out for him, he reluctantly placed his forearm in her hand, the softer inner arm exposed. "Now this won't have all of the vows and theatrics and this will most likely hurt. Are you ready?" He nodded and she began. She placed the point into the inner elbow and applied enough pressure to slice through the skin. Carefully and with the practice that she was raised with she brought the blade straight to the inner part of his wrist without cutting anything that would cause him to bleed out. "Now once I kneel you need to carefully slice from the base of my skull down the spine to the middle of my back. I know they taught you how to do this safely just like they taught me." With pain around his eyes, he nodded silently. Breathing out she turned her back to him and knelt on her knees, moving her braids out of the way. This was not how she used to envision this moment but somehow it was just correct. The sudden pain of the knife almost made her flinch away. Now she knew exactly what her elders meant when they told her it would take a certain kind of strength to prove her devotion when doing the traditional ritual of binding. It took a lot to sit there and let this happen. Once the cut was made he knelt behind her placing his forearm to its match on her back, wrapping his other arm around her to keep her up with him. The sensation was indescribable at the moment. The pain turned to a heat that did not burn, it was overwhelming and rounding at the same time. They could both feel the marks taking form as if it was pressure being released into patterns. Once it was over they fell together to their side, marks no longer touching but the need to touch was still there.

"That was not what I was expecting." Truen gasped when he could finally vocalize words again.

"Now I know what the elders were talking about. How do people do that in the middle of a battle?" She breathed.

"Adrenaline?" He responded, still breathing heavily.

"It has to be, it must be a shame to miss that feeling."

"I wouldn't say that to my brother. They were in a fight when they bonded to each other."

"That is fair, speaking of your brother though we need to get back to them. Move your arm, I need to stand." Truen moved his arm off her waist as if she burned him, or if she would bite him if he didn't, which was always a possibility. It took a few attempts for the daemoness to stand again, even then she was not entirely sturdy on her feet as she reached for her cloak.

"Our marks should darken by tomorrow, correct?" He asked as he pulled himself up as well, looking at the freshly healed scars that now marked both of them before she covered her own.

"In theory but sometimes it takes a few days according to people in different areas." She spoke without looking at him as she corrected herself. "Let's go. I have a feeling something is going to happen and I hate those feelings, they are rarely wrong." He nodded, following her from the clearing that would be burned into their memories for the rest of their lives. Rushing through the trees back to their campsite Truen couldn't see anything but her hair through the darkness, leading him. As they got closer the stench of greed reached her sensitive nose, she barely made it through the tree line around their camp before she was landing on all four paws. The growl that ripped from her throat as she arrived and put herself between the traffickers and Lux before Truen even reached the firelight made the man and woman from earlier stumble back.

"Xai," Truen shouted as he skidded next to his brother. Both Jackdaw and Lux were unharmed but the wolf was baring her teeth. Both relaxed marginally with their arrival.

"That's a shame she has been tainted with a handler, I can smell it on them now that we are closer." The man scoffed. He shook his head in disappointment. "What a shame."

"But dear, he is so cute. Maybe we can sell him too? It's easy enough to break a Solar, they have no strength to them at all. It would be better than killing him." The woman cooed and whined reaching for Truen. The noise that came from the feline could only be called feral. The child, thankfully, was nowhere in sight.

"You are traitors, and no such filth will touch what is mine." Xai hissed.

"Do not hiss at us child." The woman spat at her. She reeked of fear.

"I am not a child and you will not threaten him." The feline spat back, stepping forward and pushing them back further.

"Xai," Truen called calmly as he stepped up next to his daemoness, much to her distaste. "Would you like to take care of them by yourself? I know you have been stressed, this may help." His tone did not give away the lack of true closeness in their relationship.

"Do you truly need to ask?" She responded in turn, keeping up the illusion. The bust of power through the newly opened bond almost buckled her. It felt incredible, if not careful it could be addicting. Truen had always been strong enough, she could not deny that they were perfectly matched any longer. She had denied this for almost two decades. Once her eyes cleared they narrowed onto the traffickers, she began to stalk her prey with her wolf on her flank.

"If there is any chance you want to live I would answer my questions, otherwise we will turn our backs and let you be a plaything for our beautiful ladies." Truen's tone was so matter-of-fact that it stopped them both in their tracks, waiting to see what the next move was going to be. His voice was so cold and devoid of the heart he normally spoke with that it sent shivers through his bond, she liked it more than she wanted to admit to even herself. "Answer the questions truthfully and maybe I will consider calling her back, maybe you get to see your son again and he won't end up an orphan tonight." They began nodding as the daemoness' whined back at the thought of being recalled. "Why are a pair of Lunars trafficking Lunars? Especially daemons? They keep you and everyone else safe."

"We were summoned to the last town we were in for this daemon specifically. There is a buyer who wants her no matter what. Normally we don't go after our own." The man started.

"We already know about the gathering and the bounty." Jackdaw interrupted, sounding incredibly bored. Both daemons took another step forward causing the shriveling pair to fall over themselves. The bravado they had around their own campfire was completely gone in the face of true danger. "The King called for it, he is planning the mass enslavement or eradication of the daemon race. The King is the buyer."

"She is a pure daemon and there are not many of those left. They can kill another daemon even if they have a handler. Even a protector class of pure blood can kill anything below an assassin class so she is their best hope in wiping the wild daemons out of the kingdom." The woman cried, and one of them pissed themselves in their fear.

"What do you get out of this other than money and some meager power?" Truen asked. "Your son clearly thinks this wrong and doesn't want to be part of an entire genocide. We saw that earlier at your camp." That startled them, knowing they were being watched and they had no idea. "Do you think of him in this situation? If that bloody excuse for a King really wants to begin this war it is going to come for him at his own doorstep. You have a choice to make right now, either die or renounce yourselves as traffickers and go live normal lives with your son. To us, you and most of the members of your gathering are absolutely nothing. Your death will only matter to your son so make this choice wisely."

"We renounce." They both screamed in unison.

"If you turn your back on this kindness we will know and we will come for you." Jackdaw drawled. "Now if I were you I would run far before our ladies get bored. It is a full moon, they do look like they have an itching to run." He smiled like something that seemed to belong to a villain. They took that to scramble away. "You are too soft brother." Jackdaw dropped his smile and walked over to Lux, wrapping his arms around her neck.

"That is your opinion brother. I would rather not make more orphans in this world." Truen defended himself. "Though it is a full moon, why don't you two go off and explore? I know you two are brimming with energy. We will stay here and watch out." Both daemons nodded and took off into the woods.

"You have to be nicer to her this time brother. You can't act like you did when we were kids. You can't push her away." Jackdaw was stressed watching his brother watch where the daemons went.

"I am trying, I am trying to be as honest as I can with her without her pushing me away this time. I can't lose her again, the last time almost killed me when she disappeared. Now we are permanently bound to each other. Our destinies have always been intertwined now our minds and bodies are as well. She has always held my heart since the beginning. I can't hurt her." Truen sighed looking up at the moon above them. Jackdaw saw the spark of life he hadn't seen in his brother in what seemed like a lifetime.

"Don't mess this up or neither of you will make it, and without you two I feel our world won't make it." Jackdaw sighed, too much was relying on this. In the field of flowers, the two daemons sat in a moment of peace.

"Please don't tell me you are planning on howling at the moon tonight," Xai asked, lying down in the blooms. Just for that Lux smirked and began to howl like a child.

"We have a long road ahead of us." Lux smiled as she finished her howl. "Many problems to solve, people to save. Such a long road for us, our kingdom, our species, and our future. We have to have fun while we can and enjoy beauty when we find it. We don't have the time not to take what we want while we are sent on this crazy mission that everything is riding on. We can't let fear stop us." her tongue rolled out of the side of her mouth.

"I hate it when you have a point, come on we need to get back to the boys and get some sort of rest. Our journey continues in the morning. Fate and Time Mages don't wait for anyone." Xai huffed while standing. Every day seemed to bring a new layer of change that shook the foundation they stood on and the only way they were getting through this was together.

Chapter Four: Journey to the Mountain

Days passed as they traveled in their new normal, moving as fast as they could toward the frozen northern mountain range. The group opted to avoid as many towns as they could, hunting for their food during the day and camping at night, only stopping when it was absolutely necessary until they reached the base of the mountain trail. The final town was bustling and the townspeople tended to keep to themselves considering who resided above them on the mountain. The group had arrived the night before and chosen to get rooms at one of the inns before going up the dangerous and uncomfortable mountain trail. Xai had been too tired to even complain when Jackdaw paid for the two rooms and said it made more sense that each team should take one room, for safety of course. It wasn't until she woke up in Truen's arms that it clicked that the sneaky little shit that was in the room next door had gotten rooms with only one bed.

While camping Truen and her had been sleeping on opposite sides of the fire, the bond between them making it harder for Xai to ignore the draw she felt towards him. Now that one part of the draw was satisfied the rest wanted to be heard. Since that night she found herself reaching out to him instinctually. Here and now she refused to accept that in his arms was the best night's sleep she had in years since everything started. Xai was thankful she woke before her counterpart but there was no surprise there, he was not nor ever had been an early riser, even as a child. Though she could not figure out how to get out of his octopus-like grasp without waking him, she didn't want him to know but it seemed like waking him was the only way she was getting up. She wanted to start getting ready for the trip up the mountain which meant going to the market and getting appropriate camping and

72

clothing for the non-Lunars in the traveling party. Other races did not handle the frozen terrain as the Lunar races did, which is exactly why the High vampires chose the top of one of the most inhospitable mountains in the land to set up their village.

They would also need all blades tended to before the journey in case of wild beasts or bandits. The narrow pathways did not give the daemons enough space to shift fully and fight. It would have to be one or the other. Any sort of offensive spell would also run the risk of friendly fire which would not be helpful. Thankfully between what Lux and Xia carried with them and what the Princes had run with, they should have enough coin to pay for it all. This was not the type of area that would discount items or services based on blood or societal ranking, they couldn't if they wanted to survive.

"You are thinking too loud." The sleep-worn voice of the Prince spoke into her neck, it took all of her self-control not to shiver. His arms wrapping tighter around her, it was a good thing she did not have to relieve herself at the moment or he would have regretted his actions.

"I am planning on the market trip we have to make today, if you would let go of me I could go get started." She sighed knowing she could easily overpower him but that ran the risk of feeling that rejection through the bond.

"How are you always such a morning person?" He complained instead of letting go.

"Because someone has to get things done and if you are even remotely similar to the childhood self that is not you or your brother. We need to get things done and leave." She tried knowing it was most likely useless to try reasoning with the half-asleep man-child.

"Shh, stop being so logical." How could a man his age and size whine like such a little brat?

"Fine, keep sleeping but I still need to go to the market. If you are not going to help I am taking your coin purse and buying you a weapon I find suitable." She threatened.

"No, you like large heavy swords." He complained, eyes still not open but more awake than he had been.

"It is not my fault you can not physically handle a real sword." She teased, momentarily forgetting herself again.

"Don't be mean to me this early in the morning, it is not fair and you know it." He sighed, finally letting her go and rolling onto his back. "So how much trouble is my brother in for using our extreme exhaustion to get us to share a bed?" He asked rolling his head over to watch her reaction. Sighing to herself she sat up, letting the blankets pool around her, her tail hanging lazily off the side of the bed. Without turning to look at him she began unraveling her braids and gently working through any of the knots she had in her hair.

"I may forget that his legs and lungs are weaker than yours as we go up the mountain."

"You are not allowed to kill my brother, even if we are no longer your favorite people in this world, he is the favorite of your best friend."

"I won't kill him, cripple him more maybe but I am aware that I can not maim him too badly. He needs to stop trying to force us together so much."

"I agree, he needs to let things be and happen as they need to happen," Truen answered softly, looking back at the ceiling.

"Does he not understand his meddling is only making things harder? We have more important things to be concerned about including genocide in the process. And yet here he is trying to force a relationship between us."

"He thinks he is helping, you know this. Not that I am excusing him but he had to watch the aftermath of losing you and your sister." He said carefully, feeling her tense beside him. "We went from days of everything being easy and carefree to everything falling apart. I know after we lost our brother, Jhelum, I shut you out in only the way an eight-year-old can but then we lost your sister, and then you disappeared. That almost shattered Krutz and me entirely."

"I don't want to talk about this Truen," Xai whispered.

"I know you don't but that is why he is trying. We can't let the past keep festering between us." He pleaded, eyes falling shut.

"I know you are right, but I can't yet. With what you did, with what happened. It took years to be able to breathe correctly again, I can not bring myself to face it. I promised you we would and we will. Let us start with learning who we are together now instead of digging up the past. As long as you do not betray me again, give me a reason to trust you, and we will get there. I don't want to go down that path without knowing you will be there at the end of it."

"I guess that is fair enough, I just want to know how we got here. What did I do that was so bad for you to leave me behind? But I will wait until you are ready until I can prove it to you." He sighed getting up. "What is on our shopping list today? And more importantly, we are leaving tomorrow up the mountain right? I would like to get a bath and to get these clothes washed, I feel like they will run from me on their own."

"Yes we are resting today, we pushed a lot of distance in a little time. We will need to have our energy to get to the village safely so you can bathe. I was planning on getting you more clothes situated for the cold anyways and a bag to carry your extra items." She explained watching him stretch. They all did a rest day even if it made her skin crawl in paranoia.

"What about you and Lux?" He asked looking back over his shoulder.

"Fur coats remember, also Lunar's bodies tend to run a bit warmer which is why most of our settlements are north of the kingdom. You and Jackdaw through dress for warmer climates which are normally fine this time of year but up the mountain you will freeze no matter what time of year it is." She explained she had never been to the vampire village but she had met a few people born there on her travels to stay hidden over the years.

"Do you want me to braid your hair?" He asked quietly, startling her. She turned to look at him with wide eyes. As a child he always scoffed when she had asked, saying that was a girl thing. "Your mother taught me after you left. It gave me something to do." He shrugged, obviously embarrassed.

"Not this morning." She spoke sharply, she caught herself when he flinched away. "There is no point in an intricate braid when I will just undo it for a bath later, I am leaving it down today. Maybe tomorrow." She tried reassuring him. They were both trying but the wall was still there. He seemed to relax at the explanation. "Now you get yourself a bath and I am going to see if Lux wants to join me or if she and Jackdaw are preoccupied with each other. I know they try not to express how involved they are with their relationship so they may be using this as an opportunity."

"That is utterly disgusting and in no way how I wanted to think about my brother." He shuddered. Xai huffed out a laugh as she walked past him and to the door. "I should be back in a few hours so enjoy your bath." The innuendo was clear as she rushed to close the door. Thankfully Lux seemed to have a similar thought and was leaving her own room at the same time. "Not too involved?" Xai asked with a raised brow.

"Not until he gets a bath of his own. I adore that man but he is currently foul." She laughed clearly, with not a hint of shame. "Later maybe though." She winked walking up to her longtime companion. "What about you and Truen?"

"You two need to stop pushing," Xai warned as they walked towards the stairs, completely in sync and with no need to explain the plan. "Even though I will admit it is much easier to forget the past being able to feel the echoes of his feelings through the bond, feeling his intention is grounding."

"You know not every handler bond can feel emotions?" Lux asked carefully. She knew something was between the two stubborn individuals and their past had been alluded to but everyone, Jackdaw included, had kept so tightlipped about it. She watched the feline carefully as they walked out onto the street and directly into the market, her tail staying relaxed but the world knew that meant very little with her friend. Xai was too good at burying things and that had scared Lux for as long as she knew what that meant, trauma and betrayal.

"Yes Lux I know that only happens with a fated pair, I am well aware. A long time ago it was all I could think about but right now that can not be what I am focused on. And there is a lot of bad blood we have to wade through to get anywhere close to where you and Jackdaw are if we ever do."

"I wish you would tell me what happened." Lux huffed, it was a long-time disagreement between the two. "But I can understand where you are coming from I guess, I am just happy you two are getting along."

"Yes well as I said last the other night there is something grounding in the bond, and reassuring that he will never truly be able to leave again."

"So he left you before you left him?" Lux tried to get as much information as she could as nonchalantly as she could manage. Trying to keep the conversation going while looking through the market. The peaceful atmosphere was making Xai more talkative than she normally would be about sensitive topics.

"In a way yes he did. It was too much to bare with everything else going on at the time. My mother gave me a way out and I took it."

"Some day you need to tell someone what happened, I know you have nightmares and it affects your sleep. But you know I won't pry into old wounds like that, I've seen the damage that causes. Just please don't push him away as you do with everyone else. You two need each other to heal whatever happened." Xai knew the wolf was right, the feline did not like people getting too close. Experience after experience taught her that it would only end badly and with someone damaged beyond repair.

"Wolfy!" A cry came through the crowd, Lux tensed and growled before the name caught up with Xai. The spotted daemoness could not hold in the hysterical laughter if she tried. Bent over and clutching her sides was the most defenseless the Princes had ever seen her as they joined them in front of the storefront they had idled in front of.

"Do you honestly think you are talking to me Jackdaw? I refuse to answer to that. That is completely demeaning." The larger woman growled something low and threatening only to cause the smaller daemoness to snort ungracefully. The Princes were unconcerned about the snarling daemoness, though the sight of the other wheezing for breath made their lips twitch.

"Fangs you already answered to it." She gasped, tears streaming down her face. She hadn't laughed that hard since she was an innocent child.

"If you want to play that Spots, Truen can always call you Kitty." Lux snapped back. Before Truen could even voice his concern with the statement all of the infectious laughter was gone and a vicious hiss replaced it. Lux wasn't prepared for the complete whiplash from the entire group. Even Jackdaw looked down and away from the spotted daemoness.

"No one on the living plane has the right to ever call me that ever again, certainly not Truen or anyone of his bloodline." The strained voice that came from Xai took her long-time friend by surprise. She knew that the past that connected the three of them was long and painful but she had never seen that kind of open pain on the feline's face. Open grief and pain, her tail whipping back and forth, her eyes nothing but slits. "If that ever slips from your lips I will tear you limb from limb." Truen though knew she would never hurt him, even without the bond between them. The bond did make it easier to tell the outburst was pain and longing for the past instead of hatred and resentment. He knew what that nickname meant to her, it meant the connection, it meant the past when they were together and safe, and it meant they hadn't lost anyone.

"Calm down Kitty." He knew it was a gamble, even his own brother gasped as the words left his mouth. The chance of making things worse was a high probability but if he was right the chance of taking a step forward was a reward that was worth it. It's all depending on if any bit of the girl he knew then was still in the warrior that stood before him. He had seen pieces of her so there was hope.

"You tempt fate boy." She snarled in response but there was hope in the bond, hope, and a cry for safety. Truen could guarantee that Xai didn't realize he could feel the bond as strongly as he did.

"I am not a boy anymore little girl, I am not the boy you left behind." He knew it was a dangerous game, but a game that she responded well to. In a game they used to play, they were not truly fighting but sparring and teasing. As they had gotten older it was a game that changed too but stayed the same in their absence from the other's side. Something old to fall into in the present without even noticing. Unfortunately, the sudden laughter of the couple beside them broke the spell between the two. The audience startled Xai, bringing her back to the present and the pain. Instead of saying anything she turned and ran, ran right out of the town and into the forest surrounding the southern border.

"Xai please wait." The call of Lux was enough to make her stop running and catch her breath. It wasn't Truen who followed her so she allowed herself to be caught. "Xai please, what was that?" The wolf begged as she slowed, circling the other like she was a scared animal.

"Kitty is what my twin sister would call me." Xai bit out. "All those years ago when living in the palace wasn't a gilded cage."

"So you did live in the palace." Xai had never said it explicitly but Lux had put some pieces of her past together over the last seventeen years. "What happened to your sister?"

"You are aware that those two are the Princes of this kingdom, correct?"

"Yes Xai I am not an unobservant bumpkin from the country, that and Jackdaw told me not wanting to lie about who he was after we bonded."

"Lui and I have known the Princes, all four of them since they were born. Our parents were the head of the pack that protected the Royal Family. Imagine their surprise when there were two fated pairs then and there. As you know about Truen and me, Lui was fated to the third Prince Krutz. After the fourth Prince died of sickness when they were seven-ish everything changed. Truen completely shut me out and Krutz became volatile. I remember hearing that the Princes were planning on breaking their fate bonds because they no longer wanted to be fated to daemons and it broke Lui but it didn't sound right to me so I went to confront Truen about it. Mind you we were kids. But what I saw was Krutz pushing Lui down a well that led into the caverns below the castle as Truen watched laughing. I can still hear his voice teaching those below them a lesson about talking back to their betters. We weren't allowed to see her body. It was so badly mangled, that she landed on rocks below and they hoped she died on impact but you know how daemon bodies are. Less than a week later my mother came to me in the night with a bag packed and told me to run, run and never look back. They were planning to kill me too so that Truen wouldn't have to deal with our bond. I ran knowing that fated bonds destroyed everything I had." Xai had never told someone exactly what happened those last few days of the life she had. Behind her, Lux had tears streaming down her face. She knew her friend's past was traumatic but that was not at all what she had been expecting. But something didn't sit right.

"I am so sorry Xai. That is unimaginable, especially seeing Truen now." She tried, but the man they had been traveling with showed no capacity for that much cruelty, especially towards Xai.

"He regrets what happened, I can feel it. But I can't let the past go. Trusting him and his brothers lost me everything. My sister, my family, my home, my sense of safety and innocence. Now I am bonded to him as fate wanted and part of me wants to forget and forgive but I can't."

"I don't understand what you're going through, there is no way for me too but I want you to know I have always been and will always be here for you. Now that I know what happened I will make sure nothing happens to your happiness again." Carefully she wrapped her arms around the middle of the other daemoness and held her like she would fall apart if she didn't. Xai didn't cry, she didn't scream, she didn't pull away. She just stood there and felt her friend around her.

"I can't trust him again. Not with what little I have left of myself. I am bonded to him, I trust him to help us with this god's forsaken journey we were forced on but I can't trust him with all of me again."

"Only time will tell Xai. You are fated, if you keep punishing the bond as much as you have you will both get hurt. I am not saying hand over your heart to him now, make him work for it, but you know you will never truly be able to escape what he is to you, what he always was to you." Lux sighed. "You are bound for as many years as you have left. It is more permanent and meaningful than marriage and was blessed before you were even born. I have to believe he would never hurt you like that again, he can't without breaking a piece of himself too."

"I hope you are right."

"I am always right when it comes to this my dear socially inept and awkward friend, now let's go back to town, I left the boys with the shopping list to distract them and I am concerned." Lux smiled, releasing the other.

"Xai, come on and move, we have to go." A man's voice roared, his familiar voice laced with panic. He screamed for her to open her eyes, sounding more frantic as the seconds drew on. When she opened her eyes she realized she and the dark figure crouched next to her were surrounded by walls of fire. "Come on Xai, I am not leaving you here. I am not going to leave you to die. You have to get up please, I am begging you." The voice was so familiar to her and so close to tears but she could not see who the shadow person was. She tried to get up as he instructed but as she did a sharp pain went through her side, and she fell back to the ground. Looking down to her own horror she saw she was completely split open from shoulder to hip, bleeding out profusely.

"I can't, I can't get up. Just leave me and go, save yourself. Please just leave me here." She cried out, she could not let him risk himself, whoever he was. Her eyes burned with smoke and tears but the shadow man would not leave her. "Go save yourself." She pleaded again.

"No, I will not leave you, understand me Xai I will never leave you behind." With that, the man picked her up from the ground as gently as possible. She knew those marks anywhere, it was Truen who was with her. The pain ripped through her as he adjusted her in his arms and she screamed in agony. He was strong enough to carry her with ease which was lucky for her and her injuries. As fast as possible he could he ran through the ring of fire that surrounded them. She could not believe

Truen would run through the inferno with her securely in his arms, she couldn't even feel the intensity of her wounds.

"Why wouldn't you leave me?" She demanded through gritted teeth once he stopped running, she was hoping they made it to safety if he was no longer at full sprint. He set her carefully on the ground to look once more at her wound as she spoke at him, she couldn't even tell if he was listening to her at this point. "Why do you always insist on being with me? Saving me? Protecting me? I am a daemon, your daemon. I am disposable in this relationship. Is it for the extended life I can provide you? Is it for the power that comes with being a handler? Just tell me please because you are making no sense."

"Xai you should know me better than that by now." The tired man sighed, his voice resigned. "It has never been about the power, the near immortality, or anything else that people get from becoming a handler. It never has and it never will be any of those reasons Xai. It has always been more important than that." He caressed her face with one hand as he tried applying pressure with the other. Her blood was a highlight on his blood-covered body.

"Then why?"

"Because I love you Xai, always have and always will."

Her eyes shot open, sweat dripping on her skin, and she felt as though she couldn't catch her breath. The man leaning over her with his hands on her shoulders was lucky that even in her sleep she knew he wasn't a threat. Once she was back in the present she groaned, she loathed that dream. Nothing ever changed, only more detail was given each time she had it. Unfortunately, the object of her dreams was not making this easy on her by leaning over, her eyes full of concern and sleep.

"Get off me." She groaned, pushing him back over onto his back.

"Sorry, but are you alright? You woke me up screaming." He sighed, laying back into his bedroll. The moon was high so he had to have been back from his turn at keeping watch for only a bit.

"I am fine Truen, go back to sleep." She sighed sitting up, she knew she would get no more sleep tonight. Looking down at the man beside her, they had taken to sleeping side by side since the last village. His eyes were closed but she knew he was still awake. His brother was fast asleep across the fire, completely at ease in the small cave they had found going up the path leading to the opening of the mountain way. "Go back to sleep, I apologize for waking you."

"Xai please don't lie to me, I know you are not fine and I have a feeling the moment you get me to sleep again you are going to make Lux go back to Jackdaw and take watch over for the rest of the night. This isn't the first time this has happened since we started traveling together. I don't even need the bond to know that." His voice was tired and deep with sleep.

"If you know that so well you should have learned if I have chosen to lie to you knowing our bond will allow you to know any time I lie without fail then I don't want to tell you the truth and I won't." Cracking his eyes open he reached to place his arm around her waist, his sleep-like haze not considering the consequences of his boldened actions. "Truen please don't." Even with the plea, she did not move away from his warm skin against her exposed back. Part of her would miss this when they started up the mountain and the Solars would have to cover their skin in fear of frostbite. She would never admit it aloud.

"Don't what Xai?" He was too tired to pretend that they hadn't gotten closer and yet further from each other since the day he called her Kitty. He was too tired to pretend he didn't want to comfort her or sleep with her in his arms.

"Please do not pretend to care, I don't want your pity and I do not want emotions forced by fate." She too was tired of fighting it all. Traveling together made the resentment so much harder to hold when it used to be her barrier.

"How many times will I have to tell you I don't pity you?" Groaning in frustration he sat up as she tried to move away. "No, you are not running away this time." He spoke calmly, grabbing her arm. They both knew if she wanted to she could easily get out of his gentle hold even if he forced it. "I don't understand what I did to lose your trust. No, let's take a walk and talk about this, it is eating both of us." He shook his head, standing up as quietly as he could. He pulled her up with him and with a quick look over to his sleeping brother, he began to walk out of the cave and into the small outcropping of trees on the opposite side of the path. Nodding at Lux on their way out they continued to walk enough distance to not be overheard. As much as they cared about their makeshift pack some things needed to be said alone. "Talk to me Xai."

"I can't. For one I am not used to trusting people anymore and I have no privacy from you, you get to know my thoughts and weaknesses without my consent. You and I are bound for the rest of our lives and I can't get past what you did. Since I was chased out of the palace I have been on the run. I have been in hiding for seventeen years doing what I can to do good and protect people without getting caught and only a few months ago that all went tits up now you are back in my life and our history is getting thrown in my face again and again." She hissed, frustration getting the better of her. "I went from being in control of my emotions to feeling like I need to fly off the handle because you frustrate me. I hated touch for years and now I don't want to move your hands off of me. Your family betrayed me, you betrayed me. I spent so long now hating Solars, hating you with so much passion that standing next to you is pushing me off balance. You know we grew up romanticizing the handler bond, and being fated on top of that and knowing since we could understand what that meant. You promised to never tame me, your brother promised to ground Lui and to have that stolen from me. But this god's forsaken bond wants me to forget the feelings of pain, betrayal, and fear. To forget the feelings that forged me in the fires and what spat out the person before you." There was nothing she could do as he wrapped her against himself. He was embracing her and instead of wishing to run she wanted to hold him back, closer, and never let go. But she couldn't, she could not betray her sister like that.

"I need to know how to make this better Xai. I don't understand the things you said but it is hurting you. Losing Lui hurt us all, especially after losing Jhelum as well before her." He whispered in her ear, his voice full of grief and confusion. Slowly he backed her against a tree, effectively caging her with his body. But she did not feel trapped but protected, even though she was the predator between the two. The honesty of his words confused her, how could he not know what she was talking about?

"How can you not understand how your actions were betrayal? How traumatizing were they?"

"What are you talking about Xai? What did I do?" He begged.

"Yeah Xai what did he do?" A voice came through the trees making the two who were still wrapped into each other tense, their stance was no longer for comfort but for protection. Truen didn't think as he shielded Xai with his own body from the smug voice, a voice he unfortunately recognized. Neither had sensed the intruder coming at all, and only a few in the world could sneak up on a daemon. Xai pushed Truen off of her so she could see their opponent, instead, she saw nothing in the shadows of the forest. She heard no footsteps, only the rustling of the trees, hell she couldn't even smell another person over the scent of rain on the horizon. A shadow walker, it had to be, but that was an incredibly rare gift to possess for any mage or spell caster. "And how the world has changed, heir apparent Prince Truen being branded a traitor to his kingdom. Here I always thought you were a goodie two shoes, looking down on people like me who get paid to use their abilities. Look at you now enemy number two of the entire kingdom. I am almost proud of you Truen."

"Baye, show yourself you annoying asshole. I thought you were rotting in the dungeons somewhere." Truen growled, eyes rapidly moving through the shadows to try and predict where the crook for hire would appear. Once more trying to shield daemoness from the unseen foe.

"Nah, your brother let me out to take care of you." The words caused Xai to prickle. "But I have to say I can see why you betrayed your kingdom if it was for her. She is the finest piece of meat I have ever laid my eyes on, good on you man. I will have to take good care of her after I kill you. Keep her nice and happy." Once he reappeared on the physical plane Xai would kill him. She was not a piece of meat nor did she appreciate how he was so sure he would end her handler.

"Why don't you remove yourself from the shadows and see how easy I am to keep as you put it? Just mind my claws coward, they are sharper than someone like you could think."

Pride washed through Truen's side of the bond, always enjoying the natural confidence that came from her station.

"Such a hot-blooded woman, my favorite type to cool off. I had no idea we had the same type, my friend. Such a shame we couldn't have gotten along but I will love getting my hands on her."

"You will not touch her, not now not ever Baye." He was sure that if Baye managed to get close he would never get his filthy fingers on his daemoness. The daemoness knew this situation would not resolve itself without blood. Their arguing brought the best cover to her movements, swift and careful, removing a singular knife from the pouch on her belt. She would have only one shot with a shadow walker. If she missed it would be over.

"So touchy" the voice teased. "You must really love her. I assure you that I will treat her like a treasure once I have stolen her from you. You know I did take this job because of our past, you know you put me in that cage, but this might be better than the amazing amount of coin your brother promised for your head. Your family's coin, your woman, your life, how could it get any better." How a voice could be slimy Xai wished to never find out. Finally, he walked out, tall and broad, deep skin tinted by the night but the black marking-like tendrils over his skin were easy enough to see. Red eyes seemed to glow unnaturally, unlike the vampires that were above them on the mountain. His appearance was not what she imagined with that voice, but that was why it was a rare gift from what she heard. The shadow plane corrupted those who entered but were not strong enough, most shadow walkers died in the realm they traveled through. A crossbow hung at his side, ready for use with no arrows. The feline cursed under her breath, he was a mage, not a spell caster. He had access to materialization, they would never be able to outrun or stop bolts made from shadow. She had heard many times about when a daemon's handler was in true danger a daemon's sense of time seemed to slow. She always took that with a grain or two of salt, there was no way adrenaline could make time still only time casters could do that. And yet here she was with Truen in danger and time seemed to slow. It took only seconds for the mercenary to lift his arm and release the bolt in the short distance between them. With all the speed and strength she possessed, she threw Truen in a safe direction into the trees, taking his place at the last second knowing the shadow walker could not think fast enough to chase his target. Neither man noticed her release her knife, with an accuracy that only came with years of practice and survival. She knew the outcome the moment she moved her Prince. The knife made its target clean into the surprised man's throat, bleeding him in moments. The cry of her Prince let her know the bolt also hit, but she felt nothing. Looking down the bolt in her chest fell out of existence as its mage left this plane for the last time. She had done her job and protected her partner but she knew this was the last time. The damage was done, and the accuracy was calculated, between the upper ribs but just enough to bleed out slower giving a false sense of hope for survival.

"Xai!" Truen's scream was a sound she never wanted to hear again, a sound of total loss and devastation. By the time he reached her, she had hit her knees. Though time seemed normal again she still could not feel the pain and that was a small mercy. "Why did you do that?" He cried cradling her to his chest. The feeling of heartbreak and pain drenched the bond. His face contorted in a way that looked painful, she understood, of course, they were fated and she was dying. There was no saving her this time, no solution. She was thankful she never promised to not abandon him again though this was not her choice. She could admit she did not want to leave him, now that she was getting ripped away on the forest floor. "Oh, Gods there is so much blood. Help! Someone Help us! Please Gods dammit!" Truen started screaming at the top of his lungs.

"Don't waste your breath." She gasped, she couldn't tell if she was imagining it or if she could actually feel the blood filling her lungs. Everything was getting blurry, cold seeping into her bones. Dying was a strange feeling she decided, she had always wondered what her sister had gone through if she didn't die on impact. Truen looked down at her completely distraught, tears falling onto her face, when had he moved her to lie down? He was putting pressure on the wound but even with that, she couldn't really feel. "There is no need to cry. This was my job, remember." She struggled to speak. "I don't regret it, I regret knowing what we could have had if we had time. Don't cry." He kept trying to shush her, begging her not to speak and to reserve her strength but she knew it was useless. She wasn't scared which surprised her. She couldn't stop his tears but at least she could push the love that never left through the bond as things went dark.

"Xai, Xai, Xai." He chanted between screaming himself hoarse for help, praying someone would hear him. She couldn't die, not with what she said, what she felt. He knew he was being selfish, not caring about everyone who would be lost without her, but he didn't care he needed her. He had been trying the entire time to use the one healing spell he could use to save her but it wasn't strong enough, he wasn't strong enough. It felt like ages when Lux and Jackdaw broke through the trees around them.

"Please brother can you save her." Jackdaw had never seen his brother like this. This was the ghost of the man he knew. "I tried to but I am not strong enough, she is still warm." He pleaded for his daemoness' life like he needed to beg Jackdaw to help her. He nodded, taking the limp body of one of the few people he truly cared about, and began working. This was his sister and he would save her.

"What happened?" Lux screeched at the broken raven. He just pointed at the corpse beside her, neither had noticed it beforehand.

"He came for me, she threw herself in the way of the bolt." He whispered.

"A shadow walker comes for you and Xai dies. This is your fault." Lux screamed, her grief was obvious even with unshed tears. "You killed her. She was right, she shouldn't have been around you." She growled. Truen just sat there where he had been on his knees before his brother took the woman who meant the most to him in this world and the next. Tears fell to the ground as he accepted all the pain and blame. "If he can not save her there will not be much to keep me from killing you myself."

"Lux stop it right now," Jackdaw spoke, not yelled, his voice strained as he worked.

"Why should I, this is his fault that my sister is covered in her own blood." She argued back, not even turning to look at her own handler.

"Because if I am going to save her I need to concentrate and you are distracting me." He answered knowing her anger was not with him or even his brother. "Go take care of that corpse. Truen, come make yourself useful and help me." He instructed. Normally Truen would be taking control in a crisis but Jackdaw knew his brother for once needed direction. Placing Xai back in Truen's hold was enough to ground the elder brother while the younger worked, it wasn't much but it was a start.

"Lux if Jackdaw can not save your best friend, I beg you to follow through and end me as well. I can not live in a world that she no longer is in. It almost killed me not being with her all these years but at least I knew she still lived. Let me share death with her, please. It is my only request for you." Truen's voice was almost non-existent after screaming loud enough for the entire forest to hear him.

"You really love her don't you." She looked at the man she had traveled with for months now and not seeing him but seeing a broken soul barely tethered still.

"Since the first time, I knew what love was. Even before that. There is something about living your entire life with your fated if you have one."

"Have you told her?"

"No, she thinks I betrayed her somehow."

"And you didn't?"

"I would never, not then and not now."

"And you haven't told her? What really happened, whatever it was?"

"No, I haven't."

"You are the stupidest man I have ever met."

"That is fair."He was so resigned.

"I am going to need you two to shut up." Both stopped still at the strained voice. "My head is killing me." Xai groaned.

"Brother you saved her." Truen's voice barely supported him.

"Yes but now I am going to need to sleep almost as long as she is." Jackdaw fell back on his ass in the dirt completely exhausted.

"I am completely indebted to you." Truen pulled Xai to his chest.

"No, you aren't but let us call it even for the past shall we." Jackdaw sighed. "But we need rest."

Xai came back to consciousness with a groan. She had no idea how she was alive, though there was a dark-haired woman who said it was not time for them to meet yet. Part of her missed dying, it hurt a significant amount less than healing. "Gods Truen I hate you." She groaned again knowing that the pain of being alive was somehow his fault. She knew he was sitting next to her, but she refused to open her eyes and be subjected to light. She could feel him, smell him, hear his heartbeat somehow better than before. Memories of the night before swam behind her eyes in disgusting detail.

"Finally you are awake. I was beginning to think that you were trying to remain with the dead." He sounded relieved, almost happy.

"Currently wishing I could have stayed dead, living is painful." She whined trying to rub her eyes.

"Don't open your eyes yet, it's a bit on the bright side. We made our way back to the village so you and Jackdaw could rest in beds while you recovered. I changed your bandages a little over an hour ago. I am sorry to say your top was not saveable neither was your cloak but I sent Lux to get you a new set along with a new tunic for myself."

94

"You telling me this so I won't beat you for my partial nakedness?"

"Mostly, currently your chest is covered in bandages the healer gave us, nothing is out in the open if that is your concern. More so with the style, you prefer it will be a few days before you are going to be well enough to put it on so you will either need to embrace the bandages or wear one of my tunics." The daemoness had a suspicion that her handler would rather her in his tunic, so possessive.

I am just glad she is finally awake. That was weird she thought, that felt like it floated in her mind like she wasn't supposed to hear that. It was Truen's voice but that wasn't possible.

Get out. She responded loudly not in the mood to deal with someone who was not supposed to be in her head.

"Xai I know you don't like people taking care of you but can you not scream at me to get out? I am not going anywhere." Truen sighed.

"Truen, I didn't say that out loud," Xai spoke carefully. Opening her eyes, and regretting it almost instantly, she watched him carefully, not entirely sure where to go with this.

Truen?

Yes?

What is going on?

I don't know but I think we can read each other's minds.

That is what I thought.

Are you about to flip shit?

95

No, I am good. At least it seems like I can only hear and talk to you.

Really? Are you okay with this?

Oh, hells no I am about to lose my absolute shit.

That makes more sense.

What about you?

Not even close to okay but considering what happened I will survive.

"That reminds me, thank you for saving my life." Xai sighed using her actual voice again.

"Don't thank me, thank Jackdaw. I was useless, he used all the magic he had stored to save you. You and he have been sleeping for four days healing."

"How badly has Lux been spiraling?" She asked, already exhausted again, deciding to ignore the timeframe she had been asleep.

"Oh horribly." He nodded.

"Alright then let us not tell anyone about the sudden telepathy, and let us check on the others."

"I can agree to that for now."

"Hand me one of your tunics then." He was a little too happy about helping her dress. They only made it one more day of rest before they became impatient and started back up towards the mountain. If Xai was still wearing Truen's tunic then no one mentioned it.

Chapter Five: The Pure Blood Vampire

With the slow down of pace for those healing it took nearly three days to pass the cave, they had been resting in during the attack. They made no move to stay there again, pressing through to get to the bottom of the true mountain pass. By the time they made it to the archway in the stone, Xai was dealing with only lingering soreness. Shifting helped reduce the pain so she tended to stay in her feline form, it would also help with the temperature that would drop the higher into the mountains they traveled. Luckily for the sanity of both daemoness,' their handlers did not fight them about adding extra layers before leaving sea level. Solars were notorious for hating the feeling of extra layers and the weight it adds to their bodies. Truen and Jackdaw were no exceptions but knew when not to argue with their overly tired and sore companions. They easily headed the warnings of the below-freezing conditions they were traveling towards. Xai tried silencing the disapproval within herself at the loss of exposed skin on her Prince. Their bond had matured in the years apart.

Once we get back off this frigid rock I will take the layers back off, have no fears. A voice teased.

Get out of my head. She sighed, not used to this new connection at all.

It is kind of nice being able to hear your thoughts about me, it definitely helps with some of the insecurities the bond hasn't fixed. He sounded much too pleased.

Just remember before you get too smug I can hear your thoughts as well, this connection goes both ways.

Such a small sacrifice for such comfort and reassurance. I always wondered if you would be attracted to me as we got older.

I am not above begging you to shut up.

That could be fun.

There was no more hiding and as frustrating as it was for her she could also admit deep within that he was right, it was a reassurance. To be able to not only feel the emotion but hear the candid thoughts along with the pointed, there wasn't a guessing game on the meanings of words or actions. The extra connection was going to be undeniably in the coming days up the mountain, it would most likely be too cold for either of the solars to talk correctly. As it was they had already set Jackdaw on Lux's back when they arrived at the archway so that his weaker body would not slow them further or get him injured on the unforgiving terrain. Lux had joked that Truen should do the same with Xai, knowing that even though Xai was smaller than the behemoth of a wolf next to her. Even though he seemed to consider it for a brief moment he shut the idea down quickly inside himself and declined to say that he was fine to walk the two-day journey.

Though I would not let you ride on my back you didn't decline due to my size, did you? I know I am much smaller than Lux like this but you don't weigh more than a kit to me.

No, I know how strong you are. I don't want to take advantage of something I don't need. I am able-bodied and though I am glad it was so easy to accommodate my brother I do not require assistance with the physical hike.

The day's journey was finally anticlimactic, all random chatter and fairly easy travel even on the steep uneven path along the side of the mountain. Finally, the stress of the last few days was passing, and both metaphorically and they were moving forward. Even with the temperature dropping the mood was not, which was rare for each member. Their luck continued as they reached one of the rest points carved into the mountain face as the sun started to set. Leading them inside the stone hut the solars looked around confused. It was just a room hallowed out of the rock, a fire pit ready in the middle to be lit. Whoever maintained the site made sure to keep some cooking gear well cared for in case, even made sure there was fresh water accessible.

"What is this?" Jackdaw asked as he snooped through the shelves full of seasonings.

"It is a checkpoint," Lux answered maneuvering her large body into one of the worn divots on the floor. "There are a lot of different people that come up the mountain to visit the vampires for a lot of reasons. Not everyone can safely get through the night on the path. So the village put various checkpoints so people can safely rest until they are ready to continue their journey."

"Vampires, elves, and daemons are the longest-living races in our world. vampires are the symbol of knowledge and wisdom so they tend to have information about almost anything that people seek out. Sometimes it's for medicine, sometimes for scholars, there is apparently a lot of history and information hidden away in this city they call a village. They have kept it safe by tampering with the conditions to make them harsher and dealing with it. No one who wants to be a conqueror can survive here long enough to challenge them." Xai continued. She always admired the vampires and their cold determination to protect knowledge above all else but to also share it with those who took every chance to seek it out. "Truen, light the fire please, and fill the pot. For the rest of the night, you two need to stay within arm's length of Lux or me at any given point. We also need to keep the fire going."

"It smells like they left meat behind so we shouldn't have to use the rations the town below gave us," Lux added, sniffing towards a chest sitting by the wall.

"Why do we have to stay that close? I mean there isn't that much room in here with you two shifted but that seems a little extreme." Jackdaw asked.

"When I said they tampered with the conditions on the mountain I meant it. They have made it unsafe for those of non-lunar descent to make it safely by themselves at night. Once the sun goes down the temperature will drop to a point that a solar could freeze to death in moments without a fire or a lunar. Terras can make it a bit longer but not much. Only lunars have safe passage due to our ability to withstand the most frigid conditions and no sane lunar would challenge an entire village of an original race. The daemon and vampire villages and the human city are all safe zones for lunars and most solars and terras. Not to mention outside of this checkpoint is almost complete blackness with only the stars to help and only lunars have a vision in the dark so you might fall off the cliff's edge on the other side of the path without us."

"So either stay within your reach where we are safe and warm or die one of a few horrible deaths, got it." Truen sighed as he put a stew together with the ingredients he and his brother could find.

"Simply put, yes. And since if you die we die we would prefer you just listen to us so we can keep you alive." Lux shrugged.

"That is a general rule to follow. Don't make it hard for us to keep you alive." Xai sighed, stretching out to get into some sort of comfortable position while the Princes cooked. The healing injuries did not make it easy to be comfortable while she was still, though they were healed enough to travel with the scarring. It still hurt more than she wanted to let the others know. The last bit of healing was always the worst, this injury itself taking its sweet time to finish going back to normal.

"I will try not to make it difficult my dear Astrantia." Truen looked over at the daemoness who had closed her eyes. Aftershocks of pain moved through his chest every time she moved.

"Astrantia?" Lux asked in confusion.

"It is a flower meaning courage, strength, and protection, it symbolizes one's inner strength, one's ability to overcome any and all obstacles, as well as unkillable passion in the language of flowers. It is the flower that marks the royal daemons in our kingdom. Only the best and most loyal royal daemons get the Astrantia crest to wear." Jackdaw explained in awe, knowing that it was the perfect name for his brother to give his daemoness. "A perfect endearment for her brother."

"Thank you, have you thought about a better endearment for Lux? Maybe Clematis or some variation of." Truen smirked focusing on the pot before him and not at the wolf who might not be amused with him in a second.

"That would be perfect, maybe blue jasmine, like her pale silver eyes? It is a common name for it." Jackdaw thought aloud.

"And that means what exactly?" Lux sighed.

"If I remember correctly Clematis is a flower meaning wisdom, aspiration, travel, and mischief along with a few other things. It is commonly known as the blue jasmine or the leather flower and one variation fairly close to your eye color if memory serves me." Xai recited without taking a moment to open her eyes, finally comfortable where she lay... "My mother loved flowers, she was the one to teach us all about them." She spoke as she felt the other daemoness' eyes on her. "Also better than wolfy but not much could be worse so it is a win no matter what he does." That earned her a growl that normally would have landed her with a wolf on top of her, but she was thankful her companion spared her the extra bruising.

"Why would you both choose to call predators by the names of dainty little flowers?" Lux huffed, not entirely sure how to feel since most daemoness were not compared to pretty things let alone things that were fragile like flowers. No matter how they presented themselves, society always saw them as weapons that were sturdy and dangerous. There was no femininity to being a daemoness unless they were a honeypot or seductress, then they were just whores.

"No matter how fragile a flower may appear, it can be deadly and resilient. Never forget you are not just a daemon but a woman as well and you deserve to have a beautiful term of endearment from your partner if you want one." Truen reassured her. Xai made a soft noise of agreement, Truen had always treated her and her female relatives as women, not just females of a species. The Queen had always instilled a need in her sons to validate a person's gender no matter the race. Lux seemed to settle with the explanation and the evening progressed calmly. The fire was enough to keep the two men warm as they slept next to their protectors. The two were still awake relaxed in the stillness of the clear night. No winds, no storms, and no apparent danger on the horizon, it made the arrival of the vampire scouts seen from a great distance away. The small group of three was more surprised when they opened the door into the cutout than the daemoness' waiting for them to arrive. The Higher vampires, each one of three hooded men, made noises of disgust at the sleeping solars present.

"I thought I smelled solars on the path." One of them hissed lowly in pure venom.

"What are the likes of them doing so close to the village?" Another spat out, his tone was incredibly harsh.

"Well, they would be sleeping instead of listening to your rude comments." Xai raised her head to look at the scouts in apathy. She knew they would not do anything but their blatant racism put her fur on end. Even her hatred of what the majority of solars bought into with their racial supremacy did not make every member of the bloodlines beneath her, only those who participated in the problem.

"Do not speak to me like that, you may be a daemon but you sunk to letting yourself become a pet. I can smell the bond on you." He hissed in reply, taken aback at the cold tone from the superior threat in the area. Carefully standing, adjusting to not hurt the man who had cuddled into her side for warmth, she turned to the scouts pushing them back through the doorway. They would not wake the solars with their nonsense nor would she with the urge to tear this one apart. Lux would watch and protect them while she took care of their welcome party. Higher vampires were apex predators in most areas, only falling to daemons as the gods had intended. daemons were made to keep humans safe and vampires in check and sometimes the younger generations of vampires forgot that fact because daemons allowed themselves handlers.

"I am going to assume you have never met a daemon with how you are speaking to me boy but I would watch your tongue before you lose it." Her tone was just as uncaring as she herded them away from the others. "I will be merciful this once because you seem young but if I ever hear you call another daemon a pet without permission or classification I will personally rip you limb from limb and dangle your pieces

103

through the trees as path markers. I will bite out your throat and use it as a fire starter in your village and your elders will not stop me. I will use your fangs as accessories for my mate so he can wear them proudly as a sign of my ability to defend his and my honor. Do you understand me?" The vampires were all trembling by the time she was done with her monotone threats.

"You couldn't do that to me, I am a High vampire." His voice wavered in his fear.

"Congratulations you were born with fangs. So was I, but mine are more dangerous boys." Shifting back and completely unashamed of her nakedness she raised a brow and waited for them to catch up, her tail swishing back and forth. Forgetting how uncomfortable the healing wound was in this form long enough to prove a point.

"You are pure blood." One gasped, and the others shielded their eyes from her bare skin. The air around felt different without fur but nothing she couldn't easily handle.

"Very good and do you know what this brand means?" She gestured to the scar on her hip, knowing they could easily see it in the dark. The scar in question looks like a flower and a bow, a brand to show her status.

"An assassin class." Whispered the one who had been quiet. It was taught so many would know about the class brands for daemons, much like the symbols for all beings who use magic.

"Good boy. I can and will make good on my threats if I need to. No one would stop me. Now would you like a second chance to change the song you're singing or would you like this to be the last time you feel the wind on your skin."

"My lady, I apologize for my companion's rude comments, please spare us." The quiet one spoke again, falling to his knee before her. The others followed after him to their knees. This is one of the reasons she never spoke about her classifications, this was an uncomfortable yet common occurrence.

"Please stand, I hate people bowing to me. If you curb your tongue I have no reason to correct you and your existence in this world. I do not tolerate disrespect for the innocent. Now if you can behave I would like to put clothing on before they awaken and think something is wrong." It did not take the scouts long to follow after her back into the cut-out where she found both men awake and laying against the wolf for extra warmth. Truen's eyes went wide as she walked in completely naked and Jackdaw looked away, uncomfortable seeing his childhood friend in such a state of undress. "Truen please put your eyes back in your head, this is hardly the first time you have seen me without clothing." She sighed as she began rummaging through the bags containing the clothes she had been wearing at the bottom of the path. She could feel the obvious disappointment at the loss of skin but also approval at her wearing his tunic again coming through the bond with the almost overwhelming arousal that she had been expecting. What wasn't expected was the amount of concern that was also present. At least no shame or jealousy was coming through.

"Have attitudes been checked?" Lux asked, carefully watching the other dress in case she needed help and refusing to ask.

"They better be." Xai sighed, turning back to the vampires. "Now what do you need? We would have been in your village tomorrow, why send scouts the night before?"

"We wanted to know why solars were on the path my lady, they are no longer allowed in the village without reason."

105

Thankfully the rude one kept his mouth shut, Xai did not have the energy to kill tonight.

"Alright, please stop calling me your lady." Xai sighed feeling completely exasperated.

"My Astrantia please calm down, you're flooding the bond." Truen tried to comfort her but the feeling of being completely uncomfortable was almost overwhelming for him.

"So he is your handler my lady?" Asked one of them, completely disregarding her request. Xai shrugged it off to kneel beside him, hand on his shoulder for grounding. She tried calming herself, forgetting the force that she felt was not what he could handle without warning.

"I will take that as a yes." The snide one spoke up causing the others to stiffen at his blatant disrespect.

"Do you have an issue with handlers boy or just with living in general because I was merciful the once already?"

"No ma'am." He quickly corrected himself. "Your bond is just very strong and easily seen, you are obviously fated."

"My lady," another interrupted. "May we inquire about the reason to travel to our village?"

"Why are you treating her in such a way? It very clearly makes her uncomfortable and she has asked you to stop." Jackdaw asked instead, trying to help. His face scrunched up in obvious agitation over the dismissal of his friend's request.

"She is of pure descent. This is how she should be treated across the land. Purebloods are the lines passed down by the gods and watched over by the chosen divine." One answered.

"She does not want to be treated as such and has said so multiple times now." Lux cut in. "If you want to respect her then actually listen to her instead of pushing your wishes upon her."

"I am sorry but this is how we are taught pure blood should be treated, nothing less. This is how you will be treated in your time here and I am sorry if that makes you uncomfortable but that is how it has always been."

"Then it is time for it to change, don't you think? Pure-blooded creatures are people too." Xai sighed standing back up. She knew that no matter how much of a fuss they put up some things most likely won't change. But wasn't that the premise of this task they had taken on, to change things people think can't be changed? The scouts only nodded but said nothing else about the subject.

"Your purpose ma'am?" They tried again.

"I am looking for a pure-blood High vampire, a time mage sent me up here to collect them," Xai answered.

"Then we have been expecting you as we thought. Please follow us. We have a portal stone waiting to get us to the village."

"Why am I not surprised you have portal stones on the path?" Lux groaned, she hated traveling through portals.

"It does make solving problems easier madam daemoness." One of the scouts replied, sounding much more comfortable speaking to her.

Stay with Lux, she is currently going to be able to keep you warm until we get into the village.

Will you not shift back? You were more comfortable on all fours.

107

It will be easier to shut people up like this.

Any way I can help so you are more at ease?

Don't talk much, here you are the pretty thing hanging off me not the other way around.

Will it be safe for me to be with you in the village?

From what I know, yes, they spell the path colder but keep the village safe for everyone allowed inside. Solars included.

The portal stone was hidden only a bit further up the pathway. One of the scouts led, and the other two brought the party up behind making both daemoness' on edge. The portal stone itself was covered in glamor but once visible looked the same as all the others. A solid stone doorway with a mostly clear ice-like stable magic in the center. Only a certain kind of mage could make a permanent portal stone like these. Though slightly disoriented when traveling through they are convenient. Xai couldn't help but chuckle as she watched her three companions have to stop and wait for the nausea to pass. The vampires were less amused at having to stop on the outskirt of the village. Eventually, once the others were ready, they walked in silence into the village limits. As soon as the border was crossed the temperature rose enough to only hold a slight chill.

The stories were right though this is not a village but a city.

I have to agree with you, this place is massive and much more than a simple village.

Maybe the market will have a good blacksmith.

Didn't you just get new knives?

Does it matter? Can never have too many knives.

First, we have to figure out where they are taking us.

My guess is one of the elders if they were waiting for us then they know exactly who the pure-blood vampire is.

Hopefully, this will be simple. Then we can get out of here.

Do you honestly think anything about this will be easy? This is a journey forged by destiny and given to me, well us, by an old crone with time magic.

That is fair but let's stay hopeful.

You stay hopeful, I will stay realistic. The comment got a smirk from Truen as they walked on the cobblestone streets. It was not surprising at all that the village was crowded this late at night. Any non-born vampires had to stay out of the sun for long periods of time. The scouts nearly pushed people over in their mission to get through the streets and into what appeared to be the village center. There on a bench sat a well-groomed man, reading to a small group of children sitting on the ground. He hadn't bothered to look up at the scouts who were standing at attention waiting for him until he was done with the fairy tale he was reciting. His voice was gentle and soft, it was easy to see he did this regularly.

"Children, run along. There must be a reason these three are looming again." He smiled, sending the children on their way. He looked pointed at the scouts, his deep red eyes disapproving. "What have I said about being rude to our people and scaring our children?" His tone reminded them of a scolding father.

"We are sorry elder but we have important guests."

Elder? He looks maybe forty.

Never trust the look of most lunar races, solars, and certain terras age faster than the rest of us.

Bets on age?

Easily six hundred plus.

No, I am calling your bluff. You take five hundred and above. I will take anything below.

Deal. But what happens when I win?

One unavoidable favor that will not cause harm?

I can work with that.

"And who are these guests that you had to interrupt me for?" The man looked at the four travelers. "Ah, a pure-blooded daemon. Here for Kato are you? Our pure-blooded vampire?"

"Yes, Sir we are," Xai answered calmly.

"Please call me Yuell. I am one of the founding members of this village."

"Sir, with all respect your village is more like a city," Xai smirked knowing she was about to get the information she was looking for.

"That is a fair observation. Mytril please go and fetch Kato and Hestia for us." He grinned at the scouts. Nodding one of them rushed off across the center. "To be fair though it was a village when we came here more than six hundred years ago so it is hard to call it anything else.

Called it over six hundred.

Dammit

Never trust a vampire's skin routine.

Lesson learned.

"Your village has done well to protect itself and its people." Truen smiled.

"Thank you, young man. That means a lot. Speaking of protecting you are aware of the prophecy correct? And the next part of your journey?"

"The Time Mage led us here and then to the humans in the south."

"Very good. Please take care of Kato, he is very special to all of us and more so to his aunt and me. We raised him." As Yuell spoke those words a child came running over to him, throwing his arm around the older man's waist. A small amber-colored fox on his heels chirping away at the raven-haired boy. "Kato, how about you introduce yourself and your partner to these nice people who came to see you." The elder calmly spoke to the boy, encouraging him to stop hiding his face away.

"Hello Kato, my name is Xai." The daemoness knelt before the scared boy. He was only a child and no doubt grew up with the weight of this prophecy over his head. "I am kind of like you." The raven-haired boy looked away from his guardian enough for bright red eyes to look into a vibrant purple. "I am pure blood too." The boy gasped and the little fox started hissing at the older daemon trying to protect the little vampire. "Do not worry I won't hurt you or your little daemon. I have a handler too. I know what it is like to be like her in a way as well. So does my friend here." She said gesturing at Lux who knelt beside her friend.

Xai look at the fox's face. Taking her eyes off the boy for a moment she looked at the small daemon.

Runes of silence and shifting

They can only make quiet fox noises and can not shift back.

Who does that to a child?

"How old are you two?" Truen asked gently, putting his hand on Xai's shoulder to steady them both.

"Kato turns ten today, and Hestia, his daemon companion, is seven," Yuell spoke sadly. "Kato hasn't spoken since Hesita was bound like that. It has been two years."

"Not long after Kato and Hestia bonded accidentally a spell caster were in town." A woman spoke up as she came in earshot. "They had made some sort of nasty comment about them both being orphans and the only way Kato could get love was by forcing the bond on Hestia so she couldn't get away. Hestia rose to the defense as only a five-year-old could and the spell caster did not like her attitude or her reminding them of their own red-haired daughter so they bound her." As the woman reached them Kato reached out his hand for her. Her hair was the same raven shade as Kato's but significantly longer than his childhood bedhead. The biggest difference was her white eyes, she was blind. Xai had never seen a vampire who had been struck blind before. "I am Kato's aunt. His mother was my older sister." She smiled just as gently as Yuell. "You are here to take him with you?"

"Only if it is alright with you and them." The boy looked shocked at the feline. "Both of you."

"They are both used to people ignoring Hestia because she is small," Yuell explained as the fox chirped.

"That would be incredibly rude to do to such a fierce protector." Lux gasped comically earning a prideful hop around by the kit and a smile from the boy.

"I can even attempt to remove the runes if you would like. Even if you don't come with us." Truen offered. The offer was met by an uncharacteristic hiss from his brother that though he ignored the daemoness' did not. But it seemed neither was going to explain in front of the children who were both nodding their heads furiously.

"Do you want to come with us on the adventure?" Xai asked cautiously, trying to get back on track. "Or do you want to take a day and think about it? I know you were told about your life leading up to meeting me but that does not mean you have to come with me. Talk it over with your aunt. And we can meet here tomorrow to finish everything up?" She asked, looking at the guardians.

"It is destiny, but I would like one more night with the children." The aunt asked sheepishly, as though she was ashamed to use the out the daemoness had provided.

"That is understandable. Just because it is destiny does not mean we have to enjoy the journey. Plus that gives us a night of rest." Xai shrugged standing back up.

That was much softer than I was expecting, I know you want to get this over with.

These are children, I was not expecting children to be pulled into this.

"Then let us set you up with some rooms at one of our inns so you can rest." Yuell smiled tension that had not been noticeably drained from his figure.

113

"Maybe you can tell us any other information you may have from the Time Mage or about Kato and Hestia," Lux replied as he gestured towards some buildings on the other side of the village center.

"Of course, over some ale maybe? I do not know what information you have and what you are missing." He spoke calmly, leading us at a leisurely pace.

"If you don't mind I would like to get Xai resting, she is still recovering from her injuries," Truen spoke up, getting a growl from his daemoness and a look of concern from the elder.

"Do you need a healer? I can have one sent to your room to check on you."

"Thank you but I am fine, just sore. My handler is just a worrier." Xai reassured him.

"Please send a healer just to check," Truen spoke at the same time causing the vampire to smile.

"You two are definitely a fated pair, aren't you? I can smell it in the air around you. The young one is patient with your mate, many worry about their mates no matter how resilient they are."

"It is surprising to hear how many people can smell their bond." Lux hummed.

"High vampires can smell magic bonds, the older we are we can discern the kind of bond it is. They have a very strong and complete bond but it is somehow tainted slightly. Something akin to interference. Your bonds with your mate are fresh and new but fated nonetheless. Eventually, your bond will get as strong as theirs." Truen tried to stifle a laugh as his brother blushed at the accusation.

"What could taint a bond like that?" Jackdaw coughed out.

"Pain, betrayal, outside interference, and a few other things. Anything they could have done to their own bond would have hurt them considerably to do so. Personally, it smells like magic of some sort."

"How does magic smell?" Truen asked, intrigued.

"Like ozone," Xai replied, Yuell and Lux both nodded in agreement. Walking into the inn stalled the conversation. Yuell asked the keep for two separate rooms as the group was guests of the city and not just visitors.

"Brother, take Xai to your room. We can have a bath and a healer sent to you. Lux and I will continue to speak with Yuell. We can talk in the morning about your offer to Hestia." Jackdaw looked at his tired brother. He wanted them to rest but he was not letting the reckless decision of his brother go unchecked. But first Xai needed to be checked and Jackdaw was hoping to get a bit more information from the elder about the tainted bond. Something was wrong but for some reason, the two kept skirting the topic.

"I can handle the baths, in the morning please send over the healer." Truen sighed, knowing the morning would come with a headache but took the key nonetheless and guided his feline up the stairs to a bed and bath. He could feel the exhaustion in her silence as they entered the room.

You need to stop worrying.

You need to stop faking being fine, I can feel the echoes of your pain remember?

I can handle it.

You don't need to handle it.

I am not soft.

No one said you were. I definitely never accused you of being physically soft. But you are not alone.

This is not fair, I can't have any privacy.

It does make this easier but you already knew that. He smiled corralling her to the bed. Do you want the bath first my Astrantia?

Yes, I also want to know why your brother is mad at you.

Caught that did you?

If I have no privacy neither do you, Ruen.

I haven't been called that since you left, that is playing dirty.

I am aware of how I am playing. She grunted while removing her clothes slowly as he walked to the small partition. A larger tub sat empty but it only took him a moment to get the water flowing through the pipes that had been opened for him.

Do you still like your bath water scalding?

Yes, and you are not escaping this conversation.

I wouldn't dream of it, but first I want your healing muscles in heated water. She walked over smirking as he checked the water filling the tub. Her presence had not startled him as she walked over to join him behind the partition but her comfortable lack of clothing did. "You are enjoying this way too much." He sighed looking back into the water instead of her spotted skin.

116

"That I am, it does make it easier and harder at the same time. I never doubted you would take interest in me though, we are fated." She smirked, stepping into the tub. A groan escaped as the warmth seeped into the healing areas.

"I can almost feel you suppressing the urge to purr. Do you want me to wash your hair?" He asked carefully looking at the dual-colored strands.

"Can I trust you not to hurt me?" She asked quietly, uncertainty and fear leaking through the bond. He knew she meant more than damaging her beautiful hair or stabbing her in the back while she relaxed.

"I will never bring harm to you on purpose. Not now, not ever and I will repeat again and again for the rest of our days." The spell caster knew this would be a constant issue until their past was resolved but it got better and better every day. Even without them putting in the effort eventually, they would come back together. Subtly she nodded, lowering herself even more into the water.

"But you have to tell me why Jackdaw is unhappy with you."

"He doesn't want me to try and break another's spell. That kind of magic is not my call. Neither are healing or manipulation spells. I can control elements not people, emotions, or the magic of others. I spent many years studying and forcing myself to accept runes that do not come naturally to me. They draw too much power from me and if used too much it will backfire slightly." The way he said that was far too nonchalant for her not to hear the lie. Walking away long enough to retrieve her hair oils from their bags he was hoping she would let it slide.

"How slightly?" Of course, she didn't.

117

"Last time I broke the curse of another I was asleep for almost two weeks. It drained all the magic reserves that I had." He winced knowing she was not happy with that response without her even looking at him.

"That is more than a slight backfire." Her voice was devoid of the anger felt through the bond as he took a seat behind her, gently undoing the simple braid he had put in for her the morning before.

"It would be simple enough with a bit more of a power reserve."

"You are putting yourself in real danger for this. You know very well that spell casters are not supposed to try magic that does not belong to them.

"She is a child Xia, I can not leave her like that and neither can you." He pushed back.

"And why can we not wait to find someone who can break it without draining them completely?"

"We have no idea how long that could take, not to mention she could be a liability on this journey stuck like that. They could both get hurt if we don't attempt to fix this." He knew he had made a good point when she sighed in frustration.

"How do we make it less of a danger to you as you attempt this?"

"Other than someone sharing the burden of the drain I don't know."

"Well you can use me to help the burden, the bond will make that easy."

"I don't want to take our bond for granted. Yuell already said something was tainting it."

"We will put that on the list of things we need to get answers for." Xai sighed as Truen worked out small knots in her hair. It felt nice to have someone else take care of that for once even if she was not entirely sure where they stood for now.

"Alongside our past, the telepathic link, our fated bond as a whole, and this entire journey?"

"Exactly there on the list."

"Fantastic, exactly what I thought."

"Are we ready to take care of children though? Going forward tomorrow we will most likely become parents even if we have to return them in the future."

"Well I always thought that we would have our own children in the future but I will be honest when I say this is not what I had in mind." He admitted as he rinsed her hair.

"We are not even on the solid ground between the two of us and now we are throwing a ten and seven-year-old in the mixture." Fear leaked into her voice.

"You already sound like an expectant mother. We will handle this the same way any other parent who adopts children will handle it. We will get through this together, Jackdaw and Lux will also be there to help." The raven spoke calmly trying to reassure his daemoness.

"What if we ruin them? Or worse what if we don't then we have to bring them back? We have no idea how long we will have to travel. Let alone the war that we are about to start is no place for the children we swore to protect. What if the human is a child too?"

"That does not sound like the words of someone who would ruin a child. But unfortunately, I do not have the answers for you, at least not right now. I know without a shadow of a doubt though that we will do everything right by those children while we have them." He smiled as he braided her wet hair back, knowing she would enjoy the waves in the morning. "The water is cooling, let's get you out so I can also bathe. Do you need assistance?"

"I should be alright but can you get me a towel please so I do not get our bed wet?" He nodded, reaching beside him as she stood from the water. "Would you like me to wash your hair?" She asked with uncertainty but with the urge to reciprocate the intimacy that they had shared.

"Not until you're healed without soreness." He smiled, holding his hand out for her as she stepped from the tub. "As much as I would enjoy that, I would rather not put your healing further back. It has only been a few days even with your accelerated healing it is taking a bit for your range of motion to come back fully. Dry and go rest, I will be in bed with you shortly."

"So I am not allowed to watch you bathe but you can watch me?" She smirked knowing how to get less pure thoughts in his head.

"You can but you were always worse at keeping your hands to yourself than I was." He smirked back. Falling into banter that was a more adult version than what they had as children but just as comfortable. "As a bit of incentive, you can enjoy the view once we have talked through that list we are avoiding."

"That is cruel."

"To both of us but maybe it will work. Now go lay down." He smiled again, turning from her to drain the tub. They could feel the other's frustration and wondered who would break first.

The morning came too soon in their opinion, neither wanting to acknowledge once again they had tangled up with each other in their sleep. It happened every morning that one would wake with their head pillowed on the other's chest and limbs would be wrapped in each other. This morning it was Xai who was laying on top of Truen's chest trying to shake off the feeling of that damn dream again. Just the same as the other mornings they untangled themselves in silence. Truen had been correct about Xai's content happiness when she managed to take the braid out herself and let the black and white waves cascade over her shoulders.

"I don't want to go down to meet the others." She admitted.

"I can understand that, neither do I." He agreed.

"Is it wrong that I do not want to do any of this? I don't want to travel across the kingdom collecting people unfortunate enough to be born like me. I don't want to start a war. I don't want to be scared every day. I don't want to drag children or what little family I have into this shit storm."

"I wouldn't think you would have been chosen to do this if you wanted any of those things. You are the kind of person who will save one person by yourself every day by trying to make a difference. Do not start a war where you put innocent lives in danger. I always looked up to that and strived to be like you even when we were apart."

"I hate your father for this."

"So do I. mother said he wasn't always like this but something happened when we lost Jhelum. I don't remember, we were young when he died."

"We didn't feel young back then." She smiled at the memories before everything fell apart.

"No of course not we were big kids, dumb kids but no longer babies." Truen huffed, a small sad smile spreading across his face.

"And now here we are." Xai sighed. "And there is no way to get back to when things were easy. No matter what we do we will never have that innocence again."

"No, but we can bring back innocence to the children who have not lost it yet. We can make sure they don't have to live in a world of war and genocide. That is why we are doing this." Determination painted his voice. She nodded, steeling herself to move back into the real world of pain.

"We will see the end of this." She matched his confidence.

"Let us get going. I would like to get you checked even though I am not feeling any soreness from you."

"You also want to avoid your brother's lecture."

"That is not the point at the moment. We also need to collect the children and get them ready to leave."

"You don't think they will decide to stay?"

122

"Unfortunately I think destiny will not give us a choice to spare them." Resignation filled the air as they finished getting ready for the day. They were met at the bottom of the stairs by Jackdaw conversing with Yuell, Lux facedown in her meal, and the aunt who had never given her name looking apprehensive.

"Good morning you two, did you rest well?" Yuell greeted them calmly. "I will take you to the healer once you have had something to eat." Lux groaned.

"Did you forget High vampires hold their alcohol like gods?" Xai asked the wolf, she knew her canine friend probably spent a good lot of the night talking to the residents instead of resting like she had wanted to. The line of questions was meat with a low growl, daemons with hangovers were never fun.

"We will be taking her to the healer as well." Yuell chuckled. "Luckily we have a mage who specializes in healing here in the village. She makes sure no one stays injured or sick long no matter the cause."

"Convenient. It is a shame that is not a more common calling in magic users." Truen shrugged. "How was Kato and Hesita last night?" Truen asked the aunt.

"Well, they were very excited, my guess at the idea of getting the curse lifted. Children that age don't understand the depths of things like destiny." She spoke quietly. Yuell did not seem as happy with her this morning as he did the night before. "Though I did think about your presence in their life. As their guardian, I have made a decision that I hope you can agree with."

"Of course, you are their guardian. What did you have in mind?" Xai asked carefully. Yuell and Jackdaw grew tense.

"I want you to leave them here with me. I am their family. You can go find the other pure blood and bring them back here so Kato and Hestia are kept out of this. Destiny has no right to do this to children and take them away from me." She spoke quickly as if someone was going to stop her from speaking her mind. With the way, Yuell sneered it was not a long shot that he would have.

"That is fair," Xai spoke, shocking everyone but her handler. "We don't want to drag them into this either. If they would be safer with you then I agree with you. But they need to be safe. If not, I would prefer to leave with them."

"We talked about this last night. Destiny is demanding something of Xai, Kato, and this human. Demanding they be something to each other and by extension, their families are somewhat intertwined. There is no denying that. We don't know what Xai and I are supposed to be to Kato and Hestia but you are their family too, this is their home."

"But destiny says.." Yuell started only to be cut off by Xai.

"Honestly at the moment fuck destiny. Destiny is throwing us together and we need to take care of each other. Not just me and the other two but everyone getting dragged into this. Yourselves included here."

"Think of it as a daemon's pack," Lux interjected. "We are hereby destiny and by choice but a pack involves family and extended family to take care of each other. I see their point, if the kids are safe here we trust you to continue to take care of them while we do the dangerous part."

"They are your children through destiny and you would leave them here with me willingly?" The aunt asked cautiously.

"Why not? Would anyone willingly take children into a war? Or would they leave them with a close family member they trust? It is the same idea if you call them ours. If they are actually our children through destiny then I sure as shit would rather them here after we fix that curse." Xai shrugged sitting down next to the aunt, Lux passing her a bowl of some sort of grain and fruit. Truen sat beside her, dodging the glare from his brother at the mention of the curses. "And though I know there is apprehension on said curse removal I would like to see if we can get that done this morning while the streets are mostly clear and the healer is on standby."

"I can go get the children. I left them home because I thought you were just going to take them." She sounded ashamed.

"I understand. You want what is best for them and I respect that." Xai smirked knowing she couldn't see it.

"We can handle that after breakfast when we go over towards the healer's house. You can meet us there." Truen suggested. She nodded and silently left the inn.

"Destiny will not like this. It will correct itself." Jackdaw sighed.

"Maybe destiny will do right by the people it is screwing over for once." Xai sighed.

"No, he is correct. I can feel it in the air, destiny is not pleased you are not planning to take them along with you."

"I have a feeling we will not make it out of the village without them," Jackdaw added.

"I have packs already set up for them, I had a feeling Rosada would not let them go easily." Yuell sighed again.

"Though somehow I am not surprised you would be willing to leave them here out of harm's way."

"We will pick up extra at the healer's house then," Lux added without thinking.

"As I said they are children, I would rather fight all the gods alone than purposely allow innocent children to get put in harm's way." Xai shrugged.

"I can see you doing that." Lux giggled. The conversation turned to travel and how far south they could get by portal stone. Yuell told them that they could get within a few days' journey to Terrdia, the largest city in the kingdom outside the Royal city, but that is as far south as they had access to. That still took weeks off their travel time so they would not complain at all, even with the need of taking the portals making most of the members sick at the thought. It did not take long for the group to stroll across town with all of their bags to a modest little house outside of what Yuell explained was the library complex. A grouping of buildings containing all the knowledge that the vampires had access to. There was a woman with flame-red hair waiting for us in the garden out front.

"Everyone this is Lorell our healer, Lorell these are my guests I told you about. Truen and his daemoness Xai who was injured very seriously recently. This is Jackdaw and his daemoness Lux who decided to instigate a drinking contest with me last night in the inn." Yuell introduced us.

"Thank you for seeing us, ma'am. I am sorry that this morning was on my request." Truen bowed slightly.

"Worry not boy, it is reasonable to be worried after an injury to the one you care deeply for. The one who should apologize is the daemon who lost any mind she had to challenge an elder to drink." She smiled joyfully. Her pale eyes were full of mirth for Lux's pain. "Now I will see your daemoness before your companion's. Maybe she will learn." Stepping up carefully to Xai, inspecting her carefully.

"A few days back I took a shadow bolt to the chest, went through my lung. Other than some soreness I feel fine." The mage's smile dropped as she listened.

"You also came very close to death, a mere breath. You should listen to your handler and be more concerned with yourself." She shook her head and began incanting, placing her hands on Xai's chest, forcing magic into what had yet to heal completely. It was a new feeling for Xai, she had never assisted in healing before. It was a warm and almost tingly feeling. The daemoness had not realized she had shut her eyes and leaned against her handler until the feeling stopped and the healer stepped away. The children had arrived at some point and stood watching with their aunt.

"I need you on retainer." Xai hummed, feeling better than she had in years.

"That is what happens when you actually let things heal." Lorell sang as she walked over to Lux.

"Morning children. Did your aunt tell you what is going to happen?" Truen smiled, wrapping his arm around his daemoness without thinking. They both nodded their heads wildly causing the adults watching to smile. "Fantastic, then with Miss Lorell here I am going to try to break the curse on Hestia and we will be on our way."

Are you ready?

Take the power you need. Kneeling Truen put his hand on the small kit's face, the other hand never leaving Xai's person.

127

She could tell the moment he started, it was vastly different from Lorell's magic. It felt like electricity spreading through every nerve, the feedback through the bond was almost too much. It was over almost as fast as it started leaving both out of breath and drained but nothing life-threatening, solved with simple rest. The results were worth the discomfort, as soon as the curse snapped Hestia laughed. It took only moments for a little girl to be standing before them instead of a kit. Amber hair and bright green eyes that they had seen were much more human. Her voice was like bells, which mixed beautifully with Kato's. Yuell and Rosada had tears streaming down their faces after having to watch the children suffer in silence for so long. Jackdaw watched his brother until Truen waved him off, Xai had kept him grounded and gave him access to a larger pool of magic. Lorell watched carefully after she was finished with Lux who had been too distracted to pay attention.

"Well, that was something I would not like to try again." Xai huffed, smiling at the children. "Though worth the energy.

"Thank you." Kato looked up at them both with large red eyes.

"No problem kiddo, take care of your aunt and your daemoness while we are gone and we will call it even." She responded.

"You will come back for us right?" He sounded unsure.

"Of course, we will," Truen reassured, ruffling his short black hair. Exchanging goodbyes they went to follow Yuell to the portal stone as they planned when destiny decided to intervene. It happened so fast. Before anyone knew what was happening Xai was over the top of the small vampire, Rosada was dead on the ground, Lux had tucked Hestia away, and three scouts lay dead on the ground. Xai knew she had killed the two who targeted them, spitting something about the end of purebloods, Yuell killed the last but not before they killed his friend. Blood was rushing through Xai's veins, muffling the sounds of distress and she held her child to her chest unharmed. She had missed the bite on her shoulder as she lost consciousness. Truen learned valuable lessons at that moment. One, vampire venom is lethal to daemons. Two, his daemoness had a habit of almost dying, but she would die to protect their new child. Three, they would be spending a few more days in the village under Yuell and Lorell's care as Xai was resurrected once more. And most importantly four, destiny would not let anyone stand in its way, those deemed unnecessary to the path were expendable. They burned Rosada and the scouts who had been spelled to attack while Xai was recovering, Truen and Kato only left her side to pay their respects to the only guardian the boy ever knew.

Chapter Six: Fairies in the City

It took days after Xai woke from the vampire venom for Lorell and Truen to let her out of bed. Kato and Hestia had taken to sleeping in the bed with her and Truen, shaken to the core at losing their aunt in front of them. Yuell had mentioned they had never truly known Kato's mother because she passed in childbirth, Hestia had been left on the doorstep of the library at only a few days old. Rosada had been the only parent they had ever known. Xai was the parent they had been promised. They almost lost both in one attack. It had not taken long for Lux and Yuell to sniff out a mercenary spell caster who had followed them into the village waiting to take out the purebloods. He had used the scouts as his puppets. The feline was surprised she didn't get a lecture about self-preservation from her handler or the mage, they were just happy both purebloods survived. Though she could not do anything without a trail behind her, Kato gently holding onto her hand, Hestia with a gentle grip on her tail, and Truen as the ever-present shadow watching for any threats. Once she got cleared to travel Xai was almost unstoppable to leave. Yuell and Lorell packed extra rations and medical supplies and demanded they return when they could as they said their true goodbyes at the portal stone to Terrdia.

"We will have to spend a few days camping before we get to the city," Jackdaw explained to the children as they entered the portal. The other side was almost more disorienting than the portal itself. From a mountain with clean air to an industrial city in barren land in the distance. The temperature shift alone was uncomfortable enough to force the males to have to change clothing, let alone the acres and acres of dry cracked dirt and smog in the air. Trees were farther in the distance than the city which made the outer walls look much

130

closer than they were. Days passed in uncomfortable silence, and the air itself became unsettling the closer they got until they passed the barrier that made their skin crawl.

"This is why I hate Terrdia," Lux whined, pulling at her skin. Much like her feline companion Lux had learned never to go into Terrdia shifted no matter how uncomfortable. Xai could not help but agree with that sentiment. The discomfort was on the verge of being too much for her to deal with. She could see those who had never visited the city rub at their exposed skin, unable to put together what was wrong.

"I agree with you Fangs but it's a necessary evil at the moment. But we need a safe night's sleep, Kato and Hestia are not used to this way of life and camping out and we need to take care of them too. Truen needs to relax and Jackdaw needs to rest, they are exhausted. Just think about those open-air baths at all the inns and we might be able to get through a night or two without peril and with our skin still attached."

What is this feeling?

We have been cut off from our natural magic.

What? How? The voice came through drenched in panic.

No idea but it is the law of the city. No magic, no fighting, and everyone is on a level playing field. That is why it grew so large, and its natural hot springs.

Have you been here before?

A few times when Lux and I were younger. We could only stand a few days before the hot springs were no longer worth it. I would like to only stay the night and keep moving.

I agree with you. Though I am curious about how they do this to an entire city.

131

I do not care. I have had to deal with more near-death experiences in the last month than I have in the last decade. Please do not get yourself in trouble while I enjoy an open-air bath.

I will do my best to stay out of trouble. I would also appreciate you never having a near-death experience again, I feel as though your kits feel the same.

"Let's go find an inn with some rooms, a bath, and a tavern. I feel like I am going to need it to deal with this city." Lux sighed. And they did just that. Finding an inn was thankfully easy enough. The harder part was convincing Kato to leave with Truen and Jackdaw for the bath and Hestia to go with Lux to the market so Xai could get a bit of a nap without the children attached to her hips.

"Xai, come on and move, we have to go." A man's voice roared, his familiar voice laced with panic. He screamed for her to open her eyes, sounding more frantic as the seconds drew on. When she opened her eyes she realized she and the dark figure crouched next to her were surrounded by walls of fire. "Come on Xai, I am not leaving you here. I am not going to leave you to die. You have to get up please, I am begging you." The voice was so familiar to her and so close to tears but she could not see who the shadow person was. She tried to get up as he instructed but as she did a sharp pain went through her side, and she fell back to the ground. Looking down to her own horror she saw she was completely split open from shoulder to hip, bleeding out profusely.

"I can't, I can't get up. Just leave me and go, save yourself. Please just leave me here." She cried out, she could not let him risk himself, whoever he was. Her eyes burned with smoke and tears but the shadow man would not leave her. "Go save yourself." She pleaded again.

"No, I will not leave you, understand me Xai I will never leave you behind." With that, the man picked her up from the ground as gently as possible. She knew those marks anywhere, it was Truen who was with her. The pain ripped through her as he adjusted her in his arms and she screamed in agony. He was strong enough to carry her with ease which was lucky for her and her injuries. As fast as possible he could he ran through the ring of fire that surrounded them. She could not believe Truen would run through the inferno with her securely in his arms, she couldn't even feel the intensity of her wounds.

"Why wouldn't you leave me?" She demanded through gritted teeth once he stopped running, she was hoping they made it to safety if he was no longer at full sprint. He set her carefully on the ground to look once more at her wound as she spoke at him, she couldn't even tell if he was listening to her at this point. "Why do you always insist on being with me? Saving me? Protecting me? I am a demon, your demon. I am disposable in this relationship. Is it for the extended life I can provide you? Is it for the power that comes with being a handler? Just tell me please because you are making no sense."

"Xai you should know me better than that by now." The tired man sighed, his voice resigned. "It has never been about the power, the near immortality, or anything else that people get from becoming a handler. It never has and it never will be any of those reasons Xai. It has always been more important than that." He caressed her face with one hand as he tried applying pressure with the other. Her blood was a highlight on his blood-covered body.

"Then why?"

"Because I love you Xai, always have and always will."

The last words to leave the dream Truen's mouth were a natural alarm for the daemoness. She never slept past the confession, if Truen wasn't in the bed with her she would wake covered in sweat and almost gasping for breath.

"Xai are you alright? I can feel your panic." Truen asked, carefully entering the room childless. "I could tell you were having that dream again so I sent Kato to get food with Jackdaw."

"I will be fine in a moment. I just wish to forget the dream." She pushed knowing he would drop it like he had since he first caught glimpses of the dream himself.

"Alright, as long as you are going to be okay. If it helps you were right those baths are worth the discomfort of being here. Lux and Hestia just went down to the baths if you want to join her. I can have Jackdaw continue to watch them so we can eat when you are done." A stray thought of Truen being a partner and father swept through Xai's mind once again, the stray thoughts started when she first woke up and watched the spell caster braid their kit's hair, showing the vampire how to help. She would continue to be grateful that he never mentioned these thoughts even when she knew he heard them, pride would swell the bond every time it happened. He was every bit of the man she always knew he would be.

"That sounds magnificent." She sighed looking at the man who was still drying his hair as he paced the room. Runes on complete display on his bare chest. Sometimes she forgot how physically strong the Prince was in his own right. He had always been a hand on learner when it came to things like sword fighting and casting when they were younger so it came as no surprise that he was covered in defined muscle. It was getting harder and harder to ignore her attraction to him.

I can hear you Astrantia. You are being fairly loud in your mind tonight.

Then ignore it.

I couldn't if I wanted to, not that I wanted to. It is nice to hear about your attraction to me. Don't you feel the same? I know you are aware of how attractive I find you.

We are not having this conversation. You do not need an expanded ego just because you are attractive. I am not the only one who finds you attractive in this world.

Yes but you are the only one in the world whose opinion matters to me. But alas are we adding our mutual attraction to the avoid list with the others?

I am going to the bath and you are going to stay out of my head.

You are running away again.

You can bite me.

Only if you ask nicely. The incredibly confident comment was rewarded with a pillow thrown with amazing accuracy at the back of his head as the daemoness swept out of the room and towards the baths. He was getting more comfortable again and cockier and she had no idea how to handle it. Rushing through stripping her clothes and rinsing off she did not even acknowledge Lux already in the perfect hot water, Hestia was swimming around the smaller pool chirping contently.

Even when you run away you are still astonishingly beautiful.

Get out of my head Truen.

You know as well as I do that I can not turn this connection off. Though I can use it to my advantage. What can I say? I am feeling romantic tonight.

I am taking a bath, go feel something else somewhere else.

I don't think I want to put this off anymore. I thought you were going to die in my arms twice recently. Not to mention we now have children together.

We are not talking about this.

"Are you alright Spots? You look like you have a headache." Lux asked from where she relaxed in the pool.

"Yeah Fangs, Truen has just been up my ass recently and it is a tad bit stressful considering."

"Can you really blame him? You scared us all twice in only a short time." She whined.

"I have already gotten that lecture a few times. At the moment I would rather not have my mind on him. How about you? How are things going with Jackdaw?"

"Things are going good, especially now that the initial surge of the bond has settled. Gods above I forgot how nice these baths are." She groaned, closing her eyes and laying her head back. Chuckling Xai copied her actions and relaxed, only feeling the slight pull of Truen still actively listening.

"That is fair I am surprised every morning you two don't show with heinous marks covering you," Xai smirked at the noise that came from the other daemoness. Crude remarks always flustered Lux and it only got worse with Jackdaw in the picture.

"Oh, and how are you feeling any better? I have no idea how you keep your hands off of Truen." The wolf shot back.

"One reason we have more restraint is we were raised together so there was no surge of overwhelming lust. We also have a difficult past which allows for a bit more self-control. You were always looking for your mate, praying to anyone who would listen that your fated mate would be your handler. You saw him and did not waste a chance. You allowed yourself to fall as fast as you could."

"You can't deny you have feelings for Truen." This was a dangerous territory of conversation especially with Truen still listening, still actively checking the bond. "When will you admit you love him?"

"Probably never. No matter what I feel or what destiny wants I don't know if I can ever embrace that."

Do you love me?

"But why?"

"Even with us traveling, seeing him with you and the children, seeing him provide for the group I can't let myself trust him. Never again. Even with the man, he has grown into." She spoke carefully. "He betrayed me."

"What if he didn't?" The wolf asked.

"If he didn't by now we probably would be married and happy somewhere. That is normally the goal." It was true. Even though they had been children, Xai knew the basics of where their relationship was going before she was chased from the castle. "He would be my mate, handler, husband, and partner."

"Maybe it's time to heal and put it behind you. I am not trying to say what happened wasn't traumatic but you don't have all the information, you said it yourself everything that happened didn't make sense." Xai wanted to be frustrated with her friend but she was right and the feline knew it. She had been fighting with the urge to let the past go for weeks since they met again if she was honest. Xai could not hope that destiny would not be cruel to her, it had been cruel since the day it decided to include her in its plans. The daemoness was pulled out of her consuming thoughts as Lux screeched, Her eyes snapped open only to see Hestia giggling beside her. No danger is present only a mischievous child.

"You seem to have a growth attached to you Fangs." Xai chuckled watching the smile spread across the little girl's face.

"Your kit thinks she is funny." Lux groaned, she was Hestia's fascination. It was a good conclusion to draw that the little girl hadn't met many other daemons before let alone anything remotely canine. For the most part, Hestia watched and copied Lux's movements as best as she could. She was not a quiet child but she stayed away from talking still, preferring chirps and chitters to words. They would work her and Kato through the burdens left by the curse as time went on, Lorell warning that it could take years but it would heal eventually. They had time now with Yuell being so adamant that these were the children of a Prince and his daemoness. She still had no idea how he knew the men were Princes but she figured his age and some sort of vampiric bullshit. "Why are you up my ass? Go get Xai, she is your new guardian."

"It is because you are a wolf, to a fox kit you are fascinating. It won't be later until a feline becomes interesting to a kit. Though she will have definite advantages as she gets older." Hestia preened at the proud tone Xia had.

138

"I don't know what to call her," Hestia said after a moment looking at Xai from Lux's side.

"What do you want to call her?" Lux asked, confused.

"Grandpa Yuell said she was our mom, and her handler is our dad. But Aunty said they were strangers." The kit seemed so confused and lost while looking at the daemoness with large eyes.

"You can call me by my name, my title, or as some sort of family. It is up to you and Kato to decide. Truen and I will never force you."

"Kato and I have never had a mom and dad before." She looked over with hope.

"We would be honored but make sure that is what you want. Think about it, until then you can use our names." Xai tried to be comforting. She was used to dealing with the tiny horde that was Lux's family but none of the wolf's little cousins came close to forcibly adopting a traumatized kit and vampire. "I am going to get some food and rest. Lux, will you take the little one for food? I think you and Jackdaw are babysitting tonight." As the other adult nodded as Xai moved to get out of the water. "I have missed these baths but I hate being cut off." Lux groaned in agreement, she had returned to relaxing with the kit curled into her side. The daemoness took her time drying and pampering her skin all the while feeling the frustration and impatience of her handler on the other side of the bond. He would not be able to ambush her when she returned but she could make him wait, maybe she would get food on the way to their room just to put off the encounter a bit longer.

I already got our food sent to our room, get that ass here.

If you are going to be pushy...

Xai please get your tail in here before I come to get you. The bond was full of insecurity, fear, hope, and confusion.

Fine, I am on my way. She sighed internally. This would not be the most exciting conversation in her life but thankfully it did not feel like walking to the gallows. Their room was not far enough from the baths to overthink what she was walking into. Opening the door was not quite what she was expecting. Candles had been lit along with the already going fire. Their food was on a table that had not been there before, two chairs and two mugs of ale sat on top. Truen sat on the bed with his head in his hands, thoughts still swirling faster than she could interpret without them being directed.

"I don't know where to go from here. Please tell me where we are going."

"You were my first love and my only love if I am honest but I can't trust you. Not after Lui's death. I don't know where to go with this either. We are fated and I have never heard of a fated pair not being together or rejecting each other without death. Neither of us is dying so even with the betrayal I can not reject you. But how can I ever forget what you did? Because of you, I had to flee the only home I ever knew and go on the run. I was homeless, familyless, drowning in grief and confusion on how it could happen, how you of all people in the world could betray me. You were supposed to be the one person I could trust above my parents, my sister, my best friend." Xai forced out, sounding sad and exhausted. "I want to have the bond fulfilled but I can't let myself be with you."

"You can not keep blaming me for Lui's death." Truen shot off the bed, pacing. "Her death was an accident. I did not kill her."

140

"Truen I was there, I saw it. And even if my mind was playing me my mother would not have had me flee if I was not next. She knew how Lui died too and she chased me from the castle to save my life or I would be buried next to Lui right now." Her tail swished erratically as she stood leaning against the door.

"But Xai, how does that make sense? Why would anyone in the Royal family be responsible for Lui's death unless it was an accident? She was fated to a Prince just like you. You two were the most protected daemons in the entire Royal City." He tried to emphasize, raising his voice slightly, remembering they were in an inn with thin walls.

"What I saw was no accident, but again even if it was a cover-up it would not have been hard."

"The entire Royal castle has been looking for you since you left, hell some thought you hurt your sister. But we never let those rumors live."

"Why would I be the scapegoat, maybe that is why my mother had me run."

"But Lui's death was an accident. Why would you be in danger? It does not make sense at all." Truen pleaded. "Please tell me exactly what you saw when you saw your sister die."

"Why would I relive that with you?" Xai sighed pushing away from the door. Truen was pushing confusion and frustration through the bond.

"Because nothing makes sense. Not you thinking I would kill one of my best friends, not your mother making you leave, not my brother's crusade since her death, not the attitude in the castle after. Shit, even father has been acting completely out of character with this genocide. Something is wrong. I know it, Jackdaw was the first to put the pieces together, you have to feel it. Even Yuell said something was tainting our bond. If I am your fated mate I shouldn't be able to hurt you on this caliber without hurting myself. I have not felt anything but numbness and abandonment since the night you left until the day I saw you in the dungeon again." When he put it that way it did sound strange, the bond having no damage with the betrayal was something Xai had wondered about since they bonded as handler and daemon, opening up their fated bond once more.

"I will admit that the situation is strange. But until we figure out what is going on the complete truth, I can not be with you like that." Confusion gave way to determination.

"We will find out what is tempering with our bond." He stopped pacing, looking at her dead in the eyes. It was a look Xai had been familiar with at one point, Truen would stop at nothing to get the answers he wanted. That look had matured as much as he had over the years and had an interesting reaction. "I am going to take that as an agreement and not an inappropriate time to be aroused." He gave her an unimpressed look, though the bond said otherwise.

"Were you not the one complaining earlier that I do not outwardly admit I am attracted to you?"

"You are a pain in the ass woman." He groaned, Xai moved further into the room, towards the almost forgotten ale.

"And your brother is about to burst through that door." She could hear his unique steps getting closer and decided to take a sip of the mug as the frazzled blonde threw open the door, Kato on his heels. Truen raised an eyebrow at his daemoness who shrugged before looking at his brother. Kato looked between the two brothers before walking past them to sit on the bed and watch.

"I am going to guess you found something?" Truen prompted, Jackdaw nodded as he limped over to one of the two unused chairs.

"Yes, Kato and I were able to figure out how they make the city a magic-free zone." He nodded. "You have a really smart boy there." Looking at his new nephew proudly. The vampire smiled slightly and looked down, obviously getting embarrassed by the praise. The opposite reaction of his daemon.

"You took a ten-year-old to help you with espionage. Interesting choice." Xai commented nonchalantly.

"I remember you at your age Xai, you are not allowed to talk about things done at the age of ten." Truen shot back not looking at her but at his brother still. She shrugged as Kato looked up at her with curiosity in his eyes. "We will tell you what things she got up to at your age when you are older and can no longer challenge her stories to make worse ones." Truen already sounded like a father, Xai thought amused. The blush rising on his neck was a fantastic indicator.

"Nightmares of the Royal castle staff aside, the answer to the barrier preventing magic is in the central tower. They are draining the powers of a pixie and fairy team along with their daemons to create a forced barrier with a manufactured spell stone." Jackdaw got out.

"I am sorry what?" Xai slammed her mug down as Lux and Hestia walked into the room as well.

"That is what the residents are scared of and why they stay even when cut off from any inherent magic they have." Jackdaw continued. "According to the tavern goers every time a person or group tries to free the tower they go missing."

"Seems like the kind of thing we fix." Xai shrugged with feigned indifference, once more picking up the mug and draining it completely. Her smirk was visible as she set the mug down again.

"What do you mean the kind of thing we fix?" Truen asked, gaining a laugh from Lux.

"I have made a name for myself outside the Royal City," Xai said as she walked over to grab her cloak, she was going out and she would need all her weapons. "I right wrongs on a small scale and this seems wrong." She continued as she checked her holsters and pouches making sure her knives were where they needed to be for a delicate mission. "Should be easy enough, in and out. Lux, can you watch the kiddos for me? I need stealth, not the wolf pack."

"Got you covered. Jackdaw and I will kid-sit tonight. See you when you get back then." Lux nodded motioning for the children to go to her and shuffling them back out the door, of course, both stopping to hug Xai awkwardly before leaving. The affection made Xai only pause for a moment before continuing to get ready. A sigh came from the blonde.

"I will go with her but please don't get injured again. We don't have a healer on hand and I don't have that kind of stamina. I am still recovering from the first time." He shook his head knowing that Truen was waiting for privacy to talk to his daemoness.

"Xai.." Truen started the moment the door closed.

"You are not stopping me from going, even if you are scared." She cut him off.

"I am not going to stop you, I am going with you." His words made her stop and smile. He was just as much a warrior as he was a Prince and she knew that.

"Then are you ready to go?" She looked at him in defiance. He raised his eyebrow in response, walking past her to grab his sword. "I have always wanted to storm a tower, next it will be storming a castle." She giggled leaving the room.

"Sometimes I am reminded you are a child in an adult body." He sighed following behind her. The excitement was palpable between the two as they walked through the almost empty dark streets of the city. It was too easy to get to the base of the tower, but with the reports of people going missing the people holding the tower were overconfident. They were completely in sync as they slid into the shadows of the tower. Level by level they cleared out all the workers who had been there voluntarily. Anyone in chains or clearly scared when their saviors showed they were released without hesitation. When they finally reached the top, the twentieth level, they had found little resistance. Some of the levels were empty as they searched. Chained at the top were the creatures they had been looking for. A fairy and a pixie are locked to a spell stone, a set of daemons looking sick chained to the walls. The moment they stepped closer the pair realized the trap that had been set. Eight was the total number of armed men waiting in the wings. This made more sense than the empty floors, once the two made a significant amount of distance up the tower they focused on protecting their unwilling assets. These were most likely how they made people disappear.

"Armed guards in close quarters, interesting. I wonder how this will work for you."

"Since this should be over shortly, how do you want to get out of here, those four look barely conscious," Truen asked, knowing that they had the advantage in this situation. Xai had always done better in close combat, Truen learned quickly as he got his ass kicked as a child.

"We will figure that out when the tower is clear." She smiled, pulling out two of the knives from the thigh holster. "You know these men are very unprepared to fight against trained soldiers. I can tell easily because you seem too calm and your armor is just terrible." She smiled, throwing the first knife into the shoulder of the man directly across from her. "Time to play." It was an easy enough dance back and forth, the hardest part was keeping the captives safe. The high of victory made it easy to miss the sound of an arrow being released.

"Xai, come on and move, we have to go." A man's voice roared, his familiar voice laced with panic. He screamed for her to open her eyes, sounding more frantic as the seconds drew on. When she opened her eyes she realized she and the dark figure crouched next to her were surrounded by walls of fire. "Come on Xai, I am not leaving you here. I am not going to leave you to die. You have to get up please, I am begging you." The voice was so familiar to her and so close to tears but she could not see who the shadow person was. She tried to get up as he instructed but as she did a sharp pain went through her side, and she fell back to the ground. Looking down to her own horror she saw she was completely split open from shoulder to hip, bleeding out profusely.

"I can't, I can't get up. Just leave me and go, save yourself. Please just leave me here." She cried out, she could not let him risk himself, whoever he was. Her eyes burned with smoke and tears but the shadow man would not leave her. "Go save yourself." She pleaded again.

"No, I will not leave you, understand me Xai I will never leave you behind." With that, the man picked her up from the ground as gently as possible. She knew those marks anywhere, it was Truen who was with her. The pain ripped through her as he adjusted her in his arms and she screamed in agony. He was strong enough to carry her with ease which was lucky for her and her injuries. As fast as possible he could he ran through the ring of fire that surrounded them. She could not believe Truen would run through the inferno with her securely in his arms, she couldn't even feel the intensity of her wounds.

"Why wouldn't you leave me?" She demanded through gritted teeth once he stopped running, she was hoping they made it to safety if he was no longer at full sprint. He set her carefully on the ground to look once more at her wound as she spoke at him, she couldn't even tell if he was listening to her at this point. "Why do you always insist on being with me? Saving me? Protecting me? I am a demon, your demon. I am disposable in this relationship. Is it for the extended life I can provide you? Is it for the power that comes with being a handler? Just tell me please because you are making no sense."

"Xai you should know me better than that by now." The tired man sighed, his voice resigned. "It has never been about the power, the near immortality, or anything else that people get from becoming a handler. It never has and it never will be any of those reasons Xai. It has always been more important than that." He caressed her face with one hand as he tried applying pressure with the other. Her blood was a highlight on his blood-covered body.

"Then why?"

"Because I love you Xai, always have and always will." He looked at her with pain in his eyes. "And I always have. I will not lose you again."

"Please don't tell me I am dreaming again." The pain in her side was grounding her in reality.

"Dreaming? Is this the full dream you have been having? I understand why you were incredibly irritated every time you had it, this is terrible."

"Trust me I am already aware. And you are not on the receiving end here." She tried to laugh it off but only coughed in pain instead.

"You need to relax. You promised to stay safe and you threw yourself in front of another projectile. Jackdaw is going to be pissed." He sighed trying to be as calm as possible.

"Maybe it would be safer if I went to whatever afterlife is ready for us." Before she finished her poor attempt at a joke he silenced her with a kiss. It wasn't the most sensual or romantic but it was perfect for the moment.

"You two are under arrest." Looking up from Truen's face, incredibly pissed, Xai hissed at the ring of Royal Guards surrounding the embracing couple. Truen lifted her carefully into his arms, refusing the help of any of the guards. He walked calmly into the back of the barred carriage that was waiting for them.

Just relax, and don't do anything rash with your injury.

We will be fine. Do you know how often I have broken out of cells?

No should I be concerned?

No, but Lux will know to help those we saved and we will meet them back in a few days. It took three nights and days to arrive back into the dungeon that had changed their lives as they had been before these last few months.

Thankfully they did not put us in a magic lock cell this time someone doesn't want us to stay here long. Truen held carefully onto the healing wounds thanking all of the gods for a daemon's accelerated healing. He kept her in his lap, shielding her from onlookers even when they sat in the dingy cell. The entire journey they had stayed completely silent to those outside their bond.

"Hello, brother." A voice broke their silence.

Chapter Seven: The Past Returns

"Why are you here Krutz?" Truen growled out, calling attention to the figure who had been standing silently in the cell door. Truen curled over Xai's upper body so his brother could not see the extent of her injuries. Pushing her raven-haired handler away, ignoring his complaints, purple eyes glared at the man as she stood to face him. His hair was as red and wild as she remembered, his eyes as green and cold as a gem.

"Why if it isn't the youngest Prince." She hissed.

"I knew he would find you Xai, you are more beautiful than I remember you being." His voice made her skin crawl. "It is nice to see you again."

"I can't say the same." She retorted, her voice losing all emotion. Memories flooded her thoughts of all the happy times as children. The four Princes and the two daemoness'.

"Don't be like that darling, I have missed you greatly since you ran. Maybe as much as my brother. You were my only true tie to Lui." His expression began to edge too close to madness to be sincere.

"If you were intelligent you would keep her name out of your mouth, traitor."

"But that is where you are wrong darling."

"Stop calling her that." Truen spat out trying to push past Xai and towards his brother. She blocked his path, pushing him back.

"My brother behind you is the traitor." Krutz continued entirely ignoring his older brother.

I swear I am not a traitor.

Shut up Truen.

He is delusional.

To your kingdom you are a traitor, and so am I. But I have a feeling that is not what he is talking about, is it?

No. He thinks I killed your sister.

So that is two people who think you killed Lui. Tell me how you are not her murderer again.

"Pity isn't it brother, even with her tongue as sharp as ever she will not use it to protect you. You are the reason her sister is dead. Why my mate is dead, and I promised you that you would lose everything you love just as you did to me. Watch her as she hates you again and leaves. He poisoned your sister so that he was the only one with a pure-blood daemoness as a partner in everything. He wanted to be special." His rant became more unhinged. "Maybe I can truly make you hate him with what I have planned for you before I sentence you both to death."

Because he thinks I poisoned her, which is not what you said happened. And you said it was Krutz and me who killed her, not me alone.

"I would leave before I kill you myself so you can join her." Xai turned from the younger Prince to look at the older Prince. The bond was full of confusion and frustration at the puzzle in their past. "If you do not leave my sight before I take the three steps that it will take to reach the door you will find yourself in here with me and I am not in the best of moods."

She barely took a step before the youngest Prince took off running, the scent of fear permeating the air around them.

Was he always that scared of me?

Yes, but he has also always been a bit of a coward. We need to get out of here.

Yes and then you need to explain the storm going on in your head right now.

Do you believe me?

I don't know what to believe at the moment but you were correct on something being wrong.

Then let me make our exit. The smell of fear was replaced by the smell of magic as the stone walls began to tremble. A doorway opened in the outer stonework leading down to the familiar field.

Ah, it was you wasn't it? You were the one who broke me out last time I was here. She hummed walking through the opening and onto the path her handler had made.

Yes, though I had to be far enough away to disturb the earth below the last cell since you were in a much more secure area of the dungeon.

It is strange that we were put in the low-security section.

I feel like someone did not want us in here long but I am not sure if it was to help or to harm. The lack of noise at their escape as they walked away did not put much into the sense of security as they left. *If it helps I don't feel outside spells attached to us.*

At the moment I don't care. We need to get back to the group and that is another three-day journey by a horse which we do not have.

There are safe houses nearby so we can rest and I can check your wound.

It is fine.

I feel your pain, please. It will also give us a safe place to talk without interference. Just us. She could not argue with that. She knew that they could not put this off any longer but she did not want an audience no matter how much she cared for them.

Lead the way then, I don't remember any safe houses in the direction we are heading though.

They were acquired after you left, I chose a few hunting cabins out this way. The overly exhausted raven-haired male began walking towards the forest surrounding the royal city. They walked for hours without a single ambush or pursuer. The ease of the escape put them on edge by the time they arrived at the small log cabin in the middle of nowhere. Once we are inside it will be safe to talk aloud again. *This cabin is spelled for secrecy and seclusion, I didn't have to leave for days on end when it all became too much.*

Does the spell mean there is food?

Yes, I had a friend connect a spell to one of the overflow storerooms of the castle so no one ever noticed food got moved.

Clever. The cabin itself was small but homey in a way Xai was not used to. The entire interior smelled faintly of Truen.

"As I said I spent a lot of time here when things became too much?" He sighed, voice sounding raw.

"When what becomes too much?"

"Your absence mostly." He shrugged. Guilt sat heavy in her chest. "Don't feel guilty, something is bigger at play than

153

just a miscommunication. Finding out what it is will be worth the years apart."

"How can it be worth it if something kept us apart?"

"Because I have a sickening suspicion that it kept you from a similar fate that befell your sister. You're alive and that is worth the pain." Shivers spread across her skin at the thought. "There are two rooms down the hallway. One is the bedroom but the one further down the hall has a large bathtub in it full of clean hot water."

"You spare nothing here in your hideaway did you?"

"When you have access to the magic to make your life bearable in a time like that you take it, dear heart."

"And what of my clothing? They have destroyed another outfit by shooting me."

"You will just have to take something of mine until we get back to the city. If I remember correctly I have some coins stashed away here if you would like me to pay for a new ensemble for you?"

"I might have to take you up on that." She smirked.

"I will start dinner, you go bathe so you can get cell grime off your wound and I can look at it. We can talk during or after dinner, that is your choice."

"Best let it be after, this will not be a light conversation." She nodded walking towards the small hallway, it was easy enough to find the room at the end of the hall. The steam greeted her as she opened the door. A lavishly large pool of heated water was waiting for her, close to the size she had in her family's rooms in the castle. Xai had to admit she missed a tub so large she could almost swim in it but was still private and enclosed. Truen could only smile softly from the kitchen feeling the thinly veiled excitement that came from his daemoness. He remembered fondly how much she enjoyed the hot water when they were children. He was almost done with their meal by the time she re-emerged from the hallway. She stood there in nothing but one of his longer hunting tunics, water still dripping from her loose hair. She laughed obnoxiously as he stopped functioning at the sight of her.

"That is not fair at all Astrantia." He choked.

"I think there is nothing wrong at all." All the animosity from earlier was completely gone, almost like it was never there. Xai took stock of that internally. "And my wound is completely healed so you do not need to concern yourself with that. Scar tissue is just settling, give it another night and the soreness will be gone."

"So my instinct to make you rest in safety for a night was the correct choice." The feeling of pride that bubbled in Xai's chest at the thought her fated knew when to take care of her was almost overwhelming for both of them. "Well, that was something." Truen coughed. "Food is ready if you are ready to eat." He gestured over to the long table against the wall. The large window adjacent gave a beautiful view into the woods in the darkness.

"Are you not going to take a bath?" She asked sitting on the wooden stool, watching him bring their plates over. This was a fantasy that Xai had as a child when she thought about what kinds of getaways Truen and her would go on as adults.

"I will take a bath after we talk, I have a feeling that I will need a moment to collect myself."

"I can understand that. This entire thing is completely confusing."

"We will have to write everything we can think of that is off or doesn't make any sort of sense."

"Once we are done eating of course. This is our first real dinner together as adults." He smiled softly at her words.

"I feel like this is where we were supposed to be." He responded, watching the daemoness eat what he prepared.

"Maybe, maybe in a perfect world. Maybe if Lui was still here. But that is not the life we were given and we are only getting a glimpse of peace."

"Very true, you would never be able to sit still for long even if we were in a life of peace." The atmosphere in the cabin was truly calm and happy, it was strange for the couple but not enough to force them to leave. Dinner was full of flirting and light conversation, soft touches, and a feeling of natural pacing. By the time they were washing their plates, they were acting completely like they thought they would have, with no regret, no aggravation, and no feelings of betrayal.

"We should talk." The daemoness sighed. Her companion sighed nodding at her.

"Shall we take this to the living room then, at least be comfortable by the fire while we figure out what in the fuck is going on?" Laughing she agreed as she followed him into the next room. A beautiful and spacious room that was fairly devoid of items, just a larger lounge and a fireplace with a rug in between. The wooden walls were highlighted by the large window with a cushioned window seat, just like Xai's favorite hideaway in the castle. He remembered her favorite elements whether or not he meant to and incorporated them into his own space. "Sit and get comfortable. We have a lot to get through."

"Let us start with what I remember seeing, wait." Xai stopped, looking confused as she sat down.

"What is wrong?" Truen sounded very concerned, something was clogging the bond.

"Normally I would say that I could remember that day like I was still there. Currently, it feels like the memory is more of a story I was told than a replaying. The basics though are remembering you and Krutz pushing Lui into some sort of hole in the ground and leaving her there to bleed to death. I remember the pain and the heartbreak. You two were laughing about it."

"But why would Krutz of all people hurt your sister? They were bonded, if anyone in the world would not hurt her it would be him."

"That never seemed to be a question until now." She admitted. Thinking it through felt slimy and uncomfortable. "I don't know why because that is an obvious error in thought. It is like the thought of you willingly hurting me by hurting my sister unless she was a danger to me."

"This brings us back to the fact my brother thinks I poisoned Lui, once again hurting my brother and you but this time alone. That is completely different from your memory."

"Is it wrong I do not remember Lui's funeral at all?"

"Neither do, Jackdaw told me that as well when he first started asking me to question everything. He only remembers you two going missing. Where I remember a note telling me you thought I was not enough for you and with your sister gone to sickness you could not stay."

"Sickness, poison, and a fall all with no memories of a funeral."

"You abandoned us, you running from guilt because father said you were the reason for Lui's death, and you running from fear of us attacking you. All different reasons you left."

"mother told me that someone killed Lui and was coming for me next. She packed me a bag in a rush and sent me out in the middle of the night."

"No one in the castle knew that. That is why father said you hurt Lui because you ran you must be guilty but that never sat right with me. Jackdaw begged me to see something wrong."

"And Yuell said something was tainting the bond."

"Why do you think something is different here, something feels different here."

"I noticed it as well, the underlying feeling of resentment seems to have vanished."

"Did someone do something to us? To all of us?" Xai felt a flood of panic fill her chest.

"If they did it would explain why we are safe from the influence in this cabin. It would be an explanation as to why I always feel relaxed and I guess not drained while here. I made sure that it was protected from outside influence. In these walls, nothing can touch us and we are not weighed down."

"That can explain some things but not others. What is affecting us?" The slimy feeling was now affecting both of them, making them uncomfortable to be too close to each other.

"If I had to take a wild guess with the way we are feeling at the moment I would have to go with a memory-planting spell that is not happy we are asking questions."

"But I thought you said outside magic couldn't affect us here."

"If it was planted almost twenty years ago and we are close to breaking it the memory would be distant but the spell could still try to fight to stay implanted. It is weak here."

"Then what do we do? How do we break it?"

"From what I know this sensation is close to breaking but I have only read about them in books. This uncomfortable feeling is trying to make us stop questioning their fake memories. Though the books I read depicted this as nearly crippling so I believe my spells are holding up."

"What kinds of books were you reading and why the hell were you reading them." Xai hissed as the feeling continued.

"Because I had nothing better to do without you gone, but that is not the point at hand right now dear."

"We know the memories were implanted; there are no other explanations."

"We just need to know how and why."

"Do we need to know that information to break the spell?"

"No, just give it a moment since we know it is false and we should feel it break."

"That sounds unpleasant."

"Yes, it does." He agreed. It seemed to take an eternity for the feeling to break, like a snapping thread. Not painful but not comfortable which led both to shudder at the thought of having broken the spell outside the safety of the cabin. The smell of ozone and magic filled the space and the couple slumped together like two marionettes with their strings severed. "I think it is gone, at least for us."

"How can we be sure? The slimy feeling is gone but that could be a defense mechanism of the magic as well." Xai was thoroughly concerned about still being under another's influence.

"We can go outside and see if the bond suffers?" He suggested hoping that it was in fact over and they would no longer have to feel so far apart.

"Is it wrong that I am scared to do so? I am terrified to go outside and have it weigh back down. We have been in here for hours feeling how we are supposed to feel and not being manipulated." Xai admitted. "The hatred I felt for you was completely manufactured."

"And whoever did this to us will pay. But we have to figure out if we are free." He stood up holding his hand out for her. Trusting him she allowed herself to be pulled back through the kitchen and out into the forest. She could have cried when the light feeling stayed. They were free from the curse they didn't know had afflicted them for so long.

"I will find whoever stole our time and bond and I will tear them apart piece by bloody piece to hear their sweet screams."

"I have missed you," Truen said, watching her in awe.

"Why did you seem to see through the memories easier?" The daemoness looked at him, wishing he was as overwhelmed as her.

"My guess is the cabin kept breaking through the implanted memories. Maybe because you ran and I knew you were alive in my false past but in yours, your sister died and you had to flee. That is more traumatic. Maybe Jackdaw's constant questions were chipping at the spell. Honestly, I don't know but I am glad."

"So am I, I didn't know I could miss what I didn't know I could have." She sighed.

"Let us go back inside and head to bed, you are in almost nothing and I still need to clean up. We can make plans in the morning after we rest." He smiled wrapping his arms around her waist.

"This will not make me move faster." She returned, truly and deeply content for the first time in a lifetime. Smiling Truen let her go but grabbed her hand and walked back into the cabin.

"I am going to bathe, the fire should be lit already in the bedroom. Go get comfortable and I will be there in a bit." She nodded and let him walk into the hallway, she had no plans of letting them rest now that they were free to be together again.

As the sun rose the daemoness stretched, satisfied, and happy. No soreness that had plagued her before, only the soreness from the last few days. Truen was still asleep as she slipped from the bed, grabbed some of his clothing, and headed out the front door to take a breath of fresh air. The difference this particular morning could not be ignored. A manufactured weight that had been burdening her even though she never knew was gone. She felt fast, lighter, stronger, and more grounded than she could ever remember being. The lack of the implantation spell and all of its connected symptoms put the last seventeen years of suffering into perspective. Whoever had done this would pay, their blood would be on her hands by the end of this. But that did bring more questions to mind as she sat and watched the forest awaken around her. Who was strong enough to do this? Who wanted to break apart the Royal family and create war and genocide in Chemerica? What happened to Lui? And how did this play into the prophecy of the Time Mage?

The whole situation gave her a headache, she had always hated politics and this felt exactly like political plays. Politics was Lui's specialty, and Xai's was action and solution. Xai was a warrior, she always had been, and now she was a survivor as well. She could protect her people with her own hands but this kind of plotting was out of her league. In a perfect world, she would call for Jackdaw and Lui to puzzle through the motives and culprits. Truen would calm the people with a sense of security and charm that made one comfortable to follow his lead. Xai would take care of the problem, leaving blood in the water for the merpeople to find. The daemoness knew not all problems could or should be handled with force, her mother had instilled for the twins to work together for that reason. One was cunning and the other was an unstoppable physical force, together they were unmatched even with the other Royal daemons.

The night before had been flooded with happy memories with her bubbly sister once she finally got to sleep. Lui was smaller and more hyper than Xai, it made her unassuming even though she was as deadly as her sister. No one ever saw the smaller leopard's plans until it was too late, they were always distracted by her chewing on her tail when she was happy or her ability to shift perception away from what she was doing. They made a perfect team, and when the Princes were around the King and Queen had no doubts that the kingdom would flourish when they were of age. And then everything fell apart, no was forcibly ripped apart. Xai was sent away, Lui was missing, Krutz's mind was poisoned, and Truen lost his heart and will. The King started a crusade, the Queen became silent, and the Royal daemons became pets and weapons instead of advisors and protectors.

If the Time Mage was correct, which history, unfortunately, proved that a Time Mage had never been wrong, their little pack would fix this, Truen would rise as King and the people of Chemerica would be safe again. But as she sat here in the quiet of nature Xai knew she was not enough for this task. She needed her sister, she needed to channel her sister and learn from her. Jackdaw would help with the puzzles of politics. Truen was becoming the man she always knew he could be and his skills with his people would have a chance to shine. Xai had gotten better at infiltration over the years, and with Lux, by her side, she knew any army would fall before them. Kato and Hestia would be kept from any danger that they could, hidden away when the castle was stormed. They were Xai's responsibility now and no harm would come to them even if she never planned on having children. But that left the human.

The pure blood human was a variable. humans were supposed to be known for their adaptive nature, compassion, and stupid determination. She knew whoever the human was would be a wild card in any plan their opponent set and she would use that. If the human came with a companion like Kato had then they might get another perspective as well. But that didn't seem like enough. They were going against an army, a Royal city with two daemons and two spellcasters for sure. Though Xai had no doubts they would win, the casualties would be far too much. The more people they had, the more warriors they had the less innocent blood could be spilled. There would be no way to clear the castle or city of innocent lives before the storming. There were not going to be enough mages to set portals quickly and securely without tipping off the invasion. When the time came and they had the weapon, the hero to save them all.

"You are the one to restore what is right. You can start the restoration of the original clans. Listen to me well child, you are the key to the start, and your partner holds the gateway. You need one pure-blooded human and one pure-blooded vampire by your side with the same destiny to help you but you are the one. You are the savior of this world child. Only you can call the hero, the weapon to save us all back to our world. You have to call for the weapon of the gods. You will find your human to the south, heated by the desert, and your vampire to the north, frozen in the mountains. You must hurry, child, your destiny is calling."

"Was that the prophecy you were given?" She turned her head to see her mate leaning against the door with a soft smile on his face.

"Those were the exact words, I think they will be burned into my memory until the day I die."

"I can see why it gives you a headache. But was it really enough to leave me in bed alone?" He teased.

"If I had stayed we would not leave today to get back to the others in Terrdia." She retorted, standing from her spot. "Also I just needed to think."

"These last few years have been shit mixed with this prophecy." He started sighing."

"Mixing in spellwork that should not be there and breaking said spell that was enough to taint a fated bond." She continued.

"That speaks to power and access to the Royal castle freely enough to affect the Royal family itself."

"This is a conspiracy that doesn't sound like it stops there."

"Not if it forced a Time Mage to step in, we need to find the human."

"Which means no morning fun in a secluded cabin without our kids or siblings." She finished, kissing him gently as she passed him back into the house.

"I hate when you are right, then what is our plan? To get back to our pack that is?"

"Well unless you have a portal hidden somewhere it'll take us two or so days to get there, then my plan is don't get re-arrested when we enter the city. Then collect our pack and get the fuck out, listen to Lux and Jackdaw tease us and ask us questions about our completed bond. Then explain the implanted memory spell, acknowledge of bond snapped into place the moment the outside spell was gone and integrated perfectly with our handler bond which was a given. And then ask if Jackdaw ever had an implanted memory that he broke alone or if he was not affected."

"That is one hell of a plan."

"I liked it, not looking forward to it because I feel like the answers will give me a migraine and the comments will make me bury your brother and his mate in the desert somewhere between here and Lillia." She shrugged as she gave the cabin a

165

once over. Their packs were back in Terrdia with the others but she could put a few small herbs and such in her holsters. Hunting would be easy this time of year and though sleeping on the ground would be annoying for a few days it would make moving on easier. Truen had fire covered and the weather was warm enough at night to allow them to sleep beside each other without getting too hot or cold.

"We should head out, my Princess," Truen smirked.

"You only get to call me your Princess when you have gotten on your knees and begged me to marry you. I also demand a betrothal necklace from you." She glanced over to him in time to see the hungry expression before he calmed himself.

"Well I did two of those requirements last night, but your betrothal necklace will have to wait until I find a craftsman worthy of my Astrantia."

"That is better. Until I get the betrothal necklace of the heir apparent I am only your mate, not your future wife." He groaned at calling her his wife and there by his Queen, not getting the reaction he had hoped from her, she had won this round. "But you're right, it is time to go."

"We will come back here when I am King."

"We better, I now have fond memories." She knew she had won as he shook his head, both leaving the cabin again this time not to return again until things were safer. Traveling through the Eldar woods was simple if you knew how and even easier if you were as familiar as Truen on the rarely used paths. Most were afraid of the spirits said to roam in the woods so they used the cobbled paths or skirted the woods altogether. After two days of non-stop travel, they once again came to the walls surrounding the industrial city, relief filled them as they got closer and closer to their pack.

"Shoot" Was all the warning Xai got as she snatched an arrow from the air, if it had hit its target Truen would have suffered a grave injury. The call had come from the wall, though the shot was clean, the people she saw watching in horror were not guards but citizens of the city. Watching all those hidden in the watchtowers it was clear the people took back their town and were scared, but that made them dangerous.

I will never get tired of your reflexes.

"Shoot an arrow at us again and I will personally return it to the archer by hand in the most painful way I can think of by the time I get to you."

And there is the rage, good to see that wasn't only the spell.

No the rage towards you was the spell, the rage itself is all me.

"And by that, she means she will shove the arrowhead slowly in a place you really don't want it. Trust me I have seen her do it before."

"Do you work for the King?" One brave soul shouted back from the wall.

"Are you unobservant or are you just a moron?" She hissed back, too tired and now on edge for niceties. That was not her job. Truen shot her a look.

Can you not be a bit nicer? They were shooting at us.

And none of them would last long once I got up there so no. I am tired, I have been hauling tail for two days to get back to our pack and they decided to shoot at you not me.

"My daemoness means do you honestly think we would take down your barrier and be working for the King at the same time?" Truen sighed looking back up at the wall, hopefully, he could smooth things over before blood began to spill. She was right the pace at which they hiked was grueling and though it was a fairly easy journey they were both tired and sore from such speed.

"Let us in or I will come up there and throw you back down to talk to this one face-to-face," Xai added unhelpfully.

"Our apologies, please enter." The wall responded quickly.

"You just made it a bit harder for me to win over this city before storming the castle, you know that right?" Truen sighed as they walked into the city.

"To be fair we did already liberate this city and anyone who was there that night would have seen us. It could make it easier since the citizens have taken over."

"Not if you scare them all." The city seemed more lively than before, with people milling about as they passed.

"I lead a team of two to rescue people in their tower, took down most of their guard network, and got taken away because of a call to the Royal Guard. I think I scared them before I caught an arrow and threatened them for trying to provoke me." She answered.

"We could let the message of a savior coming to stop the King travel through the cities and towns who have people being oppressed."

"Part of that has already started. You heard them ask if we work for the King. There have been places crying he is a villain for years." Xai remarked as they stopped by the city center, where the tower now stood vacant.

"In the underground, the white leopard daemoness has been the savior just as long," Lux added stepping up behind the spell caster. The way he started was amusing for both daemoness'.

Not funny, how long was she there?

Since we walked through the gates.

"Welcome back brother, I was a tad bit worried when you were taken away." Jackdaw smiled, walking to hug his brother tightly. "You seem lighter somehow."

"We were able to figure out what was wrong with our bond. We can talk about it later." Truen answered.

"We must then." Jackdaw's smile was beaming. "Things have been moving quickly here since you two took the tower down."

"Yes Bee and Crow are waiting for us back in the inn, they are currently watching Kato and Hestia," Lux added nervously playing with a purple ribbon around her neck, the motion caught Xai's attention immediately.

"And those would be?" Xai bristled slightly at the unfamiliar names belonging to people currently watching her children.

"That would be two of the four people who have sworn life debts to you for saving the lives of everyone in their micro pack," Jackdaw spoke carefully. "They mean no harm to the children. Bee is the pixie, her daemon Honey. Crow is the fairy, he has his daemon Roc." Xai nodded then proceeded to take off towards the inn they had been staying at. Pushing past everyone in the tavern she took to the stairs. Throwing open the door to her room she could see a pixie shooting in front of her vampire child, she was red from hair to wings and was baring her teeth as if she was some sort of threat. A mousling chittering angrily beside her, most likely her daemon. Kato paid no mind as he launched himself into Xai's arms, sobs making his words hard to tell but the elder had a feeling he had been scared of losing another guardian.

"I am back kiddo. I promised death would not keep me from you how could a jail cell." Xai hugged the boy tightly. She never thought about coming home to children before, or the impact of disappearing for days on end. Lux always knew she would come back but Kato and Hestia did not. To them, she was missing and possibly never returning instead of on her way back. It could take years before the young ones would be comfortable with her taking off to do something dangerous.

"Xai?" Turning her head she could see her kit down the hall, coming from the bathing area. A blue-tinted fairy male on her shoulder and another mousling in her hand. All looked a bit like drowned rats. The moment the little girl truly recognized the purple eyes looking back she nearly dropped her companions to join her handler in the feline's arms.

"I will always be back for you two." She reassured, shushing their tears as she lifted them, walking further into the room to place them both on the bed. The newcomers in Xai's life stayed at the door recognizing this was the daemon who saved them from their torture but also the mother of these children. If they tried to interfere they would regret being saved without a doubt. Much like a handler, one does not endanger the children of a daemon, children of blood, or children of destiny."

170

"Is there any room for me to see our children too?" Truen asked, finally catching up to the reunion. The children nodded ecstatically. The raven-haired male chuckled as he joined his family on the bed, it was mere seconds before he too had a lap full of children.

Is it me or with the spell broken is the bond with the children stronger too?

Do you think it was suppressing all destined bonds, not just implanting memories?

Or making them fragile like Krutz?

I don't know how to test that outside of us.

Me neither but I am no daemon but I would kill for these children and before I thought more like we were babysitting.

"Ma'am," Xia looked away from Truen to eye the fairy carefully. His blue wings fluttered nervously. "My name is Crow, this is my fate, Bee. On behalf of us and our daemons, I would like to thank you and offer a life debt for saving us." As his bell-like voice filled the air the four bowed deeply before the daemoness.

"I will not try and sound heroic by saying I was trying to save you specifically but the entire city. You were a part of it, I need no life debt."

"Please madam, we are beings of magic. You saved us and our daemons, we are bound by a life debt." The red-eyed pixie shot up, clearly more aggressive than her partner.

"She has a point Xai, beings of magic are bound by magic law and life debts are one of those laws," Truen smirked from under the children.

"We have also heard from your companions about your mission and your blessing from the Time Mage against the King and his tyranny and we would be honored to help." The fairy forced out quickly. He was the timider of the two.

"Since we can use the help and Lux already has seemed to vouch for you fine, but just dear gods call me by my name." The two winged beings beamed in only the way the fair folk could. "But now that I have seen the kids, Lux, we need to take a walk." She nodded knowing exactly why. "Stay here kids, I will be back in a bit." The two older daemoness walked silently to the pools of water, hoping the open-air baths would give them some relaxation and privacy. The pools were empty when they arrived allowing the two to undress and rinse off before entering the hot water.

"What happened between you and Truen?"

"You really think I would allow you to distract me when I know I saw a betrothal necklace around your neck? I like the purple Jackdaw chose." Xai smirked watching the apprehension, shock, and relaxation cross Lux's face as she talked.

"I like it too. He got a Clematis flower carved into a beautiful pale blue stone."

"Good choice, I know Truen will get an Astrantia flower carved for mine but I do not know what colors he will choose."

"Wait, Truen proposed? And you said yes?" The shock was back as the canine nearly screeched.

"Well, I would not call what he did proposing, closer to devoting his entire being to whatever I want but to be fair the bond snapped into place so you can imagine."

"I would rather not imagine what you do with my brother actually, thank you." Both women spun at the sound of Krutz's voice. "But please when will you two be marrying my brothers? I would hate to miss such a joyous occasion by sitting in my own pits of hell alone." Two people stood behind him, aggressive stances putting the two in the water into fight mode. This fight was too big for just Lux and Xia as they shifted in the water ready to defend themselves against two Royal daemons. Two daemons Xai considered siblings of her own once upon a time.

TRUEN!

Chapter Eight: Brothers

It took only moments for the entire pack to bust into the open-air bath, wild eyes searching the scene for answers.

Slowly back you and Lux to us. Wrapping her tail around the back of the wolf's leg she passed along the plan. Slowly they stepped back through the water towards the others.

"Krutz, what are you doing here?" Truen asked calmly.

"Well, I followed you brother, though it was harder to judge how long it would take to meet you on the other side of the Eldar woods. I portaled of course, I knew you would come back to the city we picked you up in. I never knew Jack to be too far away from you. Though I did not know you got a daemon for yourself brother." Jackdaw was more concerned about looking over Lux as they got in reach than answering his brother's taunts.

"Hello Rien, and Razden, you two are looking well." Xai looked at the two younger daemons before her and remembered when they were young when her own parents adopted them. Her younger brother and sister looked at her in utter disgust. They were so young the last time she saw them, two orphans from two separate families taken in when the Royal castle was still home. From the expressions on their faces, Xai could tell they had been raised cold and full of hatred. The feline could still recall when Rien learned how to open her wings and fly for the first time, it was Xai she came running to when she hurt herself landing. Her sleek white feathers looked stunning in her dark blonde hair. Razden on the other hand had made the cutest cub who would follow Lui around no matter where she went. They were only seven when everything happened and the twenty-four-year-olds standing

174

before her were warriors ready to draw blood, not innocent children.

"I know she was your sister but she abandoned you." Krutz hissed, making the two daemons on his side sneer. "If you do hesitate to follow my orders because she was your sister I will have you both disposed of. I would shift and get ready to fight if I were you." He spat out. The spotted woman wanted nothing more than to rip his throat out for disrespecting her siblings like that. Part of her was thankful they listened to him though and shifted. Rien was such a majestic bird of prey, just like her biological mother. Razden on the other hand was a hulking black bear.

"What is this brother, could not handle asking the help of one of the pure-blooded daemons. I know the two of them were top of their class but they could never hold a candle to Xai and her bloodline." Truen taunted, knowing that fewer injuries to all parties would come about if Krutz was distracted or flustered. Bee and Crow took the cue to remove them and the children from the open-air bath, hopefully gathering the things left in the rooms and heading out of the city.

They are.

How would you know that?

Magic creatures can make temporary magic links.

Sometimes I love magic.

We will meet them after we can get away.

Preferably without hurting my siblings too badly.

"Like you could handle a completely open bond with a pure-blooded daemon. Xai's power would rip you apart." Krutz snapped his head from her siblings to his.

175

"We haven't tested that Truen, it is unsafe." Xai looked at her partner in both confidence and skepticism.

"Let us test it now then. Jackdaw, Lux get out of here. Xai and I will handle this. My beautiful Astrantia please shift, see if you can tap into your full power."

I will be unstable

I have faith in you. Show me the power the gods gave you to protect the world. As she shifted, reaching deep into the primal power that all purebloods feel. Many believe the feeling is a pool of power given to the original clans that are drawn straight from the gods, only the purebloods could reach the power, reach towards the gods. She could only imagine how it felt to Truen on the other side of the bond but she felt older than the world and powerful enough to end it in its tracks or protect every living being that walked along it. Can you hear me Astrantia?

I can hear you.

This feels amazing. Are you still willing to follow me?

Yes.

Do you still love me like this?

Yes.

Do you still hate him?

Your questions are getting dumb, of course, I hate the Krutz that stands before us. This is not the man he was supposed to be, I can smell the spell on him like this. He is sick, we were sick. So are my siblings. They are all affected by those who have harmed us.

Then let us end this so we can find out how to save them. Rien seemed to take notice of the difference in her sister and took the air before the feline could strike, thinking she was safe at the disadvantage she had.

I will follow your lead in the fight.

Continue to distract your brother.

With pleasure. Xai shot off the edge of the pool, feeling faster and more calculated than ever. Rien never stood a chance as the feline captured the bird of prey in her mouth, enough to incapacitate but not kill. Forcing the feathered daemon to the ground, landing hard enough to bounce her head off the stone unconscious and safe for now. Razden had no time to react to protect his avian sister from the true predator. He stumbled back, standing on his hind legs, on the slick stone around the pool of heated water, such a large creature had no place trying to fight in such terrain. Xai growled harshly at the brother who had never been a fighter as a child. She doubted he classified anything higher than a protector and here Krutz was making him fight. She had to figure out a way to get the larger daemon to shift back without hurting him.

The feline darted at his legs, swiping and throwing off the balance of the large male. When the bear fell into the water the feline pounced and pushed his head under. There was a defense mechanism within daemon biology, when being attacked and they can not fight back they will shift to their other form in case the other form had a better chance at survival. Once his head was under the water for a few moments he shifted smaller to try and get away. His sister was merciful and pulled him from the water, throwing his smaller body towards his still unconscious sister. Xai set her sights on the opposing Prince now that her siblings were no threat at all.

"You can control her?" Krutz smelled terrified.

"It is not about control, or have you forgotten that with Lui missing." Truen taunted. Can you come back to me, shift back? It took Xai a moment to pull back from the pool of raw power so she could shift back to her humanoid form. Being naked as she was before was better than wet fur in her opinion. Truen removed his shirt to hand to her as she joined him, knowing she was not ready to speak. He helped her into the fabric to protect her from the borderline lecherous view of his brother. She leaned slightly against her mate, feeling drained and unsteady. It would be a few moments before she came back to herself.

"Leave her name from your mouth brother." The redhead spat. "And what about you Xai? You used to be magnificent. Now you are nothing but a pet letting my brother control your actions." She opened her eyes and glared at the other spell caster. Truen wrapped his arm quickly around her waist, trying to keep her with him.

"Why are you stupid Krutz, do you want her to kill you?" Truen groaned. "Why would you degrade a person like Xai." He looked down at his seething daemon. "Next time he talks out of turn I will let you maul him. I can feel your desire to." Truen was talking from his ass and she knew that but Xai wanted a nap more than to continue to fight. But this was part of the fight, to fluster him enough for information or an opening to break his own spell.

"I can't believe you are in complete control of her." Krutz fell to the wet ground beneath him.

"Can we go? If I can not hurt him I would like to leave." Xai asked, sounding tired.

"Of course my Astrantia." Truen kissed her head, enjoying the height difference between them. This blatant display of affection seemed only to anger Krutz more. A scream ripped

178

through him as they walked away, but they ignored him entirely. In silence, they left the inn, walked back through the city, and were stopped by no one. Truen knew where the others were camping, a good distance in the barren land and as close as they could manage in the time apart to the edge of the Eldar woods. No one in the pack said anything as they joined around the fire, almost the entire day gone by. The group allowed the exhausted daemon to sleep, her head resting on her mate's thigh. By the time she woke from her nap, the sun had set. "How are you feeling?"

"Better, that truly drains you. That is why I don't tap into that power unless I have to."

"I am sorry I asked you to do it without it being a dire situation." Truen apologized.

"It is fine, it was a show of power."

"Do we have to worry about something similar with Kato as he gets older?" Lux asked, the boy in question sitting on her lap watching the feline.

"I have no idea. I have never met a pureblood vampire before, or a human for that matter. I only know the effects for daemons." She sighed, stretching her muscles. "We will have to keep an eye on it for the future."

"We got you new clothes while you were away if you would like to change." Jackdaw changed the subject while watching Bee play with Hestia and Honey. Truen reached his hand out to his brother for the aforementioned clothes. "Lux picked them out for the hotter weather. Leather leggings that we had modified to go to your knees to prevent chafing, a spiderling silk top with no sleeves, and a hood to protect your eyes. Even boots with soles meant for the hot sand. I hope we did well."

"I am sure they are perfect thank you." Xai nodded as Truen was handed the fabrics.

"You have had us worried recently with all of your injuries and near-death experiences. Maybe a treat or two from those who care about you will remind you to take care of yourself." Lux explained.

"Xai, join me in the woods and I will help you change." Truen gestured towards the tree line. Without thinking she followed. "Are you okay?" He asked once they were alone. The daemoness was acting almost submissive since pulling back from the power. He took it upon himself to dress his partner, she was distressed and he needed to take care of her.

"While I was coming back I realized there is a good chance that even with the spells broken within the Royal family, for those affected, we may still have to kill some people. The scent of the spell was so strong on Krutz in that form, under the smell of magic was the smell of sickness and decay. The more the memory changes the person the more it kills who they are. It was not nearly as strong on my siblings. Your father has spiraled more than your brother since this started. I have heard your mother went silent. What of my own parents? My mother was terrified that night. What if the memory is keeping them together from whatever else this spell is doing? My parents are bound to yours and are mates themselves. If we kill your father, my parents will die too."

"I am so sorry you are being forced into this situation." Truen wrapped his arms around her after getting her top situated.

"I had to attack my younger siblings. I had to drive my little sister's head into stone to render her unconscious so I knew her stubborn ass would stay down. I almost drowned my little brother to get him scared enough to shift back. When I find who did this I will kill them too." He just held her while she came up with more creative threats for the unknown enemy in their life.

"I know Astrantia. I also know that whatever you do and whatever path you follow I will follow next to you, trusting your choices."

"Thank you Truen." Xai looked up at her mate, reaching up to kiss him.

"Well isn't this a sweet scene?" Xai growled, her normal aggression returning at the sound o Krutz's voice. He was standing behind Truen's back. Pushing the spell caster behind her she hissed at the intruder. "I come in peace this time, no need to be so aggressive. Your siblings have been portaled to the castle to heal. I am unarmed and without a daemon to defend me." Guilt wrecked through the daemoness, her siblings' pain was her fault.

"Why are you here Krutz?" Truen sounded exasperated.

"To talk to Xai, not you." He retorted in a matter-of-fact tone that grated on Xai's already frayed nerves. The redhead watched the woman carefully, the sickness is clearly seen now that she knew what she was looking for. "Why are you with him, you are so powerful and you lower yourself for him," Krutz asked, sounding suddenly desperate.

"Not only do I love him but he is my fated, I am not lowering myself. We were made to be together." Xai answered carefully.

"But I love you." The redhead shouted back, surprising the daemoness and enraging the raven-haired male.

"Krutz how dare you…" Truen growled behind Xai.

"No, you don't." Xai calmly cut off her mate once she found herself again.

"Yes, I do. Face it Truen I love her too and you knew that before you left to go after her." He continued with a raised voice.

"You don't love her. You are projecting onto her." Truen argued back.

"Xai, why did you choose him? We are the same him and me. You didn't run from me you ran from him."

"But you two and not the same and you never will be." Xai started. This entire situation was sad to her. "I used to tell you all the time to stop comparing yourself to your brothers. You always had an issue with that since your magic came in and it was so much weaker than the others. You are your own person with your own thoughts, feelings, and purpose."

"Did you ever love me back then Xai?" He wasn't listening to her.

"No Krutz I never loved you, Lui loved you. And much like you are not the same as your brothers I am not the same as my sister." Xai sighed, knowing saying her name would hurt him the same as it hurt her with the spell in place. Lui was at the center of the spell and the way to break it.

"Why can't you see I love you." He cried, tears falling from his normally bright green eyes. He used to be so mischievous and now he was broken. He reminded her of a child who wanted their sibling's toy and was being denied. "This is war Truen!" He screamed again pulling an ornate dagger from his belt. It would have been a surprise that the others had not heard any of his tantrums if it wasn't for his magic being sound, most likely no one could hear them. "I will get a stealer's stone and take her once I have killed you."

"Touch him and I will be forced to kill you even if you are my sister's mate." Xai hissed, her patience gone with the threat. But he did not heed the threat as he tried to charge past Xai and toward his brother. Even as out of balance as she was, Xai managed to be faster than the spell caster. She had not given too much notice to the blade protruding from the skin of her shoulder until Truen screamed. "What happened to being here in peace Krutz." She gasped, staggering back as the pain set in, the blade must have nicked the shoulder blade.

"I am sorry Xia, I am so sorry" The daemoness was more concerned with the fact her Prince had his brother by the throat held against a tree than the metal in her shoulder. His threats were imaginative.

"How dare you harm her. You insignificant prick, I should skin you and send the pieces back to father from different cities in the kingdom. First, you claim to love my wife, and then you draw her blonde in an infantile rage? The best part of you was left on our parents' wedding bed." Truen's hands were tightening around his brother's throat, turning his brother's face red as he cut off air. Xai knew she could not let this fratricide happen.

"As incredibly sexy as this act of violence is, Truen can you drop the little slime that is your brother and help me remove this metal from my shoulder? I can't currently move the arm in question." Xai's voice brought Truen back out of his rage as he dropped the redhead like a disregarded doll to rush to his daemoness. "Just so you are aware I am keeping this dagger, you have lost privileges." She tried to bring levity to the situation as Truen examined her shoulder. "Please tell me he missed my brand new top, I just got it."

183

"Don't worry Astrantia, your clothes are fine, the seam leaves your shoulder blades bare in the back. He did not damage your top." Truen comforted her knowing that she was focusing on something small instead of another injury. He looked apologetic as he removed the blade, thanking the gods that Lux had gotten the outfit dyed black so the new blood would not stain it already. He watched the wound begin to stitch itself back together slowly, thankfully it was not the worst wound she had gotten in recent weeks.

How does the wound look?

Clean thankfully. Though I love the fact that he can not take his eyes off us. Me taking care of you like this is driving him insane.

I shouldn't find this as arousing as I do, you taking care of me. Making someone else jealous.

I will keep that in mind once you have healed.

"Get those thoughts out of that spiral Truen." Xai sighed, knowing exactly where his thoughts were going.

"Just because I was thinking it does not mean I would act on it. Unless you wanted me to." Truen smirked, placing a kiss on her bloodied skin.

"What?" Krutz cried, finally able to talk again after being strangled by his much larger and stronger brother.

"Did you not know Krutz? When a fated pair trusts each other completely they have the chance to unlock another link between them, a telepathic link. I am in Truen's head as he is in mine. I can see every naughty fantasy, every romantic thought, every mundane idea that crosses his mind. He can not hide from me, nor can I hide from him."

"No that can not be true." He cried again.

"I wonder if you could have felt this complete with Lui?" Xai dug in further. "But instead you wish to replace her with a fantasy version of me. Are you that desperate and pathetic to replace your own fated one, a fated one whose funeral you don't even remember? If it ever happened." She spoke the last bit off to the side hoping he would catch it and question.

"If he is chasing you knowing what he knows he has to be desperate." Truen agreed. "Go back to the castle brother and look for your own destiny or we will be forced to cut it short."

"You do not see me as a threat do you?" Krutz whined.

"No, not a major threat at the least. More of an annoyance that I put up with because you belong to my sister."

"I would barely even call him an annoyance." Truen shrugged.

"Well, his schemes tend to draw my blood." Xai sighed.

"I may be biased but to me, he is a tag-along twat." The snide tone Truen was taking was making his daemoness proud. "Now stay out of our way and you will live." Truen ran his hand down her uninjured arm to hold her hand, pulling her past his brother who had shocked into a living statue. The others were all sitting around the fire completely unaware of the turmoil that happened.

"Xai what the hell happened? You are covered in blood?" Lux jumped up rushing to her best friend. The other adults all looked tense, the children thankfully sleeping and unresponsive to the outburst. The wolf led her to stand back to the fire and stayed to the side of her injured friend as she checked the injured shoulder.

185

"Krutz paid us another visit again." Xai sighed as Crow came over to her.

"Can I clean your shoulder?" He pulled water from the pot. She nodded and he set to work cleaning and soothing the healing skin.

"Who is Krutz?" Bee asked, sitting with her back against the rock formation that shielded half their camp. She was watching the tensed members of the pack and the children sleeping next to her.

"That would be Jackdaw and my younger brother," Truen admitted, standing back and letting the others fret over Xai.

"He is a spoiled child." Jackdaw spat with venom that shocked the new members of the pack.

"He is sick, the spell placed on us has a hold on him that is decaying his mind." Xai sighed constantly as the fairy unwound scar tissue and knotted muscles in her shoulders.

"Spell?" Crow asked, backing away from her.

"Some sort of memory implantation with some nasty side effects," Truen explained.

"That makes sense, though why was I never affected?" Jackdaw asked.

"It's on the list of questions to drag out of the asshole who did this." Xai shrugged. "Those who were closest to my sister were affected the most. But it is attacking Krutz's mind, he has been attacking us and sending mercenaries after us with an obsession that I can not fathom." Something caught the feline's attention, a rustling in the trees. Mere seconds after Xai caught the movement Lux did as well. No one else seemed to catch the stillness in the daemoness', still talking amongst

186

themselves about the cursed spell in place in the Royal castle. An archer was in the branches, Xai could see the arrow nocked and ready to fire at a moment's notice. If she was right the target would be Lux and the shot would be clean if they were a career archer. Fear froze Xai's insides, after having to harm her siblings she could not let her best friend come to harm. There might have been more force used than necessary as Xai pushed Lux out of the way but she made it in time to catch the arrow in the same shoulder Krutz had injured. The scream that tore from Lux was gut-wrenching, the daemoness had landed poorly onto part of the rock formation. The scream sent the group into motion then the arrow flew through the air, it took a moment for the handlers to figure out what had happened. The children were startled awake and frightened by what they saw. By then the archer was long gone, missing their shot and hitting the wrong daemon.

"Son of a bitch that hurts." Xai groaned. "Lux, are you alright?"

"Go fuck yourself and kiss a raven's ass Xai." She screamed back.

"Good, you'll live."

"Her arm is broken," Jackdaw called back.

"Shit and you have an arrow in your arm," Truen added checking the damage.

Is my top alright?

Stop worrying about your gods damn top and let me remove this arrow

But Lux will already be mad at me.

Well, you did just take an arrow for her.

187

And accidentally broke her arm.

There is that but at least she is alive. Thanks to you she will heal. Now we need you to heal too. Truen mentally apologized again before removing the arrow much like he removed the dagger not even an hour prior.

"Fangs, how mad are you at me?" Xai called across the camp, watching her best friend squirm around.

"Gods above I hate you right now." She snarled back as Jackdaw set her arm. "How fucking dare you take an arrow for me? I am going to kill you." Xai wasn't sure how much was the pain and how much was actual anger.

"No more violence you two." Jackdaw snapped, Crow, already cleaning Xai's shoulder, again stayed silent. Truen watched carefully, leading Xai and Crow to sit by the fire. "Lux I know you are mad she got injured for you but without her, you would be dead so excuse me for wanting to thank her for her sacrifice."

"Do not thank her, she will think it is alright to continue to sacrifice herself," Lux growled.

"Are you two going to be ok?" Hestia asked where she and Kato were huddled against the rock. Bee was trying to comfort them with the tiny daemons. They were watching in horror at the elder daemoness' both being injured.

"We will be fine, We didn't notice an archer in time to get out unscathed. We are sorry to scare you." Xai sighed, she was covered in too much blood to help much. Her shoulder would be shot for days but thankfully both injuries obtained that night would heal easily and quickly. Lux's arm was worse, the bone fusing back together would take longer than muscle and skin. "I accidentally used too much force to move Lux out of the way."

"Usually you are very careful with your strength," Truen commented, pulling Xai into his arms and trying to let her rest. He could feel her exhaustion and pain.

"I think it was reaching into the primal pool, I am having an issue containing my power as I normally do. I feel like all my senses are over-stimulated already." Xai sighed, hating to admit such weakness bluntly.

"We will have to keep an eye on that." Jackdaw hummed, looking over at the exhausted daemoness in his brother's arms. "I think both of you should stay in these forms until you heal." Lux groaned at her mate. "I am sorry sweetheart but you know I am right. You two both need to heal and shifting will put that back."

"Well we will be entering the southern desert region soon, the fur coats will be counterproductive," Bee added.

"That is true," Crow added softly. "Lunars have the advantage in the cold but are very susceptible to the heat. We will have to keep a close watch on the six of you."

"They kept us safe in the cold. We will keep them safe in the heat. Let's get some sleep and start fresh in the morning." Jackdaw nodded looking around. "Everyone is fine."

189

Chapter Nine: Travel to the Beach

"Dear sweet mother of all which is unholy in this god-forsaken hellscape please someone kill me." Lux hadn't stopped complaining in the day since they left Terrida. The temperature continued to rise the further south they traveled. The wolf was miserable without the heat, her arm healing slower than she was used to. Crow and Truen were both trying as hard as they could to keep the Lunars cooled down by misting them sporadically.

"I might be feeling merciful Fangs." Xai hissed, between the heat and the constant passive-aggressive comments from her companion the feline was out of patience. The canine was digging into her anger instead of talking to her long-time best friend and expressing her obvious fear and stress in this situation. Her mood was trickling over to her handler who was more short-tempered than anyone had ever seen him.

"Ladies, please stop," Crow begged, the quiet fairy was at his wit's end trying to calm the tempers. "From what you have said the last few months have been stressful but you are in this together for better or for worse." The pale-haired man had found his voice in the group by becoming the mediator. Since the fair folk joined in the travels they had seen the stress of injuries and threats on the lives of the members. From the traumatized children and the impossible task given to people who were not prepared to attempt to save their kingdom. Bee herself had made comments to her surprise that the group had not had such issues before now.

"Crow is right, there is no reason to continue fighting," Truen added, once more misting everyone with water he was chilling further. "You two are best friends and this is not helping anything." He took a moment to check on the children who had been almost strangely silent all day, they hadn't been this quiet since they left the mountain.

"I suggest we try to make our way to one of the bodies of water so we can relax and cool off." Jackdaw groaned knowing something had to give before everything exploded.

"That is a fantastic idea brother." Truen tried but Jackdaw brushed him off. The raven-haired male knew what his brother was dealing with, Truen himself could feel the frustration, anger, and fear through his own bond. It took every bit of his strength not to snap back at his brother's mate for putting them in this bubble of anger. "If we are where I think we are, we are not too far from one of the smaller lakes." The idea of swimming seemed to encourage the group to push forward in the search for reprieve. It seemed to take no time at all for the daemons to sniff out a body of water.

"Finally!" Someone screamed as most of the pack took off towards the calm clear water. Something about the water unsettled Truen and Crow though. The water manipulators could feel something was incredibly wrong.

"Wait, don't go in the water!" Truen screamed, Crow, flying after the group as fast as he could. All the elder daemons stopped as they reached the sand, looking back at the spell castor. Luckily Xai had been able to grab onto Kato before he could run past her into the water, but Hestia was able to get past Lux and join Bee in the cool waves. The moment the two were in the water something began to happen, the water began to bubble and froth. Those on the beach watched in horror as the kit and pixie were forcibly separated and dragged out into the middle of the water. Their screams were of fear and pain.

"Bee!" Screamed Crow, his fear was palpable and forced Xai into action. Pushing a terrified Kato towards Truen she rushed into the water towards Hestia, she knew Crow would go to his mate first and that she had to prioritize her child. The water itself felt more like a thin slime than real water, and it was ice cold to the touch, the kind of cold that would burn the skin. Xai could only imagine how the Solar woman felt in the trap. If the cold could harm a daemon. Halfway to her kit, she heard a blood-curdling scream from the fiery pixie. She couldn't stop to look but the others watched as the winged woman was pulled beneath the water. Truen covered his son's eyes, praying to whoever will listen that his daughter, his beloved, and his packmates will get out of the water.

Hestia was screaming in fear by the time Xai got to her she had almost worn herself out in her panic. Xai still had the strength to pull her towards her body and force her away from whatever was trying to drag her down before it could. Having the tired little girl wrap her arms around her neck, Xai swam as hard as she could back to shore. Blood rushing past her ears in her exertion she could not hear how Crow was handling Bee's rescue. Truen and Kato met them on the sand, both grabbing for the little girl and wrapping her in their arms, checking her over as she coughed up anything that had entered her lungs in the trap. Handing her over, Xai turned around to look for the others, when she couldn't see them she ran back towards the shore only to be stopped by Lux.

"Let me go, I need to get them out of there." Xai tried pulling away without hurting her friend again. Instead of answering, the other daemoness just shook her head. It took the silence to begin to understand. Searching the shore for the remaining daemons she found them, but it was too late. Roc and Honey were laying in the sand, their lifeless bodies completely still just like the water they were watching. If they were gone there was no saving the fair folk they had been bonded to. This was the true risk for a daemon who wants a handler. Every daemon was warned as a child to be careful in choosing a handler if they ever chose to have one. If a daemon dies the handler could survive, if the handler died there was no chance to save the daemon no matter how strong they were. Truen held onto the children, both with tears rushing down their faces and horrified expressions.

"It is an illusion trap, there is no water here." Truen sighed.

"How can you tell?" Lux asked, her voice strained.

"I can't manipulate it, I can't even tell it is here and I am looking at it. I think Crow knew it too." They had only been together for days, since the fall of the tower of Terrida. After ten days to fit into the pack, Bee was loud and bubbly with one eye always on the children. Crow is calm and logical, always willing to help. Their daemons never said a word and had been shifted into their rodent forms the entire time since they met but they had been sweet and thoughtful, always willing to entertain Kato and Hestia.

"We can't get to Bee and Crow can we?" Xai asked, looking at Truen with a pained expression.

"No, their bodies are lost to us." Truen sighed, arms tightening around the kids.

"We have to burn Roc and Honey at the very least, we can burn them with Bee and Crow's belongings." Xai nodded looking over at Lux for agreement. "We need to do something to respect our fallen pack members." Even when at odds with each other Lux agreed to the plan, they were pack and they need to be remembered and respected since they had left this world. Jackdaw and Truen directed the children back further to be able to watch the funeral rites, the two daemonesses collected the dried wood that they could so that they could build a small pyre for the two lost daemons. They worked in silence, both knelt in the sand, as they adorned the small

193

bodies with personal items in their handler's packs. "Truen, can you light the pyre?"

"Of course Astrantia." With a small flame, he set it ablaze.

"Why are you burning them?" Hestia asked in a small voice, grabbing onto Xai who was still kneeling in the sand.

"Because in the daemon culture, it lets the daemon finally rest. We were created from the time we can waddle to protect those around us. We give our lives for others from beginning to end to others. No magic can ever bring back someone who has been turned to ash. When you burn their bodies you are letting them rest and go back to the gods, back to nature."

"We do the same with warriors that fall," Jackdaw added. "And the Royal family as well. Let those who have lived in the service of others to rest."

"Hestia, how are you feeling?" Xai quietly asked the little girl as they watched the pyre burn.

"Would you have burned me if you couldn't save me?" She asked just as quietly. Kato gasped looking at his daemon in horror.

"Well if I have anything to say about it your life will not end while I still breathe. But if you want you can be burned too when you are laid to rest. We all will be laid to rest one day, even the strongest people need to rest eventually." Xai tried to comfort them, not knowing how to comfort children who had already seen so much death. Hestia herself could have been lost with the others if Xai hadn't been fast enough or strong enough.

"Will you be burned?" She continued.

"Yes, when it is finally my time I hope to be burned with tradition," Xai answered honestly. This was her culture and she had worked her entire life so far to protect and serve. She earned her right to the practice. "It is a rite. And it can be earned just by being your natural safe."

"If we are not burned together I will make sure you are dearest," Truen promised. Kato was watching the conversation carefully but not lacking the horror he felt.

"When we burn our kin it is in respect. If you want to be burned, that is alright, the same if you don't. You were raised in a vampire's culture, not a daemon's. Knowing your new mother you will have a long time to decide what you would potentially want." Lux added. "But for now we watch until the fire goes out and we say our goodbyes. They were not with us long but they were still pack, you can be sad they are gone."

"Why was I saved and they weren't?" Hestia looked up, tears still falling down her round face.

"I can not tell you why they couldn't be saved. I can't tell you why a lot of people can't be saved from their situation. I can tell you that I was not going to let you get taken. If I could have, I would have saved them too. I would have fought as hard to bring them back as I did with you. But I couldn't and I am sorry. I am sorry you have to be so scared. I am sorry I wasn't faster than the spell to save all of you. And I am sorry you had to watch death again."

"Unfortunately I can not send for a curse breaker until we get to another city. This spell is sentient, it is a deathbed spell." Truen added.

"What is a deathbed spell?" Kato asked.

"It is a curse that a magical being utters as they die, they are notorious to break. The entire point is to take more lives in retribution for their own being taken." Jackdaw answered the spell type was unpleasant and cruel. Only the most malicious magical beings cast them hoping to drag innocent lives with them. With it all hanging over the group they remained silent until the embers burned away. The magically fueled fire reduces everything to a fine ash.

"We need to leave." Xai sighed, finally standing again. "I don't want to stay by this thing longer than we have to."

"Xai, we have entered the desert sea, it is almost nightfall. It would be stupid to travel through the sands at night. From the elements and dunes to the marauders that scour the terrain at night." Lux looked surprised at her companion.

"I don't know how any of us could want to try and stay the night here. We need to move as far as we can, as safely as we can." Xai responded with a sense of finality. "None of you are going to get hurt again on my watch. We lose no one else."

"We can at least try to get to the next hilltop on the edges of the dunes. It should give us sturdy ground to rest on and we can see it from here." Truen compromised. They hiked in a sullen silence towards the hill Truen had pointed to, he had taken the lead while Xai took to the rear of the group. Truen had the children help with the camp so they would have some semblance of normalcy. Xai kept to the edge of the camp, keeping watch from their vantage point over the sand.

You know I hate seeing you in pain. I know I can not fix it nor can I convince you to stop blaming yourself for what happened. I can't take the pain away but please don't close yourself off to me, let me share your burden. She hadn't realized she had been closing the bond between the two, naturally trying to protect her mate even from her heavier emotions.

I know Truen, I am trying. Just leave it alone for now. You know you can not make it better with me, focus on Kato and Hestia.

I will, and I will be waiting for you to come back to me. Standing up and looking back to the others she noticed he was watching her with an expression of concern. Looking away feeling like she didn't deserve it, she failed to protect people who counted on her. Her gaze fell on the wolf whose eyes were also on her. Her gaze was strangely unreadable for her longtime companion. It was the same expression and silence since they left the cursed illusion. Xai knew that the other daemoness was feeling the pain of losing their packmates, the canines of the daemon races seemed to feel pack bonds more than any other variant. The feline did not doubt that the other blamed her as well, if not for accidentally breaking her arm she would have been able to also swim out to save Bee and Crow.

The night continued to be cool and quiet. The children curled up into each other by their adult guardians, trying to starve off unpleasant dreams. Jackdaw and Lux seem to be withdrawn into each other. Xai laid her head on Truen's chest as he ran his hands through her hair. He was pushing comfort and the idea of guiltlessness through the bond, though it was tainted with mourning and fear. All the adults were vigilant and still as they processed everything they had seen and done so far, the loss today at the forefront. It felt like there was a suffocating mist of foreboding. It was as if they were waiting on the sword to drop once more.

"I can't see anything through the sand," Kato whispered to Hestia, completely unaware in the silence that adults could hear him clearly.

"What do you mean see through the sand?" Lux snapped up looking at the startled vampire.

197

"It's nothing." The little vampire muttered, the smell of fear started to tint the air.

"You need to explain Kato." Jackdaw insisted.

"Uhm…" Kato looked at Xai frightened. She nodded in assurance, needing to know what he was talking about. "I was told never to tell anyone because it would put pure-blood vampires in more danger. But each one of us was born with a gift from the gods."

"Like the pool of power for pure blood daemons," Xai added, it made sense that the vampires got some sort of connection back to the gods.

"I guess. Mine is sensing the living essence around me. In cities, it is like static, with so many people and animals. But out like this, it is easier to tell the difference. I can tell the difference between animal, magical, and non-magical energies now but I used to not be."

"You get a stronger connection the older you get," Truen added, remembering Xai and Lui when they were younger versus their parents or even Xai now.

"Maybe, my aunt's gift was a premonition. My mother was talking to animals and sentient magic from what I was told. I can kind of tell how close they are but it isn't very accurate right now." Kato explained, Hestia curled around him ready to protect him from angry adults. It was heartbreaking to see how little of the trust they managed to gain in the last few weeks was broken by a secret that they were told to be afraid of.

"You are not in trouble for keeping it from us, you were told it would put you in danger." Truen looked at the children with a small sad smile.

"As a pureblood myself I understand. Truen is right, you are not in trouble and you do not need to be afraid. But in the future, we will be training that skill so you can use it to protect yourself and Hestia." Xai added, the children relaxing from the tense poses.

"No, he never thought to tell us? He was with us for weeks." Lux snapped, causing the children to jump and Xai to glare at her.

"Lux knock it off. He is a scared kid who was thrown into this just as much as the rest of us. You're right it has been weeks, just weeks. Not months, not years, but weeks. They don't have the best track record with adults and no track record with anything outside of the vampire Village." Xai growled at the other daemoness.

"I am sorry," Kato whispered. "I can only separate energies when I concentrate and it hurts." There was no reason he should be apologizing about it and his guardians were split between going to comfort the child and scolding the adult who knew better.

"He tends to go unconscious when he tries too hard." Hestia quickly added, trying to calm the elder's anger at her handler.

"Then you are right to be careful using the ability until it is stronger. We will work on it safely together." Truen reassured them both, reaching his arm out for the children to come to join them. Both rushed to their guardians to curl up and be comforted. Truen and Xai had to continue to remind themselves that they had fairly young children with them.

"Xai?" Kato whispered, his face buried in her chest, her arms wrapped around the smaller boy.

"What is it kiddo?" She whispered back.

"I can't be sure but I think there are people nearby." He confessed. "It was what woke me up."

"Can you tell how close they might be without hurting yourself?" Xai encouraged him quietly. The expression on Lux's face was disbelief.

"A few, I can't really tell. I am sorry." Kato sounded like he was begging as if they would still be mad at him or abandon him for not being useful enough. And if that didn't bring back unwilling memories for all four adults. "They are over by the dune."

"Thank you, and there again no need to be sorry. Thank you for telling us. You stay here with Truen and the others and I will go check it out." She smiled gently pushing the ten-year-old boy into Truen's lap with his daemon. "Stay here and keep an eye out." Xai looked at Lux while standing up, waiting only a moment for an acknowledgment before the other daemoness could protest Xai going off alone again.

Adjusting her pouches and weapons in case, she walked away from the hill. Walking around the dune Kato pointed out she saw a smaller group, presumably marauders from their looser clothing. The group smelled like human men but Xai wasn't going to take any sort of chance with everything that had happened. She watched them from the shadow of the dune, maybe they would start spilling secrets like their last trackers. Maybe they were not looking to interact with their little pack, to begin with.

"Do you think they are sleeping?" One man asked another and Xai's hope for a quiet night was dashed.

"No, we are not asleep," Xai answered from the darkness scaring the shit out of the group of four. They spun around to notice the glowing purple eyes watching them. A tail flipping around with agitation, and a spotted daemon who looked ready to kill met them when they moved their torches.

"Daemon." One shouted, shaking uncontrollably in fear. They had counted on the element of surprise by keeping downwind of the daemons in the group.

"You can not hurt us, it is against your purpose." A braver man spat, though he could not hide his fear from the predator.

"Normally it would be except you are obviously planning against my pack which puts you as my enemy, not an innocent traveler."

"But you have traitors in your group, both of the traitor Princes and the cursed vampire child. You are not protecting the innocent." Another rushed out trying to persuade the daemon to switch sides.

"Cursed child? That sounds completely ignorant." She spat. "Children are innocent, there is no such thing as a cursed child."

"No, I promise that child is cursed. One of the Royal spell casters made a call to prophesy to a cursed vampire child and cursed human who is traveling with the traitor Princes to overthrow the King and murder all the Solar and Terra races. They said the daemons were innocent and to bring them to the Royal city to save them." He continued.

"The same King who has pushed to enslave and or murder countless Lunars and Terras over the last decade or so is calling for the death of a random child and human who are trying to stop him from killing Lunars? Is that what you are telling me?" Xai's tone was condescending. That propaganda being spread against them was unimaginable.

"They have lied to you." One pleaded.

"So the same man who put a bounty on my head with mercenaries has put a bounty on the head of my child and my mate as well is what you are telling me." She tilted her head at the men, unnerving them further. humans had no chance at all against even a weaker daemon, it was why they were the protectors.

"No, listen here little girl you can not hurt us." The man had such audacity to think that he could control a daemon who had no connection to him, especially when he was the threat.

"Now I am a little girl to you? I will show you what I can or can not do, human. I am in a terrible mood already and if you do not leave now I will use you as stress relief." She growled. She could feel the apprehension from her handler but she also knew he would not stop her from ripping these men apart. Unfortunately for them they did not heed her warning but grabbed their weapons instead.

"We don't want to fight you daemon, there are a dozen of us and one of you."

"You should have brought more people than." She answered, taking a moment to calculate that there was a minimum of eight marauders missing. Stepping forward towards them caused the men before her to back up. "I would call for the others, I will

"We were prepared to subdue daemons, our weapons are ready for you and the vampire with you."

"I can guarantee that your weapons will not affect me as you hope they will even if you are able to hit me. I will not let you close enough to the others to have to worry about what you have with you."

Be careful Xai, if they have poisoned weapons you could get seriously hurt again.

They were told to save the daemons not kill them, nothing they will have could kill me. But they have put a hit on Kato's head. vampire weapons won't kill me either but I will be careful.

"Daemon, why do you care so much about those people?"

"They are my pack and I would die for them." She answered, advancing again.

Astrantia please do not talk like that, we can not live without you. I can not live without you.

But it is true. I am a daemon, it is what I live for. If I fall protecting you I have done my duty by my blood and by the gods.

Fuck the gods, my love, stay with us instead.

"You are one hell of a daemon, we will give you that, too bad you are on the wrong side of history." That was the trigger. The humans did not have a chance to watch her movements once she started. The screams called the other members to come running back from their hiding places around the hill. One by one she viciously killed each threat that had made itself known. She couldn't tell how many she had taken care of when she noticed a dart needle in her side. Looking around she with her vision blurring slightly saw eight bodies, one of them must have gotten her when she dragged them to the ground. It was hard to tell considering a few of the bodies had landed in pieces. She could hear the remaining members arriving finally and feel the fear from Truen.

Stay there I will be fine. It is a sedative at most. I will finish this. She pushed through, but that was the last thing Truen got from his mate. The bond went numb and he could barely contain the fear as he handed the children to his brother. He was trying to play calm as he walked out of their sight and to where the fight had taken place. He found her lying in the sand, slowly breathing. The mangled bodies of twelve surrounding her, the exact number of marauders he knew about. That did not explain the two men kneeling beside her.

"Your daemon is remarkable."

"Come on Xai, it is time to wake up. I can feel your awareness." Gods be damned as Truen spoke to the barely conscious daemon in the bed beside him. He could feel her wish for death in the bond and chuckled. He continued braiding the hair of the seven-year-old while he waited for her to unwillingly rejoin the land of the living.

"My head feels like I took an ax to it." She groaned, opening her eyes. She noticed there was a boy child asleep curled into her side.

"I do not doubt that at all. Apparently, it was not supposed to be a sedative but a full poison that you got injected into you. Thankfully you were correct in your assumption they would have nothing to kill a daemon like you. You have been asleep for two days working it through your system." Truen explained, his eyes focusing on the intricate braid he was trying to put into the squirming girl's hair.

"Where are we?" The feline asked.

"An inn in the town of Desrtea. Only about a day or two outside of Lillia." He said finishing up with Hestia and standing from the bed. She watched him cross the room for the pitcher of water as Hestia curled up with Xai as well, being very careful of her freshly done hair. "Have some water, it should help."

"You seem less upset than I thought you would be."

"I am not happy with you risking yourself again but you knew you were not in life-threatening danger. Your protected our children though you scared us all again I can not bring myself to be as angry as if you risked yourself stupidly."

"I am sorry I scared you all again." She confessed, tightening her arms around the children before reaching for the water her mate was providing.

"Thank you for protecting us again," Hestia whispered.

"Of course, it is my job. You two were handed to us as our children and I will do everything I can to protect you. I will do anything to protect Truen, Jackdaw, and Lux too. I don't want you to have to lose anyone again if I can help it."

"We don't want to lose you either." Kato's voice was covered in sleep.

"I will do what I can to make sure you will not lose me any time soon. Do me a favor and take Hestia to bring us back some food, I am starving." She smiled, knowing that the boy probably had not left her side the entire time she was asleep. He nodded and said nothing else as he reached out for his daemon and left the room hand and hand. "What happened? You are too calm and the last place I remember was the hills surrounding the dunes at the southern edge of the Eldar Woods and the top of the desert sea. If we are only a day or so outside of Lillia we have traveled four-ish days in the span of me being unconscious for two. So what the hell happened while I was out?"

"Well, when I had gotten to your location after the bond went numb with the poison you had massacred all twelve humans. Almost all of them were in multiple pieces. I am glad that I left the children on the hill with my brother. The carnage was almost too much for me. You were laying in the sand, breathing so slowly but alive. All the blood on you was human. But there were two people with you when I arrived. The solars were incredibly impressed by you, drawn to you. They decided to help out and they brought us here at an expedited rate."

"What about them do you not want me to know?" Her irritation was growing with his aversion to telling her the full story.

"They are fallen solars." He finally admitted. The view on fallen solars or fallen lunars was not the best for most of the population. They were those of solar races that actively tried to revert to their original lunar bloodlines. They were never truly solars nor were they really lunars, they were an in-between. They were an in-between then no one wanted to truly accept.

"What kind of fallen?" She was trying to keep fairly calm but his demeanor made it clear she would not like the answer no matter her view of the fallen.

"One is a dragon rider." He answered hopefully.

"And the other Truen?" He sighed knowing he could not hide it any longer.

"An anigel." He cringed while saying it, not entirely sure how the daemon would handle it. anigels were the original solars, evolving from daemons. The evolution corrupted the

206

core being of the anigels versus the daemons, taking a fraction of the power and becoming much more bloodthirsty than their lunar counterpart. She tried standing up, being fairly unbalanced on her feet after a few days of forced rest. Truen reached out to steady his mate on her feet. "I know you have a bad opinion of anigels but please my love, they helped you and in turn helped all of us while you were asleep."

"Tell me more about them, give me a reason to trust a feathery ball of lies." She hissed.

"I know you do not like them but you need to stop with that, you are better than those bigots that judge someone based on their race." He scolded, groaning because she knew he was right she leaned further into her mate. "I never even saw the dragon until they called for her, though the anigel had their wings out when I arrived. I was cautious because they made a comment about you being remarkable. They said their dragon felt a pull to the location and then they saw you. They have been with us since and have been at odds with Lux and my brother the entire time."

"Well, then it is time to figure out what is going on now and then leave," Xai grunted standing up straight, ignoring the soreness in her body again.

"Astrantia, you need to rest still. You have been pushing yourself too far recently." Truen pleaded knowing it was a losing battle.

"Remember you are my mate even with an anigel around," She looked at him quickly, taking him by surprise at the surge of fear and jealousy through the bond. "If I catch that nasty little anigel flirting with you I will rip their wings from their body." Truen suddenly remembered every interaction they had together at the Royal castle with an anigel. They were the first solars as daemons were one of the first lunars but for some reason, it was a cultural view that anigels were better than daemons because they were not made to protect nor could be forced into servitude. It wasn't abnormal for an anigel to try to steal a daemon's mate since they could not have their own traditionally.

"First he is a male."

"That means nothing and you know it. I'm your mate, I am well aware you enjoy the male view as much as the female. I don't mind as long as it is not an anigel." If Truen didn't know better he would say his daemoness was pouting.

"I know you have no objections to my preferences, my love, do not worry though no anigel could steal me from you. Not to mention I am almost positive Mi'kal only has eyes for Dante, who is our current resident dragon rider."

"Oh ok." She seemed uncertain and that was nothing that Truen ever had to deal with before. Xai was always so sure of herself and their relationship even when the curse was in place. He helped her sit back on the bed, joining to continue to hold his vulnerable lover.

"No, I have a question that has been driving me insane the entire time you were asleep." He hurried to try to distract her from her uncertainty. She looked back at him with curiosity. "Every solar race originally came from a lunar race, correct?"

"Yes. daemon to anigel, a fairy to pixie, mage to spell caster, vampire to soul eater, etc." She nodded.

"Then what in the hell is the opposite of a dragon rider?" He asked.

"A lyear rider." She answered easily. "The natural counter to a dragon is a lyear, so when the riders split from lunars they turned to dragons and the dragons accepted."

"Lyears are not a myth? I have never seen one or a rider before." Truen tried taking in the information.

"You could have and never would have known. Lyears are the natural shapeshifters in our world. They tend to hide themselves so only those they trust have ever seen their true forms." Xai shrugged. Hearing a shuffling outside the door she looked over Truen's shoulder to concentrate, but it wasn't their children it was the other daemoness and her handler pacing outside.

"Lux you can come in," Xai called, hoping this would not be a fight like it had been before the dunes. She did not have the energy to have an emotional fight. She walked into the room in her humanoid form which caught Xai as strange, her arm should be healed and the canine always preferred her shifted form. Unless she wasn't allowed to be shifted on the premises which would be a quick reason to move from the inn to make sure her companion was comfortable. Her face was a mask which was also a red flag for the feline. "What is wrong, fangs? Isn't your arm healed? Is there a reason you are not shifted? We can leave this inn if we have to."

"Yes, something is wrong Xai. I am thoroughly pissed at you." The wolf growled, making the elemental spell caster tense around his still-weakened daemon. Logically he knew Lux would never physically harm her best friend but the normally calm and happy daemon had been acting strangely aggressive since leaving Terrida.

"Why?" Xai was confused, still not fully functioning mentally but could not think of a reason for Lux to be pissed at her. She knew she was stressed and irritated but she was the one who wanted to join on this mission and as a daemon herself and knows how daemons function.

"Because you risked your life AGAIN!" She screamed, catching everyone off guard including her own handler. "You could have died AGAIN!"

"First I wasn't going to die, if the threat had been more than it was I would not have engaged by myself. And second, you have known me for fifteen years and know I am prone to taking the hit, this isn't a new occurrence." The feline defended herself, though her handler would not let her back off the bed to confront her friend.

"It was less frequent and life-threatening before that asshole came back into your life." She gestured at Truen angrily.

"Do not blame him for any of this Lux." Xai hissed back, becoming angrier than before. She ripped herself away from her handler and removed herself from the bed. Truen himself raced to stop her by the edge of the bed, she wasn't fit to physically fight. Hell, he didn't think she was fit enough for this but there was no way to stop what the other daemon started. Once again thanking the gods that the children were not in the room, he had a feeling they had gotten stopped by their new acquaintances.

"HE LET AN ANIGEL HELP US, TRANSPORT US WHILE YOU WERE VULNERABLE!" She screamed at the top of her lungs. "ALL BECAUSE YOU WANTED TO PICK A FIGHT BECAUSE YOU CHOSE TO SAVE THE ONE AND LOST US FOUR."

"So it is my fault that we lost Bee, Crow, Honey, and Roc?" Xai went from fire to ice. "The illusion curse was my fault?"

210

"No, but my uselessness was." She backed up, suddenly unsure of the stronger daemon's stance.

"Of course, my moving you out of the way of a fatal shot made it so that I could not save five people in a matter of moments. I chose to save my child expecting that Bee's own mate would be able to save her instead of perishing as well." Lux looked as if she had been slapped.

"Well, what about those children? Kato and Hestia cry every time you get injured." She tried again. "They are only children and they love you, it would take anything above the intelligence of a rock to see that. Bringing you back unconscious again was a nightmare for them. Truen was a barely contained wreck, which made Jackdaw on edge. And for fucks sake you are my best friend. How can you keep doing this to us? How can you keep doing this to me? What would happen if we lost you Xai?" Her mask broke, and though she took a breath to try and ground herself Xai was well aware this was the closest she had ever been to seeing her best friend cry. Xai knew that if she fell it would be a chain reaction that would destroy a part of every one of them. But she could not lose them either, she had to protect them. She was a daemon, it was what she did, and she knew Lux did not know what it was like to have a daemon below you that you needed to protect in the hierarchy. All of her family was in the same classification and Hestia was not old enough to fall into a classification yet.

"I will not stop protecting all of you, I am nothing more than myself and you need to stop putting me on a pedestal. I am not some sort of savior or some sort of I don't know messiah. I am a daemon with a pack I love that I will kill for and I will die for if I have to." Xai countered. She would not be guilted out of her purpose.

"Lux please calm down, she just woke up." Truen tried to mediate, he was feeling all the anger, guilt, and fear about to break apart his daemoness.

"Stay out of this Truen." She snapped. "If you were any sort of man you would step up and stop her from doing half of this crazy shit. It is your fault you can't get her under control. You say you love her and yet you are continuously allowing her to take risks that could get her killed. You don't deserve her if you can't keep her safe from herself." Her voice was downright venomous. "You are nothing but a spoiled rotten Prince who should have done us all a favor and stayed in your castle." The canine muttered. She knew exactly where to hurt him and she kept digging in until she did. Xai could feel the guilt and absolute distraught feeling flooding the already tense bond between them.

Do not listen to her Truen.

I know I don't deserve you but I would deserve you less if I kept you in a cage no matter how gilded. I want to keep you safe, but I need to keep you happy.

Stop, we let a spell come between us we will not let a scared woman make us doubt our bond again.

I love you, dear heart.

I love you too, do not forget it again.

"Do not blame him, Lux." Xai hissed again. "Do not be cruel to him because you are scared." She snapped with the same venom making the canine back up again.

"Why? Is it not his fault?"

"Do you want to challenge me? Even now I am stronger than you and I can make it so you will never be anything but a

212

pet again." The stronger hissed. Fear flashed across the other's face knowing better than to challenge the more powerful being.

"This is too much. Jackdaw please try and calm Lux down so I can calm Xai down." Truen tried again.

"No, because she needs this. Xai hasn't been listening and has been causing nothing but heartache. Why don't you do something and control your daemon for once." The comment stung them both. Jackdaw was usually so kind, he had never referred to Xai as just a daemon before.

"I never thought I would hear something so stupid out of the mouth of my supposedly genius brother." Truen finally turned to them, clearly annoyed. The other couple was taken completely aback by his tone. Truen was normally the kind and gentlemanly type, always comfort-covered truth. "You need to work through whatever is going on in your head instead of taking it out on everyone you care about and dragging my brother down with you." Then he looked at his incredibly stunned brother. "You know she is her own person, she is not just a daemon, not just my daemon or my mate. She is a person, not a tool. You would do your best to remember that little brother before you are left with nothing but your own partner and no one else." He scolded the blonde until he was refusing to look at anything but the ground. The older brother walked towards the younger, neither daemon stopping him. "She has done nothing to deserve this ire from either of you."

I have done plenty to deserve this.

No, you have done nothing to be disregarded, treated like nothing but your race, or treated like property. Truen ended up caging his brother against the wall. Snapping out of their trances, Lux lunges for Truen only to be batted away by Xai. She landed on her ass on the opposite wall from her own handler, looking up to see her long-time friend nearly feral while protecting her mate. It took what felt like an eternity of moments for her to arise from the ground, a crack in the stone wall behind her, she was completely shocked her friend attacked her with aggression. Truen backed away from his brother, letting Lux collect him from his shock. Without looking back they all about ran from the room.

"Holy shit what just happened." Truen groaned after a moment of silence.

"I feel the need to rip something to shreds. To destroy something completely." She growled. The noise was cut off abruptly with a small hesitant knock at the door.

"Yes?" Truen answered, raising a hand to his mate to silence her for a moment, the knock was tentative and scared.

"Uhm…Xai?" Kato opened the door a crack, sticking his head in to get permission. His expression was scared and they could both hear Hestia whining behind the door.

"Yes, dear? What is it? Come in the room." Xai said softly, forcing herself to calm down. Both of the children rushed into the room, closing the door behind them. The food they had been sent to get nowhere in sight.

"Uhm…Lux and Jackdaw just pushed past us and out of the inn in a hurry." Kato sounded distraught.

"I don't think they are coming back, they were angry," Hestia whined.

"Come sit on the bed guys. Everything will be alright." Truen called to them sitting on the side of the bed. He hugged them tightly once they were in reach. What was worse for kids with abandonment issues, loved ones dying, or loved ones

214

leaving voluntarily? The sight made Xai angrier, the selfishness of the two of them was too much. "I can try and go get them." Truen looked at Xai for input. She watched the children holding back tears while pushing themselves into the man's chest for comfort. They were trying to be strong. They were so young and had already gone through so much. If the two of them no longer wanted to put in the effort to make the journey work then she would not force them. It would only hurt them all more in the future. They had not been needed in the prophecy, they could go to safety and stay there until Xai was done doing what she needed to so that everyone had a life to continue to live.

"Don't bother looking for them. If they don't want to finish the journey then let them sit it out. They are scared but still pack. If they wish to come back we will deal with it then. We will be leaving ourselves after food. We are closer now to the pure blood human and we need to get to them as fast as we can now that the castle has put a bounty on their head too."

Chapter Ten: Anigels and Dragons

Within the hour the family of four left the inn and walked out of the town of Desrtea alone. It had taken longer than normal to calm down the children and get them to eat so they could leave. Kato had been willing to leave without eating so they could leave the town they had once again abandoned. It had taken Truen allowing him to take some blood that the young vampire needed to get him to eat as well. Yuell had taken Truen aside before they left the village to explain how to take care of the child's need for blood. Since he was a pure-blood high vampire Kato did not need to eat often, though more frequently than his adult counterparts. The elder had given a full lesson to the spellcaster since the daemons of the group would never help with their toxic blood. Once every other week or so the two would sit down so Kato could feed and the two could bond together.

"Dear sweet gods, I still hate the desert." Xai groaned causing the children to laugh at her exaggerated actions. Once the words left her mouth a unique shadow cast over them.

"Told you the daemoness was alive." Someone yelled from above. "He was worried about you."

"Friends of yours I take it?" Xai looked at Truen as his amusement through the bond. Hestia and Kato looked equally as excited as the large lavender dragon landed in their path. Such a beautiful creature that many outside of the Island of Thane never got to see in person. The massive reptile was regal as they walked to face the daemoness, on their back a saddle meant for two that were both filled. In front of a man holding the reins that were larger than Truen or any man Xai had ever seen in person gently unmounted from the beast. His skin was dark and scarred, it was easy to tell he was used to dealing with

216

sharp claws on young dragons with his bulbous arms showing with his sleeveless tunic. His head was shaved and his short and well-kept beard had beads braided in, he nodded at the daemoness as he reached his hand to help the smaller figure off the back of the dragon. The other was a dainty little thing, with long white hair, snow-white skin, an ethereal beauty broken with solid black eyes, and large black wings protruding from their back.

"Mi'kal," Truen called out to the anigel, Xai would have mistaken them as a woman if not for Truen's comments earlier about them both being male. The white-haired man smiled at the spellcaster and rushed over to him completely barefoot on the hot sand and made Xai release a low threatening growl.

"Do not worry my lady Mi'kal means no harm to your mate." The large man spoke with incredible softness.

"Dante." Truen smiled looking at the larger man. "I am not surprised to see you have followed us." The winged man in an almost uncomfortably tight set of clothing bounced between the larger men. It was only uncomfortable for Xai because of how close the strange anigel was to her mate. The mountain of a man gently patted the majestic beast nodding again at the raven-haired male.

"This is Kila, my partner since her birth." He said looking between Xai and the children while scratching the scales of the happy reptile. A low purring noise came from the creature as he continued. She stretched her wings before pulling them to her sides, Xai looked at the beautiful girl, noticing the lack of horns. She was still young, maybe only fifty or so years into her life.

"Your name is Xai, correct?" The anigel bounced over bringing her attention back to him. He wrapped his arms around the waist of the other man looking over her with endless amazement. Smiling at her, Dante bent down and pressed his lips to Mi'kal's with such passion and heat that the smaller man's knees went visibly weak. It was the kind of kiss that was meant for a truly loved one, and one that you would not let into the hands of another for any reason. There was a territorial feel that made the daemon slightly jealous and has the instinct to cover the eyes of the children. Dante had no intention of letting the smaller man's interest change from him. When it was over the larger winked at the nodding daemoness as the anigel leaned against him breathlessly. She liked him and his style, and if he could keep the anigel sated like that and away from her mate, even better in her books.

Are you going to kiss me like that? Truen pushed through with amusement.

Are you saying you need me to assert dominance? Because of that the anigel looks pretty satisfied.

I am not opposed. Told you they were together and you had no reason to worry about Mi'kal.

"Xai?" Kato pulled on her pants. "Why are they kissing? Aunt said two men can't kiss."

"Your aunt was wrong. People who love each other or are attracted to each other can kiss. Two men, two women, a man, and a woman, any people in between. As long as all parties consent then kissing and other things we will explain when you are older are completely fine." Xai explained carefully not expecting homophobia from the child's last guardian. vampires were normally known for their acceptance of all.

"Does Truen kiss you like that?" Hestia asked curiously.

"Yes, though I have seen Truen kiss another boy when he was a boy himself before as well."

"Xai never was mad at me for kissing someone that was not her or someone not female," Truen added trying to help.

"We were not mated then, we were only kids so I had no reason to be mad as long as you made your way to me eventually. You can be attracted to other people and genders even when you have a fated mate." Xai explained, never wanting the children to think that attraction was wrong no matter who they were attracted to. Hestia had a mate somewhere and so did Kato and if either of them were homosexual she did not want them to be ashamed.

"I haven't seen you two kiss at all." The little girl whined, Xai forgot how little girls can romanticize anything. The kit was stubborn, crossing her arms and huffing at the unfairness she perceived at not seeing her guardian's affection.

"I do not think such displays of affection should be asked of children," Dante interjected. "Just because Mi'kal and I are comfortable with such open displays does not mean all are."

"My sweet Dante is correct, maybe your parents are not comfortable with kissing in front of others and that is completely fine. You should not ask for something that makes someone uncomfortable." Mi'kal added.

"It is not that I am uncomfortable myself but we are new to parenting and you and Kato are young. Our bond is still fresh and can be easily carried away." Xai explained to the waiting children. "Truen has never been one for public displays so I, as his partner, need to respect that. Eventually, you may see something innocent but nothing like the kiss those two just shared."

Thank you for explaining that.

219

Of course love, you were even uncomfortable with affectionate displays from your parents or siblings.

After all this time it still amazes me you notice and are fine with our differences.

We are mates of course I notice and do not care, we are mates, not identical souls. We are going to be different but complementary.

"Not to interrupt a lovely parenting moment but are we not missing two people in the group?" Mi'kal's bell-like voice brought them back to the group. He spoke softly and respectfully as expected from a resident of an anigelic city like Lowestoft.

"They decided this journey was too much for them to handle so they left." It wasn't a complete lie, Xai and Truen both knew the toll the journey had taken on Lux and Jackdaw considering the toll it was taking on them as well as the children as well. Xai herself had seen it in Lux's eyes as the worry and the fear had slowly been taking the happy attitude away from her friend. She just wasn't meant to deal with such a serious task. As long as her friend was safe somewhere with her mate, Xai could continue to move forward.

"Then where are we going?" Dante saved the others from continuing, his voice was so incredibly deep and smooth, completely the opposite of his partner.

"We are on the way to the human colony of Lillia," Truen answered.

"Why are you going down there? This is solar territory, most of your group is lunars and right now this isn't the most welcoming place for ya'll. Not to mention the heat. It could kill most of you if you're not careful." Dante sounded concerned, an unique accent coming through.

"We are looking for someone very important." Hestia helped.

"And who is that important little one?" Mi'kal asked, Xai tensing at the two strange solars asking questions about the prophecy.

"A pure human." She answered happily to help the pretty man.

"So you are the group that everyone is supposedly looking for in the solar world?" He asked carefully, his wings fluttering as Xai watched carefully ready to protect her family from these men if needed. "People are either trying to join you in your cause or stop you in your tracks."

"Seems like it," Xai answered carefully.

"That would make Truen the heir apparent and Kato here a pure vampire if the rumors are to be believed." He continued. The two males in question tensed but nodded apprehensively not knowing where this would lead. "And Xai you are pure…"

"Mean bitch you will ever meet if you are about to put my family or my task at risk." She hissed, readying herself to fight.

"Fantastic, one more question before we continue." Dante was completely unfazed by the daemon, unlike his partner who stepped back with eyes wide.

"Are ya'll really planning on taking out King? I mean no offense to your highness but that is your father."

"No offense to me, and please just call me Truen. Yes, we are though, what he is doing is unhinged and past the realm of acceptable leadership." Truen sighed.

221

"I am glad our views align then, you said to the human colony correct? That is about a day's journey. We might get there tonight." Dante walked back over to Kila as if all of that had not happened. Mi'kal looked more excited than before, wings puffing out happily.

"And why would we trust you to come with us? We don't know you or your reasoning." Dante looked at Mi'kal who had deflated with a look of regret.

"I used to, many years ago before either of you were born, on the lunar extraction team of the King's army. Your father is not the first King to try and enslave the lunar races. Your grandfather tried as well but it was wiped from history when he was corrected by your idealistic father taking the throne. But history forgotten is history repeating itself. I am not proud of what I was doing but it was that or jail for crimes committed against the crown. Mi'kal made Kila and I better. I never liked what I was doing but at least I got to keep Kila by my side, my brothers under the same rebel flag were not so lucky." He swallowed hard remembering his past transgressions. "We were trying to stop the enslavement but we hurt a lot of innocent people in the process. My last collection was a fallen anigel who had done nothing wrong but decided to fall. He disagreed with anigel culture and the dismissal of daemons." He looked at his partner again with so much love in his honey-like eyes. "He was beautiful and innocent. I told him to run and hide but he decided against better judgment to stay by my side for protection or because he liked bothering me I am not sure. I resigned after refusing to return with his wings, saying that even Kila could not find him so he was probably dead or no longer on the mainland. Eventually, I fell in love with him and somehow he fell in love with me." Mi'kal walked calmly over to Dante, hugging him tightly trying to comfort the walking mountain. "I could not hurt Mi'kal then and I won't now. Years ago my old team found us in our house living a peaceful life and decided that they needed to turn us both in. They burned down our farm and forced me to fight them. Now we are both in danger, I don't want either of us to live in fear anymore. Kila was the one who brought us to you so she seems to think you are the key. I have learned to trust her over the last ninety years of our life."

"It is my fault Dante has to look over our shoulders every day and I want it to stop so we can live our lives," Mi'kal added, looking at Dante with devotion.

You look at me like that when you think I am not looking. Xai absently thought.

"Shush you, it is no skin of me to stay beside you every day even if today would be our last.

They are disgustingly in love.

I have heard your thoughts about us, my Astrantia, and so, are we.

"He has given everything up for me. To save the life of someone he did not know and had no reason at the time to protect and tolerate. Now he suffers consequences that should not rest on his shoulders."

"I understand how Dante feels Mi'kal, to him you are worth it. Every moment, every danger, every spark of happiness and hope." Truen interjected looking at Xai.

"How could you possibly understand?" Mi'kal looked over not understanding, thinking Dante's devotion to him was rare.

"Because dear heart the Prince here has given up everything and became the traitor of the kingdom to save his daemoness." Dante nodded at the spellcaster in solidarity. "He is as ready as I am to burn the world down for the one he loves."

"My family, my throne, my life, my kingdom. I threw it all away for Xai and I got two children in the process." Truen agreed. "I would do it over and over again for all of eternity without a thought. Without her, my life is empty and meaningless. I have a feeling that Dante feels the same about you."

"If you can understand the need to give up everything for your love then we would be happy to allow you to join us." Xai sighed, knowing the kind of heart it took for the devotion Dante and Mi'kal shared. To burn the world to promise the safety of others was what they needed. "We will need all the help we can get when we finally turn to storm the castle."

"If it is a fighter you need I am your man." Dante puffed out proudly.

"By the way you look fantastic for a ninety-year-old." Xai nodded at the dragon rider who smirked back at her.

"Why thank you ma'am though I think Mi'kal looks much better for sixty." Dante winked at his partner. "Such a baby face."

"I'm seven," Hestia added, joining the conversation again. "Kato is ten." Mi'kal looked at Xai wide-eyed again not realizing just how young the children were.

"Tell me about it," Xai muttered in response to his horror.

"So young to be out here in the middle of all this turmoil." Mi'kal was able to choke out.

"We are ok, Xai saved us and our elder said we were their children through destiny so we are safe," Kato said calmly enough. Dante and Mi'kal looked at Xai for more information.

"Long story that would make sure we would not make it to Lillia today." Xai sighed. "But maybe as we continue our little adventure we can explain what has happened thus far."

"That is a fair compromise. Since destiny seems to be bringing you to those who need you I feel as though we will be traveling together for a while." Mi'kal nodded. "Though I do not feel envious of you for being in the grasps of destiny."

"Let's get going because this sun is frying me." Xai sighed again uncomfortably covered in sweat. Truen jumped to action and mist the three lunars to try and cool them down.

"Unfortunately Kila can not carry all of us who can not take to the skies on their own." Dante started, but he looked at the children with a mischievous glint in his eyes. "Do you two want to see something dragons like Kila can do?" Xai couldn't help but laugh as their eyes lit up and their heads began to bobble. "Dragons like Kila who are purple are made of pure magic, that is their element. It allows them to do things like this. Kila laghedi ghidea (Smaller size)." The dragon, who to this point had been laying in the sand sunbathing while the others talked, looked at her rider and made a chirping noise before shrinking before their very eyes. Her saddle and harness shrunk with her, clearly embedded with magic as well. By the time she was the size of a house pet, she scaled her rider with practiced ease to ride on his shoulders. Not at all what any of them were expecting from the reptile and rider.

"She's so cute." The little girl squealed, getting a scrunched-up face from the tiny creature at the volume. The kit ran over to the large man making hands at the now child-sized beast.

"Maybe you can play with her later little one but now we have a bit further to go today and we do not need any of you getting sunburned in this heat." Dante smiled kindly and gently

225

at the excited child. Hours passed with ease as the two newer adult members of the group swapped stories of the past with the other adults. Their humor meshed well as they tried to keep the hike through the sand moving. Halfway through the day, while the sun was directly above them Truen took to carrying Hestia and Dante took to carrying Kato, Kila walking happily alongside her rider occasionally bouncing around the group. As time passed their conversations touched on any safer topic they could think of, they even talked about Dante's and Mi'kal's lonely wedding, how to care for a young dragon and a young vampire, what it meant to be a pure-blood daemon, and what the kit had to look forward to as she grew into her own fully realized daemon.

"How much longer would you say we have until we reach the walls of the colony?" Truen asked randomly as the sun began to set.

"I would say maybe over the next dune or so." Dante guessed not sure himself. "We have to be close enough to be seeing it soon."

"Truen," Kato called, reaching for the other man.

"What is it kiddo?" Truen asked, walking closer to Dante who was still holding the drowsy vampire close.

"There are people pacing up ahead." He muttered in pain. If his gift was warning him through the sand again it would explain why he looked like talking hurt.

"Do you know how many?" Xai asked gently.

"No, we are too close to the colony." He muttered burying his face again in Dante's shoulder. Mi'kal was having the time of his life watching his husband take such good care of a child. Xai rubbed her hand on the back of the tired boy, trying to convey her thanks and pride. She hoped deep down that there wouldn't be another fight.

Marauders?

I don't know but I hope not.

We have Mi'kal and Dante to help at least.

That is fair but I am too tired for another fight.

Can you smell anything? Or is the sand making it challenging for you as well?

Unless we were closer all I can smell is you, dragon, and sand.

"Could it be a marauder?" Mi'kal asked, sounding concerned.

"Too late in the day for them, they won't be out until the moon is up." Dante tried comforting his husband.

"What about hunters? Or worse?" Mi'kal clearly wasn't comforted.

"What could be worse than a hunter? I used to be a hunter and I can't think of something worse?" Dante sounded slightly offended at the idea of something being scarier than anyone in the traveling party.

"There are plenty worse than hunters. That being said I am going to see if I can get closer without getting spotted so we know if it is safe or not." Xai sighed knowing she and Kila were currently the easiest to move through the shadows of the dunes. The men all nodded their heads knowing that even though she was still tired she was still the quietest no matter the circumstance.

Please be careful.

I will try. Carefully walking up the far side of the dune, keeping in sight of the others. At the top of the mound of sand, the daemoness saw the outer part of the colony at last. Kato was correct though at the feeling of the pacing people, two of them pacing across the pathway into the colony.

Nothing we have to worry about physically, no need to fight. Xai stood up and kept walking to the top of the dune, no longer trying to move with stealth.

Who is it then?

"Luxan Rose, GET YOUR ASS HERE NOW!" Xai yelled over the sand. The pacing figured startled as they looked up at the dune. Lux slinked with hesitation towards the other daemoness at the top of the dune, her handler not far behind. By the time they stood in front of the feline, the others had also joined from behind. The three men were waiting for a cue from the woman they had been traveling with all day.

"Why are you here?" Truen was not giving them a chance to apologize as his hold on his kit tightened. If they were not going to apologize to his mate and their children he did not want to hear from them. He was still too raw and angry from the fight earlier that day, Xai was feeling similar. The scent of regent was potent on the two before her, neither would look any of the others in the eyes.

"When we left we talked, instead of letting the feelings continue to fester," Jackdaw spoke to the sand, adamantly refusing to look at his brother. "You were right. We were wrong to let our fear blind us, corrupt us, and make us take it out on you and Xai."

"Spots we are sorry, no I am sorry. I am not used to being so scared all the time. If I am this scared I can only imagine how you feel, how you have felt for the last almost twenty years living on the run and putting yourself in danger to protect anyone you can. The fight was my fault not yours and not Truen's and I am incredibly sorry." Lux was trying to muddle through the apology that she had been practicing for hours. "I shouldn't have snapped at you, especially right after you woke up."

"I did deserve part of it, I have been reckless. I have gotten injured a lot and you all have every right to be scared and angry with me." Xai stopped Lux's rant in its tracks. "I need to remember that I am no longer alone in this, and this prophecy is much bigger than me. I shouldn't have taken on those marauders alone and I know I was clouded by the anger and guilt of losing Crow, Bee, Roc, and Honey. I am sorry I have added extra stress to this already fucked up situation." Stepping forward, Xai wrapped her arms around the shoulders of the other daemoness. It took a moment for the canine to realize she was getting hugged by her friend and reciprocate.

"We hoped we would find you around the colony when we realized the mistake we made." Jackdaw finally found the strength to look up to his older brother. "I am sorry brother. And Xai I am sorry for what I said to you, how I regarded you."

"I know little brother." Truen relaxed, shifting Hestia onto his hip to pull his brother to his side.

"Truen I am also sorry I keep blaming you for things changing and things happening around us." Lux looked at the raven-haired male.

"I will forgive you for now Lux, but I can not continue to be the scapegoat every time you have an issue with change in your life. I have been in Xai's life since the beginning and even though you were there when I wasn't, I will not be leaving again. We are each other's fate and nothing will tear us apart again."

"I understand, I do. I want to thank you for protecting Xai from everything you can, including me. I said spewed absolute shit to you and you took it but when I turned on her you would not take my bullshit any longer. You are an amazing man to her and your children and they deserve nothing less." Letting go of his brother Truen reached out an invitation to the other woman to touch in a way they hadn't before. The thought that the very tactile Lux had never actually touched Truen without being forced stunned Xai for a moment as the canine accepted a hug from her handler.

"Though when they are completely awake you both owe an apology to Kato and Hestia. We were not the only ones you walked out on." Truen looked harshly at both his brother and future sister. Both nodded vigorously knowing they had been the ones to hurt the children that morning.

"And you must make your peace with Dante and Mi'kal traveling with us as well. They want to help and so far they have given every reason for us to trust them. They have helped with the care of the children in the harsh heat. Their reasons for wanting to take down the King is one I can get behind and if they wish to tell you they can but I will not force them since you decided to leave for the day." Nodding again the two looked over to the new men of the group. "Now let us go find an inn, we have a pure-blooded human to find in the morning. Tonight we eat, rest, and drink."

Chapter Eleven: The Pure Blood Human

Mi'kal was the one to find the inn with pure determination, to everyone else all the buildings in the colony looked almost entirely identical. The colony felt abandoned if not for the cold purple mage fire burning at all the street posts and the same eerie color shining in the open windows of each building. Xai could see the sea on the edge of the colony, she would have to investigate it in the morning.

"There is an inn over by the docks, we can see about rooms there. I know that the colony is known for their mineral baths, not heated like in Terrida but relaxing in its own right." Mi'kal sounded like a frequent visitor to the town.

"Then tonight we eat, drink, maybe bathe if we have the energy, and rest as I said. Tomorrow we can look for the human, enjoy the mineral baths, and swim in the sea. We will most likely be here for a few days as we talk to and convince the human to join us unless the Time Mage has been here before us like she did in the vampire village." Xai yawned. Incredibly sharp teeth showed as she did, startling the anigel.

"Sounds like a beautiful plan." Truen agreed, swapping the hip that was carrying the sleeping girl.

"How would you like to set up rooms?" Dante asked.

"If we are lucky we can get four rooms so we can each have some breathing room. Each couple can sleep together, obviously, and let the children share a bed." Xai explained eyeing each of the couples. "It makes it easy and allows for some alone time for each couple." The men nodded and the anigel continued forward to a beautiful and large building towards the shore. It was strange, a clear difference between the inn entrance and the tavern on the same level. The two men walked over to a small desk with a bored-looking elven woman. The tavern on the other side of the half wall was already rambunctious as an older grandmotherly woman moved with impressive grace and speed. Focusing back onto the tanned younger woman with trancelike white eyes the daemoness watched a visible attitude and fear cross her face as Dante stepped up to her.

"Ma'am we would like four single rooms if you have them." He said softly with a smile, trying not to scare her with his size.

"We will also need food and drink but we can get that at the tavern after we are settled," Xai added nodding at the older woman who had stopped to greet the strangers in her town.

"We can get things ready for you dearies." The elderly woman smiled before walking back toward the kitchen.

"Only siblings and of-age couples can occupy single rooms, it's in policy so we don't get unsavory types." The elven woman replied in a snappy tone.

"Well, ma'am my wife-to-be and I am well above age." Truen stepped forward, handing Hestia to Xai forcing her to step away from the woman. "And our children are siblings, we just want a bit of alone time." He said with a smooth charm that always seemed to work.

"My husband and I are also above age if you are worried," Mi'kal said, holding onto Dante's arm, Kila wrapping around their legs.

"My betrothed and I as well," Jackdaw added with a polite tone that the daemoness would not have been able to achieve in the face of such blatant disrespect to the group.

"We would thank you for helping us find rooms," Truen spoke again, laying on the charm once more for the now flustered woman. "We have traveled all day and our children are exhausted. We have business in the colony tomorrow and all need a moment to relax."

"My apologies sir." She stammered out, red flushing across her tanned face. "Your rooms are this way, I can bring bathes to your rooms if you would like." She almost threw herself from behind her desk to rush down the hall, waiting for the group to follow. "These four rooms back at the end of the hall should be exactly what you are looking for and close to each other."

"Thank you we will take our baths in our room," Jackdaw spoke calmly.

"As will we." Mi'kal nodded along.

"I think we will bathe later, and the children in the morning since they are completely asleep." Truen looked at Xai. "Dante, can you help me tuck the children in?" He asked taking Hestia out of Xai's arms. "Xai and I are going to relax a bit before going to get a drink." He announced to the group, dismissing the elven woman.

Oh, are we?

I can feel your jealousy, my love.

I do not know what you are talking about. She turned and walked into the closest room ignoring the others as she did so. She knew it was immature to be jealous of Truen being charming with another, he wasn't even flirting. But the elven woman was a such unique beauty, someone who she could see one day looking beautiful with a crown. That had been on her mind for a while, if they are successful Truen will be King, he

233

is the heir apparent. She is his mate, she would be Queen, and part of her always knew that she would be. She is a leader and warrior, not a Queen.

You are my warrior Queen, my love. Truen walked into the room, *childless and calm. He wrapped his arms tightly around her waist.*

I do hate you can hear all my thoughts.

"I know you have been having nightmares about the crown recently." He responded out loud.

"We are getting closer to storming the Royal City and I am worried about a title." Her insecurities seemed silly out loud.

"A title you were given as a child and thought was taken from you." He reassured her. They were raised to know that at some point in their lives that Truen and Xai would take over the throne. The daemoness had even been given extra etiquette lessons in preparation until she was chased from the castle.

"I had given up any thought of ruling the Kingdom and now it is almost in front of me again." She admitted, remembering the tiara that the Queen had made for her for the tenth birthday of the Princes.

"I think you will do beautifully, you were always meant to be my Queen, prophecy or not." She knew he honestly believed that.

"I won't look good in a crown." They always made her uncomfortable. The Queen always said she would find a style that didn't make Xai's skin crawl.

"I think you look absolutely stunning in anything or nothing at all." His voice lowered into a more seductive octave.

"Ah, I see since we are alone you are back to being your flirtatious and horny self." She sighed leaning back against him. She enjoyed the onslaught of arousal through the bond, and the interesting images he came up with focusing on her in a crown. They hadn't been together since the cabin. Gentle-loving kisses and small touches were one thing but it had been days since they had enjoyed more than a chaste touch.

"The moon is close tonight, and full. I was thinking maybe we should go for a late-night swim, just the two of us. Wash the sweat and sand off that way while the town sleeps?" He mumbled into her neck. She smirked knowing that he was asking her for permission, always following her lead.

"Some days you have the most wonderful ideas. I would love a midnight swim." She agreed.

"My only regret is not being able to swim naked with you, the colony here is not nearly as comfortable with nudity as the rest of the kingdom."

"Well, we both have smalls that will dry." She smiled. He chuckled letting go of her. They walked back out of the inn and to the shore down the walkway. The moon was rising the colony was quiet, and most of its residents were asleep or back in the tavern. It felt to them like they were teenagers as they looked for a secluded spot on the sandy shoreline, the water is calm as the tide rolled in slowly keeping the temperature lower than it had been on the other side of the town. Finally finding a rocky alcove they stripped to their smalls, Xai thought it was strange for the forced modesty but was thankful it was only one piece of cloth. She walked into the water first enjoying the water on her bare skin. Wading out until the water covered her exposed chest she turned back to the man watching her from the shore. She wasn't that far out but the bright light of the full moon made the distance feel so much more.

You look like you belong in the water, like a mer.

Then do you want to join me so I can drag you out further into the water?

Such a tempting threat, dragging me away to your people as a prize.

You would be quite the prize to bring home to show off as a trophy.

Such a temptress.

Just noticing this? I have been tempting you this entire time. You seem to like submitting to my will very eagerly.

What can I say, I want to be in service to my beautiful and powerful daemon Queen.

Trying to charm me more Princeling? Why don't you come in? Do you not trust me?

"I trust you more than anything, my Queen. As if in a trance he began to walk into the cooler water and to his daemoness. From his view, she looked like one of the goddesses herself. Her bright purple eyes glowed in the dark. The moonlight shining on her dual-colored hair made the darker section look like a voided halo and the white almost blinding. Her spots looked like ink on her paler skin. To him, she was worth praying to, on his knees. Her beauty could not be matched and neither was the dangerous nature that she held even when almost completely bare in the water of the open sea. He waded closer to her, slowly reaching where she was on a sandbar.

"Took you long enough." She smiled, the moonlight making her look feral.

"You are ethereal in the moonlight, I had to soak in your radiance."

"You already have me darling, but I will admit you are also breathtaking in the moonlight. So incredibly handsome." She pulled him closer, catching his lips with her own. Even with the passion between the two, she pulled away before he could pursue it any further. "You will have to wait until after our swim, I refuse to enjoy your body in the presence of fish." She smirked, making him groan. Pushing away from him she got a mischievous look in her eyes giving him only a moment before she splashed him with water and then swam away right after. By the time the moon was high in the sky, the two of them had tousled and chased each other around the safety of the alcove. Enjoying their time releasing energy in a childish way for once, as they should have over the years. Eventually, they rested together in the shallows just enjoying the water on their lower halves. They talked and traded stupid stories while enjoying watching each other's bodies in the moonlight. Innocent arousal passes through the bond. The two lovers enjoy their time together strengthening the bond between them.

"I have put it off as long as I can, but in the moonlight some of your scaring is visible and I need to know the stories."

"Do you not wish for any mysteries between us?" She teased wondering if she could trail him off.

"I will trade you scar for scar, I want to know every secret your body holds."

"I would watch what you say before you get no stories and we cut this evening short." She raised her eyebrow causing her mate to groan at the idea. Growing his resolve he began to trace a nasty scar on her left hip.

"What about this one?" He asked with a low voice.

"Lux was there for that one, it was when we met. I tried to pickpocket her father so I could get food. I had been alone for two years at that point and was starving. He didn't think twice as he batted the thirteen-year-old me away. It wouldn't have been that bad of an injury if it wasn't for the fact I hadn't had food in days or clean water. I hit a stone path wall leading out of the town near their pack lands. It split my hip on one of the rocks, when I didn't get up he brought me home on his back and had his daughter help take care of me until I regained consciousness." The first thing I saw was a very unamused Lux and a much more amused man watching me. The rest is history." It was a good memory for Xai even if she had been terrified when she woke back up that day. Reaching out she ran her fingers down a scar that went from the small of his back and around to disappear down into his smalls. "I know the large scar on your back but if we are trading stories I want to know where this one came from and how far down it goes."

"That one was a 'maid' in the castle. You already know it missed anything you would consider important." He smirked. "She was actually from a small village somewhere and had been paid to kill me. Apparently, there was quite a bounty out on Jackdaw, Krutz, and me. We found two other people who had been paid from smaller no-name villages. Each one of them was given a different Prince. They were told they could stop my father if they killed off the bloodline because his sons had to be just as bad if not worse than him."

"She huh? Was she pretty to be able to get a knife all the way down here?" Xai asked, teasing him again. He knew she did not truly care about his past lovers when they were apart.

"She was too young even if she was pretty. She caught me in the baths that you love so much. She thought I would still be soaking and planned to slit my throat but I had something I had to do so I was drying off. I was able to fight her off for the most part but she caught me on the way down to the ground. My mother was a nervous wreck for weeks after that incident.

Finding her meant the others were found before they could attempt their assassinations."

"I bet she didn't let you out of her sight for weeks." Xai sighed thinking about the Queen. "Honestly even with the spell in place creating the wall between you and me, I missed your mother more than anything. Your mother and my mother were the only two I missed."

"It hurts to know that you were forced out for someone else's plans. She misses you too just so you know. Jackdaw and I are the only ones our mothers will talk to besides each other. They both want me to bring you home safely. They miss their daughters and your absence has left a hole for both of them just like Lui."

"I hope we can save them both, I do not want to lose them more than I already have." The mood dampened at the thought of the older women they left waiting for them in the castle waiting to be saved and reunited with the children they love so much. The sounds of oncoming footsteps stilled the conversation as both adults looked to see another couple approaching them on the beach. They had not been the only ones who thought a late-night stroll by the water would be romantic. The other couple had yet to notice them watching from the shallows but as they got closer Xai smelled something off about the approaching couple. The man walked with purpose before the smaller woman behind him. The woman was hesitant and timid, leaning away from the man but following him nonetheless. Xai didn't smell fear but apprehension and resignation. Xai listened carefully as the man's voice carried over the sound of the waves. He was talking about their wedding and how he would turn her into a respectable wife. How he would make her daemon stay out of the house and in the barn where it belonged. Finally, the man looked over and saw the two in the water watching them, a feminine figure in front of a masculine.

"You two in the water, come here." He shouted, seeming to think he had some sort of authority. Xai cared little about him but noticed how the woman flinched as he raised his voice. "You are not supposed to be in the water after dark." Looking at her handler for acknowledgment before they both stood, Truen was easily larger than the other man who puffed his chest out as he noticed the same. Truen remained calm and unaffected by the other's bravado and remained behind Xai. Truen never thought a show of force was needed, he never had to try and be a bigger man to a stranger. He knew he had power both politically and physically. The dark-haired man before them looked completely unremarkable even in the dark but the way the smaller woman looked at the ground was more telling than anything.

"And how may we help you?" Xai looked the smaller man up and down clearly unimpressed. He smelled lightly of solar, obviously a half-breed with a chip on his shoulder.

"I have nothing to say to an animal like you." Xai was taken aback by the nonchalant audacity of the young man. "You have no place here lunar and I will not lower myself to converse with the likes of you." Xai released a hiss at his words, causing him to startle. As if in an instinctual reaction he went to strike the feline across the face only to have his hand caught by the larger man.

"I would think again before raising a hand to anyone let alone a woman before I remove your hand myself," Truen growled. Xai looked at her nonviolent mate without a bit of surprise. He had never taken it lightly when someone threatened his woman.

"Croden, please stop before someone gets hurt." The small woman pleaded beside him, even looking up her features were shrouded in shadow. He ripped his arm out of Truen's grasp, rubbing the area as if Truen had burned him somehow which would be entirely within the realm of possibilities for the elemental spell caster.

"Do not speak out of turn, Dremira. I will make a proper woman out of you." He snapped at the woman who looked immediately back to the sand. "I follow our King, and he says all lunars are scum so they are beneath us, nothing but animals and lesser beings." He huffed. "They need to know their place or get extinguished."

"You know boy." Xai started, knowing calling the younger man a boy would get a reaction. "There are no solars without lunars. The gods didn't make them, they made us. Solars forced themselves on the rest of the world. "

"Xai, no need to stoop to his level. He is a local and for now, we shouldn't have them upset with us until we are done doing what we need to." Truen tried to calm her down, even with his own aggression flooding through the bond. "No matter how tempting, someone like him is not worth your time."

"You do not need to protect me from the likes of this thing." The imbecile snapped. "But I think you should get a new daemon and put this one down. She is too mouthy to do anything correctly."

"I would never cause harm to my partner. She and I are equals and I will warn one only once more about watching your tongue." Truen threatened. Xai should not find his protective nature attractive.

241

"Then you are a bleeding heart and can die with the rest of their kind and others like you." Xai stepped in front of her handler again.

"Was that a threat little boy?" Xai hissed again.

"What if it was?" He huffed thinking he had an upper hand.

"I would say you wouldn't stand a chance. I wouldn't even need to try to kill you and scatter your unimportant body in the water, maybe a school of mers could make use of the pieces."

"Please, Croden, let us just leave these people alone." The woman begged again, this time pulling on the sleeve of his tunic.

"Shut your mouth Dremira!" He shouted, turning and slapping her with the back of his hand before anyone could react. He struck her hard enough to make her fall back into the water beside her.

"Oh, you are going to pay for that." Xai began to stalk towards the man as Truen rushed to help the now crying woman up, pulling her behind the angered daemoness. His bravado quickly melted away as he realized he had crossed a line and was now in danger.

"What is going on out here?" An older voice came down the shore. Whoever it was spoke with authority. The young man spun around thinking he was saved and took off to meet the small group before they could arrive in the alcove.

"Elder, help me. That feral lunar was threatening to kill me and has taken Dremira from me." He cried. The older man, an older human from what Xai could see pushed passed the young man until he and a few town guards stood before Xai

242

and Truen. They were still protecting the woman not knowing if they would also be a danger to her.

"I was not threatening you boy, I would have. You laid your hand on this woman and hit her so hard you knocked her into the water." Xai hissed. The Elder looked at the crying woman who was being held tightly against the spell caster.

"And who are you?" The Elder asked carefully, barely taking his eyes off the woman.

"I apologize, sir. My name is Truen, I am the heir apparent of the kingdom of Chemerica." The local's jaws all seemed to drop. "This is my consort and future Queen Xai. We traveled all day to get here so we were taking a late-night swim to relax before going back to our room at the inn. We were interrupted by these two, mostly this man here with his derogatory remarks about lunars and women both. He tried to strike my consort and threatened my life. He was warned to curb his tongue and walk away but he decided to strike his companion instead. We have no tolerance for that kind of behavior so my consort reacted."

"We have business here in the colony but we were going to wait until morning to attempt to complete said business." Xai continued watching the young man carefully.

"And your daemon threatened this boy?" The guard asked, somehow only focusing on that piece of information.

"My consort," Truen emphasized, surprising every witness. "Did in fact threaten him after he threatened me, she was going to do much more than threaten after striking this young woman." He carefully released the woman so the others could see the large bruise forming in the moonlight.

"Did Croden really do that to you Dremira?" The Elder asked the woman softly, his voice dripping with sadness. "Dremira please."

"Yes he did...father." The woman still refused to look at her father. The older man's eyes hardened as he looked at the younger man.

"Take Croden into custody." He told the guards whose hands were suddenly on the young man. "Not only is your betrothal to my daughter null and void but your crimes against the heir apparent and his consort will be decided tomorrow. Take him to the jailhouse." The young man struggled and spit as he was taken away. "Your highness, can you two kindly get dressed." He looked at the two in their current state. "Dremira, darling, please go home and have Crazden take care of you." He spoke softer again to his daughter. She just nodded, stepping away from Truen, walking quickly but silently past her father and back towards the colony. The Elder waited calmly for Xai and Truen to redress themselves before speaking again. "Thank you for protecting my daughter, she is all I have left in life. I thought he was a good man when he asked to court her traditionally."

"Of course, it is my natural calling to protect," Xai responded as she finished dressing. "Though we did not mean to cause trouble this late at night, we were just hoping for a late-night swim just the two of us."

"I was already concerned because Dremira was not home yet, we live on the shore so her daemon Crazden heard the commotion and became concerned."

"Why didn't he come looking for her?" Truen asked knowing what it was like having a worried daemon.

"Croden refuses to let Crazden go on dates with them, now we know why if what you said was true." the Elder sighed. "Before it gets too much later in the night though, may I ask your business here in the colony? I am the colony alderman."

"We are looking for a pure-blood human. We were told by a Time Mage that they would be here and we have a feeling she was already here to let you know we would come and for who." Truen answered, watching the man tense at his words. The color drained from his face and he stepped back as if he could run from them. "You know who it is, who we are talking about." Truen sighed. He nodded reluctantly looking out onto the water.

"The pure-blood humans do live here, a few years ago a Time Mage blessed us with a visit and a prophecy. She pointed at my daughter and said she would be the one to help call upon the savior. The girl you saved is the one the Time Mage chose." His voice broke. "She is only twenty years old. She is too young for this kind of responsibility." He knew he had no choice but to let his daughter go out and face the world. "She is not a fighter, as you saw she is a gentle girl, a passive soul." He was trying to reason with whoever was listening but he knew deep within that it was her time to go.

"Sir, if I had a choice she would stay here with you and live a normal life. The pure vampire we have with us lost everything and he is ten years old, his daemon is only six." The sympathy in her voice was thick. Xai would have rather stayed in the cell in the Royal Castle than drag these innocent people into a prophesied war. "I don't want any of them to see the horror that we will. I am not sure what kind of savior we are calling but even if it doesn't work I myself will be trying to set things right. The king has set bounties on purebloods knowing that there are some of us who have been sent to stop his genocide. People are hunting her already she is no longer safe here."

"Our mission can not wait any longer. We have to save the lunar races considering they are the only ones who can protect the terra races from being next in the extermination. There are so many innocent people being murdered and enslaved. We either roll over and wait for death to come to us or we fight back." Truen added.

"I know, I know this is important and bigger than just my baby girl but she is my only child." The man was completely resigned. "The Time Mage made sure her mother and I understood. But she is all I have after my wife got sick and passed away when Dremira was only twelve."

"I swear that mage told everyone before me," Xai muttered.

"You were the last piece of the prophecy, my dear Astrantia." Truen ran his hand over her mark.

"Let us all rest tonight and then we can all talk tomorrow. We don't have to leave tomorrow but soon. We need to make our way back to the Royal city so we can stop this nightmare." Truen reasoned.

"I understand, I will see you both tomorrow." The Elder sighed, turning to walk away.

"Let us go back to the inn as well." Truen sighed.

"At least we still have time for the rest of our plans."

"You still have plans tonight?" Truen asked with a raised brow.

"Well, it is said that something magical tends to occur to lunars in love under the full moonlight when they are at their strongest. Also our most unstable and vulnerable. I have heard that especially when mated there is nothing like a night with your daemon under the full moonlight. I am curious if it is true or just rumors from those who think of nothing but dangerous and raunchy sex." She teased, the mood shifting back instantly.

"Then I guess we need to find out for ourselves." He pulled her closer, smirking. "I suggest going back to our room."

"I suggest running." She smirked back tilting her head.

Chapter Twelve: What do you mean Bunny?

"Xai…Truen… We have visitors in the front of the inn."
Lux's voice sounded far too amused so early in the morning.
Xai stretched, truly enjoying the feeling of the inn's sheets on
her skin. Truen was face down on the pillow beside her
looking just as satisfied but like he got mauled by a wild animal.

"Take your time waking up love, you had a long night,"
Xai smirked as she slid from the bed to find where they threw
her clothing the night before. "When you have enough
strength to get up please go check on the children, I will deal
with our visitors." He just groaned in response. Smiling to
herself she left the room to see an equally satisfied wolf.

"Truen can't get up to handle business?" She asked, unable
to keep the grin from her face.

"He will probably have an easier time than Jackdaw this
morning but otherwise he is completely useless." Xai retorted
as they began to walk to the front of the inn.

"Good to know those old women were correct about the
full moon." Lux sounded smug. Pacing in front of the inn was
an incredibly petite woman in a loose linen dress, brown hair
braided simply, earrings glittering in the sunlight, and a bruise
disrupting her lightly tanned face.

"Good morning Dremira," Xai called out, startling the
woman out of her thoughts. "Sorry Truen is still asleep, we
went to sleep kind of late last night and he is not an early riser
without reason." Lux choked on a laugh at the explanation.

"You are the daemoness from last night." She said
excitedly, her blue eyes bright in the sun. She seemed much

248

calmer and happier than she had when they met last night. "Thank you so much for last night."

"What happened last night?" Lux asked with a raised brow.

"Truen and I went on a late-night…swim and Dremia here and her former beau interrupted. We ended up showing the bigot that he was wrong and Dremia ended her relationship with him hopefully after he struck her in front of me." Xai explained.

"Does he still draw breath?" Lux asked surprised.

"Only because the alderman saved him with a jail cell and charges." She retorted.

"That sounds about right, and you have ended your relations with that kind of scum correct?" Lux asked.

"Yes thankfully father understood why I had been reluctant the entire time and agreed that he was not a good fit for me or anyone in the colony."

"I am glad, you should not be tied to that kind of man, no one should." Xai nodded.

"You yourself are betrothed to the crowned Prince are you not?" Dremira asked cautiously.

"Yes, I am. He is also my handler." Xai looked at Lux in confusion about the question.

"My handler and betrothed is the second Prince, Advisor to the Crown Prince Jackdaw," Lux added.

"It is always strange to hear Jackdaw's full title." Xai scrunched her face.

"Isn't Truen Crowned Prince Truen Heir Apparent," Lux asked making a face as well.

"Technically the third Prince is General of the Crown Prince Krutz." Xai hated the full titles. "We also have titles, but I never cared to remember them past consort to the crown." Lux just shuddered at the thought of having a title for herself. "Sorry, was there something you would like to ask about my betrothal?" Xai looked back at the very curious human woman.

"I am just excited to meet a daemon betrothed to their handler and so happy. I am so sorry where my manners are. My name is Dremia Hulim."

"My name is Xai. the pure-blood daemon. As a pure-blood human, you know what that means."

"I am the pure human, I have waited for you for a very long time. Is the pure vampire with you already?"

"Yes he is also sleeping, the hike in the sun took a lot from him and his daemon yesterday," Xai explained.

"I have been thinking of what the Time Mage said to me about helping you bring forth the savior of our people since that day. I know my father is scared but I can not think of anything I would rather do with my life than help you save the kingdom I love from the Tyrant King."

"And your father thinks you're not a fighter, I see a warrior in you." Xai's words broke a huge smile across Dremia's face.

"My father is afraid because he lost my mother so early and she was sick for a long time so I have no siblings. But I have kept my ears out for all the rumors and the strife happening across the kingdom and my heart can not handle it.

The pain, the suffering, the fear, it should not be here. I want to help stop it all."

"Any ulterior motives to high tail it out of the colony?" Lux asked.

"Not any longer, Xai saved me from the oaf trying to marry me for my bloodline."

"I wouldn't want to marry him either." Xai snorted. "When will you be ready to leave? I have a feeling your father will try to postpone us leaving."

"If my daemon is allowed to come with us we can leave by nightfall when it is cooler." She looked like she was trying to pull her daemon through a loophole in the agreement.

"Why wouldn't your daemon come with you?" Xai asked, confused. "One does not separate a daemon and their handler. Why would we try to make you?" Her excitement was palpable. She suddenly took off with impressive speed across the sand pathway. The daemoness looked confused at each other before following the bare-footed woman. The human had made a decent distance before throwing herself into the arms of a man only slightly taller than her with just as slight of a frame.

"Crazden...oh Crazden I have wonderful news." Xai was not surprised that such excitement had accentuated the simple beauty she had hidden the night before. The man in question had caught her easily, it was clear that she threw herself at him regularly. The man himself was hard to look at with his female counterpart being on top of him but his long black hair was easily seen, and so were his pointed ears. The feline was able to catch a fond look in the dark eyes that reminded her of the man she left back in bed at the inn. This man loved the woman he was holding off the hot sand. She was watching the scene with a soft fondness. A daemon and his mate sharing the good

251

news. But if she was his mate why was she being courted by another? Her line of questioning was broken by the obnoxious sound of Lux sniffing at the air.

"What is your problem?" Xai looked at her companion, noticing her pupils blown out. "Lux?" She asked cautiously.

"I smell a rabbit." The wolf growls, getting the man's attention. His face blanched as fear spiked in the air. He set his handler down carefully but tensed reading to bolt away from the predator. Slowly he backed away from his handler clearly planning to draw the predator away from her. Xai just sighed knowing that if the man were to run the wolf would chase.

"Don't do it," Xai said loud enough for both of them to hear her if only one paid attention. Her voice seemed to break the trance and he took off into town shifting mid-stride.

"Bunny rabbit." She growled again, sounding far too excited. He barely got to the corner of the house behind them when the wolf started to chase after him, thankfully shedding her clothes as she ran before shifting, though now her clothes littered the path.

"I feel the need to apologize for her. She grew up in pack land so some more natural instincts tend to take precedence. I promise to pack members she is harmless." Xai groaned.

"She is a wolf?" Dremira asked, completely stunned as they watched the daemons run through the town that was slowly waking up.

"Yes, she is. Our youngest daemon with us is a little fox kit, you will meet her later. Both may or may not terrorize your mate there until he plays with them. Growing up the rabbit family on the pack lands would let the pups and kits chase them around to get their energy out." Xai sighed. "I hope he doesn't mind that he just made friends by being fast prey."

"He has never gotten to play with other daemons even when we were children, he is the only one our age in the colony. It might be good for him if she does not give him a heart attack first." Dremira looked thoughtful.

"Let us see if we can get them back over in this direction before I need to wake up her handler." Xai whistled hoping that the canine would answer to it, even if to tell the feline that to whistle to her was derogatory to canine daemons. It seemed to give the rabbit enough of a distraction to dart back to his handler, Lux on his tail having the time of her life chasing him. As they got closer Luxed looked over to Xai and the expression on the other woman's face made her stop in her tracks. Finally realizing what she had done the wolf slunk back over to her companion and sat, knowing she was going to get scolded. "You know that was a mean thing to do to him, correct?" The wolf nodded. "Go get your clothes and your handler while I try and convince them that you are not reliant on your instincts." Lux nodded again and walked off, picking up the pieces of clothing she had left behind. The wolf passed their largest companion as she went back to the inn.

"Do I want to know?" Dante asked, looking over to Xai.

"Lux forgot herself for a moment." Xai looked back to Dremira who was no longer surrounded by her daemon. "Is he alright?"

"He is a little more unsure now but otherwise fine, he went to go cool off. I am sure he will be back shortly."

"Dante, this is Dremira. She is the pure blood we have come looking for."

253

"Well then welcome, my name is Dante and I am the resident dragon rider. My husband is back in the inn." His smile was kind as always.

"I do apologize but you are the biggest man I have ever seen." Her eyes were wide as she looked over the seven-foot-tall man.

"I get that a lot, dragon riders tend to be bigger than your average person." He chuckled. "I actually came to get you because your children are awake and giving your man a hard time." Looking at Xai who sighed. Of course, while she was out was when the children decided they wanted her and not Truen. Thankfully Crazden crept back over to his handler, though he was looking around wildly in case the wolf would still be ready to chase him through town again.

"Dante this is Crazden, our new acquaintance that Lux just tried to run into the ground." Xai introduced the small man to the living mountain. Xai had to stifle the laugh that threatened to escape when the small daemon looked straight up at the dragon rider. The petite man looked more terrified of the man than the wolf who had chased him.

"I would love to see her handler's reaction to that, seems like he will not find that as funny as she did." Dante huffed with a smirk. Shaking her head they meandered back towards the inn where the newly dressed Lux was getting once again scolded by Jackdaw as Truen watched on with amusement.

"Where are the kids?" Xai asked as they got closer.

"Mi'kal took them swimming in the water," Truen answered, kissing her forehead as she got closer. He didn't even attempt to cover the markings from the night prior.

"See I told you." Dremira nudged at Crazden pointing at the daemoness and her mate.

"Are you her handler spell caster?" Crazden asked with a stern tone that Xai wouldn't have pictured coming from him.

"It has been a while since someone called me spell caster as a title," Truen commented, taken a bit aback while looking over at the other dark-haired man. "But yes to answer your question, I am her handler."

"And you two are betrothed?" He asked like he could not believe the idea.

"Yes, she is my Queen and once this is over she will be everyone else's as well," Truen explained with no hesitation.

"Is it on her own accord?"

"Why wouldn't you ask her that?" Truen looked completely confused on why the man was asking him instead of the independent daemoness next to him.

"Because you are the handler, you can force her to do as you please." He pressed.

"You try telling her what to do, I would love to see how that works for you." Truen scoffed, causing everyone who knew Xai for more than an hour to laugh. "This woman has complete control of our lives, and I need to emphasize that daemons and their handlers share a partnership. One does not have complete control of the other."

"No matter what you were taught, your handler needs you as much as you need your handler, especially if you are mates like Truen and I or you and Dremira." Xai pointed out. Crazden's face paled as she said it aloud. "You never told her, did you, that she is your mate."

"And what does that mean?" Dremiria asked, looking directly at her partner, arms crossed over her small chest. Xai only partially felt bad for outing the man. He looked absolutely terrified, refusing to look in the direction of his handler.

"A mate for a daemon, or any lunar really but most importantly daemons is a part of their soul. Some say our mate is the one who keeps us from going feral even with all the power the gods gave us. They are our hearts and we would give anything to them, anything for them. To have our handler be our mate as well is the ideal connection. It doesn't have to be the case, our vampire Kato is not the mate to his daemon Hestia but Truen is mine and I can tell that you are his." Xai explained carefully. "Not something you want to be outed, I do apologize."

"Were you ever going to tell me?" She asked the rabbit. "We could have been together this entire time? You made it seem like we could not be together, you convinced my father that I needed to marry someone else."

"You deserve better than someone like me." He muttered.

"Technically she was born for you," Lux added unhelpfully.

"Not only am I prey Dremira but you are a pure-blooded human. Not to mention I am almost ten years older than you."

"For someone who is normally so smart but you can be so stupid. I love you and I always have, we already share a mark. Now I am being told I am meant to be with you by a stranger sent by a prophecy." The tiny woman looked ready to assault her daemon for being stubborn and self-loathing. "I was not going to marry that oaf or anyone who is not you. You can't make me, father can't make me."

256

"Oaf? That is a kind way to say he is an abusive prick." Truen muttered into Xai's hair.

"Why would age matter? You are human, he is a daemon you age differently. Social status or bloodline doesn't really matter either. Love doesn't care, destiny doesn't care either." Xai spoke.

"If you are worried about the age I am thirty years older than Mi'kal, my husband," Dante added hoping to help.

"You are only nine years older than me." Dremira snapped, sounding completely frustrated with the man. "And I might understand much about daemons but I know even a prey daemon is stronger and more protective than anyone who abusive could ever be. I am assuming that nasty bruise on her face is from the other man, how could you think someone who would willingly do that is better than you?"

"Not him, anyone who would treat her right. I am just a half-breed daemon."

"Like that makes a difference, a daemon is a daemon. We are strong, we are loyal, and we will give anything for those we love. You have a special lady here so take care of her like you are supposed to." Xai shrugged. "She has an important task and she needs you by her side."

"You're only twenty…"

"And you are only twenty-nine, stop making excuses." This woman had determination, Xai could see why the Time Mage chose her. Now that she was near her daemon she was not taking any shit, no longer the meek and beaten down woman they saw last night.

"When did you become bonded to each other if you don't mind me asking?" Jackdaw asked, suddenly changing the direction of the conversation.

"I had seen her around when we were children, she was being bullied and I kept standing up for her. Once her mother passed away from an illness she began to spiral. I asked her father for permission as a long-time friend and the only daemon in our age group. She needed someone she could rely on, and someone who needed her. Dremira is needed in this world so I needed to make sure nothing happened to her. I didn't know what fated mates were until I was eighteen or so, she was only nine. I felt like I was taking advantage of her so I never mentioned it."

"He had been my best friend since I can remember, and I have had a crush on him since I knew what that was. After he asked my father permission to be my daemon he asked me and I couldn't have been happier. But he never fully opened the bond, I know that you are supposed to feel each other's emotions through the bond but I have never been able to feel his."

"I didn't want you to know so I closed my side," Crazden explained sheepishly.

"Well you better fix it because I know now and we are leaving the colony," Dremira said without any room for further argument. She walked over to her daemon who had not moved a muscle since he was caught in his omission and stood in front of him. "No more hiding from me."

"As happy as I am for you two you should get all your affairs in order before we leave." Xai interrupted. "Go make amends and be careful opening the bond, you don't want to overwhelm each other."

"Do you still want to leave at nightfall?" Dremira looked over at the feline.

"It would be helpful for the temperature to be cooler while we travel," Jackdaw answered.

"If you can get everything together I am sure we can make it work." Xai nodded. "Plus I do not think I could convince the children out of the water at the moment, they have never seen water at sea level before.

"Were we like that?" Truen asked, watching Dremira pull Crazden back towards their house, the man acting in a mix of fondness and a pout. There was going to be a long conversation between the two while they got their things together.

"When you were around five, you asked me to marry you. It was absolutely adorable." Xai recalled the tiny Prince toddling about with a fist full of flowers pulled from his mother's garden. He had seen a proposal for one of his cousins earlier that week. Growing up knowing that the daemoness that was three years older would be his wife he decided to propose in only the way a small child can.

"Do you remember your response?" He asked, not even the slightest bit embarrassed to know he had been gone for his daemoness since he started becoming his own person.

"I said yes, of course, you willingly evoked your mother's ire to bring me flowers."

"Will I have to outdo myself when I get your betrothal necklace?" He asked, kissing her neck, wrapping his arms around her tighter.

"I told you, on your knees, preferably begging." She teased, causing Lux to groan and Dante to laugh.

"You have your work cut out for you." Dante shook his head.

"Didn't you two get enough last night?" Jackdaw sighed, refusing to look at his brother again.

"I am going to see if I can get us some more supplies." Dante walked back into the inn, presumably to get Kila.

"We should go watch the children play since we have the day," Xai said, leaning further against Truen.

"Xai, I actually have a request since we have found all of the components of the prophecy," Lux spoke up.

"What is it?" Xai rolled her head to look at the other daemoness.

"Can we stay a night or two in Garmsby? We have to go through it on the way towards the Royal city anyways. Plus we need to figure out the last part of the prophecy."

"How long has it been since we left home?"

"Almost a year, the last five months have been non-stop."

"Time has flown by then, it seems like less time since we have been back. It would be a safe place to plan."

"We are about to face a huge fight once we get back to the Royal city and I have no idea what will happen once the fighting starts, let alone this weapon you are supposed to be finding," Lux said calmly.

"The others have all been told there is no weapon, only a savior," Xai mentioned in response. "You are the one to restore what is right. You can start the restoration of the original clans. Listen to me well child, you are the key to the start, and your partner holds the gateway. You need one pure-blooded human and one pure-blooded vampire by your side with the same destiny to help you but you are the one. You are the savior of this world child. Only you can call the hero, the weapon to save us all back to our world. You have to call for the weapon of the gods. You will find your human to the south, heated by the desert, and your vampire to the north, frozen in the mountains. You must hurry, child, your destiny is calling." She recited. Pulling away from Truen she sauntered over to the path leading to the shore. She wanted to watch the children but did not want them to hear this conversation. The others followed without question.

"We gathered everyone together, what is left?" Truen asked in frustration. Xai removed her shoes, choosing a rock to sit on so she would put her feet into the water.

"I have no idea, if this is a prophecy then someone has to have the next piece." Xai groaned as the others got comfortable around her on the sand. They could easily watch Kato and Hestia swimming with Mi'kal. "I hate all of this, every person has a singular piece and it all stops with mine. The Time Mage turned into dust so there has to be someone else who has a piece that we are missing."

"Some of us might not return from this fight, everyone is aware of that, correct?" Lux sounded resigned.

"Are you scared?" Xai asked.

"Absolutely terrified." She admitted.

"Good you should be, we should all be. Those who are storming the castle, even if we don't find a to bring the weapon, might get seriously injured." Truen agreed.

"We could lose," Jackdaw added.

"Losing is not an option. Even if we all fall we can not leave the King in charge." Xai looked over the water. "Our kingdom and our people will not survive if we lose."

"We have something to fight for, something to die for, and more importantly something to live for." Truen tried to reassure them all. "They do not, they have something holding them back. We will win."

"We have to find the missing piece, the one thing that guarantees our victory by prophecy." Kato's laugh was heard over Xai's words.

"I have faith that you will find it my Astrantia, we all do, if we didn't we wouldn't be here."

"We already have people who wish to fight with you, with us. You are stronger by yourself than just about any other being in the Royal castle." Lux had no doubt in her even with the fear. The day passes peacefully as they watch the children. Eventually, Dante joins them on the shore, deciding to put his feet in the water as well. Kila ran off to play with the children and her rider's partner. He informed them of the supplies he had gotten, and in return, they filled him in on their current plans and concerns. He added his own thoughts and expertise reminding them all that this was not his first act of rebellion against the crown. It felt like no time had passed at all by the time they had to call the others back so they could eat before leaving the colony with the last people they needed to find. As the adults ushered the tired children into the inn they were stopped by a scream in the direction of the town square. Taking off Xai didn't look behind to see who had followed to see the man from the night before had Dremira backed against a wall. Villagers watching but doing nothing to stop him.

"Croden, back away from me." She tried being forceful, but her fight from earlier was gone, and her daemon was nowhere in sight. "How are you even out of your cell?"

"I have friends everywhere, and you should remember that before trying to disobey me again." He sneered. It didn't take long for him to notice the advancing daemoness' though, neither of them could keep growls contained.

"Back away from her you insignificant little preed." Xai forced out in her growl as she stalked closer. Truen walked menacingly behind her, lightning crackling across his skin. Lux flanked her with ease.

"This has nothing to do with you lunar." Condescension dripped from his voice. "You put it into her head that she could leave me. She will not leave here, she is not important, she is just a woman." Tears started to fall down Dremiria's face but her expression turned determined. She knew her daemon was close by and her new companions would not let harm come to her. Never again.

"I will leave here." She spoke strongly surprising the aggressive male. "I do not belong to you, I am my own person. You are a weak poor excuse for a man and I hope my father punishes you with life in prison."

"If he doesn't I will." Truen gave her a smile. Xai quietly watched, Crazden walked through the gathered crowd like a shadow. Those who noticed him gave him a wide berth. The locals knew something was going to happen.

"Let her go." The low growl surprised the daemoness' at the veracity. That was not the growl of prey or a daemon for that matter. Both daemoness stopped growling and continued to watch cautiously, pushing their handlers back with the crowd. The man turned and slapped the daemon across the face, he didn't even attempt to stop the blow.

"You have nothing to do with this." He laughed. "You are nothing compared to me, know your place, lunar." Croden looked the unassuming man up and down, continuing to laugh uncontrollably. "Do you think you can be with her? We all know you lust after her, you are obvious and pathetic." A series of small snapping caught the attention of the daemons. Almost instantly the small man was no longer there, but instead a large golden dragon, his scales tipped in black. He snarled, putting his face a mere breath away from his mate's abuser.

"I said let her go." There was that growl again. Xai almost laughed when the smell of urine permeated the air. "Leave." He snarled again. The man couldn't, he was scared stiff.

"Crazden." Xai turned to see the Elder looking calm, though his guards were terrified. "Let us get him out of here. The guards that let him out have their own cells now. Dremira is safe again because of you. Thank you." Without taking his eyes off the man before him the dragon nodded. As quickly as they could, the guards moved between the apex predator and the criminal to remove him from the scene and get out of the way. As soon as the man was gone Dremira walked to her mate and placed her hand on his snout.

"Thank you, my love." She smiled. "You saved me again." Placing a kiss gently on the side of his face it was clear she was the only local that did not feel fear in his presence.

"With the pointed ears I thought half daemon half elven, I did not think dragon." Xai nodded as she walked over to the man, with no fear at all.

"My father was a golden dragon and my mother was a daemon. Are you not scared of me? Everyone else is." His deep voice was confused.

"I am a pure-blooded daemon, I am one of the few creatures in the world that could match you and have a good chance to win." She shrugged, taking him by surprise. Though he felt better knowing that there was someone here he could not hurt, that could stop him if he went feral like his father had at his mother's death. "Now we also know you could easily eat Lux if she gets a little too nippy. It would be no one's fault but her own at that point."

"I will have to mourn her for her own stupidity." Jackdaw shook his head.

"That being said now that the fun is over I think we should leave early." Xai sighed. "I am ready to get this over with."

"That is fair we have a kingdom to save," Truen smirked. It was almost time for this to end.

Chapter Thirteen: A Night Alone

Garmsby was an unassuming city that had an atmosphere for couples. Between the Eldar woods and the outer coast sits the city. It was just close enough to the desert to remain a contestant temperature and set optimal conditions for all races.

"I hate it here," Kato whined. He had been pouting in the room they had paid for since they had gotten to the inn. Xai couldn't help but smirk as she got ready for a trip out into the market with Truen, they decided to take a night in the peaceful city to go to a local restaurant for dinner just the two of them.

"Why do you hate it here? Lux and I grew up around here so I may take offense." She smirked at what the ten-year-old boy could possibly be thinking.

"This town is made for couples. There is nothing for Hestia and me to do here." He complained.

"That is not entirely true. During the day there are plenty of family activities. We got here closer to evening so the couple's activities have begun. Tomorrow we can do family things if you want. We will probably be here a few days until we figure out what to do next."

"It isn't fair, I don't want to be stuck in the inn room with Hestia all night while you go out to get food."

"I am not canceling on my mate because you are feeling needy. I know that doesn't feel fair to you but when we find your mate and are at the age when it will matter more to you, you and Hestia will both understand what Lux and I mean by the need to bond with your mate."

"I don't understand why it is so important, maybe I don't want to find my mate." He was still pouting.

"You are only ten, just a child. You will not be saying the same when you are older or you find them." She turned to look at him. "Mates are important to daemons and vampires, nothing would survive without them."

"What do you mean?" He looked up at her with confusion and curiosity.

"You do know that the gods made daemons and then vampires the strongest creatures in the world, correct?" He nodded. Everyone was taught that daemons were the strongest deemed by the gods themselves. "The reason mates were created and why most lunars have them where others don't is because the gods needed a way to balance our power, to make sure we were connected to the world they built so we may protect it and not destroy it. Mates make us want to stay and create a better world for them, without which we would go feral and do nothing but destroy. Truen keeps me at peace like every mate will do. It is one of the reasons thought to explain why it is so very rare to see a daemon or vampire mated to their same species."

"Then how are there still pure bloods then if daemons are not mated to daemons and vampires are not mated to vampires."

"The way it is explained by those who talk to the gods is that pure blood is a branding from the gods on a line of people or a person than something that can be passed down. A random daemon child can be born pure-blooded or like myself have two pure-blooded parents. The pure blood gene can also be erased from a line even with two pure-blooded parents."

"How do the gods decide that?"

"If I ever meet one of those who have a title given by the gods I will ask but honestly I do not know." She explained.

"Titles given by the gods?"

"As a pure blood, I am surprised you were never taught of them. There are four people who are directly connected to the gods. mother Nature is the title given to the human woman chosen by Terra herself. Arch-anigel is a male anigel who serves Sol. And Luna was special, she chose a daemon but she is the only one of the gods who switches between male and female every time the title is passed on. Saten is for the female daemons, and something else is for the male."

"Who is the fourth?"

"Only the gods and those with the titles know. But apparently, they have not walked in our mists for centuries. No one remembers the last time they did. History calls them a weapon of the gods, and I have a feeling deep within that is who we are meant to call upon. They have no loyalty to any specific god but to the original clans, to the people."

"Are you scared to call out for whatever we are needed for?"

"A little, I will protect you and Hestia, but whoever says they are not scared of war or battle is either lying or someone who enjoys spilling blood. That is where this is all heading, war to protect our kind and remove the rot from our kingdom."

"And yet you're going to spend the night out with Truen?"

"Yes, because it is needed. Balance will let us win, if we are too scared we will make mistakes and everyone will lose in the process. We need to remember what we are fighting for. I am fighting for Truen, for you, for Hestia, for every other member of our pack. We are fighting for every lunar and terra born on our land and in our waters. I am going with Truen tonight and we are taking you two out tomorrow to remember what is at risk. Our family is at risk if we were to fail and I can't let that happen."

"You will take us out tomorrow?"

"Of course, you are my child kiddo, you are part of my balance as much as Truen is. Tonight will just be Truen and I as adults and tomorrow will be the four of us." She could tell that he was still struggling with the entire idea. It wasn't the idea of their new found family that he was struggling with but her idea of family. Kato and Hestia had always been left out of traditional family activities, not that Yuell did not try but his aunt was incredibly paranoid after the prophecy was given before Kato was even born.

"We were never taken out for family time." that stopped the daemoness in the middle of braiding her hair.

"What do you mean?"

"Aunt would only let us go out when we were called after Hestia was cursed, she said the prophecy was a curse so she tried to keep us hidden until you showed up in the village. Yuell tried to let us be part of the village but aunt always got mad." She took two steady steps towards him and wrapped her arms around the boy whose eyes never left the ground. "I mean we couldn't really complain when I was born pure blood under a prophecy."

"Oh kiddo, that is not normal even for pure-bloods. I am so sorry you were not allowed to be a child." Xai cooed. "After this war is won we will have more time and safety for you and Hestia both to be loved children. Hell, you will be the Prince and Princess of the kingdom but much like the current Queen all the crowned children will be children before royalty." This was not what she expected at all. "I am not sure how to help right now but we are going to fix this once it is safe. I promise you that Truen and I do our best to be the parents we can be for you."

"But what if we lose you too? You said we are going to war and that some of you might not come back."

"I understand you are scared, I am too but we can't believe we will lose or we will. I need to assume that we are going to win. If I have to continue to remind everyone of that so we have the faith to win I will every day. I will continue to remind you every day as we move forward." She looked down at him. "Even if I fall, Truen will not, I will not allow it. You will not have to start over with your family again."

"When will you be back tonight?" He quickly changed the subject, too exhausted to continue talking about the next few challenges in their pathway and what that means for the entire pack they created.

"After you have gone to bed I hope. I know that we can get you some blood from the tavern downstairs. There is a decent size community outside town. Mi'kal and Dante will be watching you two tonight." She stepped back from him, watching the child closely. Somehow he looked both deflated and tense at the same time, she had no idea what to do. She wished she could ask either her mother or Truen's for help. She never thought her and Truen would be parenting without them. There is a large part of her who prays that the two women who raised them all as long as they could will be saved in the raid that they are planning.

"Did Truen buy you this dress? I haven't seen you in a dress since you came to get us." The dress laying on the bed was a light piece of spider silk, her favorite fabric to feel on her skin.

"Yes he did, this was the kind of slim dress that I used to wear to gallas and such when Truen and I were younger. Not the style I would wear around the court but the same fabric. daemons tend to have sensitive skin when we are not shifted so you will notice each daemon has a type of fabric or two that they will always gravitate towards."

"I never thought of that, Hestia tends to like wool." Kato nods thinking of it.

"That is a good thing to notice, maybe tomorrow we can find her something made from wool in the market." As she changed into the dress finally she looked into the mirror to see how the shimmering black silk poured beautifully over her spotted skin. The low v cut-out resting just above her navel, the skirt flowing to the ground. If not for the slits up either side it would be an uncomfortable cut since she would not be able to take complete strides. "You will all be safe here tonight." After lacing her shoes for the evening, a dainty pair of sandals she walked back over to her son and placed a gentle kiss to the top of his head. It seemed to startle the boy only for a second. "We will be back in a few hours so try and behave." Finally looking up at the daemoness the small vampire gave her a pure child's smile, fangs out and all. It caused warmth to spread through her chest. She never wanted that smile to go away now that she had seen it.

"Have a good night." She smiled at her son again before leaving the room that she was sharing with her mate. Said mate was waiting, leaving against the wall looking as a Royal should. He looked breathtaking in his black and gold suit.

"You are absolutely stunning my love." Truen looked her up and down like a man who had never seen the sunset before. "You always turn me speechless with your beauty."

"And you are always such a smooth talker dear heart." She smirked knowing that her mate was a weak man.

"I have to find some way to keep up with how you make me feel when you quirk your eyebrow like that." Truen reached his hand out for her, like the gentlemen he grew into. "You are right, I am a weak man especially when it comes to you."

"As long as you are aware of who is in charge in our relationship my dear." He guided her through the crowds of people as they walked to the restaurant he had chosen for their night out.

"Of course you are, I would never try to challenge your dominance between us." He was confident in his position as they were led to a private room. He had thought of everything for this evening. "How is Kato by the way? I heard a bit of your conversation." He asked as he pushed her chair to the table.

"I am not sure."

"You seemed torn on something." He added nonchalantly as he took his seat across from her.

"He confided in me that he and Hestia were almost completely locked away and kept as a trinket. Yuell tried to get their aunt to agree to let them be children but apparently, she thought the prophecy was more of a curse than anything else. It seems to me like she blamed the prophecy for the death of her sister thereby punishing the children by being overprotective."

"I wouldn't be surprised. It is not a terra concept to punish what one does not understand." From the doorway soft music started to play, Xai could easily tell it was a live performer.

"My favorite song? I am surprised you remembered that little bit of information."

"Even with the spell in place dear heart, there wasn't much I forgot about you as a person. I never stopped thinking of you even when it was painful."

"You grew into quite the romantic my Prince."

"I know you like the gestures even when you say you don't. You are also a romantic my queen."

"No sharing secrets like that. I have a reputation to maintain."

"Like you are not a caring mother to our adopted children that were thrust upon us?"

"Exactly like that."

"We will take care of them Xai, after we figure out what the hell is going on in our kingdom and what the gods have in store for all of you they will get to be children."

"That is what I promised Kato, I just hope that we can fulfill that promise and make it through the next few weeks."

"It does not seem that only a few months ago we were still under the influence of that nasty spell."

"And in a matter of days, we will be fulfilling the prophecy whatever it is, and raiding the Royal City."

"Exactly my love. How did things change so fast?"

"If I ever find the gods then I will ask because I am blaming this entirely on them at the moment. Maybe they can help us or at least their mouthpieces to figure out what is going on after the raid. I don't know how they have been silent in all of this."

"That is a good point, a prophecy from the gods, and their mouthpieces are surprisingly missing." A soft knock interrupted the conversation. A small girl, no more than a teenager, bowed as low as possible.

"I am sorry Your highness, I know you asked for no intruders or staff unless the food was ready but we have a guest who is very determined to send a drink to your consort." Her bald head still lowered as she shuffled towards the table, gently placing an ornate glass of dark red liquid inside. Xai recognized the light scent of the high-end alcohol.

"You are fine dear but we can not accept, That drink is Vampura correct? A very sweet gesture but Vampura contains the venom of a high vampire in it, neither of us can drink that. Kindly send our apologies and regards." Truen spoke kindly, not to frighten the human girl more than she already was. Xai thought she would hurt herself with how fast she nodded her head and rushed back from the private room with the drink.

"You already ordered food?" She raised her brow, looking back at her mate. "Why am I not surprised?"

"I told you I would take care of everything for tonight. I made sure they started some of our favorite dishes the moment we arrived."

"That would explain the lack of staff and our drinks already adorning the table, though it does not explain who would know we were here with the intent to give poison or a well-meaning and expensive mistake in a crystal goblet."

274

"Let us hope for a simple mistake and not a clumsy assassination attempt. I promised Hestia to keep you safe tonight."

"Is that the only reason my dear?"

"No, selfishly I would like a peaceful night with you and a peaceful day that you promised the children tomorrow. There has been so much stress and fear, so much death and fighting that I would like a night."

"I do not think that is selfish with everything going on, though I also do not think we will see a night of peace until you wear the crown."

"I knew I would someday but I did not think it would be us who had to remove it from my father by force."

"Me either if I am honest. When we were children he was such a sweet man with love for all that called his kingdom home. But the man who sits on that throne now is not the man who raised us."

"No, after Jhelum died something happened. I wonder if he is under a spell as well."

"I hope so as horrible as it is to say, I would hate to think our childhood was a lie. My father was always a cold man, there will be no love lost but I would hate to lose our mothers. Or my remaining siblings."

"Hopefully we can save them. I would like to try and save my father as well if we can. I am even less prepared to run the kingdom than I am to raise children with you."

"So far you have been a fantastic father to those children. You have learned well from your parents."

"You have been doing well as a mother as well, do not sell yourself short."

"I learned from our mothers, though I wish I had their advice at the ready for those two. I never thought, when I allowed myself to imagine, that we would adopt children though somehow it makes sense for us."

"Raising children who had no one else to treat them like children, children who were given too much on their small shoulders or curses. That does sound like us, giving shelter to those who could not get it themselves."

"If we never had more children I would be at peace with that since we have the two of them."

"I would be as well, but if we have more when everything is settled I would not be opposed either."

"Why good sir what kind of woman do you take me for? I demand a grand ceremony showing the world your devotion to me before you even attempt to bed me with the purpose of more children." She teased. If she were being truthful she did not at all care about grand ceremonies. A quiet gathering of those they cared about in the gardens belonging to the Queen would be enough for her as long as the world knew that her mate was hers and hers alone. Her words got the effect she was hoping for as Truen let out a truthfully indignant snort at the idea. His laughs drowned out the soft lute music playing still. Neither paid attention to the door once more opening, assuming that it was a member of staff waiting to interrupt once the crowned Prince could breathe again.

"I must say I was almost offended when the waitress returned the drink I bought you with an apology. But how can I stay mad when you two are having such a good time" The jovial atmosphere dried up instantly as they recognized the voice.

"What is it that you want, Krutz? Can't you see that your brother and I are busy?" Xai sighed without looking at the youngest living Prince. She had just told Truen she did not think they would get a night of peace and this thorn in her paw just needed to prove her correct.

"Should I feel honored you remember my voice without so much as turning around my dearest Xai?"

"No, you should leave. We were having a nice time and you are a little too smug for this to be a coincidence."

"So rude, my beautiful forest flower. Am I interrupting something?"

"Yes you are, a night out between those who are betrothed to each other, who are thoroughly mated." Xai finally turned to look at the Prince who would never be king. His face reddened as he tried to compose himself poorly.

"I would rather you not be so dismissive of me my sweet. I have only come to talk and I would rather you not test my temper as you did last time we were together."

"Are you talking about where you stabbed me?" The reminder caused both men to growl at the memory. "To be fair I would rather you stop with the ridiculous pet names for me. I am not your daemon nor am I your mate or betrothed."

"I would watch your tone if you want your winged pack members to continue to be safe. I just want to talk."

Winged members?

He could not take on Dante, Mi'kal, or Crazden alone and he is not with anyone. He is doing his stealth spells.

"Which members do you have your eyes on?" Xai spoke carefully.

"Do not fear I will not attempt to harm your children. But your fair folk pack members are under surveillance and one wrong move can have them removed permanently." Her blood began to boil at the younger Prince trying to bluff with the dead members of their pack, threatening them. She could feel the anger flowing freely through the bond.

"Do not make ideal threats and bluffs Krutz, that is not how you get what you want." Xai hissed. "And do not use those who have already been lost as pawns in your schemes." The color drained from the other's face.

"Brother we will give you one chance for the talk you say you want before we have you removed or worse. Join us for dinner and be civil or I will not stop her again." Truen spoke calmly, though Xai knew better. "Go place an order with the staff if you haven't already and have someone bring you a chair."

"Thank you, brother." He nodded, rushing back out the door.

"Why are you giving him a chance?" She sighed again knowing this would be a long conversation. Truen stood, moving his chair to sit next to his mate so his brother could not and would not come between them, even figuratively.

"Because if we can get the spell to break on him maybe we can save him, maybe it could lead to what actually happened to your sister. We know Lui is in the middle of whatever this is and he is her mate." He had a point not that it helped any. One more member of the Royal family saved would be a blessing, even if it was the clever but assholish youngest Prince. She did miss his sense of humor. It didn't take long for Krutz to return with a staff member carrying a chair.

"They said the food would be ready shortly." He tried to sound confident as he sat down at the edge of the table across from the couple.

"What did you wish to talk about little brother? Speak clearly and quickly before we decide to cut the evening short."

"Your brother is giving you a chance, do not waste it," Xai added to Truen's calm words. "No more manipulation or you will go from a nuisance that we wish to save to an enemy we must strike down with the rest of those who threaten us.

"Of course, it was wrong of me to lie to you. You very rarely fell for it." He considered. "I have felt strange since we last spoke as if there is a war in my head. You mentioned a spell and I want more information."

"We are not entirely sure brother, Jackdaw was the first to notice the inconsistencies." Truen started.

"All we know is that for some reason false memories and feelings were given to each of us, all being different. Once you start questioning them the spell starts to fall apart but it does try and fight back." Xai continued. Part of her remembering the cabin fondly.

"What do you mean different?"

"I remembered my sister being pushed to her death by you and Truen, the hatred and betrayal I felt overriding the instincts to be with my mate until we were together again."

"I remember Lui getting sick like Jhelum and Xai running off abandoning us when you and I needed her." Truen hated those false memories. He and Xai were both trying to comfort each other. "You remember me poisoning Lui."

"But none of us remember Lui's funeral, only that she was gone." Xai mourned her sister for so long and now she just wanted answers. The conversation lulled momentarily as the staff brought in the food finally.

"We don't know why Jackdaw wasn't affected but everyone else in the castle seems to be, especially our families. Someone is trying to tear the Royal family apart and the kingdom as well."

"How do I break it?" Krutz asked. "If you are correct before it takes my mind over again with false hate and grief." He seemed to want to focus on pushing his food around his plate while his head was swimming unnaturally.

"Go to Quin, my friend. He specializes in nullifying magic. If anyone I trust can help break it he can, he inadvertently helped break ours."

"Once broken for yourself please try and help the others. My siblings, our mothers, even our fathers if you can manage."

"And Lui? Is she alive? Where is she?" He sounded desperate.

"I am hoping to find out. Maybe we can bring her home with us. But you need to get that slime off you and help us if you want more."

"Where is Quinn hiding these days?" Krutz asked, trying to sound nonchalant and once more failing.

"He has a cottage outside the Royal City, and if you try to cross us he has done nothing illegal and since I left I have had no contact with him so you could not haul him away," Truen spoke harshly.

"I will try not brother, I want the pain and the war in my head to stop. Before the pain, it was like a fog. Now I want it to stop and answers." Krutz sounded a mix of desperate and miserable.

"We felt the same way when the spell was weakening. For once in the last almost twenty years please trust us, little brother. We are not the villains but victims fighting back." The rest of the dinner was silent as they ate. Xai and Truen both bid farewell to the other who walked away in a daze. The silence followed them back to the inn even with the crowds among them. The light atmosphere from when they left was completely gone, though there was more hope. The hope grew as they reached their room to find their child curled in the middle of their bed, laying under their cloaks like it was their lifeline. Smiling each of the adults went to move one child.

"Welcome back mother, father," Kato mumbled slightly awoken as he was lifted.

"We tried to wait up for you." Hestia yawned, her words barely audible.

"Thank you dears, sleep now and we will have a family adventure tomorrow." Truen smiled, kissing both foreheads after they were deposited back in the center but this time comfortably under the blankets. This might not have been a peaceful night but it was a night full of hope.

Chapter Fourteen: Seeing Ghosts

"Truen, Truen! Where are you?" Everything was darkness, not even her enhanced eyes could cut through the void.

"Xai! Where are you?" His voice was faint and strained. The daemoness tried to follow the sound of her mate's voice but it was hard to track. She kept calling out to get more clues about his whereabouts.

"Truen, where are you!" She kept crying while panic set in, he had been silent through the last few calls. She could not feel him at all in the darkness or through the bond. It was as if the bond never existed between them.

Over here love. She let out a sigh of relief as the telepathic link was still there, leading her to him finally. From the darkness she ran into the throne room, they were back at the castle. There he was leaning against the throne, his arms wrapped tightly around his abdomen, blood pooling on the stone beneath him. The color had fallen from his skin. His face scrunched in pain with each breath. His beautiful eyes were still defiant as he stared at her in the doorway. His eyes darted away, bringing her focus deliberately to the shadow figure standing in the middle of the room. The shadow person's back was to Xai as he held Krutz by his throat on the ground, distracted and none the wiser of Xai's presence. As quietly as possible she snuck to her mate, only making it halfway to him before she fell to the floor vomiting blood. The shadow turned to watch her retch, not lowering the Prince until she was done spitting.

"Welcome, you finally made it Xai Lurra." The shadow spoke in a low masculine tone.

"Put him down." She growled in response. The dark figure shrugged but did as she asked, throwing the young Prince like a child's toy away from her and his brother.

"I was trying to explain to him that you, your mother, even his own mother never loved him. No woman would." The shadow gave in explanation.

"What the fuck are you talking about?" Her words forced her to cough up more blood.

"Well his mother never really loved him so she had to die, it was only logical." Moving the shadow pointed at a female form with dark hair laying on the ground in nothing but her light blue night dress covered in blood. Next to her in a heap a white-haired body looking broken and bloodied. Even from across the room, Xai knew who these corpses were. "Of course, your mother fought to protect his mother only proving she never loved him either."

"Are you delusional? Who the hell are you?" She hissed through the pain.

"I am not delusional, you foolish little girl. None of this would be happening if you all followed the script. Who I am is not important at the moment. What is important is the next arch of the story."

"What the hell are you talking about? You killed innocent women for what? Hurting all these people for what?"

"You will know when the time is right if you stop interfering." The shadow continued to pace the throne room.

"I will continue to interfere."

"You will not win against me Xai. I don't know who you think you are but my plans will be followed through as the best-laid stories always are. The hero, myself, of course, will win. You can not defeat me by breaking the spells I had cast or trying to kill my puppet king. You don't get to make it to the end of the book."

"So you are the one behind all of this?"

"It is my story that is being told. How I saved the world."

"You are destroying everything."

"I beg to differ, child. I am saving my world. You do not see the bigger picture of the world." The shadow made no sense.

"I will not let you win."

"You do not have a choice in that matter. I will stop your little prophecy in its tracks and leave you to watch those you love die slowly. You had a chance to live when I had you sent away but you chose to come back. I do hate it when the characters have a mind of their own. You can not change my story at will."

"Fuck your story, it means nothing to us, we are not characters we are living beings."

"That is the same thing your sister said before I got rid of her." The voice sounded almost saddened as if that was not the conclusion he had wanted.

"You did it!" She screamed, only causing more blood to rise in her throat. "You are the one who stole my sister away from us. You made us blame each other for losing her."

"She needed to be out of the way, for my plan to work, for everyone to be saved. You were in the way too, being too stubborn for your own good."

"You are insane, you must be. To think of living people as nothing but props and to kill anyone who doesn't listen to your asinine plans for what you alone think is best for our world."

"Unfortunately I have no time to explain it to you, my dear. I need people who will just follow simple instructions to help me usher our world into peace away from the gods and their destiny."

"Are you missing the ability for thought, you are killing people for a crusade for gods who may or may not exist. If they do exist they are GODS you complete imbecile."

"Always so rude. You know nothing of my plans child. You will fall into what I need you to."

"I will need you to release my sister if you don't mind." A bell-like voice came from a person who had not been there prior. Xai almost thought her neck would snap at the sound. A beautiful white-haired woman checked on her Prince. "Close your mouth Xai, your drooling blood. I know I was the more lady-like twin but have some decorum." Purple eyes met purple eyes as Lui finally looked at her sister. "Now shadow you are not welcome in my sister's mind or dreams. Be gone." The shadows vanished in an instant as if her command broke the spell. The blood was gone from the daemoness' lungs and she could breathe clearly again. The ghostly image of the long-gone daemon child floated through the room. Checking first on her mate and then her sister's before coming to stand before Xai herself looking as she remembered her.

"Lui?" The elder daemoness asked carefully as if directly addressing the spector would collapse the illusion.

"How old are we now Xai? It has been so long since I cared." She asked with the same gentle smile she always wore.

285

"We became twenty-eight since the snow fell last winter."

"That would make our boys twenty-five then. Impressive. It is hard to think of yourself as an adult when you are a child. You look amazing, your spots faded a bit though. I always loved how your spots were more pronounced than mine."

"A lot seemed to fade when I lost having you by my side," Xai admitted back.

"I am sorry sister. You must believe that I didn't want to leave your side. Or Krutz or anyone else. I didn't have a choice."

"No one ever blamed you sister. We blamed me, we blamed Truen, we blamed Krutz. We blamed everyone who was innocent and grieving because of someone else's lies. And I will find who did this all and tear them to shreds."

"I know you will. Always the wild one, the one with a sense of justice and loyalty that went deeper than any ocean. To have that broken in you is too much for me to handle. The fire in your eyes is smaller than it ever was and that alone makes me want to taste blood with you."

"You sound like a friend when you say that."

"You made a friend? Outside of us? Even more impressive. Tell me about them." The childlike wonder hurt Xai deep in her chest but she could not say no to the one person in the world she had left to miss.

"Her name is Lux, a snarky little daemoness, wolf pup actually. Her mate is Jackdaw surprisingly enough. They are good for each other, and she is nothing like we ever could have imagined when talking about Jackdaw's mate when we were kids."

"Then she must be something special. I am happy for you both then. You needed someone when I couldn't be there with you."

"I wish you could meet her. I could never bring myself to tell her much about you. It always hurts too much, like remembering I was missing a limb."

"One day I will be able to know her and for her to know me. Do not worry about that dear sister. Soon that pain will pass and it will be forgotten."

"I will never stop missing you, never stop hurting for you. I would rather hurt than forget you, Lui."

"I know, but you will understand soon. And when you do you can tell me all the new and amazing things I have missed in my time away."

"Will I see you more than?"

"Of course, now that I am free to finally reach out to you again I will never let that connection go. When it got taken from me I felt like half of me was ripped out."

"I have felt that way since the day you were taken."

"I know, and I am so sorry. When I was taken I felt nothing for so long. I don't know where I was but there was nothing until recently. I worked so hard to make my way back to you, to them."

"I will do everything in my power to never let our connection fade again no matter how far we are from each other."

"When the war comes to a head you will not have to fight alone. I will be beside you in one way or another."

"It won't be the same without you there in spirit and body."

"Do not count me out quite yet sister. But it is time for you to wake up, I'm afraid. I can't keep you here with me either."

"Please don't send me away yet Lui." Before the words were out of her mouth the room started to fade to black.

"Soon Xai." Was the last thing she heard.

Her eyes shot open, searching widely in the darkness of the inn room they had acquired hours before. A cold sweat covered her body as tears ran down her face. It felt so real to her, from the blood in her lungs to the presence of her sister.

"Dear heart, are you alright?" The sleep-heavy voice of her Prince was enough to ground her.

"I didn't mean to wake you." She coughed out. His arm warped around her waist, pulling her into his chest.

"You are not normally one for tears, I promise it is no hardship for me to comfort you when they come."

"Are you normally this romantic when woken up?" She groans curling into him.

"Depends on why I was awoken I think. Tears get romance and comfort, other reasons can cause much more interesting responses."

"How can you go from comfort to horny I will never know." She shakes her head as she groans into his skin.

"It is a skill most men possess, my love." He smirked. "Do you wish to talk about the dream you had? You were crying so steadily."

"I was in the castle, you were calling to me. Some sort of shadow man was over you and hurting you brother."

"Then Lui showed up." Truen finished her thought. "That was my dream as well, I could only see you though. I could only feel the pain and the coolness of the stone floor."

"Do you think Lui has something to do with us seeing the same things?"

"I don't know my dear, do you think Krutz had the same dream tonight?"

"With Lui there, we can only hope. Though I need to find out who the shadow man was. Who is he to try and defy the gods and treat us all like puppets in his games."

"Do you even believe in the gods my dear?"

"I can not say if they are or are not real, to be honest. With everything that I have seen in life if they are, they do not care about any of us." She sighed pushing up from his grasp. "I need some air, go back to sleep if you can. I will return when I can." Slipping from the bed she reached for the tunic he had thrown on the end of the bed as he got ready for bed hours before.

"I will wait for your return, my dearest."

"Sleep Princeling. I will return to you before dawn." She reassured him as she slipped through the door. When she made it to the porch of the inn the rain was pouring from the sky. It was why they had stopped in this no-name village. The night air was a comfort even with the moon covered by the clouds. If any of the deities truly existed it was nights like that she could believe it. The moon had always shown her the way through life. If there was anything she believed in truly it was that. Her compilations almost made her miss the woman walking up to her from the other side of the porch.

"You seem lost in thought child, anything that you need the night to listen to?" The woman asked, startling the daemoness. "My apologies, I didn't mean to startle you."

"You're completely fine, I just didn't notice you joining me. I think the night already knows my concerns, the issue is I don't entirely know what to do about them. The darkness allows me to think about those issues and try to sort through them without any sort of judgment or conflict."

"That was an amazing outlook on things." She smiled gently. The daemoness looked the woman over, blackened-haired speckled with silver strands. She seemed like she had seen more of the world than anyone Xai had ever met. "I know you might not care what a strange old woman has to say but the air around you is full of destiny and you seem to be drowning in it."

"You would not be the only woman who has told me that in recent months. The last one turned into dust though so I hope that will not happen with you too. I might start thinking that it is personal." The woman laughed sweetly, clearly amused.

"You are funny. Now come with me, a child who is lost in her own destiny, come inside with me where it is dry and safe."

"It's not the time in my life to be dry and safe." She smirked at the woman who seemed to approve of her answer.

"No, I guess it is not. Do you want your next steps?"

"I am starting to assume every time a strange woman comes up to me that it's something to do with this damn prophecy." Xai groaned in frustration. She turned back to the storm.

"That seems to be the case." She didn't seem offended by the frustration. "But maybe I can help where the Mage could not."

"How so? How could you help any more than her other than giving me the next piece, the piece she left out?" Xai turned back and watched the woman again. Her eyes were black but somehow had so much life in them.

"Well, it wasn't her information to give, unfortunately. You are now ready for the second part of the prophecy. Now that you have everyone you need beside you, you can move forward."

"I am sorry but it is too late to be talking to me in riddles." The daemoness sighed.

"That is fair enough, you have had a rough go of it so I shall be kind to you. Do you know what you are in this mess?"

"I am the pure-blooded daemon," Xai answered.

"You are a pure blood that is true but also you are mixed in blood."

"How can I be pure and mixed?"

"That will have to wait, child. But know that you have the possession of the weapon of the gods, a powerful champion who can save us all, gods and creations."

"What are you talking about?"

"Go to the village over to the west. You will be given what is necessary to awaken the champion. Please remember that you are everything we need. You brought a pure-blood human, a pure-blood daemon, and a pure-blood vampire together. More importantly, you brought a pack together who will risk it all to help you and help the land."

"Who are you?"

"Do you really want to know or do you want to figure it out yourself?" She asked with a smile.

"I am done figuring these things out alone."

"I am Luna, goddess of the moon, night, and creature of the Lunar races."

"You are not making that up are you, you are serious. The night that I admit that I don't think the gods would help any of us here you show up to help?"

"I am never that far away from my children, neither is Terra, or Sol. Normally you don't need us."

"Then why did this happen, why was any of this allowed to happen?" She pleaded with the goddess, trying to understand.

"Because something went wrong. Sol, Terra, and I were separated from each other. We can't reach out to each other nor can we access our celestial powers. We got locked into our mortal forms. Someone is pulling strings behind the scenes for years and hiding from us in a way that we did not know was possible. We are not omnipotent gods, we don't know what is happening in our own world. But our champion can help us. Our speakers can help us. You are the one I was able to find because you are my creation. The champion is the fighter for us all, even the gods. We need your help Xai."

"Then why be so cryptic about everything?"

"Because I don't know who is doing all this. I don't know where the others are. But the first step to our safety is to awaken the blood of the champion and stop the genocide. Then we can find the others and free ourselves."

"That is understandable. I never thought a god could be so vulnerable."

"Gods are not perfect Xai. We make things and we take care of them. We fail and we miss things. We make mistakes and sometimes our creations twist themselves into monsters. That is why we made fail-safes to protect the innocent lives we created. We are not malicious gods like some others."

"I can understand that."

"You need to face the trails to awaken the blood though."

"And what are these trials?"

"They will be reaching into the magic in the blood. I don't know what exact trials you will have but I will be beside you the entire time. I created the champion, I created the daemons and the vampires. I will not leave you to face these alone."

"I thank you for that Luna. That takes some of the foreboding off of this endeavor but not all of it."

"I understand my child. I truly do. But understand I am not asking this lightly. Every generation has the potential for a champion but we have not had to call upon one before. The first was one of a kind and he lived among the people for centuries needing to solve no true problem. I was hoping to not have to call another but the blood continues to manifest in case of emergencies. This is not something we ask for or risk lightly."

"I couldn't imagine a benevolent set of gods would want to request such a thing."

"I do apologize for doing this to you or those who are traveling with you. I apologize that things got this far without us realizing."

"We do have free will, and as you said you are not omnipotent. You talk as though the gods are their own race so how could you be in control when you are just as much a living creature as we all are."

"You are more understanding than most Xai, I am glad you were the one that was chosen."

"With everything that has happened, I do not have the luxury of not being understanding."

"That is very true, I wish it wasn't."

"I have a feeling nothing in this life will ever be easy until the shadow over us all is taken care of."

"I agree, and I will see how we can help each other solve that particular pain in the side."

"I don't see why we can't continue to help each other."

"I hope you continue to think that once the trails are over. When this is all over." The goddess' smile turned sad. "Please remember that we did not want this either."

"Remind the people of that when you are free again."

"We will try. I am just hoping we get to that point. A world without gods is doomed even if the gods choose not to interfere with what they created."

"Just because you are currently trapped in this body doesn't mean you can be melodramatic. God or not you have an obligation to what you created like any half-decent parent." Xai sighed again. "You are strong whether or not you have access to your full powers, I can feel it from here, the underlying power."

"You will make an amazing Queen when this is over." Luna, her smile losing the sadness. "I have been working on fixing how you have been wronged over the years."

"You don't have to."

"But I do, I have been trying to fix things for years, we all have. You are part of who we are as gods, I have told you this. But we have to protect you as much as guide you."

"I can't let myself hope for things to get fixed from the past but I look for a shining future once we get through this."

"You will make it through this."

"I know I will, I don't have a choice but to make it through. Too many people are counting on me."

"That is no way to make your way through a war. You need to have something to live for."

"I live for those who need me and to keep the memories of those we lost already alive."

"And you wonder why you were chosen Xai. You have all the reasons to be mad at the world and mad at us and yet you are trying to move forward."

"What is the point of being mad at the gods or mad at the world for the mistakes of a select few who have put everyone else in danger? Am I happy about being put in this situation or in the middle of a prophecy, not in the slightest. But it is the life I was given and I refused to do nothing with it."

"Thank you for not squandering the gifts I gave you."

"When do the trials start?"

"When you want to start the trials, call for me. You have time to prepare. Go back to your Prince and rest now my child. There is a lot of work to do until we are all free." Finally, the daemoness felt the weariness that had escaped her since she woke up from the dream. Nodding to the goddess she walked back into the warm air in the inn and back to the room her Prince was waiting in. As she crawled back in next to him the tension left her, his arms reaching back for her and bringing her body back to his where it belonged. Dreamless sleep followed shortly after.

Chapter Fifteen: The Preparations

Going home had never felt so foreboding to the daemoness'. It had only taken mere days to return to the forest that they had lived in for so long. Xai had called the portion of the forest where Lux's family resided at as their home since she was found and taken in by the crazy pack. It hadn't taken as long as they would have hoped for the Princes to realize how close they were traveling to the royal city. They had decided as a group to walk and keep as far from the main roads as they could and they are as far away from possible attention as possible. That did not stop the judgmental looks from the men the daemonesses were avoiding looking at. Lux was happy enough without looking at her handler, feeling comfort in her home forest.

"I have missed these trees more than I ever thought I could." She sighed happily.

"I will have to agree with you there. I never thought I would miss these woods." Xai nodded standing beside her best friend.

"You two were right here the entire time?" Truen asked in a strained voice.

"The whole time!" Jackdaw shouted in disbelief. The two could not figure out how frustrated they were at their future wives being so close all these years or if it was a more amusing set of circumstances.

Do you really think I could have been that far from you this entire time?

297

"In my defense, I knew nothing about any of you growing up and Xai refused to talk about anything for the longest time after we found her." Lux threw her hands up in defense.

"This place is amazing." Mi'kal laughed as he watched Dante play in the trees like a child, each of them had felt the safety that Xai had all those years ago when she had fled. Something about this part of the Eldar Forest felt like home should like nothing could hurt you here if the trees had accepted you as one of their own.

"I have to agree with you but unfortunately we are here for more dire reasons than to play here. As much as I would love to tell you all to relax and feel at peace here where peace found me I can't and I am sorry." Xai sighed watching the wonder fade from each member of her pack and gather around her. "Though I would like to say that it is almost the summer solstice and I have not forgotten your birthday Lux, hopefully, we can stop and see your family before this shit show that is about to happen."

"What shit show, in particular, are you talking about at the moment?" Jackdaw asked, wrapping himself around Lux.

"Taking on your father and his army." Xai sighed again knowing no one disagreed with her but also that no one wanted to walk headlong into what could be the turning point in their history, in this war against innocent people. "I know we won't have to fight your brother but I am not sure about my little siblings. I also don't know where our mothers will stand. I know my father will stand with yours without a thought. Our best bet is to attack during the full moon. I know it will give the daemons in the castle an advantage as well but by default, we will have the advantage. My father will most likely be the only pure-blood daemon to stand against us. Honestly, Truen, Jackdaw, Lux, and I can handle the Royal

Forces. It doesn't even matter I trained with many of them and have seen more actual fights than them but we have the bonus of handlers now."

"With all of our expertise and the fact they are not expecting us, we can easily take on anything they throw at us. That is even with Kato and Hestia sitting out. Crazden will be a bit more vulnerable if he and Dremira join in the fight but that is up to them. " Mi'Kal added in.

"I know I might not help much but I will do what will help the most." Dremira spoke, "I don't want to be a burden or keep Crazden from the fight if you need him."

"You are not a burden," Treun responded. "Honestly I would prefer you and Crazden watch and protect the children. If someone finds out who they are to us they could try to use them against us, if we know someone who cares and will be protecting them then it will be easier for us to lay those thoughts to rest while we are fighting for us all."

"Truen has a point. If we know that those who can not fight are safe then it will make it easier for us all." Jackdaw agreed, knowing that if more people agreed it would sound less like a placation to the non-fighting members of the pack.

"We do need to come up with a strategy though. If we want to strike on the full moon to give us an advantage that is only weeks away, the moon is gone now. Do you think we are even close to ready to take the Royal Guard?" Dante asked honestly.

"I think we definitely need a plan and some training to work together. Even if we were always meant to work as one unit through some sort of destiny it would be a fool's errand to try and start a battle without never even having spared together. I am not going to put our lives and our cause in the hands of the god's prophecy alone." Truen explained.

"I doubt anyone was disagreeing, that is why we are taking us somewhere where it will be safe for us to spar with people who have different ways of fighting. Where Lux grew up is full of daemons that the Royal family never knew about from all over the kingdom. I know Lux's parents themselves were warriors at one point. When they found that I was training with the guard and the knights at the castle they came up with a training plan to incorporate what they knew too. It is one of the reasons that Lux and I have different fighting styles. I have a mix of the Royal styles and a northern style that her parents taught me." Xai explained.

"My parents were always saying that daemons who were not docile should all know how to fight. Even the most submissive of us are predators and protectors." Lux shrugged, she had always been uncomfortable with anyone bragging about her parents.

"I can not wait to meet the people who raised you and saved Xai." Jackdaw smiled, placing his hand on her arm trying to take away the tension the canine was feeling. It was not as helpful as he was hoping but it did make her smile.

Is there a reason why she is so uncomfortable?

Lux has never been a big fighter but her parents were both warriors at heart. It was a bit of contention when they found me since I was a warrior. Lux and I got into many fights when we were kids because she thought I was going to replace her and I thought her parents were annoying. In truth, they knew I was traumatized and were trying to give me structure and distraction.

I am glad you took the time for each other.

So am I, I almost lost her back then. And almost losing her back in the desert brought back a lot of resentment and insecurities.

I am guessing on both sides?

I would guess so, I am waiting for her to finally explode and actually tell me what is going on in that head of hers.

"I would say that Lux's father would be a fantastic help for structured training, I know most of us to have a background in fighting one way or another but Truen is right we need to know not just how to fight for our lives but fight alongside each other for everyone else as well," Xai spoke calmly. "I know Lux takes after her mother who is a brilliant strategist so the two of them and Jackdaw should take the lead on the battle plan. I would trust any plan Lux and Jackdaw come up with to lead us through a battle into not just victory but with as few casualties on both sides as possible." Xai continued, looking directly at her best friend and sister as she spoke her praises.

"I know we are still a few days out from where the patch of forest where my family resides is but we can rest there and figure out the last of preparations before we head out to the castle." Lux conceded without releasing Xai's gaze.

"Besides a plan and learning how to work together, what else could we possibly need?" Dante asked. "I know we came in late to this party but what else could we possibly need to storm the castle?"

"We need the weapon of the gods," Dremira answered, looking a little dazed, almost like she was caught back in the grasp of the prophecy. "The weapon that needs the sacrifice of the pure-blood human, the pure-blood daemon, and the pure-blood vampire."

"What sacrifice?" Lux snapped her head to the human.

"That was not a part of what I was told." Xai was caught completely unaware with this new information.

"We are not sacrificing any of you." Truen sounded appalled, looking frantically between his soon-to-be wife and their son.

"No we are not, Luna did not mention a sacrifice, only that we were needed together. The old Time Mage said nothing either. Though both were cryptic and vague about everything they never said any of us would have to be sacrificed."

"But we need to, we need the weapon, that is what they told us." Dremira sounded resigned like this was the part of the prophecy she had always had to carry. It was as if she always knew this is what was going to happen and was surprised the rest had no idea.

"Then fuck the weapon and fuck the prophecy. We will do this with or without their weapon." Xai hissed at nothing but the situation. "No one and I truly mean no one is getting knowingly sacrificed for this shit."

"But it was the decree of the gods." Dremira protested again.

"I don't care about the gods, I never have," Xai responded while looking over all of them. "The gods can all come to me personally to protest a lack of a weapon, a lack of a sacrifice and I will tell them each by name to kiss my ass."

"I would expect nothing else from you." Lux scoffed.

"Neither would I." Truen sighed shaking his head with a smile knowing that his soon-to-be wife would stop at nothing to protect their little family even face the ire of the gods to do so.

"We will win without their weapon, I do not doubt that at all." Mi'Kal smiled. "I have complete faith in our leader and in us all. We have too much on the line and too much experience between us all and our allies to lose to them."

"Exactly, I have faith in us and our cause, and if the gods will no longer give us their blessing then we will make our own." Jackdaw smiled.

"The gods can't help us now anyways so if they want their weapon they can do it without us." Xai sighed.

"What do you mean?" Dante looked over at the daemoness.

"In the last town, we stopped in I was greeted by a cryptic woman who came out of the shadows in the night, made no sound through the rain but commanded the night air," Xai admitted. "Luna, goddess of the night and creator of the Lunar Races as a whole." Many of the members gasped watching her in disbelief. "I didn't say anything to anyone before anyone gets haughty. At first, I thought it had been a dream, but since I have been having those visions and messages at night I thought nothing of it but a piece of the prophecy. What she had said made no sense anyways to be fair."

"What did she say?" Truen asked carefully vaguely remembering the night in question, the night they dreamt of Lui together.

"First she apologized to me and in regards to all of us. This was not in their plans. Something changed, someone changed the rules who wasn't supposed to be able to. This is that person's doing. Sol, Terra, and herself were separated from each other. they can't reach out to each other nor can they access their celestial powers. They got locked into their mortal forms. Someone is pulling strings behind the scenes for

303

years and hiding from them in a way that no one knew was possible. They are not omnipotent gods she admitted to me and they like walking around amongst the creatures they created, but somehow they didn't know what is happening in our world. But their champion can help them, they need their weapon against whoever is doing this. Their speakers can help them, whatever that means. I was the one she was able to find because I am her creation. The champion is the fighter for them all, even the gods. That is pretty much all she told me."

"Was there anything else about the prophecy? About sacrifices?" Kato asked quietly.

"I am sorry darling she did not." Xai knelt in front of her little boy wishing once more she had all the answers. "She mentioned to me that I will have to take trials to awaken the weapon or the champion whatever it is we are trying to find."

"What kind of trials?" Truen asked, reaching out for Hestia to bring her to him.

"I don't know, I have a feeling there's still a piece or two of the prophecy that we are missing, and at this point, I don't care anymore. I was serious that I refuse to have anyone sacrifice themselves because of gods who get outdone by a creature they created. If their champion needs sacrifice then they can do it without us. They can stay in their mortal bodies until the next generation of pure-bloods is ready for them."

"You would defy the gods for us?" Dremira asked in shock.

"I am willing to storm the castle and finish a war to better the lives of people I have never met. Do you doubt my ability to tell the gods to shove it up their asses for people I care about, for my family?"

"No, I have no doubt you would burn down the kingdom for us or something equally as stupid." Lux sighed.

"And never forget that. I am willing to throw a lot away for those I love. You included fangs and never forget that. I will take it as a personal slight against me from the world to lose any one of you, and those we have already lost will always mark me in a way only grief can. The guilt is almost suffocating and I will not let it happen again. I will not let anyone else be lost. Not to death, not to arguments, and sure as shit not to the gods."

"Only you." Jackdaw finally broke the stunned silence with disbelievable laughter.

"I am not going to lie, dear heart, I am glad you stand beside me and not against me." Truen joined in. The rest finally relaxed again with amazement and agreement that someone as strong and dedicated as the daemoness that they follow would be crazy enough to fight the gods for them and win. That fighting against her would be a nightmare, they collectively almost pity their enemies. To be on the other side of her ire or her weapons would be a death sentence even now.

"Xai, can I speak with you for a moment in private?" Lux whispered as she walked past the other daemoness. Xai knew this was going to be the conversation she was waiting for from the other. What was truly bothering her sister? Silently Xai followed her father into the woods, hoping for their privacy to be respected by those with sensitive hearing in the clear air.

"Is this where you tell me what has been bothering you for weeks?" Xai sighed when they finally stopped in a dense cropping of trees.

"If you knew something was wrong why didn't you say something?" She snapped, Xai knew her well enough to know she was looking for a fight.

"Because I have known you for almost a whole lifetime Lux. If I confronted you you would deny it. But if I wait for you to confront me we can work through it all."

"Oh, you know me so well do you? Then you must know why I am so damn mad at you?" She growled. Xai refused to rise to the challenge.

"I have a feeling, I know that it started around when we lost Crow, Bee, Roc, and Honey. I know I have no idea how to fix it. I know we have been so godsdamn stressed and I have no idea what I am doing. I know it has been harder for me to deal with any of this with you being at arm's length. I know that I want my best friend back before we go into this and I would do just about anything to fix whatever is between us."

"I don't know if you can fix this Xai."

"Then what is it? What is causing you to be so distant from me?"

"You are being such an inconsiderate and ignorant asshole!" She suddenly screamed.

"How so? How am I being inconsiderate? I can agree to being an asshole, I always have been through and that has never stopped you before. No matter how I pushed you away for so long you were always by my side. Then you beg me to join me on a mission I didn't even want to be on with people I had avoided for so long. Because of you I accepted my destiny and accepted my place besides Treun and ever since the colony, no before that you seem to have been disagreeing with everything I do. Did you think destiny would be without pain?

306

Without bloodshed and battles? Without loss and grief." Xai seethed back, barely containing the hurt and fear.

"I didn't think you would be so willing to throw your own life away for this, for people you just met and for people you have never met before." She retorted.

"You and I have been trying to protect those who have been dealing with this injustice. How is it you never minded going in and saving slaves and those who were being repressed one town and city at a time? You were okay with street scuffles and running from guards, putting ourselves in as bait and trying not to end up executed. How is ending all of the suffering not better? It was always for people we never knew."

"Because this IS different!" She insisted.

"But how is it different?" Xai pressed.

"Because We are in the middle of something so much bigger than before."

"Then what would you like me to do about that?" The feline pressed again.

"I want Jackdaw and me to sit out the raid." She huffed, pushing out her chest in defiance.

"Bullshit and you know it. You nor Jackdaw want to send us in there alone, not knowing and definitely without you by our sides." Xai scoffed. "Not including the simple fact that I know you well enough to know you have been ready for years to storm the castle and tear out the throats of anyone who hurt me alone let alone innocent people. You have mentioned how much you would love to redecorate using their entrails. And don't get me started on Jackdaw, he has been training with his brothers since they could walk on their own and hold a

307

weapon. He would never let Truen and Krutz fight without him. They are a unit. Ignoring the fact that this fight determines his soon-to-be wife's and soon-to-be sister's safety in this world." Lux stayed silent, finally deflating. Her eyes no longer met Xai's but a tree behind her. "You are not tamed, you are not a lap dog, you are not someone's pretty little housewife with not a thought between those ears. I know I always said that to have a handler meant to give up our wildness and become a tamed caged animal but you helped me see I was wrong. You proved to me that even with a handler neither of us are the type to stay out of a fight or draw blood before someone else can. Hell fangs you tried to eat a living fire-breathing dragon not too long ago."

"But Xai what if I want to be a housewife?" She whispered.

"Then be one, that doesn't have to conflict with that wild spirit inside you. You can be a warrior and a housewife. Many have done it before you and many will do it after you. But don't lose what little thought you have to do it. Don't break yourself to live in a black-and-white world. We are fighting to live in every shade in between, for everyone."

"But mother said one could not be a warrior and a housewife. That she was a warrior before she was a wife or a mother."

"She was wrong. Wait until you meet my mother or worse the Queen. She is a fierce woman not to be trifled with but she is still a mother. Why did you come back, Lux?" She sighed again.

"Jackdaw made me."

"Bullshit, you can't be made to do anything you genuinely don't want to do." Xai shot back.

"We have known each other for so long." She finally spat out. "All these years we never had more than a spat. I have never seen you like this. And I have been pushed so far down on your list now that you have Truen and your children. What do you want me to say? I am jealous and scared."

"Yes, that is exactly what I want to hear." Xai breathed out, finally. "Because that way I can remind you that you are my sister in all but blood and we are doing this together. You are seeing the me I was before someone decided they needed to destroy my life melding with the me you have always known who was nothing but shattered and ragged pieces. As much as I hate to admit it, this is the me that is finally healing and piecing myself together not for myself but for all of you."

"But I can't be your number one, Truen is. And somehow you have children now." She all about whined,

"And Jackdaw is yours. I am sorry Lux but I love you but not like that, you are not my type. Though do you think I am jealous of him? Oh god no. He can cuddle you at night for warmth, you wet dog."

"Oh go kiss a raven's ass Spots." Lux barked out a laugh.

"And wait until you have your own children, I know you want them, they shift the world. It doesn't change how much you care about the rest of your loved ones but they shift your perception of love." She smiled, reaching out for her counterpart. "Just because life changes doesn't mean I will leave you behind. We are getting older, we are allowed to add to our family. We are allowed to take on dangers together."

"I hate that you can make me feel better and laugh when I am pissed off at you." She sighed pulling the smaller daemoness into a hug. "You are better at it than even Jackdaw and it is not fair."

"And think about it we aren't even bound to each other. Plus he has some ways of calming you down that I don't. Maybe he should be reading more books if he can't get that to work." His words caused the canine to snort into her shoulder, laughs racking through her body.

"Please stop." She begged.

"I don't think I will if it keeps all those insecurities out of your mind." Xai smiled gently. "I much prefer you snorting than brooding. What can you say? I am a sentimentalist." Xai smirked, earning another snort.

"I don't even think you know what that means."

"No, I don't think so either. That seems more your area."

"You are more the type to burn the world down for those you love instead of sentiment." She lifted her head, wiping away tears that had gathered in her eyes from crying.

"Oh definitely more likely to commit crimes against the world for you all. I mean isn't that what I am doing? Crimes of treason against the crown because they hurt people I care about for some reason."

"You have emotions Xai, I have seen them. You can't hide it from me any longer."

"Damn, how will I ever go on with my plans then."

"I am sorry Xai, I know I have been difficult for weeks."

"Try kind of an ass but if I didn't adore you I wouldn't have put up with it for so long so no harm and no foul. Let us move past it so we can fight side by side as we were meant to."

"Agreed. Let us tear through their defenses and leave no questions about who is the victor."

"That is my strong daemoness."

"But what do we do now?" She asked earnestly. Between meeting a goddess and learning about a sacrifice Xai had no idea.

"See if we can find a way to get the whole prophecy and go from there. Maybe I can find Luna again and stop with this cryptic one-piece-at-a-time shit. We need to know the whole thing and what it means. Someone has to know if we don't find her again."

Are you two doing alright?

Get out of my head Truen, this is not for you.

Will you tell me later?

"Probably not," Xai mumbled out loud not really wanting to answer him.

"What was that?" Lux asked.

"Oh, I was going to say maybe another Time Mage but probably not with how rare they are." She caught herself, thankfully it had been a thought in her mind for a long time. "I mean all this started with one and if we were lucky it would end with a clear answer from one but I doubt it."

Probably not now stop.

"That would make it easy wouldn't it."

"I told Luna I was tired of missing pieces of this damn thing. She told me that the trails will be reaching into the magic in the blood. She didn't know what exact trials I will have but she will be beside me the entire time. She created the champion, she created the daemons, and the vampires. She will not leave any of us to face these alone. But I needed to understand she was not asking this lightly. Every generation has the potential for a champion but they have not had to call upon one before. The first was one of a kind and he lived among the people for centuries needing to solve no true problem. She was hoping to not have to call another but the blood continues to manifest in case of emergencies. This is not something they ask for or risk lightly."

"I wonder what this champion is then. What are they trying to get us to awaken?"

" I have no idea and then she said this to me which I am even more unsure of. She said that she had been working on fixing how I have been wronged over the years. She went on to say she had been trying to fix things for years, and they all have. That I am part of who they are as gods, She has told me this, that I am some larger part of this plan to awaken the champion. But they have to protect me as much as guide me. I have a very bad feeling that I have more to do with the champion than just being the pure-blood daemon."

"Do you think you might have to be the one sacrificed to awaken the champion?"

"Or worse I am the one that holds the blood of the champion and the others have to be sacrificed for me."

"We will only know with more information, but you are right, how do we find the whole prophecy?"

"I don't know but I am serious about telling the gods to shove it if there needs to be sacrifices."

"I know, I have no doubt if anyone would do such an inane thing it would be you." She smiled something sad. "Though, I think we need to let the others know about what she told you."

"I know it's just hard to process everything that might be important and what means absolutely nothing," Xai admitted as they were walking back to the group. The dual-colored daemoness smirked when she saw her Prince pacing back and forth. "You can calm down, no one ran off and no one is dead. Everything was worked out."

"You have no idea." The brothers rushed to their loves to check them over, the bonds from the daemoness' had been a fluctuating mess of emotions the entire time they were gone.

"I think I do actually." Xai smiled at their antics. Dante chuckled a bit causing the rest of the pack to look at him questioningly.

"What it was an amusing choice of words. She said 'I think I do' and considering they have a telepathic connection that is amusing," Truen and Xai stiffened as heads snapped to them with different expressions of shock and confusion.

"You have what?" Jackdaw asked in a tone too calm not to cause shivers through the bodies of the couple in question.

313

Chapter Sixteen: Separated Pain

Jackdaw was not one to get upset very easily but the glare he was giving his brother made everyone back away from the physically least intimidating member of the pack. If the blonde spellcaster could, Xai was sure he would have killed her and his brother on the spot.

"I don't know why you are surprised brother, You know Xai and I have had that kind of connection when we were little. I mean yes it closed as before we were six or so but it was still there. I mean both of them were connected to all four of us."

"How did it come back Truen." Jackdaw hissed.

"When Xai died protecting me in the forest before I brought her to you I tried to save her myself."

"But you are no healer and you know that." Jackdaw continued remembering the panic and the blood.

"I know I am not but I tried pushing every ounce of magic I had to give into her, hoping that maybe we would at least make it to you in time. I couldn't lose her again." Truen admitted. "Years ago I had etched a healing rune into myself that took just enough to channel through it. That seemed to reopen the connection."

"Is that the scarred rune on your chest?" Dremira asked carefully, reminding the brothers that they had an audience.

"Yes, that one. I am an elemental rune user, I know I shouldn't have tried wearing other runes but there were points for one reason or another I had the compulsion to try. I have never rejected one but it hasn't been easy."

314

"That is very dangerous." Xai and Lux scolded him at the same time.

"What kind of connection is it?" Kato finally asked.

"Well, when certain daemons, strong daemons, are born there is a rumor that their best choices for handlers have a natural connection to the daemon. Sometimes it is a telepathic link, sometimes it is empathic, and there have been others reported but it's still rare. The thought is it will help bring the strongest pairs together. There also seems to be a correlation between those that are fated to each other but there is not a lot of evidence since it isn't a truly common phenomenon. I know I had a connection to both Truen and Jhelum when we were children but it was short-lived from what our mothers say. It is honestly why I was always closer to them while my sister was closer to Jackdaw and Krutz."

"Have you been having private conversations this entire time?" Mi'Kal asked.

"Yes we have, it has been easier to handle our complicated bond since the connection has been opened again. There has been a lot more trust and misunderstandings." Truen admitted, looking directly at his brother.

"To be fair there are many things Truen and I discuss that none of you need to be privy to," Xai added, watching the blonde carefully. Anger was clearly etched into his face which was completely foreign to the daemoness. Even with their time separated, she had known these men long enough to know she had never seen the anger on Jackdaw's features, it seemed that Truen knew why it was being directed at them. "And you can kiss my tail if you think I will say everything out loud to you all when I have this option."

"Xai," Lux whined as she looked between us along with everyone else. "What is going on?"

"Honestly I don't know but these two do," Xai answered, trying to reassure the other daemoness that she just mended ties with. It seemed they were not the only two having tension between them for some time. "So are you going to enlighten us about the reason you are so pissed off about our link being opened again?" She quirked her eyebrow at the younger Prince.

"Really Jackdaw what is the problem with it?" Lux turned her attention to her own handler. It was obvious that his anger was physically making her uncomfortable. "With everything else going on and all the stress put on their bond isn't having an extra layer of understanding a good thing? Don't you want them to have an easier time at it? Especially when someone spent so much time and energy trying to keep them apart?" Her expression was morphing into suspicion as he remained silent. "Jackdaw what is wrong with it?"

"Don't worry about it, my love." Jackdaw tried to subdue her worry.

"This is about your connection with Lui isn't it?" Truen cut through his mediocre placation.

"Truen, silence." Jackdaw hissed.

"What does this have to do with my sister?" Xai insisted. "What connection?" Even if it was to the memory of her sister, if he was using her friend as a replacement she would tear him apart and leave him for scraps. Truen's anger that was being pushed through the bond was not helping her reign in her own rage at the possibilities,

316

"Nothing in the way you think Xai." Jackdaw snapped at her. "She and I had a different connection than what you're thinking."

"As interesting as this is, we are going to remove the children from the blood bath." Dante interrupted gesturing away from the camp. Xai nodded thankfully not knowing what was about to happen. This was unknown and this was not something she wanted the rest of her pack in the middle, especially the children.

"Then please tell me what you mean, explain to me what you meant because at the moment it sounds like you are replacing one of my sisters with another and I refuse to let you use either of them like that. I have had enough people fucking with our bonds and our family to let you do it too." She growled. She had known Lui and Jackdaw had been close like she had been with Jhelum but to what extent she apparently didn't know.

"Xai I want answers too but please don't hurt him." Lux pleaded. She didn't know where to stand. One person was her soul but he was making it sound like her sister needed to protect her from him.

"I am not going to hurt him because that would hurt you. But he needs to hurry up and explain what he is talking about and why he is so damned angry about something Truen and I were born with before I decide not hurting him means he needs to be paralyzed from the neck down so he doesn't hurt anyone else." Xai sighed trying to calm down. "I would also like to know why one of my oldest friends was keeping some sort of secret connection with my twin sister."

"If it helps, I only know part of it. Only that there was some sort of connection. He was affected when you two disappeared too, but not in the same way. He was in some sort of pain and his disorder got worse."

"Are you going to say anything?" Truen prompted his brother. "Or are you going to sit there in your resentment?" Instead of rising to the bait, the younger stayed silent.

"If you're not going to man up and tell me what is going on I am going to assume that you need to grow up and become a man that Lux deserves but you will mean very little to me." Xai hissed again, becoming impatient. But as he looked to the ground with his rage going nowhere she lost all ability to look at him, he was more pathetic than she had ever seen someone she cared about. "You know what I am done with this for now. You are pathetic and if I look at you any longer I might do something that I will regret." She looked at her own Prince and laid a hand on his arm, his tense muscles relaxing slightly at her touch. "I will be back but I need to step away." He nodded without looking at her, his eyes never leaving his brother. She walked away, separating herself from the problem for just a moment. She had never seen Jackdaw so angry, and below the anger so afraid. Something was amiss and it was serious but now he decided to show his stubbornness and risk what for a connection that was as old as them all. When she heard him trailing behind her she did not slow. It was cruel to do in such harsh terrain, a forest floor was not easy in a rush for anyone but his body was weaker than others no matter how he acted.

"Xai please wait!" He screamed after her.

"Why your brother allowed you to follow me I have no idea but unless you have something to tell me about my own sister that you both decided I didn't need to know you need to go back to the only person here who will continue to care about your opinion."

"I don't know how to explain." He pleaded.

"Then come back to me when you do. Lux's opinion of you is more important than mine. Even your brother's opinion is more important than mine. Explain to them first." Xai called back still walking away from the blonde.

"No Xai I need to explain this to you." He pleaded louder. She finally stopped to face him as he leaned heavily against a large tree. He had had a hard time of it through the woods, gaining small cuts through the brush on his chase.

"Go back Jackdaw." She commanded.

"NO, YOU DON'T UNDERSTAND!" He screamed at her, startling her with the volume and desperation of his voice. It was enough to make her stop and watch him again. " Do you know how much pain I have been in since that day? I love Lux with everything in me and more just as Truen loves you, but Lui and I were connected the moment she was born, just like you and Truen. We shared one mind. We knew what each other was thinking, feeling, what they wanted, everything. It was why we were so close. When she died, part of me died with her, I felt so incredibly empty, and there is a void in me only she can fill. I act so soft and carefree but I wake up in the middle of the night in a cold sweat, I worry about Lux so much and I hate it. I don't want either of you two to feel that again. I know it is a rare gift to be connected like that but I was hoping it would stay sealed for you two. I am jealous and terrified of it, I'm terrified of how much I hate you have that back and what would happen if you lose it again."

"And you really don't think I don't know that feeling? Or did you think losing Jhelum did nothing to me? Or did you forget that my connection with him was never closed like mine and Truen's did? The day that he died I felt it. I have never been able to fill the emptiness that he left but it doesn't mean I wasn't rejoicing about the return of the link with Truen." Xai countered. Sometimes it felt to her that no one remembered the loss of Jhelum the same they did for Lui. Jackdaw seemed taken aback by that. "Now I know Lui was taken from us strangely and I hope to any god that may listen that Jhelum died peacefully in his sleep due to his illness and not in whatever mess ripped us apart. I don't know what actually happened to Lui and I have only prayers that Jhelum isn't in the middle of this as well. And if he was killed with the same intent as Lui then I will promise to burn them all down with every bit of grief and righteous anger that I have." Xai sighed." At least this time if Truen dies I die too."

"But if you die he has to live with the worst pain imaginable for the rest of his miserable life once more." Jackdaw shot back.

"I refuse to leave him by my own will." She retorted.

"You didn't leave on your own will last time either." He bit back. "And you were ready to do so again many times before the bond was forced into place by circumstance."

"I can not leave him again and that is not including the rest of the pack or our children. I have too much to stay for, to live for."

"I have lost a brother and a sister already. Your leaving almost killed Truen last time, he became incredibly reckless and a danger to himself. Now if something were to happen he would not survive. If it didn't kill him physically it would emotionally and mentally."

"I know that now. I have felt the residual pain and insecurity." She knew that there was more than Truen let her feel, and the spells added to this mess made everything more complicated. A passing thought in her mind wondered if the spellwork made the separation worse if that was part of the sabotage.

"I grew up with you, it killed both of us as much as it killed you when Lui died. Then you left Xai, Truen got the short end of the stick, he had a really hard time. He had nightmares every night, waking up covered in sweat, and screaming, crying out your name nightly. He would go and start unnecessary fights and make sure he got himself injured just to release the anger he stored in himself. He closed himself off from everyone, he was angry, hateful, quiet, and not himself he wasn't Truen." The blonde explained. "He was a shell. And he was actively trying to break himself. And I know he never told you about how it affected him. Why would he tell you the one woman he has ever loved the pain she caused him? This is what happened, when I overheard Krutz say there was a black and white-haired demon in the dungeon of the castle I knew it was you. I took Truen even though I knew that there was such a large chance it wasn't you and that would have killed him even more. But in the end, it was you, and as soon as he saw you Truen came back, you revived him. You brought him back to life just by looking at him. And he has grown more and more every day he is with you, every time you two had a fight he ran after you without hesitating, he has opened back up, and you are taking the walls he has built and destroyed them all."

"Why are you telling me this now?"

"Because we are about to go into battle and you opened up the last link that binds you two together. There is no separating you two ever again. There will be irrevocable damage if you fall. If you die in front of him there will never be a way I can save him from the abyss." Jackdaw sighed. "You need to know what it was like for him."

"And how would you do that?" Xai asked skeptically as the blonde tried walking closer to her.

"A potion I had made a long time ago." He admitted.

"You have resented me a long time haven't you, even knowing that I was just as much a victim." Xai sighed as the younger Prince pulled a small vial out of the pouch of his belt.

"At one point yes, until I started piecing together what was really happening. Honestly, I thought I was going to need to use it to break the spell holding you two apart but you two fixed that yourselves."

"You were going to drug me if I wouldn't listen?" She looked at him in shock.

"I had to plan something." He shrugged.

"And here people think you are the morally straight brother."

"Oh, gods no Truen has me beat on that any day, though his morally straight stick up his spine is more flexible with you around." He handed out the vail as an offer. The grayish liquid inside looked viscous and ominous.

"You are not trying to kill me, correct?" She asked as she reached for the vial. The vial itself fits easily in her palm. The cork was pushed in as tight as possible.

"Of course not, again you are like a sister to me and just as much of a victim. I have made this concoction many times, even took it for myself to understand him while you were away. I adore you Xai but I still think you need to understand what he went through before you get careless in the fight. What he felt then was before you two had all your bonds in place."

"I will not deny I want to know what pain he has been hiding from me, always acting like the time apart doesn't matter because it is over."

"I know Truen is going to be furious with me for giving that to you, he doesn't even know that I have been carrying it around this entire time."

"How long is this good for?" Xai asked in curiosity.

"It is stable for years and years so you are safe, I brewed this batch months before we found you. I had a feeling I would need it." Nodding apprehensively she used a claw to pop the cork. The smell was nauseating though not the worst smell she had ever experienced.

"Then once I drink this you need to drop the anger-covered fear. If you are going to be scared then just be scared." Xai gestured with the vial. Her words seemed to startle the blonde.

"Xai if you are doing this just to make me feel better please don't do this, this should be to understand my brother not to clear my fears."

"It is a dual-purpose adventure. Onesies so I can understand that self-sacrificing prick that I love and also to make you understand the lengths I will go through for your brother when I am not being spelled. I can't have you holding onto this much fear or resentment that you look ready to go toe to toe with your brother in a losing fight because of some honestly inconsequential news." Before he could argue she knocked the vial back like a shot in a tavern. "That is foul, good sir." She shuddered. She would have rather licked a corpse than taste that again. "Now how long does it take to take effect? Because if it is not soon I will find a way to get this aftertaste out of my mouth." She grimaced to his surprise.

323

"Before now it has been a pretty instantaneous effect, how are you not feeling it?" He asked cautiously.

"Best guess you have never had to dose a daemon with this, sadder guess the spell didn't interfere and I can't tell the difference between my pain and his under the spell."

"Is it wrong of me to hope the spell isn't interfering with the pain felt? I hope that it wasn't making it even worse for my brother and I ended up blaming that on you and your connection to him."

"Blaming her for what brother?" Truen's voice spoke calmly but not without anger. Even Xai hadn't noticed him arriving behind his brother, so the potion was starting to take effect within her. That had to mean the spell had made Truen's suffering worse on purpose, like her own paranoia. "I felt something interfering with the bonds and I find my brother offering my soon-to-be wife poison."

"Only a mild poison in the potion dear." She hadn't thought of her words as her vision began to darken. "And Jackdaw it was a daemon dosage issue for future reference." She bit out, pain starting to work its way up her limbs. All of her nerves were beginning to light up, pulsing sporadically.

"Jackdaw what did you give her?" That was the last thing she heard before the ringing started. Her vision left and for once she was thankful that Truen had followed, he would keep her safe while she waited this out. The overbearing self-hatred and guilt were nothing she wasn't accustomed to but the pain was nearly unbearable and she had died before. The sharp stinging in her limbs, the crushing weight in her chest, if this is what he lived with for all those years she did not know how he lived through it. She was familiar with the voices telling her how much easier it would be to end her own suffering, that she had brought this upon herself as well as the suffering she brought onto her partner. It was her fault they had lost Lui and Jhelum. She felt the fear of watching Jackdaw get weaker and give up, she felt the guilt of watching their mothers suffer and the remaining brother break. She could not feel anything outside of herself. She could only hear her own heartbeat and the incessant ringing.

Xai... Xai I need you to focus on my voice.

I can't.

Yes, you can, you are answering me right now. I need you to focus.

I can't, the pain won't let me.

Tell me what you feel.

You know what I am feeling.

No that is what the spell and the potion made us feel. Push past it and what can you feel? It was such a strange request but she tried to push past the pain, using his voice to center herself in the effects of the potion.

I can feel the wind on my skin, it is like small blades.

Not ideal but what else.

A pressure on my arms.

That is me, I am holding you in place, You were trying to claw your skin.

Small spots of pressure on my skin.

That is me again, I am kissing all the spots I can reach as gently as possible.

It doesn't hurt.

325

That is good. My touch should never hurt you, nor should my memories. I need you to come back to me.

I can't yet, you were so alone. And it was my fault.

No, it was the spell's fault. Never yours, we are all victims and we will get our retribution. Now I need you to open your eyes.

I can't everything is black.

You can Xai, open your eyes for me. Let me see those beautiful purple eyes that I love so much.

I can't Truen.

Please Xai, it will be alright. I have got you here with me, you are safe with me. I promise it will be over when you open your eyes and break the spell.

"Sweet shit." Her voice sounded hoarse and broken to her own ears as she blinked her eyes open, the sun's light trickling through the leaves did her no favors but instead of darkness came the beautiful forest that she knew so well.

"Welcome back dear heart." Truen's voice sounded soothing to her battered senses. Looking towards him she found she was leaning her entire weight against him on the forest floor, his face only mere inches from her own. His eyes looking like honey in the sunlight were full of worry. Somehow laying here in the dirt with him felt new again. "Please never take potions my brother gives you again. You two will be the death of me."

"Was that really what you went through while we were apart?" She whispered, feeling more vulnerable than she thought she would while dealing with his pain.

"I will not lie to you, love, yes it was. But please remember that there was a spell involved making everything worse for us all."

"How did you make it through? Back to me?" The phantom feeling of the potion made her shiver slightly, carefully he held her tighter.

"Because I think a part of our bond would not yield to the magic, no matter how bad it got I never lost the feeling of being with you again. Time in the cabin helped a lot when everything got too much to bare. Jackdaw helped too since the spell was never impacting him for whatever reason."

"How can I make up for the time lost? I need to do something." She pleaded.

"Xai calm down, you were in pain as well, if you knew it or locked it away along with all your memories of me like I hoped you would when I said those horrible things to you before you were made to leave us. I suffered the consequences of my actions that were not my own, we both did. Anyways I have you back now and that is all that matters to me. I have you back by my side where you belong. The spell is broken on us, no one can separate us again. I made my peace with that long before you could my love. I have had time to know there was a spell without the fast-paced life of war and prophecy. Though I am not happy about it if this helps you come to terms with what happened then so be it. Eventually, we will have to deal with everything without interference or adrenaline influencing our acceptance. We can not use the threat of death as a way to escape the trauma we endured forever."

"You are too wise for me right now, though don't be too mad at your brother I did take the potion of my own will."

"Yes, but he shouldn't have had it and the fact he still had it after the spell was broken at the cabin is something he and I need to discuss at length. I can not have him manipulating your protective nature and need to make your family happy and comfortable to do dangerous things." Gently he rested his hand on her face. "We are as safe as we can be for the time being and we need to continue to temporarily put aside what happened back then so we can face the threats in front of us together as one pack."

Leaning into her space he gently pressed his own lips to hers, the kiss was slow and meaningful. Nothing like the ones they had been sharing recently when the others were not looking and certainly contained more vulnerability and emotion than those shared in the night when they have their own room at the inns. The potion had stripped away any lingering paranoia or doubt that she had not known she still harbored. As she sat there in his lap surrounded by tree roots and birds kissing him like nothing had ever come between them knowing that for years through pain and lies this man waited for her, fought for her, and came back to her when he had no reason to was a realization that not only shook her to the core but settled her. There was no doubt about their future. It seemed like a lifetime before they separated. "I will say the bonds between us feel lighter and more solid than before."

"They do, there may still have been some reminisce that that foul concoction stripped away along with my tastebuds." Calmly he wiped her face of the tears she hadn't known she had cried. "Are you ready to go to see the others? Or did you want to hear the surprise that I was going to wait to tell you?" He smiled gently knowing she was still too overstimulated to see the others.

"What surprise?"

"Well since we are in the Eldar woods I figured while the others go to Lux's family we could make a side trip for a day or two towards the underground city to obtain a few accessories for you." He put calmly.

"What kind of accessories?" She asked, her eyes going wide in a way he hadn't seen since they were children. He would use to distract her after having any sort of fit when they were little brats, younger than their own children now.

"Well we are about to go into a battle and you don't have appropriate armor nor weaponry, and do not tell me your knives or claws are good enough to storm the castle alone with. You have trained with your swords and you should go into this with your best possible skills on display." He tried to refrain from chuckling as her tail began swishing back and forth in excitement.

"Do you know where the underground city is?" She asked, trying to sound uninterested, but he knew her too well to fall for her nonchalant voice.

"No but I know you do, and so does Lux." He smiled at her.

"The main entrance is at the shore of the lost lake." She nodded along, he was finally seeing the pieces of his love that had been missing.

"Oh lovely a lost lake in a dangerous forest." He sighed, getting the response he had been hoping for.

"Don't worry Princeling I will protect you from the big scary monsters in the forest."

"I think I would rather deal with the big bad scary monster. But that is not my issue with the underground city dear heart. That is where my mother's family lives."

"Then they must be amazing people like your mother, she had to have gotten it somewhere." She reasoned.

"I don't know how they will take Jackdaw and me since we are my father's children. The last I heard is that they blame him for stealing my mother away and locking her in the castle. I have no idea how they would react if I was in the city, but for you, I will risk an uncomfortable meeting. I doubt they would be violent since I am her child as well but it will probably not be pleasant."

"If they hate your father as much as we do then we should be fine, but I will keep you safe."

"Why do you think it will be fine if we have a shared enemy in my father? My mother is still in the castle and may fight against us because of our fathers."

"But Well think of it this way, your mother is basically a slave in the castle is she not?" he nodded. "We aren't fighting your mother, we are fighting your father, and if we win this your mother and everyone else are free. Anyways she is a saint in her own right. They won't be fighting her if they decide to join us. The underground city is a mage city anyways so we should be able to find someone to help us find the rest of the prophecy." Xai stopped for a moment as something dawned on her and she looked at her betrothed in shock. The smile on his face showed he knew exactly what information she connected together.

"Yes my mother is a mage, father put a cover spell over her to turn her while she is on the castle grounds she is a spell caster. It is one reason she is not allowed to leave the castle grounds. If she does the spell will break and everyone will know that the king who hates lunars with such passion has their other half who is, in fact, a lunar in her own right, and his sons are all half-lunar."

"Have I mentioned I hate your father recently?" She hissed, throwing her arms around his shoulders.

"I know my love. If you wish to stay here I can go inform the others we are going to be away for a bit and let your sister chew on her mate for a bit for what he did to you. Then we can set off for the city, we should be able to meet back up before the solstice with the others as long as nothing goes wrong." He said gently as he tried to stand with his daemoness clinging to him. It took effort and assistance from the tree behind him but he managed. "Rest here and I will be back in a moment. I will leave Jackdaw with any explanations as his penance."

"Be quick about it then." She sighed letting him go, her tail gave away her pout as it wrapped around her subconsciously. He was happy to see once more some things never change.

"Of course." He said as he kissed her forehead and stepped back towards the way he had come, back towards their pack.

Chapter Seventeen: Road Block

It had only taken them the rest of the day to reach the shores of the lake hidden in the forest. Trees grow deep from within the water obscuring the sun and making the perfect habitat for the predators to swim in the deceptively deep waters. Lights shimmered on the underside of the water as Xai watched it suspiciously, she made sure as they reached the shore they never entered the ring of sand around the water's edge.

"We can make camp here." She said pointedly, never looking at her Prince. "Can you make your sense of hearing dulled in any manner?"

"We would be more comfortable on the shore, wouldn't we? And yes I can in theory but why would I need to, wouldn't it be dangerous to not be able to hear as well as normal? We are alone out here."

"I don't want to give them any ideas." She nodded at the water, ripples forming from the curious creatures darting back and forth.

"Who are you so worried about?" Truen asked finally looking at the water.

"This is one of the largest concentrated colonies of merpeople in the kingdom." The daemoness explained. "And they always sing louder at night."

"Are you truly that scared of a few finned beings to warrant all of these precautions? I thought kitty cats such as yourself loved to fish." He smirked and thought that he was funny.

"Ah, I see you have found your unique sense of humor again after so long." Xai sighed, side-eyeing the Prince. "Now do us all a favor and put it back where you found it." She smirked as he huffed indignantly.

"Always so mean to me." He sighed, always the dramatic one when they were alone.

"Yes well, you chose me so you have no one to blame but yourself." She shot back, glad to be back to bantering, glad that the pain of the potion was gone and she felt more herself. She had a feeling that the potion did more than what it was supposed to given the circumstances but it was not enough of a hypothesis to bring up to anyone. Just somehow cleaner, maybe leftover residue from breaking the spell that held her captive.

"I believe I was not the only one who chose us to be together my love, not that I would change anything about that at all." Truen smiled wearing that love-sick expression that sometimes made his daemoness uncomfortable. The idea of someone loving anyone that much, knowing she felt the same as he did.

"I would not change it either and I will kill whoever tried to ruin it. I will not lose us again which is a very good reason to keep your Princely yet shapely ass here on the grass where the Mers will not think of you as easy food during the night."

"Why are you so worried about only myself, jokes aside we never learned much about those who dwell and hunt in the water."

"To be fair their spawning ground is normally kept a secret from most. They do their best to hide their communities away from those who might try to hunt them or capture them, many rich assholes have tried to make them pets forgetting they are sentient and dangerous predators."

"Like daemons."

"It is a common misconception from solars I have noticed, for some time they have forgotten their place in the cycle of life. Only predators your kind has are anigels."

"More and more am I finding myself disgusted with my people."

"Don't get too hard on yourself you are making a conscious decision to change and learn, you are helping us free those enslaved and the long process that comes after waging a war on your father and usurping him."

"I know but it doesn't seem enough, you are gathering people to fight and I am along for the ride."

"If all goes well you will be the next King. Your work comes after I put that crown on your head. Remember that, you are an incredible fighter but you are a diplomat first and foremost. Your brother can collect information, and Lux can comfort people."

"You inspire them, inspire change and revolution. And that is what we need. Once you get me that crown I can dig through all the paperwork he hides telling me where the enslavement camps are and who bought daemons and other Lunars."

"See already making plans to fix things I didn't even think of, I am here to fight and bring revolution as you said, it is your job to fix the damage and promote the change to stay."

"For me to fix anything I need to know as much as I can, tell me more about Merpeople since we are here, while we set up camp. I am assuming the Underground city is somewhere around here?" He nodded, starting to map out a spot for a small fire. His interest poured through the bond.

"Yes, the Underground city or the hidden city of Mages has an entrance around here. They have many but they all went dark when Mages started getting imprisoned and enslaved years ago, what did they call it, ah that's right permanent placement of magical use. Those who were taken were either deemed useful and given to nobility or deemed useless and killed. So most mages went into hiding in the city. Supposedly there are also hidden or hard-to-get cities for other species too just like the vampire city and the Underground." She answered while gathering wood from the forest edge so they could continue the conversation.

"You don't know them all?" He asked, looking up from his makeshift fire pit.

"Other than the wilde that holds the fairies and pixies and the cities we have been to most are a secret for a reason, I mean most of them are hiding themselves or something to do with their culture. Hunting other races isn't new with your father." She shrugged, depositing the wood next to him so he could build the fire how he wanted to.

"What is the point in any of it?" He groaned honestly not understanding the thought process of any of it. She smiled at his frustration for others suffering while he kept his hands busy with a menial task she never thought she would see a Prince do, but somehow this was all him.

"Well I know daemons are pets or for protection, mers are kept for pets or killed for their scales. vampires get killed for their teeth for some reason, and fairies and pixies for their magic, or their wings. Do you know what Mages are kept for, there are so many stupid reasons why so many races on every side are getting hunted or enslaved. And the worst part is it is the same few races who think they are superior for no real reason." Disgust flooded the bond along with astonishment at the horrific truth.

"Spell Castors and Soul vampires have always been arrogant but who else?" He spat into the fire as he lit it.

"humans, Elves, and anigels mostly." She shrugged as she finally sat down on the bedrolls she had laid out. "Somehow they found some kind of entitlement in the last few centuries if it is to be believed and it has all led to this. enslavement, genocide, and in some places torture for entertainment overseas is a thing." She sighed again. "It is not just here in our kingdom but in our world."

"Then we start here and then fight for the rest, I can make a sanctuary for the refugees here while you storm the rest of the world." He said as if this was a fact of what would happen.

"Let us not forget I have to either stop the gods or help them in the process. At least stop whoever they can't control." She laid back to look at the darkening sky instead of her Prince.

"One step at a time?" He asked turning to her. "I don't know how we will accomplish it but everyone has faith in us so we should try and make our goals come to fruition."

"At least one of us has a positive mindset on this." She looked at him again, his sun-kissed skin was illuminated by the fire behind him. If one did not know they would never assume him to be a Prince or any sort of nobility, not now at the very least. Even without his title, she knew deep within he would be standing next to her trying to save a kingdom that would have wronged him if he had not been born with a crown.

"Tell me more about Merpeople, we went off on a tangent before." He prompted, sitting beside her on the dirt.

"Well for one they have both gills and lungs meaning they can breathe above and below water. Their vocal cords are infused with magic, that is what makes their songs so dangerous. For some reason, daemons, vampires, their Solar equivalents and of course other Merpeople are immune to the magic in their songs. That is why I am not worried about me being close to the water or having an option of sound suppression if they begin to sing. You could be easily manipulated to take a swim with them or make an easy target if they were to climb onto the sand. Dirt is too hard on their underbellies."

"That makes more sense and is incredibly terrifying." He admitted shuddering while taking an uneasy look at the water.

"From what I have been told by them Merpeople also don't need to sleep, like vampires. But their song gets more powerful under the moon which is why they are more dangerous at night."

"I mean the moon controls the tides so I am not surprised by that." He responded.

"That is true, they in my opinion are the most terrifying of the Terra races. I used to have a friend who was a Mer years ago, unfortunately, they were stolen while we were in a town getting something. He was left for dead after he was stripped of his scales. I didn't make it in time to save him because it was common for him to wander off but I got to comfort him in the end. It is one of the reasons I started looking into the enslavement and the trading of living beings. If someone would have stepped in when we were children he would be here helping alongside us."

337

"What was his name?"

"Ronan, he had beautiful red and golden scales. He gave me one when it was shed, I keep it in one of my chests in Lux's parent's house. He had made it into a necklace for me but I could never wear it after his death." It had been a long time since she had talked about or even thought of Ronan. "His family used to be in these waters but I don't know if they still are. I have been a coward since then. This whole mission of justice started as thinly veiled revenge."

"When all is settled we should come back here and see if his family is still here. Tell them all you accomplished in his name, to make things safer for you all." Truen tried, pushing into her.

"Maybe, I am not sure if they would want to see me." She sighed watching the water.

"You said it yourself, you were children."

"Lux thought it was the funniest thing that a cat and fish were so close that he thought it was hilarious that a dog was friends with a cat, neither of us talked about him since he died. I think that was the first horrendous thing that happened in Lux's life and she wasn't there. Thankfully she didn't have to see it."

"I wonder if my mother knew his family?" He said thoughtlessly.

"Why would you say that?" Xai asked looking up at him again.

"Mother said it was a secret but she is from the underground city originally. Before she herself was stolen by my father's family to be his bride. My mother is a very

338

powerful elemental Mage in her own right." Truen smiled thinking about his mother's excitement when he showed a capacity for elemental magic without runes, and even happier when runes made his natural ability stronger. She had been happy he and Jackdaw could hide their Mage blood with runes.

"How did your father's family even know about your mother? If she is from the Underground how did they find her?" Xai asked watching his face.

"I don't know, neither ever talked about it. Other than it was my Grandfather who brought my mother into the family none of us ever knew. And when we asked it upset mother so we didn't often. We have no idea who her side of the family is, she was forbidden to talk about them once she was in the castle. Their past is as much of a guess to us as why my father hates Lunars so much. Maybe not just him either but it is hard to tell since the last King and Queen died before we were born and once again no one was to talk about them or ask about them."

"That is so strange though," Xai responded.

"It is and I would love answers. Maybe we can get them before you kill my father, or maybe my mother has answers and when he is dead she can speak freely. I do know there are a few Lunars he likes, my mother, your mother, you and he was actually sad at your sister's death and your disappearance." He listed. "I guess part of it was that he couldn't hate or sell off those who completed the souls of his sons. Plus he found your attitude refreshing every time he reminisced about you."

"Well, I hope that works in our favor as I kick his ass all over his own castle. I wonder if my killing him will put a damper on his approval of me. I would truly hate for his death to put a strain on our in-law relationship." She smiled as a laugh punched out of Truen, he had not been expecting such a ridiculous thought to come from her mouth. The dry sarcasm of her words had him laughing harder than he could remember laughing before. "I hope this doesn't change his view about me because as you know I care so highly for your father's opinion and approval."

"You are perfect so have no fear, nothing could sway him, except maybe a noose but that is up to you my love." He finally caught his breath and leaned down to kiss her.

"Ah, there is my morbid humor rubbing off on you again, much better than your other jokes." She smiled when the kiss left them both a bit breathless. The sun setting behind the trees, the dark night sky giving more ambiance to the fire, and surrounding forest noises created an atmosphere they could enjoy. He smiled at her again.

"Well, something of yours had to." He smirked as she groaned, the return of his horrible puns. It was bad enough when they didn't involve juvenile innuendo. But for some reason she never wanted him to change.

"Careful lover boy, any more bad jokes and whatever you want to happen deep in the forest will be nothing but another one of your fantasies. Behave a little and we might be able to make a Mer blush."

"And what would be behaving? What would make me a good boy in your eyes Princess?" He teased back.

"Do you truly want to play this game?" She asked, sitting up.

"It's one of the few games that we both win." He shrugged, trying to look as innocent and unaffected as possible.

"I think your honesty deserves a reward." She smirked, "Stand back and remove that poor excuse of a shirt." She nodded at the nearly translucent tunic that he had been wearing since they entered the forest.

"How is this a poor excuse for a shirt, I will have you know that I very much like this fabric. It is soft against my skin and very light." He made a show of being offended as he stood gracefully.

"And you know it will catch my eye every time the breeze shifts through the trees. It is like you want my attention." She continued watching him as he lifted the fabric. Her tail swished back and forth in interest.

"I never said I didn't want your eyes on me. I am not the type of man that will not admit what he wants." He shifted slowly lifting the fabric off of his skin and over his head. "I do not mind being on display for you at all."

"Did you know that your heartbeat accelerates beautifully when you do as I ask?" She purred, causing a shiver to roll over his skin.

"I am aware." He admitted his back still to the fire. The crackle of the wood is the loudest sound in the darkness but not the only one. "I do enjoy doing what pleases you, I like it even more when we will not be interrupted. And out here we are alone with not a soul to bother us." She knew he shouldn't have said that aloud.

"We have been getting only a few passing moments to be together don't we, without interruption." She sighed. He looked at her confused. Knowing that she had been just as lustful as himself then the bond went cautious and frustrated.

"We have been interrupted haven't we?" He groaned, stepping to reach for his tunic.

"Unfortunately so my love, but thankfully it is not the kids this time." She sighed standing up off the bedroll. "Though those who thought this was a good moment to watch need to know they are in danger of never knowing the pleasures of the flesh again for denying me my beautiful specimen of a man."

"Why does this continue to happen?" The Prince pouts watching the annoyance roll off his lover as she watches the shadows of the forest.

"At this point, I am beginning to believe it is the gods messing with us or something. Because armed men are a little much to stop premarital sex. And trust me you would not be saving his virtue at this point. It is much too late for that." She growled into the shadows.

"You both need to come with us." A gruff male voice responded, not at all rising to the bait.

"We don't NEED to go anywhere. We are free people and unless you want to explain why you thought interrupting us was a good idea we will not be following you anywhere. I am more likely to feed you to the residence of the lake than follow any sort of suggestion from someone still trying to hide from a daemon in the dark." Xai did not like to be interrupted, especially during her time alone with her Prince.

"You need to come with us." He repeated from his shadow.

"Fine let us try this again, who is 'us'?" Xai groaned in frustration.

"We are the guard of the Underground city and you have been summoned by the High Priestess." He responded. Xai threw her head back and sighed.

"Kill the fire and help me get our stuff, unfortunately, we do need to go with them. Though I am complaining to the High Priestess about their timing." She said looking back at Truen who nodded. They both knew this was their chance to enter the city even if they had other plans. "You could have come in the morning, you know." She looked back into the shadow watching the massive mountain of muscle that was the standing point of the group. He reminded her of Dante's build, completely solid. This was what the city had for soldiers. "Stay close to me, Truen." She spoke plainly as the guards beckoned them, blatantly showing she did not see them as a threat but they held no trust just because they were giving them access to the city. The mountain nodded and started walking back in the shadow. The daemoness carefully wrapped her tail around the Prince's wrist so he could follow as they walked further into impossible darkness. What seemed to take far too long they continued to walk in the darkness, her eyes barely straining but the man who was relying on her continued to stumble and struggle silently as they finally left the forest and entered a cave. "How much farther? My companion does not have night vision like some of us."

"Not long, almost to the temple." The man responded. Soon enough the other four guards broke off and went in separate directions as they entered a tunnel system. Once the others had left they started seeing torched lining every so often in the stone corridors, it was enough light to allow Truen to have a steady step finally. Then the torches started being stationed closer and closer, the daemoness was not surprised that she could see light at what seemed to be the end of the tunnel when the torches became only a few steps apart from each other. The light was almost blinding as they walked into a

343

large carved-out cavern in the middle of the stone. The entire city could be seen from the entrance they had entered. The guard guided them to the center of the city, past the onlookers, and towards the massive temple in the center, a temple devoted to Luna herself.

"Oh, she would love this if she doesn't already know it is here," Xai whispered to Truen who chuckled quietly.

"Mi'lady, High Priestess, I have brought you the intruders as you requested." The guard spoke calmly as he dropped to a single knee in front of the wooden doors of the temple. As if on cue the doors flung open in a dramatic fashion that made the two-toned daemoness roll her eyes as hard as she physically could. A woman walked out in true Mage theatrics. She looked incredibly familiar to the feline, familiar but off. Her bright blonde hair and fiery green eyes were intelligent and judgmental. Her robes were long and flowing but her round face pulled memories.

"Who are you, boy?" She asked in a cold, raspy voice. "You remind me of someone from long ago." She pointed at Truen with a long finger. Truen himself stood there in shock.

"My name is Truen." He responded when he finally found his voice again. The Mage began circling them as Truen continued to look like he had seen a ghost.

"Who are your parents?" She demanded earning herself a growl from the daemoness, only held back by the Prince's hand on her arm.

"King Crawden of Chemerica, the betrayer of his title." He closed his eyes to center himself as the Mage hissed. "And Luaratana, Daughter of Mages and Queen of Chemerica." He finished opening his eyes to stare directly at the woman who was now looking at him in shock. "And with the way you look like my mother and brother, I would assume she is your kin."

"My sister." The woman breathed in shock. "Luara is my sister, she was stolen a lifetime ago. You are truly my nephew?" She asked in disbelief. It dawned on Xai that he was right, where Truen took after the Queen with his dark hair and bright eyes this woman looked like the Queen if Jackdaw had taken after her instead. The family resemblance was impeccable, clearly, the Mage line was much stronger than the royal line if only one child had looked enough like the King. Without the caution, the Mage's eyes softened the same way the Queen's did when she had watched over all the children when they were small.

"Yes, you have two other nephews as well, unfortunately, my one brother died years ago or you would have four of us. This is my betrothed Xai. My brother Jackdaw is also betrothed. Unfortunately, Krutz, my last remaining brother lost his daemon mate at the same time we lost our other brother." Truen explained.

"Last time I saw my sister she hugged me and told me she loved me, that her choices would keep us all safe. It wasn't until much later that we got word that she was to become Queen, married into that horrible family. We never were able to get answers on why or even how it happened." She confessed.

"We don't even know how my mother ended up with my father, no one is allowed to ask about it or mother's past before she became the Princess to the Heir Apparent," Truen added, not trying to add to the sadness of the situation but he couldn't help it.

"Is she at least happy?" His Aunt asked with hope in her voice.

"She has gotten to raise eight children altogether with her best friend in the world. She can not stand my father or his actions but has been bound to the castle and to silence about his actions. And regrettably, she and Xai's mother, my mother's best friend and personal daemon, did lose two of us over the years. But I do know that she has been happy with us kids, and the fact we were so intermingled with each other. We will free her though, both of them. We will free everyone from the silence and oppression my father created. That is part of the reason we are here, we need your help or someone's help from here."

"You are the ones who have been waging the war and changing the tides? We have heard the whispers and rumors. Even the divination Mages have been talking about those who will bring forth the savior and end this blasted suffering." She looked in awe.

"Xai is the one with the prophecy." He nods.

"Your daemon you mean." The guard finally spoke again, his voice full of disdain earning him a hiss from the feline in question. He was smart enough to stand and step out of quick strike range. "Are you by choice or by force, girl?"

"That fact you insulated that fact that I could be forced is almost as insulting as the fact you assumed that his character is the same as his father after hearing him talk about his mother." She hissed again stepping towards the guard, only to be held back once more with her Prince's gentle touch, her ears though remained flattened and her tail swishing with agitation.

"No Solar blood can be trusted, especially the spawn of the King who has damned us all." The guard spat back with no sight of how much danger he was in, Truen would only be able to hold her temper back for so long. One did not insult her Prince and come through unphased.

346

"Watch your tongue before I steal it from you. He is the only thing that is currently protecting your vile perception from painting this temple's walls." Her voice was still and calm, her Handler trying to calm her through their bond but he even knew that it might be a lost cause if the guard did not still himself.

"Mistress?" The guard whispered, eyes looking desperately at the priestess who was watching this unfold. Fear colored his dark eyes.

"You know better than to insult a daemon's Handler or mate Barrada, you face the consequences of your choices." The Priestess answered his plea, definitely the Queen's sister. The guard nodded and tried to steel his eyes as he looked past Xai and to Truen.

"Then calm your pet boy." He tried to speak with authority only causing Truen to groan, he had added fuel to the daemoness' fire. The Priestess herself shook her head and sighed, muttering about awkward buffoons who never learned.

"She truly hates being referred to as a pet so you might want to apologize, not to mention she is her own person and no one has a prayer in this world to honestly sway her in her pursuit of violence when the mood takes her." Truen sighed side-eyeing the guard, looking him up and down in pity. "You have begun treading into the dangerous water and provoked the predator. Apologize to her before I decide letting her pent-up energy out on you is better than waiting until we are settled to restart what you interrupted earlier." Flashes of his fantasies and emotions danced behind her eyes, she could tell without him saying a word that he rather she did not waste all her energy on someone so unworthy.

Continue to be a good boy and we will see darling.

347

Only if you don't paint my Aunt's temple with her guard dear heart.

You drive a hard bargain but I do want an apology.

And you deserve one, I hate that he thought talking to you in such a matter was appropriate. Though I have noticed you are less likely to tap into that legendary temper of yours after we have had alone time.

Of course, it's harder to be violently angry when I have had to work on wearing you out. Harder not impossible mind you.

"I apologize for my rash words then." The guard grumbled obviously less interested in apologizing and more disgruntled in the obvious dressing down he was getting from his Priestess in nothing but facial expressions. "I should not have provoked you or your Handler."

"Good man Barradra." The Priestess nodded, "They need our help, and as much as I hate to admit we will need their help as well. Now my nephew and niece can you forgive my idiot?"

"I will if she does, she was the one he wronged. I will not stop her from taking a pound of flesh if she so chooses for those who spout such filth at her." Truen spoke eloquently, his diplomatic tongue once more showing itself. The Priestess looked at the feline.

"If I catch him again talking such disgrace I will deliver his tongue to you in an ornate box." She answered looking at the Priestess who was taking responsibility for the man's misstep.

"I expect nothing less from someone such as you, my dear." The Priestess nodded, clearly approving of the daemon that had become part of her family line. Strong women seemed to thrive on the Mage side of the bloodline.

"Thank you, dear heart." Truen sighed in relief, softly kissing her hair behind one of her ears, causing them to twitch in annoyance.

"You definitely have my sister's way with words, child. She was always good at calming and scolding at the same time. When she was still here she was known as a force of nature, one you wanted to be behind and not against. No matter what you had done she would talk you down worse than a mother ever could." The blonde woman smiled in nostalgia.

"He is very much like the Queen, sometimes the resemblance can be terrifying if for some reason they are teaming up against you. No one, no matter how stubborn, can stay standing against them as a team." Xai sighed looking at the other woman again, her guard had been dressed down enough to no longer catch any bit of attention as long as he continued to keep his mouth shut.

"And your magic?" She asked, head tilting, in the same way, all the Princes did when they were curious. And an interesting connection to a woman they had never once met.

"Elemental, just like my mother's magic from what I know. None of us have seen her use much of her magic over the years." He answered.

"That is a shame, her personality was not the thing about her that was a force of nature. Maybe if you can free her like you say you want to she can fight beside you." She sighed, "But that is enough for tonight, come I will set you up here in the temple. It is late at night, almost morning if I can tell correctly and you will now always find refuge here in the city. Both of you have a place here. For now, you can rest, then tomorrow we can listen to your requests and see if we can help each other. I have more questions to ask of my kin who have never gotten to know." She smiled turning with a flourish and

349

striding back into the temple. She didn't even stop to make sure the two were following her, they in fact did follow her through the temple. Its stone corridors were almost as much of a maze as the tunnels to the city but eventually, it seemed she stopped at a random room. "Here, a guest room far enough away from anyone else so I do accidentally hear too much about my nephew in the cover of the day." She winked before strutting away.

"What is with Mages and theatrics?" Xai huffed out earning a chuckle once the Mage was out of sight. "Don't laugh because now I know where you get it from." She shook her head and threw open the plain wooden door. The room itself was basic, a bed large enough for two drawers and a desk, a fireplace on the far wall. Basic comforts were better than nothing. "By the way did she ever tell us her name?" She looked back at him as she sat on the bed.

"No, but we can ask tomorrow, I have to look into some of the smiths anyways while we are here. A promise is a promise." He smiled at the thought of why they had come here, to begin with.

"Ah yes you promised me a present." She smirked, "Now I think I held up my end of the bargain, there was no blood spilled and we finally have peace."

"Whatever you wish dear heart." He smiled back.

Chapter Eighteen: Grandmother

"Truen, Truen! Where are you?" Everything was darkness, not even her enhanced eyes could cut through the void.

"Xai! Where are you?" His voice was faint and strained. The daemoness tried to follow the sound of her mate's voice but it was hard to track. She kept calling out to get more clues about his whereabouts.

"Truen, where are you!" She kept crying while panic set in, he had been silent through the last few calls. She could not feel him at all in the darkness or through the bond. It was as if the bond never existed between them.

Over here love. She let out a sigh of relief as the telepathic link was still there, leading her to him finally. From the darkness she ran into the throne room, they were back at the castle. There he was leaning against the throne, his arms wrapped tightly around his abdomen, blood pooling on the stone beneath him. The color had fallen from his skin. His face scrunched in pain with each breath. His beautiful eyes were still defiant as he stared at her in the doorway. His eyes darted away, bringing her focus deliberately to the shadow figure standing in the middle of the room. The shadow person's back was to Xai as he held Krutz by his throat on the ground, distracted and none the wiser of Xai's presence. As quietly as possible she snuck to her mate, only making it halfway to him before she fell to the floor vomiting blood. The shadow turned to watch her retch, not lowering the Prince until she was done spitting.

"Welcome, you finally made it back here Xai Lurra." The shadow spoke in a low masculine tone. She remembered him from the last time.

"Put him down. We have been here before, put him down." She growled in response. The dark figure shrugged but did as she asked, throwing the young Prince like a child's toy away from her and his brother.

"I was trying to explain to him that you again, your mother, even his own mother never loved him. No woman would. But still, he wouldn't listen to me." The shadow gave in explanation.

"I still have no idea what the fuck you are talking about?" Her words forced her to cough up more blood once more.

"Well his mother never really loved him so she had to die, it was only logical. I shouldn't have to explain this to you again too." Moving the shadow pointed at a female form with dark hair laying on the ground in nothing but her light blue night dress covered in blood. Next to her in a heap a white-haired body looking broken and bloodied. Even from across the room, Xai knew who these corpses were. "Of course, your mother fought to protect his mother only proving she never loved him either."

"You are delusional you know that right? Who the hell are you? You never said who you were last time we were here." She hissed through the pain. She had never had a dream like this before. This one changed, she could actually talk to him. Her last prophetic dream was just repeating itself every time she saw it.

"I am not delusional, you foolish little girl, I told you this last time. None of this would be happening if you all followed the script. Who I am is not important at the moment. What is important is the next arch of the story I told you. I need you to follow my story plot."

"What the hell are you talking about? You killed innocent women for what? Hurting all these people for no reason? You hide behind your delusions for a lack of actual reasoning."

"You will know when the time is right if you stop interfering." The shadow continued to pace the throne room.

"I will continue to interfere. I can promise you that until I stop you I will be nowhere else but the thorn in your side, the character you can't control. I will never stop no matter what you do to me."

"You will not win against me Xai. I don't know who you think you are but my plans will be followed through as the best-laid stories always are. The hero, myself, of course, will win. You can not defeat me by breaking the spells I had cast or trying to kill my puppet king. You don't get to make it to the end of the book. I will erase you from the story if I need to, you are not that important to the story."

"So you are the one behind all of this?"

"It is my story that is being told. How I saved the world."

"You are destroying everything. I do not see at all how you do not see that."

"I beg to differ, child. I am saving my world. You do not see the bigger picture of the world." The shadow made no sense.

"I will not let you win."

"You do not have a choice in that matter. I will stop your little prophecy in its tracks and leave you to watch those you love die slowly. You had a chance to live when I had you sent away but you chose to come back. I do hate it when the characters have a mind of their own. You can not change my story at will."

"Fuck your story, it means nothing to us, we are not characters we are living beings."

"That is the same thing your sister said before I got rid of her." The voice sounded almost saddened as if that was not the conclusion he had wanted.

"You did it!" She screamed, only causing more blood to rise in her throat. "You are the one who stole my sister away from us. You made us blame each other for losing her."

"She needed to be out of the way, for my plan to work, for everyone to be saved. You were in the way too, being too stubborn for your own good."

"You are insane, you must be. To think of living people as nothing but props and to kill anyone who doesn't listen to your asinine plans for what you alone think is best for our world."

"Unfortunately I have no time to explain it to you, my dear. I need people who will just follow simple instructions to help me usher our world into peace away from the gods and their destiny."

"Are you missing the ability for thought, you are killing people for a crusade for gods who may or may not exist. If they do exist they are GODS you complete imbecile." So only some of the conversation could be altered. Most of it had to stay the same, she only had so much strength to change the course of action.

"Always so rude. You know nothing of my plans child. You will fall into what I need you to."

"I will need you to release my sister if you don't mind." A bell-like voice came from a person who had not been there prior. Xai almost thought her neck would snap at the sound. A beautiful white-haired woman checked on her Prince. "Close your mouth Xai, your drooling blood. I know I was the more lady-like twin but have some decorum." Purple eyes met purple eyes as Lui finally looked at her sister. "Now I have told you before shadow you are not welcome in my sister's mind or dreams. Be gone and stay gone this time." The shadows vanished in an instant as if her command broke the spell. The blood was gone from the daemoness' lungs and she could breathe clearly again. The ghostly image of the long-gone daemon child floated through the room. Checking first on her mate and then her sister's before coming to stand before Xai herself looking as she remembered her.

"Lui?" The elder daemoness asked carefully as if directly addressing the spector would collapse the illusion. "You are back?"

"One of the few good things about this dream is I can find you." She sighed, her hand swiping through the air clearing the scene. The pain was gone and so was the castle. They were standing clean in an open field. The clearing was full of tall grass and flowers that Xai had never seen before. "Now that I got that cleared up talk to me sister, what has happened since we last spoke?" They stood staring at each other wearing simple braids and cotton dresses, they were soft but nothing that she would ever wear.

"Nothing much sister but what are we wearing?" She smirked as her sister sputtered. This was only a vision of what would happen if her sister was with her. Sputtering and cussing about Xai's fashion sense and lack of lady-like decorum. Swirling around acting carefree and ridiculous. Suddenly she stopped and looked at her sister with a sad but comforting smile and Xai knew this time with her would soon be over no matter what either of them wanted.

"It is time for me to go again Xai." The white-haired woman sighed, stepping back to her sister again. "I am sorry I spent our time being silly."

"I would have you no other way, you ridiculous woman. Even if it is only for a fleeting minute in a dream it means more than life itself to see that if you were here with me you would still be as silly as you always were. Silly and fierce." Xai spoke quietly with reverence as she wrapped her arms around her sister. Lui was slightly smaller than Xai now instead of being the same size as children, a fleeting thought of if this would have been accurate if she had lived went through Xai's mind as she held her sister as close as she could. "I don't want to let you go."

"But you have to for now sister." Lui leaned back placing a hand on her sister's spotted face, her own never got a chance to grow in. "This will not be the last though I promise my sister."

"When will I get to see you again though? These dreams are no guarantees." Xai sighed once more, pulling her closer again.

"I will see you when the final battle of this chapter happens my sister. Come hell or high water no one would be able to stop me from standing beside you when you start the war to fix the wrongs that have been dealt to us all."

"Lui!" She gasped as she sat up suddenly, a silken sheet pooling around her bare body. A cold sweat settled on her skin

356

as she willed her breathing to steady. She looked around wildly in the darkness of the room at the temple. Truen watched beside her, hand raised like he wanted to reassure her with physical touch but thought better of it. The fireplace was all but embers across the room.

"Your sister again?" He asked in a whisper, wanting to catch her attention but not to startle her.

"You could not see that one? You could last time." She looked at him, her eyes glowing in the darkness but that never scared him.

"No this tonight I was having a peaceful dream of the future." Finally, he reached out and laid his hand on her arm, somewhere safe in case the panic was still taking hold. Thankfully the tension and panic melted from her with the touch.

"It was different this time and I got to talk to her." She admitted, leaning back into his touch. The daemoness felt the exhaustion creep back in as the panic left. She laid back down deciding to use his chest as a pillow, allowing his heartbeat to ground her and the arm he wrapped around her to provide comfort.

"Do you want to talk more about it?" He asked unsure of where this would go.

"No, it was not significant, though she said she would see me again before we waged war. I thought we were ending a war but maybe she is right and we are ending a struggle by starting a war."

"That is one way to think about it. We have been with people who are willing to help and otherwise hiding when we are not starting a revolution in cities. We will have a lot of work after if we win this siege on the castle. One might call changing the minds and hearts of an entire kingdom a true war."

"I think she was trying to tell me something more but I don't think I understood her meaning."

"If she did, knowing your sister the way I did, I would say she will make sure you understand her meaning one way or another." He reassured. "Have faith in here where ever she is. Even from the other side, Lurra women are a force to be reckoned with." He smiled gently placing a gentle kiss on the top of her head. "You are tired though dear heart, let us try and get some more sleep before we start our day of commissioning, threatening, and other errands." His words earned him a snort from his bedmate and a kiss upon his bare chest before she snuggled further into her chest and they both drifted back into sleep. Thankfully her sleep was dreamless after that point. They woke up still entangled with each other.

"Do we have to get up?" Xai whined into his skin.

"We have a meeting with my Aunt to see if there is someone who can help with this prophecy, I need to drop off a commission, and I would like to see if we can find out more about my family." He answered.

"So yes we do." She sighed as she stretched. Her body made popping noises as she stretched as far as she could go. Sitting up finally she looked around the room which seemed to be lit with magic, to simulate daylight. "I think your Aunt would like to see us soon." She sighed again looking at something on the desk that had not been there the night before.

"And how do you suspect that?" The Prince asked, still laying flat on the bed watching his love.

"There is new clothing sitting on the desk with a note on top of it. I am truly hoping that is not a dress I see."

"Knowing mages it probably is my love." He smiled finally sitting up. As she left the bed and walked towards the desk completely bare he just watched, enjoying the view of the spots that decorated her skin and her tail on full display.

"Stop staring at my ass and get up, If I have to put on clothes so do you." She huffed. "I swear if this is a dress I am making you wear it." She said poking the fabric.

"I would look stunning in a gown." He smirked, "Depending on the cut, mind you, I don't have the chest for certain styles."

"You are such a tramp." She chuckled turning back to him.

"Don't be mad because I would look better in a gown." He goaded, finally standing just as bare as she was. "Now you are staring dear and I am feeling objectified." He smirked.

"Oh dear, you are such a woman." She laughed.

"Are you mad I am sexier?" He pressed walking towards her.

"You could never dear, I am a daemoness, by default of the gods I will always be sexier."

"I will not deny that." He smirked again kissing her. "Now let us see what my Aunt chose for you because I see black silk and I don't think that is for me." He smiled knowing that whatever it was she would look stunning, but he hadn't seen her in a gown since they were children back when he could not appreciate it. He lifted the silk fabric and watched her expression drop.

"What the fuck is that, it looks like a single piece of silk." She asked in fear.

"It is because it wraps around your hips and we cross it in the front pulling it over your shoulders and letting the chains fall over your back keeping it in place." He smiles, he had seen some of the guests of the castle wear designs similar in the last few years.

"So it is a fabric torture device with chains." She answered.

"Simple, light, and easy to move in or remove." He corrected. "We are in their city so you may as well wear what they ask before we ask for help."

"That is easy for you to say, you got a tunic and some pants. I got silk." She grumbled handing it to him to help her into it. "I can't even hide a weapon in this." She groaned.

"You don't need weapons here, we were promised safety. I think this was more a gift for me than anything. If it helps we shouldn't be here more than another day depending on the commission, then you can put pants back on and we can go and meet up with the others." She continued to mutter under her breath as he got dressed in his own clothing. "Would you like me to braid your hair? I can do something simple to keep it from your face." She nodded, a dusting of red crossing the back of her neck as Truen began to work his fingers through her hair.

"I have never had someone do my hair since my mother." She admitted as he made quick work of her loose curls.

"I practiced a lot on our mother's while you were away. I didn't know why but I felt like I needed to. Even helping with my brother's when they kept their hair longer. It was a way to keep my hands busy doing something creative instead of destructive." He shrugged as he did a simple braid collecting all of her hair. "I know this isn't my most impressive work but I feel like you wouldn't want to stand here that long for me to do something intricate."

"You are right I would hate that, especially in a dress."

"You know when you wear the crown you occasionally will have to wear gowns." He smirked as she got tense again.

"Can't we outlaw gowns while we are discussing treason?" She pleaded.

"No, we can't, dear heart." Truen laughed while finishing her hair. "Many people actually enjoy wearing them and I won't take away other people's happiness for you."

"Why not?" She turned to him pouting, her tail up on her shoulders like a scarf. He just shook his head and ignored the question while finishing getting himself ready. Once he was done there was an impeccably timed knock at their door. "Mages I swear. " Xai sighed, opening the door to see a small woman who refused to look at them.

"The council is ready for you." The small redhead squeaked.

"The council? I thought we were just meeting your Aunt?" Xai looked at the man behind her.

"Lady Naratana is on the council of Mages, they agreed to see you for your request." The woman answered in a soft voice.

"Always expect a Mage to already know what you need." Xai sighed. "And I guess we know your Aunt's name now."

"I have a feeling that like my mother she hates being addressed by her full name." The Prince shrugged and shrugged for the little Mage to show us the way. The maze of the temple was walked silently. Once they arrived at what seemed to be a random set of doors the red-haired Mage nodded and silently took off back from where they had come. "Here goes nothing." He looked back towards his love and then opens the doors with the authority that only the heir apparent could accomplish in a strange territory. Within the room sat a small handful of people some of which the two recognized. The Aunt sat in the middle closest to what appeared to be a alter in the middle of the room. Behind her was her Guard from the day before, though he refused to look at those who entered the room.

"Welcome Treun and Xai." Naratana smiled gently. "I would like to introduce you to all the members of the council. Closest to you is our master blacksmith and enchanted weapons maker Gram. If you need some sort of weapon made he is your man." She looked pointedly at her nephew. The man in question was stout and bulky, hair as red as the woman before that lead them here. His eyes glow golden even in the light of the room. He nodded to them.

"I hear I will need to talk to you later Prince Truen." He spoke deeply and gruffly but with no aggression.

"Beside him is our seer, Milya." Naratana continues gesturing to the blonde person beside her, the person was completely androgynous. Their eyes were white but they seemed to be staring through them both.

"Your journey is not yet over and I apologize." Even their voice was impossible to tell.

"And the last member is the person you will want to talk to the most. She is my mother and your grandmother Clarita.

She is a Time Mage and she can help with the prophecy that has been bestowed on you.”

“Your mother also wants to meet some of her grandbabies in person Nara don't make this more ominous than this needs to be.” Gram laughed deeply.

“That is very true, I always want to see my grandbabies.” A melodic voice came into the room, and a shorter stouter woman stormed into the room like a tidal wave, all grace and aura as everyone stepped from her path. When she finally sat on the seat on the other side of the altar from her apparent daughter Xai finally got a decent look at her. There sat the older woman, runes tattooed into her skin, over her face, and down into what was covered no longer with ratty cloth but a gorgeous silken gown. The runes covering her face gave away her specialty, she was a time mage, one of a few born every few centuries. Looking up in the dimming light the woman had eyes like the night sky, no white just black from corner to corner, it was like looking into the void itself. A face the daemoness would never forget even when it had a smirk she had never seen directed at her.

“Really it is you?” The feline hissed, ears flattening and tail thrashing about angrily. The Time Mage just smiled wider and her daughter sighed.

“What did you do, mother?” The Priestess sighed, rubbing her temples.

“Hello, child it is good to see you again on the path I sent you on.” She cooed.

“You gave me this damn curse and then died, I saw you die. You turned into dust.” Xai shot back not enjoying her flippant tone, she was the one who gave her the Prophecy, to begin with.

"Oh, dear worry not about that. Changing what life cycle we are in is a gift of a Time Mage, just wait until I can teach your brother all about it." She looked wistful at the idea of teaching Jackdaw, the obvious Time Magic carrier.

"You have no reason to look so nostalgic, old woman, you have given us all nothing but pain," Xai growled back, being barely restrained by her Prince who was just as angry and resentful towards his maternal grandmother.

"You have every reason to be pissed at me child, even more so to resent me." The older woman sombered up. "I know you all have been dealt something that no one should have and I took it upon myself to deliver it to you knowing where it would lead. But it needed to be done and without guidance, the path would have been paved in more blood and suffering than it was. I am truly sorry for having to send you to your destiny but I will never regret doing it. I know you came here seeking help both to understand the prophecy and to aid in your rebellion against the crown. I can guarantee assistance and some understanding. Give us until tomorrow to return to the rest of your group and we will have everything together for the raid on the castle and the war to begin."

"So this will be a war?" Truen finally spoke up.

"Yes dear, I am sorry but this will be the first battle of the war that will plague you for the rest of your lives. This will be a war against the silence. A war to redeem those who walked the path with no disregard for those harmed. And most importantly a war to remember what has happened so it shall not happen again. Not all of these will be fought with blood and steel."

"If you will give my mother and me sometime today we can come up with as much information as we can and a plan to help with the raid if not after. I know that this is taking up precious time but we also need to be prepared for the final stages. Gram would love to work on any commission you have my dear nephew and that should be able to be finished before you leave tomorrow. Xai we will need your assistance here with us but we shall keep Truen safe if that is alright with you?" The blonde asked, more like pleading with the daemoness. Xai doubted that she had known what part in all of this her mother played.

"Fine, but I will not be cordial just because her daughter helped raise me or I am bound to her grandson," Xai answered the Priestess, her eyes never leaving the old woman.

"That is understandable." She sighed. "If you all would excuse us."

"Of course My Lady." The guard walked around from behind Nara and towards the Seer. "Milya I will guide you through the city since it has become busy in the streets."

"You worry too much Barradra but if it makes you feel better." The pale person shook their head and left their hand out for the guard to take. "Just because we are powerful doesn't mean that we need babysitters."

"I like taking care of you all." The guard grumbled seemingly embarrassed. The rest of the Council just smiled softly as they watched the soft scene that seemed to be a regular occurrence. The pale one lifted themself from their chair and followed the guard from the chamber. Gram shook his head and lifted himself from his own chair.

"Come on Prince Truen, we have something dangerous to make." The large male smiled almost ferally. He laid a large hand on Truen's shoulder. "Don't worry about him Darling, I will make sure he stays in one piece. I would never want to see the bad side of someone as fearsome as you." She nodded at the good-humored man.

Try not to kill anyone Dear Heart, even if they were not my family we need them.

Trust me more than that love. He just smiled and left with the craftsman.

"Now that it is just the three of us, what is the current plan for the siege?" Nara looked back at the daemoness as she gestured for her to sit in the seat that Miyla had vacated. The feline sat gingerly in the wooden chair, it was not made for someone with a tail but did not want to be rude.

"Is the chair uncomfortable for you?" Clarita interrupted before Xai could answer her daughter. "We don't have long-tailed daemons in the city often so we didn't think about that."

"It is not the biggest issue we have here." Xai pushed back uncomfortable with someone blatantly worrying about the physical differences in her body. She was used to the hate and the fear about her claws, teeth, and spots but not often are people concerned about the comfort of her tail or ears.

"No it is not but we can make your life more comfortable while you are in the city, you will be back eventually. You will be family here." The grandmother insisted.

"Is this your way of saying that we will survive the raid?" Xai pushed back again changing the subject back.

"As long as nothing changes with the future then you should come back. You are the beginning and the end of this war."

"That is not ominous at all." Xai sighed causing Nara to laugh.

"That is is, do you have a plan so far?" She asked.

"Next full moon take the castle and sting up what is left of the King, save all those we can in servitude including my family and your sister, and take the stolen crown on Truen's head where it was always supposed to be."

"That is a concise plan if nothing else and puts us at an advantage." The Priestess nodded approvingly. Something simple was easier to add to.

"That plan will work, we need to figure out who will be assisting with this." Clarita nodded. "We just need to finish the prophecy and bring forth the champion."

"Now it is a champion? What the hell is the full prophecy." Xai groaned, hating this entire thing.

"Bring forth those chosen to be pure from those who were here before. Together their sacrifice will bring forth the champion ordained by the gods to save all creations made." Clarita recited. "That is the full prophecy from what the gods gave us."

"And that translates to a pure human, daemon, and vampire." Xai nodded. "So what is the Champion and what is the sacrifice?"

"From what I can gather the sacrifice is a bit of blood and a small piece of soul to bring forth the Champion." The older woman answered. "Not a sacrifice of life thankfully. I don't think that anyone they would have chosen as the Champion would allow for sacrifice but I also believe that those chosen to be those who bring the Champion to our world would be willing to sacrifice themselves to save everyone else."

"That is very true." Nara nodded along. "From what we have been seeing in the glimpses we get from the altar flames."

"But what is the Champion?"

"The Champion is a creature called the Hybrid. A perfect mix of the original three races. Strength and invulnerability of the vampires. Raw power, speed, and veracity of daemons. And the adaptability, creativity, and compassion of humans. Together make someone who can take on the world for the sake of those who need them and not for any other reason." Clarita explained.

"So Dremira, Kato, and I need to come together and sacrifice a bit of ourselves to bring rise to the Hybrid. How will we know it worked?"

"I will help you bring the Hybrid forth but I think you misunderstand, you will not be one of those to sacrifice part of themself."

"What do you mean? If I am not to help then why did you send me on this gods damned journey with this prophecy. Not to mention it put me on the map for the gods to ask favors of me." Xau shot up from the chair, beginning to pace back and forth through the chamber.

"Did you just say the gods are asking favors?" Nara asked in shock.

"That is because you are the Hybrid." Clarita shot back at the same time. The collective shouting of 'what' from all three women as they looked back and forth at each other. "Okay let us start with yours Xai. Did you really meet the gods?"

"Luna specifically, she came to me to ask for help," Xai answered slowly. Shock still clouded her mind.

"What did the Goddess need?" Nara asked in disbelief.

"Her and the others are trapped in their mortal bodies. Someone trapped them. It's why she sent the prophecy to someone who could send it in motion. Because …I am her creation….that is what she told me."

"She told you that you were the Hybrid with no way of you knowing." Clarita looked at her daughter.

"Someone is trying to take the gods out of the picture so the gods are trying to bring balance back."

"This is bigger than we knew. Now I understand what they meant by the war was only just beginning. I thought it was to change the hearts of the land but now there is something else."

"We will have to see if the other Mages who can help can find out about the gods and who is behind this." Nara nodded. "There must be something we can do."

"Occasionally I have been having prophetic dreams, I see something that may happen. One did one has not passed." Xai started to explain, she knew it started random but she had something for them. "The one that I had recently the first time Truen could see it too, but Lui was there my sister who was taken at the beginning of this nightmare. But also there was a shadow man saying that he was the one who was the hero of this story and I wasn't following his scripting. What he says to me changes slightly both times I have had this dream but he may be a connection to the one doing this. Especially since the first attack one could on us was the loss of Lui and Jhelum. It almost destroyed both families and each of us was given different memories of what happened."

"Do you know what everyone was told?" Nara asked.

"The King thought that I killed Jhelum somehow even though we had a connection similar to Truen and mine. Truen thought I abandoned him after Lui was lost. I honestly thought Truen and Krutz murdered Lui in front of me. Truen thinks Lui died in an accident. I no longer know what happened to my sister. Krutz thought Truen Poisoned Lui and so he was going to try and replace her with me or just kill me to watch his brother suffer. I was told the night I left that mother thought King was going to kill me and that he killed Lui. Jackdaw thinks Lui Killed herself and I ran to save myself and to hurt Truen in the process."

"That is strange. We can add it to the list, maybe there is a trace of the spell that we can track."

"We can go to the next problem once we hold the crown." Xai nodded to the Mages. She knew it was important but one mountain of a task at a time.

"Of course. Plus we need to know if we can find all the gods and how to help them back into their celestial forms." Clarita nodded.

"Oh nothing to it then, any other impossible tasks that we want to add to my list?"

Chapter Nineteen: Surprise Heritage

By the time Truen had gotten back to the room that day Xai had already been asleep sprawled out bare and in absolute chaos on the bed not even covered with either blanket, between the stress and planning she was not able to stay awake to see him. The raven-haired male smiled softly at the woman in his bed. She had been under an extreme amount of stress which was understandable with everything going on in their world. He set down the blade that he helped with during the day on the desk. He had worked with Gram all day on the easy design and the enchants on the sword that they had made for Xai. He pulled off the sweat-soaked clothes he was wearing and wiped himself down, hoping not to transfer too much sweat to the sheets. He walked around the bed and carefully rolled the woman he loved more than anything onto the side of the bed he knew she would be more comfortable to wake on. As gently as possible he placed the blanket on top of her and proceeded to climb into the bed next to her. He pulled her body to his own and arranged them into both being comfortable. He knew he could not physically protect her but he would do anything in his power to protect her. It might only be her reputation or emotions or even keep her from nightmares like tonight.

When she woke hours later she smiled into his skin, limbs tangled together under the covers. Not a single nightmare had plagued her. It took effort to slip from his grasp and stand beside the bed. As she stepped around she stretched, relishing in the pull of muscle and the satisfying popping of joints realigning. The fire had died hours ago but the stone room was far from cold even this far under the ground. Walking towards the seek she saw the project he had been working on the day before, she could feel the pride and exhaustion through the

371

bond the entire day as she worked with the Mages on strategy and understanding of the prophecy. They had finally come up with a plan of action after trial and error all day and were ready to head back to the others to try and bring forth the Hybrid. They had not been able to track down any of the gods in mortal form but had a theory that it might be easier once the Hybrid was awakened. She stared at the beautiful piece of weaponry and couldn't help but feel a disconnect that this mythical weapon of the gods was in fact her. She was a daemon, she was raised a weapon but not like this. The sword before her though was perfect even though simple. It did not surprise her that Truen had remembered that she preferred a longer blade and a smaller guard, closer to a traditional elven style mixed with a human style. daemons didn't traditionally use blades, finding their own bodies enough of a weapon but she had always liked to have the option of not relying strictly on her daemonic side to take on her opponents. That seemed to make a bit more sense now knowing what she was hiding in her blood.

"Do you like it?" A sleep-deep voice asked from behind her.

"It is beautiful, you did a fantastic job on its love." She cooed back looking at the raven-haired man who was face down on the pillow clearly feeling the effects of working in the forge the day before. Poor little Princeling had never been allowed to attempt something so menial labor before. Not that traveling by foot across the kingdom wasn't taxing, she corrected herself mentally.

"I mostly helped make alterations to a blade already made, Gram made me focus on enchantments. He is the smithy, not me." He groaned rolling over onto his back on the bed. "It took a lot more than I thought it would but I am glad that you like it. It came out as I envisioned it." Truen grinned towards the ceiling.

"It is beautiful and I can not thank you enough for giving me something like this before the battle. You will have to tell me the enchantments before I take it for a test run at the castle."

"I don't believe that is a test run dear heart but more so the first main event." Truen chuckled sitting up with a groan. "Though I do feel better with an enchanted blade by your side. It is not much in the ways of enchantments. I focused on it not dulling, not breaking, or being stolen in battle and used against you. I know you do not need help from magic to fight so I figured not defensive but longevity enchantments, protective ones would be better."

"Thank you for trusting me with our well-being." She smiled in this gentle moment. They would not have many more until they won.

"I know I will also be beside you giving you as much strength as I can and performing any offensive magic we may need during the siege." He smirked, finally standing from the bed to join her before her gift. "I don't need too many forms of magic interfering with one another."

"That's fair, I can't say I understand what a magic user goes through." daemons rarely had magic even when they were mixed in blood. "But I want you to know how much I appreciate this gift. We won't get many more moments like this once we leave this room. We can't stay in the underground any longer, we have to meet up with the others and try to awaken the Hybrid. Until that crown is on your head we will not see softness again, we will have no time for it if we want to live until then."

"I know my love. It won't be long now though, the full moon is not that far off and we will make it through." Truen reassured her as he wrapped his arms around her bare skin. A shimmer of magic was felt through the air, not aggressive but a shift in the air, that broke the couple apart. Clothes laying on the bed that had not been there moments before, different from the fashion of yesterday but still not the clothing they had arrived in. "I am guessing that this is their way of telling us it is time to go?" Truen sighed stepping back towards the bed. A lower dipped tunic with long sleeves and black pants had been laid out for him again, this time an addition to a belt full of pouches and a vest in a striking shade of blue were included. Two pairs of dark leather riding boots sat beside the bed no doubt in the perfect sizes. Shaking her head she decided to venture to see what the Mages had chosen for her today. Dark fabric pants were better than the gown from yesterday to begin but the leather vest top was confusing. Wouldn't they want her more covered than less? No sleeves were attached but there were leather bracers instead. The vest itself had a high back and a hood, somehow it reminded her of a travel cloak mixed with a corset without the shape or constriction.

"What the hell is this?" She asked as she held it up towards her mate as he put on his pants, lacing up the front. A disbelieving chuckle escaped him before he could stop it. "What the fuck is this... this... is a scrap of leather."

"I don't know my love, all I can say is you can have my tunic but it isn't much more." He continued to laugh as she grumbled at it but put it on. "I can tell you it is enchanted at least I am just not sure for what."

"I don't know but this is ridiculous." She groaned more as it fit perfectly and provided more ability for movement than she thought with it being leather. "I hate that they keep giving us perfectly fitting clothing."

374

"Mostly because this is not in any sort of fashion you would choose my love."

"We are supposed to be waging a war and sieging the castle and they sent me this?" She muttered as Truen finished getting dressed.

"There is probably a reason for it that will make sense, not that I am complaining. I love seeing the spots on your skin, sometimes I wished they were more pronounced."

"Of course, you would, most would rather my spots are not visible all the time and yet here you are breaking the mold once again."

"What can I say, I am in love with every part of you." He smiled at her wistfully.

"Even the part of me that is about to kill your father and put his bloodied crown in your hands?"

"I would expect nothing less from my daemon Queen."

"You call me your Queen before you even hold the title of King?"

"I would gladly bow before you with no crown or title and call you my Queen. Kingdom or not I will spend the rest of my life devoted to you no matter where we are or how much blood you have spilled."

"You are a woman's dream, you know that?"

"As long as I am your dream, my Queen, I am blessed." He smiled wider, taking the moment to kiss her. "Now that we have cleared that up shall we go and see why my grandmother has put you in such a beautiful ensemble?"

"She better have a good reason or I am going to suspect she may be as perverted as her grandson." She raised her brow. "Then again it might be a family trait and I should be more concerned." Xai shook her head removing herself from his hold and finishing getting everything together. The belt she had been given had the perfect placement for the new sword she carried. As frustratingly perfect as everything was once again she couldn't be more thankful. Once they had both deemed themselves ready they opened the door to see Truen's newfound family waiting patiently.

"They look fantastic, the tailors did wonders," Nara commented looking them both over. "Both sets have been enchanted as you must have guessed. Truen yours will help against projectiles and magic. Xai yours are meant to work with your daemonic blood and should not be destroyed if you must shift, hopefully, the items themselves should allow for more movement as well. More armor or fabric would more likely deter from your natural speed and flexibility. One of the tailors will be going with you and mother to see the rest of the raiding party so they can try to have something for everyone who is risking their lives for this. Her name is Mari, she will meet you at the doors of the temple."

"Are you not coming with us?" Truen asked his blonde aunt.

"Not now. I still have to see if I can find the gods but once you have the castle mother will let me know and more Mages will come to help with the transition. It is time for the Lunar races to stop hiding in the darkness and help save ourselves." She nodded at them. "I will be there to see you and my sister as soon as I am able."

"Then we shall see you soon." Xai nodded back. If Nara was anything like her sister she would want to fight but they all knew her magic was not suited for combat. "I will have this over with before the sun rises on the full moon."

"That will be sooner than any of you think, mere days in the grand scheme of things." She urged, her anxiety about the situation coming through her words.

"Then we have spent too much time here. We still have to gather the troops, plan to overthrow the government, and raise an ancient weapon all in mere days." Xai smirked confidently.

"Fortune smiles on those who have been burdened by destiny." The elderly mage added for herself. "But we need to head out, let us retrieve Mari, and then let us go meet my other grandchild. Nara dear can you open us a pathway outside the temple to where we need to go?"

"Of course mother, it should be simple enough."

"How would you be able to do that considering you have no idea where they should be?" Truen asked.

"Blood can call to blood if you let it my dear nephew. Your brother is there is he not? He is as much my sister's blood as you are. Mages can always find family if they reach hard enough. As long as nothing interferes as it does with your mother I should always be able to find you."

"That is good to know." Xai sighed. "If you can get us to the others that would save us a day or two of traveling especially with two extra people."

"Of course, follow me and we can have you all on your way." Nara turned gracefully and strode back down the hallways.

"She has always been dramatic." Her mother sighed following behind, causing a surprised laugh to force its way out of Xia's throat.

"At least you were not the only one thinking about it." Truen teased while pulling the daemoness behind him through the halls.

"So it's either a Mage thing or a family thing, fantastic. I will never escape it with you." She shot back. By the temple, doors stood the same redhead girl from the day before.

"Mira, are you ready to go?" The blonde asked gently, obviously trying not to startle the girl.

"Of course Ma'am I am ready to do anything to help the High Priestess and the new King and Queen." She rushed out in a surprisingly squeaking voice, her nervousness was not subtle at all.

"Good, now all of you be safe I am begging you. I know you are being blessed but do not take that as assurance. The future and destiny can always shift." Nara said, wide eyes looking at each of us. "And for the sake of us, all do not leave a single one of those bigoted bastards standing. Protect each other and those who are innocent and rain the wrath of a thousand lost souls on those who deserve it."

"Of course, I would never leave a war half-finished," Xai smirked, earning a chuckle from the woman who did not stand before them a High Priestess and a powerful Mage but someone sending the people she cared for to war. She nodded again, tears in her eyes as she opened a pathway.

"This should get you to the edge of the clearing of the daemon colony where your pack resides at. Be safe all of you and I shall see you soon." She tried to smile as she stepped out of the way but managed to kiss each of them on the forehead as they tried to pass her. Her own way of protecting them Xai was certain. The daemoness didn't look back as she went through the portal and was greeted with tall familiar trees, dirt pathways, and a clearing that was lit in the evening sunlight. She could see the others sparing across the clearing of tall grass and flowers just like those in the village had done when they were younger. Lux stood beside her father as they watched the others spar together.

"They look like a fine group. More than I expected to be gathered. How did you find two dragons? I have no idea but I am not disappointed." The Time Mage started to ramble, reminding Xai of Jackdaw anytime he was impressed.

"Well let's go say hello then shall we." The daemoness smirked, crouching slightly. Truen shook his head as he held back knowing exactly what his mate was about to do. He watched as Xai skirted the clearing in the shadows of the trees and covered her approach with the sounds of the village and the forest. The two Mages lost sight of her quickly but he never did, she was hunting her best friend and this would not end well.

"She is going to get in trouble for this." He sighed smiling to himself.

"What is she doing?" Mari asked quietly looking for the feline from behind the man's shoulder.

"She is about to pounce on that other daemoness over there. That said daemoness is Lux, my brother's mate, and partner. She and Xai are best friends and this is common but about to cause a scene. Watch behind Lux for a moment, I can feel Xai's impish excitement so it shouldn't be too much longer." He was right of course as they watched in fascination, never having seen daemons freely exist before since for the longest time villages like this stayed hidden even to other Lunars. A flash of darkness sprung from the tall grass faster than any of them could track catching the daemoness who had been correcting forms unaware, the two women ended up on the ground rolling around and shouting like children causing everyone else in the area to stop what they were doing expecting a hostile presence. Truen nodded at the two Mages to follow him as he walked out of the tree line and across the field to wear the two were wrestling still in the dirt.

"Welcome back brother." The blonde male walked over to him calmly smiling at the ruckus. "Somethings never change."

"No, they don't. We are getting ready to raid the castle and kill our father and Xai still couldn't resist ambushing Lux given the chance."

"To be fair I think it would be the same if the roles were reversed. Lux would do the same." Jackdaw smiled. "Though I see your trip was successful?" He asked nodding at the two behind his brother.

"More than you can imagine. And Xai is back in a better headspace after your little lapse in judgment." Truen looked pointedly at his brother still not willing to forgive completely, at least not yet.

"That is good, I would not want my mistakes to have permanent effects." The smaller flinched away from his brother.

"Stop glaring at your brother Truen." Xai finally joined them with a bright-fanged smile on her face, knocking the dust easily from her new outfit.

"I already tore into him Princeling," Lux added walking along beside her. "Now who did you bring with you?"

"My name is Clarita, I am the mother of the High Priestess of the Underground city Naratana and Queen Luaratana. I am the Time Mage who carries the prophecy and your grandmother." She said pointedly to Jackdaw who paled.

"You were the one to bring me the prophecy," Kato exclaimed running up to the adults and throwing his arms around the feline in the process. "Welcome back, we missed you." He chirped, Hestia not far behind. They took turns giving both adopted parents a tight hug.

"We missed you too, hopefully, you behaved while we were away." Truen smiled picking up the little girl.

"We were," Kato promised.

"You have children?" Clarita choked out in awe. She had great-grandchildren.

"You brought them to us to be fair." Xai shot back as she watched the others join. Dremira was pointed at the Time Mage and whispering to Crazden. "I am assuming you have met her too Dremira?" The human nodded. "She is here to help us finish the prophecy and to explain some missing parts. Behind her is Mira who is a tailor from the Mage city who is willing to help us get ready for the siege."

"Hopefully you won't run off to save the world without saying hello to the rest of us first." A gruff voice came from behind the daemoness. Lux smirked knowing that Xai would get an earful from her father, not to mention her mother when she got a hold of her.

"Of course, not Sir, just wanted to see my pack and children first." She spun on her heels to see the large lean man who had his arms crossed but was trying not to smile too hard for her to think she was in actual trouble. Lux's father was more of a father than hers had ever really been, but that had not been her own father's fault but the King's who took him away all the time. The man before her opened his arms and waited, she stepped to him to get engulfed in a hug that felt like the safety a child should know. This was the man who found a traumatized child covered in blood and mud trying to steal food and brought her home to take care of her with the rest of his children per the request of his daughter.

"Your sister has informed me of the wild path you have found yourself on. I am not surprised, to say the least, nor can I think of a better person to lead the charge. I am proud of everyone you have gathered and everything you have done so far. Let us here help you as well. Whatever you all need if we can do it we will." He released one of his children. "I know you don't want me to go with you but I need your mate to get a good shot in against your father while you are at it, for me."

"Of course Sir," Truen answered stepping up to the daemon. "I know you have met my brother but I am Truen, Xai's mate and partner. I would be happy to get some shots in for you while we are at it."

"Good man." He nodded letting the daemoness go. "What needs to happen now? I know we only have a few days left." He asked Clarita, turning everyone's attention to the still-shocked Time Mage whose eyes had not yet left the children hanging off her grandson.

"Grandmother?" Jackdaw prodded getting her attention.

"My apologies, seeing my grandchildren with children of their own made me lost in thought, I have missed so much yet this prophecy brought everything together in a way we never thought. It has brought an entire family back together that had been separated in a way that was unnatural."

"But how would we have all found each other without it?" Mi'Kal asked from beside Dante.

"Destiny would have found a way without bloodshed and terror if it had not been interfered with." She answered looking at the angel. "It is a little overwhelming being able to feel the sorrow of the path we were forced on and the grief of the lives we could have had. I have lived long enough to feel the paths come and go. Some for better and some for worse."

"How do we continue on our path?" Dante prompted gently hearing how overwhelmed with emotion the older woman was.

"First we pull forth a Pure Blood daemon with a bit of help from Xai's blood since she is already a Pure Blood daemon." The Mage answered, finding her determination again.

"I thought Xai was the Pure Blood daemon for the prophecy?" Dremira asked, panic entering her tone as she looked around. Uncertainty spread through the group at the thought of getting so close and missing a component right before the battle.

"Do not fret my dear we have the daemoness that we need right beside us." She turned to look at the canine daemoness beside the feline. "You, my dear were the one I didn't need to call to since I knew you would follow Xai to the end and fulfill your part of the prophecy without complaint."

"I am the Pure Blood daemon?" Lux spat out in shock, eyes wide as she looked between Xai and the Time Mage.

"I didn't even know until we were trying to decipher the full prophecy and I asked about who the daemon was if it was not me." Xai looked at her sister.

383

"If you are not the daemon what is your part?" Kato asked looking at his mother.

"She is the weapon little one, the god's champion," Clarita answered with pride. "Your mother is the Hybrid." All eyes were once more on the purple eyes daemoness as she sighed.

"Yeah, I also learned that with the Mages too. We have been looking for me apparently." She groaned. "Stupid prophecy could have been more clear, to be honest."

"That does explain some of the things Luna said to you though." Lux countered.

"That is what I said," Xai responded. "How do we pull the Pure Blood ability forward?" She asked turning back to the older woman. "We didn't talk about that while we were planning in the council room."

"She would need to ingest a small amount of your blood, simple as that. The potency of your blood should awaken hers." She said simply like she didn't just tell them they needed one to feed the other blood.

"Not to insult the vampire we have here but that is disgusting." Lux choked out.

"I am not sure how that is simple." Xai echoed.

"Well, it is simpler than awakening the Hybrid. That will take blood from all of you and then the trials." She answered.

"And what are the trails?" Truen asked his grandmother.

"From what I know once we start it will not be a smooth process. From what I was able to gather from the writings left from the gods themselves and left with the Mages who died long before even I was born she will drink the blood and then for all purposes die. Part of the trial is her making her way back to this world and you will not be able to help her I am afraid, your bond will be temporarily sealed while she goes through the process. Now the other trials are unknown but once she awakens she will need time to rest and heal from the ordeal, Truen dear you will need to watch over her as she does. She will need to feel safe so she doesn't lash out." The old woman explained looking at anything other than the group watching her. She knew this was not what they wanted to hear.

"Of course, I will, I will not leave her side at all." Truen sounded offended the woman would even suggest that he would think about leaving her side.

I no longer think you should go through with this

I figured you'd say that

Yeah well, I don't want you to be in that much pain. Did you know about this?

I knew some of the information about the trails and that it would be unpleasant. Luna told me I would not walk through them alone but I did not know about the dying portion if that is what you are asking.

If I had my way you would not attempt this but I know you are going to go through it no matter what I say.

I have to try and protect us all, that was the entire point of this.

But you are going to die.

At this point, I don't think death wants to keep me. I will be back with you soon enough.

We have come too far for this to be the point you give up on us all so you better be Xai or I will come for you myself.

As if I would let you Prineling. You are just going to have to trust in my strength once more and my determination to come back to your side.

I feel like we have proven to the gods and those who oppose us that nothing will stand between us no matter how much they try. I have all faith in you coming back to me, I am just hoping it is in one piece. She smiled at him, hopefully reassuring him that she would stop at nothing to end this and stay beside him in one piece.

"Then let us get this started. As disgusting as this is for daemons we don't have much of a choice Lux. How long will it take to affect her." Xai asked.

"Should not take long at all. The notes for bringing forth a Pure Blood says the blood is awakened almost immediately though the changes could take time. But for what we need it will be fairly instant." Clarita explained.

"You ready then Lux?" Xai asked, looking at the other daemoness, she stood there unsure but nodded nonetheless. Unfortunately, the Time Mage had been right in thinking Lux wouldn't hesitate to step into the prophecy.

"Then please Xai may I have your arm?" Clarita asked reaching out for the daemoness. Xai stepped forward and extended her arm, everyone watching closely. "Jackdaw, my dear grandson, please prepare to steady your mate in case." He nodded and stepped forward with a very apprehensive Lux.

"I will do my best to support her." He spoke as calmly as he could manage to make the daemons and his blood family smile. Dante stepped up and smiled gently as he reached out his hands to both children who had yet to leave their parent's sides. This was not something any of them wanted the children to be underneath even if Kato was soon to be dragged into the next stage. Clarita looked uncertain as she held Xai's arm.

"I have this." Xai sighed as she reached for one of her blades that she had been able to keep during their stay in the underground. Without hesitation she sliced into the meat of her forearm, the wound itself was nothing but enough to pull blood quickly to the surface but it made the Time Mage flinch and Truen's hold on her hips tighten. "Go for it Lux, just make sure to seal it." She shrugged.

"Only a little bit will do," Clarita added watching in horror as her instructions were followed. Lux carefully latched onto the wound, taking in a swallow of the blood before she cleaned and sealed the wound.

"Simple as that, right?" Xai asked as she took her arm back and examined the healing wound.

"It should be but I must say I wasn't expecting that." The Mage clarified.

"Things are much bloodier up on the land than in the Underground. You have to understand what we are willing to do to stop the carnage. You gave us these instructions knowing blood and death were in the cards." Xai shrugged slightly amused at the squeamish nature of the older woman. "Strangely enough her drinking my blood was not the weirdest sensation I have ever felt. It was a weird tugging sensation I will give it that."

"Your blood also tasted different than I imagined. Not as disgusting but not something I would do willingly ever again. I don't understand how vampires do it." Lux added rubbing the blood from her mouth and winking at her nephew who returned the wink by sticking his tongue out at her. Xai looked at the other daemoness and could tell it was working. The starting changes were subtle but knowing her for so long Xai could tell. Her animalistic features became more apparent, especially her eyes. Even in her human form, she had a more dangerous aura, the aura of a wolf, of a predator. "That being said I feel a little lightheaded but nothing too dramatic. I think I can continue if you think it is working." The Time Mage nodded.

"The next part I will need all of the Pure Bloods to come towards me, and we need a clean bowl or cup." She looked at Lux's father. He nodded and jogged off to the house closest to the clearing, his own. "Once he is back I will need blood from all of the Pure Bloods and an oath."

"What is the oath?" Dremira asked, walking closer with Kato on her side, both of the daemons standing back uncertain.

"I, state your name, the Pure Blood blank vow to bring forth the Hybrid to protect us all. I swear my oath and loyalty to the champion that I bring forward to our world." Clarita recits. "That is the oath that the gods left us according to the ancient Mages. This needs to be said as you add your blood into the mix. Now we only need a small amount from each of you so nothing much but enough to mix into a swallow for Xai."

"Simple enough." Lux nodded as she watched her father come back with a small clay cup in hand. As he got close enough he handed the cup to the old woman and stepped back to watch again. "Xai can we have your knife?" The feline cleaned it off of her own blood and handed it to the other daemoness. This was the crossroads for each of them, the part where the prophecy came true or died with her.

"Before we begin Truen darling can you go into the treeline and make a structure to keep you and Xai safe while the changes happen? We will not be able to keep her in the village just in case. Something simple should work, we can bring you food and water until it is over but we don't want Xai to think either of you are unsafe until she settles back into herself. We need you far enough but also close enough so the treeline should be fine as long as no one crosses the clearing unless they need to until you exit on your own."

"I would rather be here for this," Truen spoke in defiance. His grip tightened again on her skin.

"Truen please you do not need to see this and you will need the shelter." His grandmother pleaded.

I don't think I can let you go through with this

I will be fine

You cannot promise that

Fine I will be fine when I return to you

You cannot promise that either

Go now.

But I don't want to leave you.

Go now Truen.

But my love please don't send me away.

My Prince I do not want you to see this, none of us do.

I don't agree with this.

I know you don't but please I need you to make us a nice shelter for while I am resting.

I know you are manipulating me right now but fine I will make you something safe for us to rest in while you are recovering.

Please promise to be there when I wake up if I wake up.

389

You will wake up, you promised me you would never leave my side again and you can't go back on it now. We have been through too much.

I do promise Truen, I am just scared.

I am too. But did you ever really think I would leave your side, ever, especially now

Say it, I need to hear you say it.

I promise to be there when you wake up

Okay good, now go. She could feel him hesitate. Just do it please my love. I will return to you soon enough. He nodded and let go of her stiffly. He looked at no one as he walked alone across the clearing and back to where his aunt had deposited them through the portal.

"You did well sending him away." Clarita nodded watching him.

"We need to hurry before he decides not to listen to me at all." Xai forced out passed the fear feeding back and forth through the bond. Nodding the Pure Bloods present stood before the Mage. Lux held the knife figuring she would start, she was the one with Xai from the beginning and the last Pure Blood of the prophecy.

"I, Lux, the Pure Blood daemon vow to bring forth the Hybrid to protect us all. I swear my oath and loyalty to the champion that I bring forward to our world." Lux spoke proudly cutting into her palm and letting the blood drip into the cup. She cleaned off the blade and handed it to the little boy next to her. Quickly she licked her palm to seal the wound.

"I, Kato, son of Xai and Truen, the Pure Blood vampire vow to bring forth the Hybrid to protect us all. I swear my oath and loyalty to the champion that I bring forward to our

390

world." Kato echoed flinching as he cut into his palm, tears falling down his young cheeks at the pain, but the fire in his eyes made Xai so proud. Like his aunt before he let the drops of blood drip into the cup before cleaning the blade and handing it to the shaking woman beside him. Once it was over he reached his injured palm to Xai who reached for a piece of fabric from Clarita to avoid poisoning herself with the young vampire's blood. She did however spit on the rag to rub the saliva into the wound to seal the injury without hurting either of them.

"I, Dremira, the Pure Blood human vow to bring forth the Hybrid to protect us all. I swear my oath and loyalty to the champion that I bring forward to our world." Dremira spoke proudly as she continued to shake. Following the lead of the other two and let the blood of her palm run into the cup before handing the knife back to Lux and her palm to her own partner. Once the blood was collected Clarita swirled the mix together and handed the cup to Xai. Every one of them watched as they took the cup and breathed deeply while looking at the dark liquid inside. For once the powerful Dameoness was hesitating with fear.

Xai?

What?

You had better come back to me, to the pack, to our kids.

I'll see what I can do. She tried to push through some humor that neither felt.

Xai!

No matter what happens I love you Truen and I wouldn't have changed any of it, not if we couldn't stop the sabotage. I would take the pain and the hurt to have our little family all over again, to have you by my side for just a little bit longer.

…Xai…

Hopefully, this won't be our final goodbye but know that I will do everything to come back to you.

Xai that is not funny. Please stop sounding like this is not going to work like you won't come back.

Well, I guess it is time for me to die again. I know I promised you I wouldn't do this again but I am going to have to break this promise.

Xai!

In one fluid movement, she knocked back the liquid like it had been a foul liquor she didn't want to taste. It left a warm feeling in her throat that she tried not to think about. It only took a breath before she couldn't feel the bond, she couldn't feel Truen at all. Before the panic could spread the pain rushed through her. She could feel every drop of blood in her ignite. The pain was almost as all-consuming as losing Truen all those years ago or losing her sister. For a moment she thought she could power through the pain.

"Xai!" She turned to see Truen rushing back across the clearing. Dante tried to intercept him but got thrown with incredible strength for his efforts. Not even Mi'Kal was successful to stop the Prince from getting to his mate. By the time he got to her side her eyes had gone blurry. He caught her as her legs gave out and her body went lax. As her hearing and her sight finally failed her all she could hear was his cries and only see his tears. Then everything was gone, she was gone and only she could make her way back.

Chapter Twenty: Hall of Judgment

Truen couldn't move as he held her body, he could without confirmation that she was gone. Once again he was holding the corpse of his mate and he just had to wait. Tears fell down his face completely unrestrained as he watched her lifeless body looking for any sign of movement. The numbness was taking over his entire body in a way that was eerily similar to losing her the first time.

"I am not even mad you threw me like a child's toy," Dante spoke up a careful distance away. "Though I am mad you have been holding that kind of strength so close to the chest." He was trying to lighten the mood while the Prince's brother ushered the kids away with the help of his own daemoness who looked almost as helpless as the Spell Caster on the ground.

"Truen please you two can not stay here." Mi'Kal pleaded softly. The raven-haired male was still unresponsive even as the rest of the group watched on uncertain of what to do. Even his grandmother was at a loss of what to do, she knew all they could do was wait and hope Xai pulled through. No they all knew she would come back to them the question was would she come back in time? "Let us help." The anigel stepped closer only to have the normally even-tempered to spin on him with a glare that could rival his daemoness'.

"You will not touch her." He hissed with all the pain and anger that he was carrying.

"Don't do this to yourself." Mi'Kal tried again as gently as he could, trying to placate the man but none of them besides Jackdaw had a reference close enough on how to deal with Truen this way.

"I will take her somewhere safe. I don't need your help to take care of my mate. I promised her she would be safe when she woke up, and she will wake up, I will be there beside her like I promised." He stood carefully, never once stumbling with her weight in his arms. They had never before considered the Prince a threat before but this blatant display of strength without his daemoness awake by him made them reconsider. Prince Truen may be as much of a threat as his mate, but he would be a threat no one saw coming. He did not stagger once as they watched him walk into the forest.

The forest itself was silent as he walked into the shade and protection of the trees. Where he was originally going to bunk down with her seemed too vulnerable now so he continued to walk. She seemed both too light in his arms and too heavy as he carried her secured to his chest off the beaten path. He knew he just had to wait for her, she was strong enough to come back to him, as she had before and she will again. The inhabitants of the forest gathered on his invisible path. daemons of all kinds and ages bowed their heads in respect. vampires who had been called to the forest looked down and away unsure of their standing any longer, some feeling discomfort and others trying to hide the fear crushing them. The elves that shared the forest fell to their knees and prayed. Many of those who they passed cried as the aura of sadness and uncertainty followed the strange man who carried a daemon who seemed to have been lost.

None knew who they were but knew that the world was darker now. Truen himself was silent throughout the journey. Eventually, he was left alone with a stillness that felt as if the forest was mourning, she was gone only temporarily and yet was causing such grief. The cries of the forest and its inhabitants were enough to make Truen pray for the first time since she left and he begged her to be returned. In the current safety of his mind, he prayed and begged for them to bring her back to him. The world needed her but he needed her more. He was certain he was the reason that the sun was covered by clouds the moment she fell and why the rains had come so suddenly but he couldn't care enough to control his magic. If he had to weep at her death, even if she would return, then the world had to cry beside him. The world put too much on her and would suffer by his side until she was returned to him. He would force the gods to bring her back to him if he had to. He had every ability in him to be a bigger villain than his father could dream of. Even the shadow man would have nothing on him if his mate was lost to him. He would protect their pack and destroy everything the gods cared about until she was alive in his arms again. Or until they could find a way to stop him and bury him next to her.

He would not live without her again without a fight and he could promise anyone who was listening of that. Eventually, after walking around the forest for what seemed like an eternity Truen found a cave that was suitable. Walking into the natural stone structure and assessed the decent-sized dwelling. Nodding to himself he pushed some of his magic into the ground forcing soft plants to sprout from the barren dirt forming a patch of luscious green that was comfortable enough for him to lay her on gently. Even lost to him she deserved comfort. He made short work of making the cave inhabitable for a time. He was lost enough that none would dare to try and track him down until they both came back. It pained him to leave her long enough to bring back firewood so they could have warmth for a few days.

Each time he left for another reason caused anxiety to spike through the pain even when he knew it was necessary. He hunted to make sure they both would have food, he gathered wild herbs and vegetables for the same. Magic allowed him to make a fire and a pool of drinking water but he knew he couldn't use his pool of magic for everything, especially when his emotions were pulling his magic out of his control once more. He remembered the storms he created when she ran, it took his mother to fix the rivers and the earthquakes. He couldn't have cared less at the time, he tried so hard to not let negative emotions control his magic after his mother showed him the true damage he caused back then. He had never thought of himself as having such an ability for destruction or cruelty but without Xai by his side, he found he easily could. It scared him at one point when his father had told him how proud he was of the actions. Then he turned the destruction inwards and almost killed himself in the process. Jackdaw barely saved him from himself, only Xai could truly do that. Only Xai could save the world from him.

Xai felt like she was underwater. It was hard for her to move but possible. Closer maybe to treading water than being underwater, she decided. Everything around her was blurred, nothing had color or feeling at all. Maybe she was suspended in the air? She couldn't hear anything, opened her mouth to scream and nothing came out. There was no sense where ever she was. She only vaguely remembered how she got here. Something important and drinking from a cup. More importantly, she remembered someone crying, someone she had to get back to.

Don't worry my child. A beautiful voice filled her mind, filling the silence. It was a voice that was familiar. A voice she had heard before somewhere. I promised you that you would not walk this path alone. *I am here to help you through your trials just as I promised I would. You will make it through.* Before her vision cleared. A woman was there. She stood proud and tall, her skin as pale and luminescent as the moon. Her hair was long and somehow darker than the void they were in. The dress that draped over her body was like the night sky, full of stars that moves slightly depending on how she looked. Xai looked back at her face to notice that her skin was devoid of colors that were not gray or white, except her eyes, they were a deep black that felt endless, unlike her hair. Through all of her beauty, she was blank, empty, as if a fragment of what she truly was. *Do you recognize me Xai?* She tried to shake her head but couldn't muster the strength to do such a simple task. *I know you can speak with your mind, you do it with your Prince all the time. The void can only take from you what you let it.* Suddenly memories of Truen flooded through her, returning to her. He was who she needed to return to, he was the one who was crying.

I remember how I remember now doing this with Truen.

Good, do not let the void take from you or you may not get it back. I can only help so much with that aspect. Keep him in your heart and you will return to him. Remember all you can and you will come out stronger than we ever imagined. Remember your friends, your children, your pack, and your purpose. More memories flooded through her in a rush. *She remembered it all, the prophecy, the plan, how she got here, and those she needed to return to.*

Luna?

Yes my child, remember me as well and let me help. We need to get you through as fast as we can to save the others from both the saboteur and your Prince, he is willing to burn the world for your return.

I do not doubt that. He wouldn't be my mate if he wasn't as dangerous as I am.

I need to rethink how I match those who have the ability to become the Hybrid. She shook her head with a hollow smile.

If my opinion matters I think that you need someone as willing to protect the Hybrid and fight for them while they fight for your world. I know I forget that I am mortal. He reminds me and reminds me what I have to fight for.

That is fair, you are quite wise. Sometimes it is hard to remember that those who we have chosen can not remember that they are worth fighting for as much as they fight for others even when they didn't need to be awakened. We can talk about it when we get to where we are going.

Where are we going?

To the hall of judgment. It is where the dead go to determine if they get punishment or paradise of their choosing traditionally. The judges are the ones we need to see.

Why are they important if I am not truly dead?

Well if you do not pass their judgment you will stay here for one, and two the judges are all those before you that held the power of the Hybrid within them. Those who came before you and their mates stay here and help others, they have the choice to rest in a paradise but most can not think of resting when others need help, especially others in their own unique situations.

If I don't pass their judgment I could remain dead? Why didn't you warn anyone of that?

We had, that is why there are usually two candidates per generation, one is chosen and one in reserves. Apparently, the Mages didn't write that down. Your Hybrid partner disappeared years ago when you were both children so you were the only one we had. If you pass though you are no longer mortal by the sense of daemons though, and neither is Truen if it helps.

I know you are a god but you better pray I make it back to him.

Trust me for many reasons we are all praying to each other for your return. Between the one pulling the strings and your Prince, I thought of forcing the change through but if you don't pass judgment your body wouldn't handle it anyways.

Is it only those who were potential Hybrids that I have to impress?

Impress, yes only those who would have been where you are now. But they are not the only ones that will be here to see you. The current speakers of the gods are here too.

I have heard of them before. I thought they were myths or people who were zealots who thought they were important.

Oh, many who claim that are just that but Sol, Terra, and I all have one who helps us. Though this will be the first time I will have been able to see them since we were trapped. Thankfully the awakening of a Hybrid seems to have bypassed whatever spell has been put on me. I was hoping but I wasn't sure when I told you originally. She admitted.

I guess I am supposed to be glad that celestial power versus magic did not make you a liar.

Me too honestly. Now Terra's is called by the title mother Nature, she is always a female human. Sol chose a male anigel called the Archanigel. Mine is a daemon and their title changes depending on if they are male or female. Currently, she carries the title of Saten but the man after her will be Devile. These are the people you will work with to preserve peace, they will actually be helping a lot finding us and finding the saboteur once I can talk to them.

Anything else I need to know about before we arrive?

I did find information on your family that might help you understand some things.

Such as what? What gossip about my family could be so important now?

Your mother and father are not mates.

I could have told you that.

They were mates to each other's siblings. Your mother was meant to be with your father's brother and your father's mate looked incredibly similar to your mother, it was her friend. When the two of them died your mother and father wed in respect for them and your mother gave everything, and began to hate all that stood for hope and greatness. They both lost everything, then in their hatred yet respect they had you and your sister, and lost your sister. She was supposed to go through this with you but as I said she was lost. But she has gone through something similar to what you are about to, she has wanted to reunite with you and Jackdaw and the young Prince. So she passed and no wanders waiting for you to awaken, looking for you, and now she will know and she will find you, once you cross through the gate and awaken.

So you are saying not only my pack and mate wait for me on the other side but my sister does as well? And this is all because of a freak accident that took my parent's real mate?

Remember why you fight and you will find out more and how it all connects back to each other.

I will don't worry.

Do you see the gates? Behind the goddess, there was a set of large metal gates that had not been there before. It was the only thing in the surrounding that had definition or color.

Behind you yes.

Then you are ready for judgment. I will be beside you. Even when you can't see me I walk beside you.

Then let us get this over with so we can get back and kick some ass. She smiled and gestured to the gates. Finally, Xai's body began to move and she did not hesitate.

Days had passed since Xai fell and Truen did nothing besides take care of her body and stand watch. She looked so peaceful to him but that peace only tore through him. There were times he could swear that he felt something in the bond, longing, and determination. He tried sending something back when he felt it but he couldn't. A dream of her floating in a colorless void haunted him anytime he tried to sleep. The last few hours he got he heard whispers of a conversation though and one of those voices belonged to his lost heart. It was haunting him, he didn't know how much longer he would keep it together, he knew already his storms were flooding areas before he stopped them. If not for those whispered conversations he would have already started out against the world. He couldn't yet because Xai would be mad when she awoke and he wasn't here next to her.

He had a promise to her to keep and it was more important than the promises that he made to the gods if they did not return her to him. The Prince didn't know how long to wait with her lifeless body. Three days had already passed at a slow and agonizing pace. Occasionally he would wonder how the others were if they were safe from his grief. He knew their children were, his magic would never hurt them. He knew that as much as he knew his magic would never hurt Xai. He knew that he would have to go for Kato and Hestia before he laid waste to this world if and when he had to. But he didn't know if the others would work with him or try to stop his wrath. Truen knew that he hid his rage from the entire world except for Xai who fed from it and turned it into raw power. Part of him wondered if anyone other than his brothers would see it coming.

Maybe he could take care of the shadow man in the process and take care of Xai's task while holding the world hostage for her return. The forest never returned a counterargument for his musings as he sat in the otherwise silent cave waiting. Unbeknownst to him those who knew him better than others prayed for the storms they knew he created to cease before he did damage that they could not recover from before he came back to the mild-tempered man they knew and adored. The gods themselves pleaded with his mate to hurry in the trials before they were caught in the storms as well.

One moment Xai was walking towards the gates and next she was in a room made of light iridescent stone. Along the center wall, there were seven empty chairs that she could not quite call thrones but ceremonial nonetheless. There in the direct center and two on each side are slightly separated. She could only guess those were for the people she was waiting for, the people she was part of. Another blink in time and the seats were occupied. Each entity is robed in color. The three in the center were in ornate robes; one in white, one in green, and one in purple, the others all in simple gray fabric. Each body kept its hood up to obscure what they could, masks covering their faces.

A wing mask for the anigel who speaks for Sol? An ivy mask for the human who speaks for Terra? Very on the nose for both of you. At least the daemon's mask of patchwork is interesting and begs for questions. She sighed. Those wearing gray wore plain masks, she could feel their amusement and surprise at calling the titled ones out. The green-shrouded woman threw her head back and laughed in delight, her laugh like bells on the wind; soothing and dramatic. The daemoness snorted in amusement at the one in front of her.

Of course, the daemoness chosen had to be a spitfire. The Angiel sighed, clearly amused. If you pass the trial then we will look forward to working with you Xai Lurra.

Of course, she is a spitfire, how else would she have gotten this far? The daemoness countered, the human woman finally calming herself enough to breathe.

And what is the trial then? Xai asked impatiently. I thought there were many.

There were many, you passed most of them so far my child. You only have one left and it is the trial of intent. The human answered sweetly

You willingly followed the prophecy to save the innocent. The anigel added. *That is determination.*

You were willing to forsake everything for the bonds you made during the journey, even defying the gods to keep everyone safe. The daemoness continued. *The trail of compassion.*

This entire journey through you drinking the poison to bring you here is the trial of determination, though that is set outside of any of our control. The anigel sighed. *That is the longest trial and the one that starts everything.*

The trial of strength was getting here and remembering why you need to go back. The daemoness added in once more.

All of these things are the core essence of the Hybrid, but the trial of intent will determine if you are the right choice of those who carry the ability. The human finished. *The trials start the moment you are needed, many of those who COULD become the Hybrid never needs to be so the trials never start and they make it through their life in peace. Unfortunately is to bring peace not live in it. Only times such as these will start the trials. You are not the only one who had the ability to become the*

Hybrid but you were the one we have been cheering for. You have passed every trial without the help you would normally receive and with flying colors.

Never have we seen someone so worthy of becoming an awakened Hybrid, those you see around us were the closest anyone has come before you. Most though never were called for so they held onto the core essence with no trial. The anigel gestured around to those shrouded in gray, each nodding. *They wanted to help past their death even though they were never called upon so they help with the passage of those lost to our world.*

Then my brethren I thank you for your service, let me make our names and our title known. You will not remain in the shadows just because you never received your chance in the light. Give me my final trial so I can fix what I left behind to be here. I need to get back. Xai spoke clearly, standing straight and determined.

As you wish daemoness. We will ask you questions and you shall answer. Honesty is your best choice for your brethren will be judging you. They are the ones who will decide if you belong with them or not. The daemoness spoke, and the smile she wore behind her mask could be heard in her voice as she watched her kin. They were clearly already proud of the candidate in front of them.

Then ask me and judge me, I have things to do, people to protect, a kingdom to save, and a war to win. They all nodded, she felt that was the correct answer to have given them. The four in simple robes stood and stepped closer to Xai, she readied herself for whatever they would ask.

Have you ever wronged a person? One asked. She could not tell which one.

Yes, I have, I have purposely and accidentally wronged many, maybe even inadvertently. But such is being alive, no one is innocent of such a crime. She answered impassively. *I can almost guarantee even if it was not the intent all of you before me have done wrong by many as well.*

Do you regret it? The voice came again, it was hard to tell if it was a different person or the same since the voice was coming from many directions.

Some I do and some I don't. If they were wronged by accident or as collateral then yes, I can honestly say I regret it, But there have been many instances no matter how small the wrong was that they deserved what they received. Justice is not always clean nor served with respect.

If we let you return to the land of the living with or without the power of the Hybrid would you continue to wrong people on purpose? They continued.

Most likely. I can not think that no one will consider what I am about to do to the King as anything but a wrong. If it is to save those in need I will bear the burden of wronging others. Think what you will but it was already said you lived in peace and not war and death. Wrongs will come, people will die, and people are already dying who were innocent and did not get retribution for the wrongs committed against them for existing. Xia answered calmly.

What are you so impatient to return to if not those you wish to free? What could be as important as those in need of rescue? Luna herself had warned her not to forget what was important outside of her duty. Her attachments were what would get her back, not her powers.

For one thing, my presence in the world has been a call for hope, and whispers of plans and my name have been shared throughout the land. I am a point of hope and I can not let that be ripped from those who need it, the people who were supposed to be being protected before we got to this point. But that is not what I am desperate to get back to as selfish as it is. She sighed. *I need to get back to the family that I built, my pack needs me. Lux and Jackdaw, my siblings and best friends, can not hold down everything alone. I know they are strong but not strong enough to lose another person and keep the pack together meaning they would all lose each other as well. I need to get back to my children Kato and Hesita who I would not have found without this damn prophecy. I need to get back to Dremira and Crazden who need freedom from the overbearing society they were raised in but don't think they deserve it. And I need to get back to Mi'Kal and Dante who were ready to lose everything to fight by my side because of what I stand for. I need to get back to the Mages in the Underground still hiding but they welcomed us as strangers and family that had been lost to them. And sure as shit do I need to get back to my mate, my heart, and my Handler who is probably ready to become the biggest threat to the world we are all supposed to be protecting. I have always known the danger beneath his skin if he thinks someone he loves is in danger. He would be willing to destroy anything for me to be returned to him and there would be no one alive who would be able to stop him before he had destroyed almost everything.* Xai cleared her throat, not expecting so much emotion to come through. *I also feel the call of my sister who was lost to me. Lui will only come back to me on the battlefield so I need to get back to her as well. I live, I fight, I survive for my pack, my family, and not least but definitely, last I need to get back for Chemerica as a whole.*

And if you can not save your Kingdom? They asked with a sense of finality. The question made the daemoness smirk something dangerous causing those who stood before her back up and those who were still seated lean forward in anticipation.

That isn't an option. I will free my people or die trying, even in death though I promise you now that I will not stop until they are free and safe. Something in the room settled at her final answer.

Then there is no reason to push this off longer Xai Lurra. Welcome to the Hall of Judgment Hybrid. You are the first of our kind worth awakening. We look forward to standing beside you for eternity. You have been tested and you have passed them all like the goddess Luna expected. They sounded relieved.

I had no doubt in her. Luna's voice entered the chamber, standing beside Xai out of nowhere. *You will get used to the way time works here once you have awakened and are not a visiting soul I promise. That being said, it is time for you to return to your world while I discuss with the speakers. I will be with you soon Xai and do ask your mate to calm the storms. We have no reason to ever want to have him become the villain in our world.* She smiled at Xai, placing her hand on her forehead. It is time for you to wake up. The daemoness' body began to feel warm finally before everything went dark once more.

Truen felt unbalanced. Almost as if he was being judged through the bond that had been sealed to him. Five days since Xai had left them and he was beginning to believe that she would not come back this time. Five days of storms and flooding. His pool of magic was finally beginning to feel a dredge on his body with the size and severity of the storms he had conjured without care. He watched the stillness of the forest, feeling the heat of his fire on his back. He couldn't continue to watch her still body any longer. It was an illusion as if she were just sleeping peacefully on the bed he had created for her.

"I hope you haven't drowned the world while I was away love, the gods themselves had to ask me to stay your magic claiming and I quote 'We have no reason to ever want to have him become the villain in our world.'" Her voice startled him from his thoughts. Spinning around he looked straight into the purple eyes that haunted his dreams in the most beautiful ways. She was stretched out comfortably, resting up on her elbow watching him from the foliage bed. For the first time in days, the storms calmed, and sunlight started to peak from the clouds. Xai was back in the world and she was more dangerous than she had ever been. For her and her alone he would be a tamed man, and maybe that is what the world needed. Both he and the world needed her to walk the land and she had fought death and judgment itself to make sure she could be here for those who needed her.

Chapter Twenty One: The True Hybrid

It took Truen only moments to rush to her side. Tears welled in his eyes as he placed his hands on her and watched her breathe. For a moment they said nothing as she reached for him, pulling him down on top of her so she could hold him. For such a strong man she knew that by design she was the weakness in him. If someone who could be a Hybrid was a threat by definition of the universe then their mates were guaranteed to be as well. It was true that she had always known the cruelty that he could be capable of, how could she not when she had known his father for so long? Truen and his brothers had terrifying control of natural phenomena from elements to time to gravity like Jhelum. That was not even discussing the intelligence and the skills in battle that came with being members of the Royal family. The boys she grew up with were all dangerous, Truen the most of all and it was easy to forget when he was like this with her. By her side he was compassionate and gentle, he never truly wanted any sort of control though he was good in a room of people.

It is part of what made them work so well. He was a threat that she quelled and she was a threat that he empowered. Together their morals brought each other back from the edge of what made powerful people truly dangerous. She held him as he broke apart in her arms. The bond had reopened upon her awakening and she could feel the fear and doubt that her absence had caused. He had not been entirely sure that she would come back to him, she could feel the regret for letting the darkness closer to the surface and letting it spread his magic while she wasn't there to keep it at bay. He felt weak and relieved now but soon there would be regret in not being able to trust her return or his willingness to destroy everything to get back to her side. A deep-seated part of her was proud of the power her other half held at his fingertips knowing that he would stop at nothing for her and their children. For such a good man to be willing to do something so easily for her protection, the strength he would be willing to expend until he didn't have to anymore.

"I am here my love, no need to threaten the world anymore. We are supposed to be saving it, remember?" She teased carefully when his breathing returned to normal.

"I will do what I need to so I can insure your return to me." He mumbled into her shoulder.

"I know my love. But you got impatient for my return and you probably scared our pack and possibly our mothers since they know your magic." She continued to rub her hands over his back letting him cling to her form. "How long did the storms continue?"

"You were lost for five days, I gave up control the moment you fell." He barely whispered, embarrassment flooding the bond not that she needed the bond to tell as the back of his neck tinted red in embarrassment. She smirked knowing that giving up control the moment she fell caused more embarrassment for the man than some of the other things she has seen him do throughout their lives. "You don't understand, when you left this world to face the trials something went through the world. On our way here there were Elves, vampires, and daemons alike who stopped and cried. I was numb to everything but something changed in the air and everything knew that you were gone. I am not sure they would know you were back but hope seemed to die with you." He argued against his blush into her neck.

"I am sorry you felt that, that anyone felt anything in this instance. I knew I would be back the moment I regained myself there. Luna was there to help as she promised. I did not know I would be gone for so long. Time works strangely there when you are a soul. It felt like only moments for me." She reassured him. "I was always coming back to you I just didn't think that it would take that long in your eyes."

"I couldn't feel anything except small wisps from you while you were gone."

"Part of me wants to apologize for the stress that this put you under but we both knew I was going to have to do this. I know we were not prepared for the entirety but we knew it would happen."

"I know I don't want an apology dear heart I just need to confirm that this is not a hallucination."

"No, it is not I am back and here to stay until we end this. Though we can not leave them alone for too long. I was gone long enough to make the full moon in a handful of days. We have to see what has changed while I was away and create the final plan now that we have access to the prophesied weapon that we have been tracking for months." The reminder made the Prince finally release his would-be wife and look at her. The differences were subtle but there. Her eyes burned like a purple fire that was alive, her spots darker and more pronounced, her fangs sharper like a vampire's. Her aura had been dangerous before but now he could feel the power in the air around her that made him want to listen to any request she could ask, not that he needed help doing such but now it felt like a life or death decision instead of one of pleasure. Somehow even her natural colors seemed more extreme.

"You look the same but also different, you feel more powerful." He breathed. The bond had reopened for both of them and the power he could feel from his daemoness' side was almost overwhelming. Together they would not be able to be stopped on whichever path they went, at least that is what it

411

felt like. He had never felt such power before and it was all residing under his Queen's skin.

"That is because I am the same my love just tapped into the celestial power that I was born with. Now I have access to the power the gods set aside for the Hybrids and I know who my potential allies are on the other side." She chuckled at the awe in his voice. "To be fair though I can say the same for you, this is the first time I am ever seeing you with scruffy facial hair. It looks good on you my mate, more rugged. I might have to convince you to keep it for a time."

"I love you." He breathed out. The bond was full of adoration, pride, and unsurprisingly lust. She discovered his love of her power early in their reconnected relationship, back in the cabin. He loved that she would have no problem at all stopping those darker thoughts, he was no danger to anyone with her around because he had no chance against her.

"I know you do dear but what happened to no more soft moments until that crown was on your head?"

"You went from one of the most powerful daemons in the kingdom to one of the most powerful beings in the world. I don't have any doubt that you could storm the castle alone and slaughter all those who stand in your way."

"But would that stop you or any of the others from tearing your father's corrupt court down person by person on the night of the full moon?"

"No, but now I know none of the casualties will be on our side. They can't be with you leading us."

"Just keep in mind dearest that we have been warned many times that this is the first battle of this war. This will be the easy part I fear." She sighed pushing him off gently onto the foliage bed. Carefully she lifted herself, standing for the first time in days but also standing in her physical body for the first time with so much extra power coursing through her veins. "I will need to get used to this as well so I don't hurt anyone I care for or do too much damage to things that don't warrant the carnage." She smiled, clenching and unclenching her fingers. "It feels like the first time I tapped into my Pure daemonic blood, I got used to it relatively soon the last time, and I will do so again now. She looked back at him still laying there where she left him. "Are you ready to get back to our pack or do you need a moment more?" She asked gently.

"I just need to quell the magic that I laid down while you were away then we should be able to make it back in a few hours. Though I wish to know if losing you caused such a rift in the world to which many people felt your loss do you think they felt your return?"

"I am not sure, to be honest, I don't even know how they knew that I left the living world even for a moment." She shrugged watching him leave himself. With a mere flick of his wrist the babbling pond that she had not noticed in the cave dried, and the fire she had noticed died. "Sometimes I forget how much magic you possess." She chuckled at him. "Maybe that is the connection, those that have magic inherently in their blood whether or not it is like yours. Elves, daemons, and vampires all have a small bit of magic in them, some even being able to harness it like the Mages or Spell Casters. This forest is also embedded in magic, it is why so many colonies and villages can hide in it without detection. This forest has also been known to protect those who live here hence why many Solars will tell others that the forest is dangerous and haunted but as you can see many do not have any such issues or concerns."

413

"Meaning that if it is a connection to magic many through the kingdom or the world would have felt your death but would they feel the hope return with you?"

"I don't know but they will when we put the crown on your head and I stand next to the new King of Chemerica." She smiled again. He stepped to her and hugged her tight against him again before breathing deeply and releasing her.

"Do not give me that look, you have not had to deal with your mate die on you multiple times. This was exactly what I wanted to do when we were reunited but I held back. I no longer need to hold back and I refuse to do that to myself ever again." Her smile softened at his determination.

"You don't need to hold yourself back Truen, we are long past that. We have more than our share of trials, tribulations, and sabotage in our relationship. Never again, we were born mates and that is what we will continue to be."

"Together we will turn this kingdom around. Together we will be on the throne, wearing the crowns, and leading our people." Truen smiled.

"No one can stop us from setting everyone that we can free," I told those who set to give me judgment that failure to save our people was not an option. Not now not ever. We will storm the castle, we will remove your father, then we will set to set those enslaved free and bring back those that we can from who were stolen."

"Let us not forget to stop the shadow and save the gods in the mix."

"Or politics but I am leaving that to you." She pointed back to him.

"But of course, your thought in diplomacy is that most politicians and court members are morons."

"I haven't been proven wrong yet on that." She quirked her brow at him. Her amused expression was sharper and more attractive than before. "Let us leave before you get too distracted by the changes to my appearance and we don't leave until sundown." She smirked again. He sighed filling the bond with begrudging acceptance to make her laugh as he gestured to the entrance of the cave they have inhabited. They laughed and joked calmly on their walk back to the village, the journey back empty of all of those who had watched Truen pass on the way there. Part of Truen hoped that when the tremor went through the world it came back when she had or the world would continue to be without will or hope for a few days more. It had not taken nearly as long as Truen remembered to return to the clearing outside of Lux's childhood home. He could see the people gathering in the streets of the small village enjoying the sun for the first time in days. He caught the sight of his brother watching the treeline knowingly as soon as individuals came into view. His blonde hair was untied and waving around in the gentle breeze. Lux stood beside him watching as well, the wolfish smile crossing her face as she saw them first whispering something to her mate. "We have been spotted already, I am assuming the Pure Blood transition for Lux has helped that along."

"No doubt at all. Though I can not wait to see any of them I am excited to see the children, I might need to apologize to them if I scared them with the storms." He sounded apprehensive for the first time about his actions while away in their cave.

"You are their father, you are a good father so they probably knew they were in no danger if they knew it was you." She reassured as they made their way across the clearing.

The feline could hear her friend calling for the others announcing their return. The entire pack was collected by the time they strolled across the field.

"Welcome back you two." Lux smiled. "I see that you survived. Congratulations on somehow becoming more dangerous." The dark-haired daemoness smirked.

"Of course fangs what would you have me do? More Pure Bloods in the world? No, I have to be unique." The daemoness teased back. The newly branded Hybrid looked over her friend. Her normally silver eyes were now molten gold, and her hair was now patterned the same dark timber as her coat instead of a flat darkness. Her ears could not be hidden anymore without glamor much like all other Pure Blood daemons. They twitched with the sounds of the forest and the village around her. Sometimes Xai forgot the basics of not being a Pure Blood versus being one. She had no doubt her friend would need time to get used to the heightened senses and the power under her skin.

"Oh you are definitely unique Xai, you will never have to worry about that." She snorted reaching out to hug her friend. "But we aren't the ones you should be checking on first." She stepped back to see the two youngest members of their pack looking around apprehensive. Xai knelt down in the mud with her arms wide and no words, that is all it took for her children to run to her.

"Oh my darlings, I am sorry you had to see that. I am back though with no plans to leave you again." She hugged them tight to her. She lifted them into her arms so the Prince could join in the moment.

"And I am sorry little ones if my storms scared you," Truen spoke softly to his children. "I wouldn't let them harm you but I know they can be scary, I never wanted you to be scared of my magic."

"They didn't scare us." Hestia protested with large ember eyes.

"We wanted to stay with you while we waited for mama to return," Kato said stubbornly. Xai and Truen looked at each other in surprise. The children had taken to calling them mother and father but something so innocent as a mama? That was new.

"Uncle said that Papa was suffering alone and that is why the storms came. Why didn't you bring us with you to watch over mama together?" Hestia pouted, and both of the children refused to let go of their parents. When they had left they had to deal with something that would make a hardened warrior shudder and they came back to their children being even more like children. This only steadied Xai's resolve to get their children into a world that was safe.

"I am sorry then little ones. Your uncle was correct and I don't know if I could have taken care of you while I was watching over your mama. I wasn't strong enough to do both and that was selfish but I needed you to be safe while I couldn't keep you safe." Truen explained taking Hesita and Kato into his own arms, holding the children closely.

"We as a pack looked after the children and each other while you were away. We tried not to let them worry or think that they were missing anything. We are glad you have returned to us. We were worried you would not be able to return to us all this time" Mi'Kal smiled happily. "And seeing your transformation does bring a lot of relief as well. The fulfillment of the prophecy bodes well for all of us"

417

"Yeah, kid you had us worried as hell, though I am a little upset with your Prince here." Dante nodded light-heartedly towards Truen who had set the children down. When Xai looked over at him he just shrugged.

"What could Truen have done to upset you, I know it wasn't the storms though they are something to behold when he unleashes his magic."

"Yeah, that was more than I thought he had in his arsenal." Dante chuckled placing his hand comfortably on Truen's shoulder. "Nah I am more taken aback that he threw me damn near across the field to get to you. Your man was hiding more physical strength close to the chest. We could have had some sparring matches skin to skin."

"Watch how you speak Dante or I might get jealous of the images you are creating while talking about Xai's mate." Mi'Kal teased, his face impassive but his blacked-out eyes twinkled in mischief making his partner drop his hand from the Prince and wrap around his anigel's waist. The anigel let his blackened wings puff out a bit in defiance.

"I would never think such things of another love." He backpedaled before placing his face in the pale man's neck. Once he could no longer see his lover's face the anigel let his smirk break across his face.

"To be fair Dante how did you not know that he was physically strong?" Xai sighed trying to cover her amusement to play along. "You have seen him carry me with ease. I am not some human, no offense Dremira, or an Elf. I am sure the only ones here who are heavier than the daemons in the area are the dragons. Though Crazden doesn't count since he is part dragon part daemon." She could see the others try to stifle their laughter as he lifted his head she quirked her brow at him. "I know you are used to your feather-light anigel but they are

418

just as light as a feather compared to anything not born for flight."

"She isn't wrong." Lux joined in the teasing. "Especially larger daemons like Xai and I. Crazden would more than likely be lighter than us if not for the fact he is part lizard." She smirked at the taller quiet man. She only earned herself a playful glare in return which was a massive improvement from how they had met. Dremira was forced to hide her smile behind her hand to keep the ruse going.

"Honestly you have no one to blame but yourself for assuming the mate of a daemon would be weak just because he is a magic user."

"You are all assholes." Dante sighed thoroughly embarrassed at the assumption.

"Ah, but would you have it any other way?" Jackdaw asked innocently.

"Shit no. If you can't tease each other there is no true trust." He sighed with a smile finally standing back and stretching.

"What a nice reunion, do you think that a few more faces could be added in?" A melodic voice crossed the field from the same direction that Xai and Truen had entered. The voice caught everyone's attention but only made three stop dead in their tracks. "Now that was not quite what I had in mind. Then again it has been ages since I have seen you three. How different you two look, my boys." Slowly Xai and Truen confirm their suspicion. The hooded figures stepped not far away, only three people. Lux tried to step in front of Jackdaw but he stopped her in both of their disbelief.

"You are a ghost to be fair." The other figure, a man, answered that causing Mi'Kal to tense as well. The woman laughed in a way that brought memories flooding back in Xai. The daemoness stepped forward carefully causing the smaller figure to tilt their head. Xai stepped again into the shrouded one's space, removing her hood and letting white hair fall down her back, white ears with small tan tips twitching back and forth in excitement. A huge smile was across the fair skin that was spotted with light tan marks similar to the daemoness before her. But what caught everyone's attention was the familiar purple eyes that missed nothing no matter how relaxed the strange daemoness before them seemed.

"I told you I would be here." She hummed.

"Lui?" Jackdaw's voice broke as he spoke the name that haunted him.

"Hello darling, I hope your mate has been treating you well?" She looked around at her sister happily. "I look forward to meeting her, Xai has told me a bit about her."

"Mama?" Kato called carefully from Truen's side.

"Mama? You gained children and didn't decide that was important to tell me in the dreamscape." Her sister snapped back to the stunned Hybrid's face, the smaller smacking her sister's arm before making a beeline to the children. Carefully lowering herself to her knees in the dirt to be on their level. "Hello, little ones. My name is Lui, I am your mama's sister. That makes me your other Auntie. I knew your dad? And Uncle growing up."

"You grew up with papa?" Hestia asked from behind the still-stunned Prince's leg.

"Yep, I have so many fun stories from when we were your age." She scrunched her face getting the children to laugh. Xai turned to watch as Truen came back to his senses and hauled his childhood best friend off the ground and into his arms, hugging her like he had done her sister not long before.

"I can't believe you are here." He whispered as he let her go.

"And I can't believe you are trying to grow a beard yet here we are." She teased removing herself from his arms. She turned to look at Lux suddenly more seriously. "You are the one who helped those I was taken from and I can never thank you enough for that. You stood beside my sister and you helped raise up who should have been my Handler. I would like us to be friends and fight beside each other. But first, may I hug your partner?" She very calmly waited for Lux to respond knowing how important this moment was between the two of them. This was the catalyst of the sabotage returning of her own free will from wherever she had been held. This was the void Lux had tried to fill in Xai's life before realizing she created her own space. This was the woman who had held every right to be her mate's first daemon. And here this small powerful woman was asking permission to hug one of the people she missed the most in the world.

"Well we are to be sisters aren't we?" Lux sighed nodding her head at the smaller woman. Lui smiled brightly before all about bouncing towards the blonde and holding onto him for dear life. "She is your other brother's mate correct?" Lux asked Truen with anxiety in her eyes.

"Krutz, yes she is the mate to our feistiest brother. And don't let her smaller stature or bubblier personality confuse you she is in fact as dangerous as Xai always has been." Truen smiled. "But you have nothing to worry about her and

421

Jackdaw, there were always best friends. They had a similar bond to Xai and I thought from what I know it was more empathetic than telepathic. The Lurra children and the children of the crown were raised to be intrical to each other, there was not a time where you couldn't find a group of us together. Though as you know that all changed when Jhelum died and Lui was stolen, to be fair until right now we all thought she was dead. Even Xai did and she had spoken to her in dreams."

"Do not worry Lux you are as much my sister as she is. I have said as much multiple times with multiple people yourself included."

"I know, but it will take a bit of adjustment and I don't think the heightened everything of the transformation for myself is helping. I can smell how dangerous she is. Not as dangerous as you but still. She is a predator that can pass off as prey." Xai looked around at their grouping. Most were watching the reunion in silent interest except for Mi'Kal who had yet to remove his eyes from the second hooded figure who had yet to move away from Xai. The daemoness could feel the man beside her discomfort with the anigel watching him. The third had remained a few steps back as if they were waiting for a reason to step in or run.

"Please tell me it is true." Mi'Kal's voice sounded nearly as broken as Jackdaw's only moments before. The man beside Xai shifted, and the smell of ozone and down reached her, an anigel. "Asher? Please tell me that is you." The anigel pleaded holding onto Dante for support. The darker man looked between them as if he was hoping the answer was the hooded anigel was the one his partner was looking for. Lui looked over from her entanglement with the blonde Prince who was still clinging onto her like she was going to vanish before his eyes…again.

"You know Asher?" She asked carefully, obviously unsure of how to act until she knew the answer. She was protective of this one, Xai could guess her sister was protective of both of them.

"Asher is my little brother. We lost our other siblings and only had each other. I would have done anything to protect him and we were as close as could be. But when I fell I could not take him with me. It would have killed him, it almost killed me. I asked Dante to help me find him but not even Kila could find him." His wings lay limp showing more emotion than he had before. Normally Mi'Kal was impassive, keeping emotions close to his chest, occasionally teasing or comforting, he was mischievous, not emotional. They had always attributed it to anigel society and this sudden shift was unlike anything anyone outside of Dante or Kila had ever seen. The dragon herself finally showed herself from under Dante's jacket to comfort her other person's palpable distress.

The man beside Xai dropped his hood and let his piercing blue eyes stare into the dark depths of the other anigel in determination of whatever he expected, his brother's tears not what he thought he would meet. Dante held Mi'Kal to him noticing how uncomfortable the younger anigel was at the older's desperate attempts to get to him. Looking him over he was taller than his brother and though their features were incredibly similar the differences were more noticeable. His skin was tanner than his pale brother, and his face alone was littered with scars. He appeared to be thinner and less muscular than his older brother but it was hard to tell with the cloak still firmly wrapped around him. His light blonde hair was shorter than his brother's long white hair and much more unkempt. He held so much more color than his brother and Xai could only wonder to herself if that was just their natural difference or did Mi'Kal lose more than his anigelic eyes in his fall.

"Hello, brother." The anigel Asher finally spoke again, his voice slightly thicker with emotion than before. A sob tore from Mi'Kal at the words. Asher looked back towards the last remaining hooded figure who still stayed behind.

"May I touch you?" He asked quietly. Once the younger gave a nod Xai stepped out of the way and closer to Truen who had been watching as well, hell they all stopped to watch another emotional reunion that no one on either side had expected. Once she was out of the way Dante loosened his grasp on his lover and let him run to his brother. The normally graceful man almost fell over himself to get to his brother. They collided and almost ended up on the dirt together if not for Mi'Kal's wings balancing them. They watched as the elder brother wrapped his arms tightly around the younger, the younger blonde hesitantly returned the hug only to cling just as desperately a mere heartbeat later.

"I never thought I would get to see you again Mi'Kal," Asher spoke quietly. Before more could be said a truly broken noise came from the black-winged anigel. Everyone was brought to alert at the noise. Dante looked ready to pummel whatever made his lover make such a noise.

"Asher, where are your wings?" Mi'Kal gasped.

Chapter Twenty Two: Family Ties

"Brother do not ask that question." Asher looked pained at the question. He refused to look his brother in the eyes.

"Asher please where are your wings?" The elder begged.

"Asher you need to tell him what happened." Finally, a voice came through the last person, a tall man from the sound of it.

"Razden, please do not interfere." Asher looked back at the last remaining hooded figure.

"Actually I would like to know too. I know I have never pushed you for the information but I would like to know." Lui added finally stepping away from Jackdaw and back into the arms of her sister. No one wanted to step in between the two siblings reuniting in a heartbreaking way. No one had stopped Lui and the others why would they interrupt this, obviously the anigels needed it.

"Please do not ask me again," Asher begged his brother, Mi'Kal's eyes searching his brother's face.

"It is because of me, they punished you for my fall didn't they." Tears ran down his face. The pure anguish on Asher's face gave it away. "I am the reason your wings are gone."

"What do you mean?" Lui asked carefully, looking between the fallen anigel and her sister.

"I am sorry Xai Dante and I were not entirely clear on why I fell. It wasn't my choice." Mi'Kal looked back at the pack that had included him, that called him and his partner's family. "I was cast out long before I met Dante. Honestly, I had hoped back then the fall would have killed me and they would have left it at that. I hoped that my brother would maybe get pity but nothing more for my crimes in anigel society." Asher gasped at the implication of his brother's words.

"What did you do?" The last remaining figure asked, swiftly removing his hood to watch the elder anigel holding desperately onto his brother. The man was an elf with dark skin and haunting gray eyes. He was wearing almost as many scars on his face as Asher. The dark skin showed the scars vividly and told a horrible story that made pure rage flood through Xai's veins.

"It was just Asher at the time. We were both young but he was still considered a child and I an adult. We had lost our parents and our siblings to various causes. At the time I was barely holding onto myself. I had a child who was traumatized and grieving, outside of that I had only one friend through the end of it. That is wrong he was my lover." He sighed looking back down at his brother who had buried his face in his neck. Kila decided to wrap her miniaturized body around the younger's shoulders barely startling him while looking between Mi'Kal and Dante who stood back helplessly. "I thought he would help me through this even though we were not matched. He had been my friend since childhood and stood beside me as we lost everything. Something you all need to know about anigel culture is that homosexuality is a crime, one does not crave their own sex. Now this friend and I fought it for so long before we laid together or attempted our relationship. We kept it as secret as we could. But as we got older our views started to shift. He hated daemons or anything not Solar. I thought that people were people. I always have been flirty when I am comfortable as you have seen and he could not stand me giving affection to anyone but him. I know now that he was abusive but then we were in love and I had

426

him and a child that needed me. And that was my crime."
Mi'Kal looked directly at the elf as he said it.

"What do you mean?" The elf pushed not accepting the
heartbreaking information the anigel had already offered to the
people he cared about and strangers alike.

"Razden!" Asher shouted whipping himself around in his
brother's arms, disrupting the small dragon in the process. Kila
ran back to Dante who had tensed, anger burning in his
normally joyful eyes towards this strange elf.

"I need to know what was his crime that you bare the
punishment for." The elf ground out. Mi'Kal surprisingly
relaxed at the force of the elf's words.

"My crime was refusing to give him away. Do you think
you care for my brother enough to question me? I loved him
enough to die for him. He was never supposed to bear my
punishment." That caused the smaller anigel to flinch from his
brother in horror. But if it was the horror of the simply put
truth or the implications of his words. "If you don't think I
can't recognize the look in your eyes as you look at my brother
you are mistaken, boy. My crime was sympathizing with Lunars
and more specifically daemons. My crime was not giving away
the child who needed me when he needed me the most. My
partner went to the guards and told them that I tried to tempt
him into my bed, that I was taking daemon men into my bed
when I got the chance.

They came looking for me. He had given me a death
sentence for disagreeing with him. He told me that he would
tell the guards it was a misunderstanding if I sent Asher away
so that we could terrorize an enslavement camp of daemons."
He looked back to his brother. "I sent you to play with your
friends and set up an agreement with a distant relative that I
was friendly with to care for you and I ran. I knew the guards

were looking for me so I let them find me. I knew I was dead if they caught me but if they did everything would be aired out at my execution and they would drag you through the worst of it. Instead, I waited for the guards to get close enough to see me. I sliced my wings and threw myself from the bridge system back down to land. The fall should have killed me but I became a fallen instead. I was so confused when I woke up alive and with dark black wings instead of white. I soon found I lost my blue eyes and they were replaced with black orbs staring back into my reflection. I took my time to hide and heal. Then I became a problem. I released all the enslavement camps that I knew about."

"That was when the King's hunters were sent out to take care of the pain in the ass fallen anigel who was disrupting the slave industry," Dante spoke up finally stepping to his partner and placing a hand between his wings.

"Once Dante and I became a team I asked him to see if he could find Asher but we could never locate him. I hoped that our relative had taken him to keep him from the shame of his remaining sibling committing suicide. I did not know they would make him pay my price. I knew what I was doing would hurt Asher but I thought he would be better without me and at his age, if I wasn't there someone would take him in and he would be happy. He would find his other half and live happily without me."

"This was not your fault brother." Asher looked between his brother and Dante.

"What happened after Asher?" Mi'Kal put his hand on his brother's face cupping it gently trying to urge the truth that they all needed to hear.

"After you fell your friend heard and was angry that you didn't give in to him. I promise I didn't know you were romantically involved with him but he called you slurs. He said he was owed retribution. Long after your fall, I became a shell but our relative tried so hard to raise me with kindness. But she acted like I was cursed. But he found me and told me he had been looking for me for what you owed him in death. He never forgot. He and his friends held me down and cut my wings off. They left me to die but my caretaker found me. She said it was for the best and brought me to the ground and while I was barely bandaged up she wished me luck and left saying I was as useful as a human now. With everything that happened, I blamed you." He cried. "I am so sorry I blamed you. I thought you were dead and you left me. I was left behind again and again. I lost everything including my wings and I said the most heinous things to you. I said I was glad you were dead." Mi'Kal tensed at that and so did Dante who was remembering helping Mi'Kal through episode and episode of trying to kill himself for thinking he failed his brother or even for loving the dragon rider himself. To hear that the one person he tried to live for had blamed him was almost too much.

"After everything went wrong Dante found me, I thought that he would be merciful and kill me, the most beautiful person in the world would end the suffering," Mi'Kal whispered.

"I couldn't kill you Mi'Kal, I was there to end the suffering though."

"I know that Dante." Asher and Razden looked at the two of them.

"Brother?"

"I am sorry Asher for all I did, but I would go through it all again if it meant I could be with this man again. I know you know the feeling. Meeting the one you are meant to be with

429

even after all the pain and all the rejection. I never wanted you to be in pain but it seems like we needed our own paths for what little happiness this world can hand us."

"Brother?"

"As I said if you think I don't recognize that look on your elf's face you are insulting me. That is the same look that Dante looked at me until he was certain I was safe from myself. Even though we knew we were meant for each other he refused until I was healed. He wanted me to be happy with our little life before adding in something like a soul bond into the mix. It is a look of love and desperation and helplessness."

"You matched with this man?" He asked in such a quiet voice that even the daemons had a hard time hearing him.

"Yes I did and I could not be happier in that aspect than with him by my side. I have our little family that we made and if destiny lets it and you agree I can have you and your fated along with us as well. Once this is over maybe we can have peace." Asher looked back at Razden. "But it looks like you two need to talk more about that. It has been enough of an emotional day if I say so myself." The anigel finally showed one of his more common noncommittal smiles.

"I agree," Xai spoke up. "As much as these reunions were needed especially to remind us all who will be fighting that we each have something to come back to from the battle I think we all need to rest."

"We have my auntie's old house, she passed some years ago and it is large enough to still accommodate everyone. It is where the pack has been staying while waiting on your return. My family kept it in case either of us came home with a family or a pack of our own." Lux offered. "It is only a little bit away." Nodding towards the village. Xai smiled as everyone move quietly. She and Truen scooped up the children as they stepped with the group. Their family had grown and yet it had not, more so repaired the missing pieces that others didn't know were missing.

"Did you say that your partner is a hunter for the King?" She could hear Asher behind her.

"I was," Dante answered for himself. "But your brother was the reason that I couldn't go on not caring about the consequences. I couldn't hurt him then and I can't let anyone hurt him now."

"I agree, no one shall hurt Asher here or on the battlefield." Razden nodded, hopefully warming up to the bigger male.

"It is surprising though." Mi'Kal started. "How close our fated partners are to each other. We seem to have a similar type little brother." The intense sputtering in response made smiles cross the faces of many of the pack members on their magically cleared trip across the village. Xai recognized the house in question and remembered the older woman who lived there before they left. It felt like they had not been gone long enough for such changes to happen back in the village that they used to call home.

"My father will meet us in the morning for sparring. Then we can plan." Lux said looking over to Xai. "We kept one of the rooms downstairs by the door for you and Truen, Jackdaw and I have the other. Everyone else is upstairs. There was a handful of extra rooms so needing one or two depending on how our newest arrivals want to share will be fine."

"That is up to them," Truen answered with a shrug of the boy in his arms.

"I think the boys need a night to themselves so as long they don't need to bug big brother they should be fine in a room and I can take a bed to stretch out in," Lui interjected.

"You were always such a bed hog as a child. I would be surprised if that changed. Though remember little sister we have to discuss things tomorrow. Plans and where you were all this time." Xai chastised switching which hip Hestia was seated on.

"Of course sister. We wouldn't want to miss any more emotionally charged conversations before a battle."

"Of course not, where would the fun in that be," Xai answered in a flat dull tone that earned a few chuckles. "Now the better question are where are the kids sleeping?" Xai asked. That seemed to be the incorrect choice in questioning as the children began to cling to their parents without reason. It took time but eventually, everything settled for the night. Feeding the entire pack with an actual kitchen and not rations was a battle in and of itself, but eventually, everyone got fed. By the end of the night, the adults had a few sips of the alcohol stores and headed to their rooms. Hestia and Kato had been tucked into Truen and Xai's bed so they would sleep comfortably between them in safety, reassuring the children through the night that their parents were there.

The morning started easily enough with most of the pack pulling themselves begrudgingly from bed and the others being morning people. Xai sat with her tea and watched as the others became awake in a safe and comfortable setting. Not some strange city, no traveling, no prophecy, and no missing pieces. It was strange but comforting. If not for the looming battle the domestic style of the morning would be nice, even picturesque.

"Are you ready to be under my father's tutelage again?" Lux asked as she sat beside Xai.

"Oh, gods no that man is a hard ass when it comes to teaching. But I must say I wouldn't have minded this being the end of the journey."

"I thought the same way but the longer we were waiting it felt incomplete, not the pack with the missing members yourself included but something else. Something bigger was missing. I know we have heard it already but now I know what you were saying when you keep hinting at your feeling like this is the beginning, this is only part one. It is like something is pulling me along that I can't ignore. Is this what you, Kato, and Dremira were feeling the entire time."

"That is one way to explain it. It was hard for me to put into words then but now I can say it is the sense of destiny pulling on you. And we have only crossed the first hurdle that brought us all together." Xai sighed. "That being said who is joining us today now that I am back I doubt your family will stay away."

"I am not sure. Obviously, father will be there and he wants to be formally introduced to Truen and I quote 'Only a father should be introduced to someone trying to court one of my children'. He did the same to Jackdaw. I thought Jackdaw was honestly going to cry for a moment. Truen has managed to escape it so far but not for much longer."

"As expected from your father." Xai nodded, smiling at the ambush Truen had no idea was coming by the well-meaning warrior.

"I do expect my brothers through, they have missed you and have no idea about Truen at all."

"So Truen is not only walking into a trap with your father but he is bait for your brothers. Interesting, do your brothers know about Jackdaw?"

"No only mother and father know about Jackdaw or Truen, mother is excited to finally meet Truen."

"Your mother will scare him more than your father."

"That is what Jackdaw said as well." They both laughed as they watched the morning routines commence around them.

"By the way, I meant to ask where did the Mages go while we were gone?" Xai asked finishing her tea.

"Their grandmother went back to the city to help their aunt I think she said. And the little one has been helping the tailor and armorer in town and has sworn that everyone will have something before we head out." Lux answered putting her cup down as well.

"As long as everyone who will be joining the festivities that night will be covered that is fine with me," Xai responded as they continued to watch the others from the lounge. One by one each member became more and more ready to go back to the field and read in the lounge area. Together they made their way well-rested across the village once more to the eventful clearing that would never be forgotten by any member of the pack. Standing at the edge once more was Lux's father. He stood there in his glory. A mountain of muscular tanned skin with a mustache that had always made the daemon's children laugh at the thick bug on his lip when they were younger and black hair that had started to gray over the years. He stood in the field with his arms clasped behind his back waiting. A bell-like laugh rang through the air coming from a skinny, pale, built woman with blonde hair, and brown eyes, in a blue skirt and green skirt and bare feet. Lux's mother, the woman who raised Xai after she left the castle. This woman was as much her mother as Truen's or her own. As soon as they were in range the woman rushed beside Xai and hugged her tightly.

"You made it back to us my dear. You had me worried I would never get to hug my child again." She whispered in the daemoness' ear.

"I am sorry I didn't mean to worry you or anyone else," Xai reassured her, placing a kiss on the older woman's temple as she returned the hug. "Thank you for taking care of everyone while I was away."

"Of course, your pack is wonderful though I need to meet your Prince. I met Lux's and to know you got yours first I am intrigued by what he is like."

"Well, here he is." She gestured stepping back. "Truen this is Marsona, Lux's mother, the woman who adopted me after I left the castle. She finished raising me where our mothers could not." He reached for her hand on introduction.

"Pleasure to meet you, ma'am, you did a beautiful job with both of them. Smart, loyal, and compassionate to the core." He smiled at her placing a soft and respectful kiss on her hand.

"Don't forget smart asses, my boy. You are proper and polite but there is no reason to lie to an old lady like me. I know my girls are a handful." She laughed, the sound of bells filling the air again. "Truen this is my husband Eleraz, this is my children's father." Truen turned to the older warrior.

"Hello sir, it is a pleasure to finally get to meet you. I know we have spoken before but no formal introductions have been made." Xai was proud of the impassive but polite face her Prince was making, the bond was full of insecurity and anxiety at the closest thing he had ever come to meeting the parents of his partner. He had grown up with her mother and her father's opinion only mattered to the King and that was barely a passing thought. Eleraz just stared at him silently.

435

"Don't be a mean old man." Xai laughed while walking over to hug the hiking daemon. "He has done everything right according to everything you told us all to expect. Even when I didn't want to hear it."

"I will take your word for it, my little spitfire, if you haven't killed him yourself he must be worth something. You are far less trusting than your sister." She could hear a squawk of protest from Lux behind her. "Don't complain Lux you know it is true. You never had a reason to be distrustful. We were able to do that for you in a way we never were for Xai."

"Under no fault of your own," Truen added. "There was too much that was overlooked when Xai and I were children, and the fact that we were all attacked like that as children is horrid in its own right. But I never want it to happen again and I will make sure it doesn't happen to our own children I can assure you."

"You have a good man here Xai." Marsona smiled.

"I know, all the Princes came out pretty well. And somehow both of my sisters are mated to the other two which I have no idea how that worked." She threw a smile over to Lui. "That would be the infamous little sister right there."

"Welcome to the family dear." Marsona smiled even harder wrapping her arms around her husband's waist. Lui smiled looking back.

"Is that the love of my life I see?" A masculine voice boomed from behind the house beside the clearing. Xai tensed and let out a sigh as a man rushed out to her side ignoring everyone else to crush the daemoness to his body. Truen stiffened beside her, anger pouring through the bond at Xai's annoyance.

436

"Maxi if you do not put me down this very moment I will take that as a sign that you do not like your body in its current arrangement and you are asking me kindly to correct that error and rearrange it for you," Xai spoke in a very calm tone. "And if I don't do it I have no doubt there is someone very close by who would like to help with that in a much more natural way."

"Who would think they could stop me besides you my beautiful flower?" The man huffed as he set her down. She looked into annoyingly familiar silver eyes. Years had been kind to the buffoon, she could see why the rest of the village thought he was worth fighting over but she never had been interested in obvious reasons. That easy smile he always sported meant nothing compared to Truen's especially when Xai was convinced that Maxar had no thoughts to rub together in that thick skull of his. She was just the one that didn't want him so to him she was a challenge, not a true romantic interest.

"Oh, I know he can." She stepped aside to show an impressively angry Prince. "Meet Prince Truen, my mate and partner." She smiled watching the smile that never left no matter how many times she rejected him fall from his face. "Truen darling this is Lux's twin Maxar. Max this is Jackdaw's brother and my known mate since he was born. I always knew it wasn't you no matter how much you wouldn't listen." She shrugged looking back over to his parents who were shaking their heads. They had tried talking to him about it over the years but he never gave up on Xai no matter what anyone said, Xai included."

"Honestly I would love to see Truen spar with you brother, I think we could all use the entertainment of him wiping the clearing with you." Lux interrupted equally frustrated with her brother.

"Oh come on, it was just a joke from when we were kids." He backtracked. "Calm down, I don't want to hurt a Prince or whatever he has told you he is." He had his hands in the air with a sign of surrender as Truen wrapped his arms tightly around her waist.

"I am going to kindly warn you the once." If Truen could have growled Xai would have been sure he would have done so while talking to him. "Unless she wants you to touch her I would refrain from doing so or I might consider you on the wrong side of the battlefield." Magic crackled in the air around them proving his point. The sparks of electricity in the air caused Max to back up further and Lux to cackle uncontrollably.

"Now I officially approve." Her father grumbled with a smile on his face.

"Now will I approve?" Another voice joined. Joining was another large man with sandy blonde hair who walked up watching the group cautiously. "I am much harder to please than you when it comes to my baby sisters."

"Play nice Gaze, your sisters are adults who can make their own decisions." A voice reprimanded. A proud woman stood beside him with her long dark hair tied tightly back. Her white eyes see more than anyone wished. She fit perfectly beside Lux's eldest brother, with enough no-nonsense attitude to combat his overprotective nature. It would be completely over with when he realized he was already an uncle. No one would be able to stop him from protecting Hestia and Kato or spoiling them.

"Thank you Nirea," Xai called over to the woman who nodded in return.

"It is good to see you back Xai." A red-headed woman joined as well. Bright hair looked like it was a fire in the early morning light but green eyes that looked like emeralds.

"Same to you Loon, I am assuming you already saw your favorite cousin again?" Xai smirked.

"Of course. I saw Lux the moment she was in town. You were the one I kept missing though now the reason to join is more interesting than just catching up."

Who are all of these people?

Well, Loon or Looniva which she hates is Lux's cousin. She is one of the more standoff people in Lux's family.

Alright, I will let her come to me.

Gaze is Lux's older brother. He is incredibly overprotective and he loves his little sisters, it was all of his siblings but Max has pissed him off since he started trying to pursue me. Beside him is his handler and match, Nirea, who is a stealer, she was not actually his original handler.

Really? I have only had the one experience with stealers before and that was at the beginning of our journey.

Yes his original handler found out they were a matched pair and knew it so she tried to kill them both, Nirea found out killed his handler, and became his handler herself, only a stealer can do that as you know and it is not something that is talked about often.

Oh, that is absolutely horrible. I will not pry more though.

Good idea, occasionally they will discuss it but do not bring it up unless they do.

That is fair. I can think of a few things in our past that are the same.

And the moron is Maxicar Lux's twin brother.

He might have to die

I know, no one would probably stop you which is the worst part.

"So are you going to introduce your newcomers to us?" Gaze asked pointedly looking at Truen. "Especially the one who thinks he can hang off Xai like he has not a care in the world?"

"Nirea already told you to play nice." Xai looked at him plainly. "This is Truen and he is my Handler and partner. Technically betrothed I guess, he is also the Heir Apparent and Jackdaw's brother." Xai spoke proudly. "He is my mate."

"You are betrothed?" He bellowed.

"So is Lux and she is betrothed to Truen's brother." She sassed back before remembering Lux hadn't told Gaze yet. She looked at her friend in horror as the color left the canine's face. Gaze's, and the rest of the family's, attention shifted rapidly between Xai and Lux.

"Xai," Lux growled.

"Fangs I am so sorry." Xai threw her hands up in surrender. If one of them was going down with their Prince they both were. At least they could escape Gaze together. Lux did not by her sincerity.

"Go kiss a raven's ass spots." She ground out watching her brother carefully.

"Language Lux dear." Her mother chided trying to keep her giggles from being noticed.

"Now that we have all that out of the way." Lui started bouncing in the middle of the chaos. "I think it is a beautiful time to plan a siege don't you all?"

Chapter Twenty Three: Straight for the Castle

Days passed in a flurry of arguments and plans being rewritten. Many messages sent to allies across the kingdom were sent in secret to see who could gather for the full moon only days away. The atmosphere in the daemon village was calm yet deadly. Most of the village was ready to fight with them on the night if they needed to. Eleraz and Lux had taken to helping those who had never been in a fight let alone a battle before. Xai and Lui focused on sparing and helping those more experienced learn how to counter those who had been taught by the royal guard. Truen and his brother were in charge of strategy with Marsona and what those staying back would do. Mira had been working long hours finishing armor that would help each person individually, the poor little Mage was working harder than anyone thought she would be capable of but they were proud of her.

Dremira had taken it upon herself to coordinate with any healers that would be assisting outside the battlefield and back in the village as the seriously injured were portaled back out of the danger. Mages arrived to help with the planning, but they were only the first. Xai had honestly been surprised by how many had hurried to them when they received their invitations. The news of not only the siege but the return of the Hybrid had caused a surge of hope and rebellion. Those who could not leave their areas swore to fight back with them, and plans of evicting those loyal to the corruption from their cities, towns, and villages were a shock. Xai and Truen both had not realized that their presence had brought back the strength of their people, just knowing that the heir apparent and the Hybrid were going to battle for them gave the courage to the civilians to fight in their own ways. Following the Mages many small squads of fighters that had offered themselves to the rulers of the new kingdom. Vampires were sent by the elder, Yuell, with a message for the children about how much he missed them and how he was so proud of them and the family they created for themselves. Following the vampire was a group of humans sent by Dremira's own father to her surprise. Elves and Spell Casters joined as well to everyone's surprise. Dante just smiled when the rest of his squad of Dragon Riders landed to fight beside him once more without question, some even more excited to meet Mi'Kal to the awe of the anigel. A few Lyear Riders even graced their war party. By the days leading to the raid, everyone stood together as one. Daemons, vampires, Mages, humans, anigels, Spell Casters, elves, dwarves, pixies, fairies, Dragon Riders, and Lyear Riders all standing side by side. Every race was present in one way or another ready to fight behind their would-be new King and Queen.

With the plans finally ready and the full moon approaching every person who was preparing themselves for blood readied themselves. Xai could feel the pressure of the kingdom's fear, if they failed this fight then they would all fail. Originally they were only expecting a handful to fight beside them though not an army of their own behind them, and the masses to be waiting in the wings for their smaller but just as important fights. Their plan had been simple enough. They would arrive outside the city and prepare. Mages who were non-combative would pass messages or portal those who needed it. Medics and strategists would stay in the treeline with the Mages. Then there would be the squads who would be fighting. Seven groups of eleven or fewer depending circling the city to wait for the signal.

Xai would walk through the front gates like she was always meant to. Once everyone who needed to was in the city they would keep the city clear and with that Xai's path to the castle. Once they were inside they would be on their own. It would be easier to tell who was innocent or enemy that way since Truen and Xai knew their way around the great halls and who to look for. Lui would meet them inside when she got her area cleared so she could fight with her mate.

She watched as those she knew and those who were still strangers said their goodbyes in case they fell. The next day they would be leaving to put everything in motion. When the sun set and the moon rose they would attack. Krutz would be waiting for them in the walls to hear their entrance. Lui had decided to keep her return a beautiful and 'romantic' surprise for the battlefield in her own words. Xai chuckled at her choices instead of questioning her sister. Lui had always been more dramatic and romantically inclined than Xai, Xai would rather just get to the point of the matter when her mind and heart were her own.

Somehow the thought of her sister thinking more about her reunion with her mate instead of the bloodshed and lives that would no doubt be lost tomorrow settled a part of her that she had not thought about. For this entire journey, no all of these years of fighting, had led up to this battle. As the Mages said this would be the first of many but this would be the one to start it all. They were as ready as they could get and this may be the last time these people saw each other. They had gathered all in the clearing for one last evening before their lives changed or their lives ended. A large fire roared in the light of the setting sun as food and drinks were passed around. The sounds of laughter and stories could be heard, no one here was regretting where they were even if they feared what they could face tomorrow. Together all of these people would risk it all to protect their home and share one more meal with each other in case they were losing everything for those they had never met.

"If I could get everyone's attention for just a moment," Xai shouted as she climbed on the stone fence of Lux's childhood home. One of the parents squawked at the reckless behavior as she walked on the loose and uneven stone, it only firmed her determination to have such an easy domestic moment on the eve of battle. Once she had everyone's gaze she smiled. "I don't know how to quite thank you all for being here. Most of you are strangers or people we met in passing on this ridiculous journey. Yet here you are ready to stand beside us tomorrow. Even though I hope this will be a seamless attack since we have the element of surprise I don't think it will be. There has been a lot of discord and whispers since a Time Mage sent me on a journey for a bullshit prophecy from the confines of a prison cell. Every town we visited, every city we helped, and every pack member we gained spread hope and ideas. I expect that the King is prepared for something, though he might know what. Our person inside the walls has been informed to get those we need to protect to safety when the sun sets but he hasn't been privy to what the King has been doing as of late. All he sends back is the King as became paranoid and secretive to all but his daemon companion. Now I know many of you will not enter the castle until the King is dead but I want you all to know to be careful, we are not sure how many guards, soldiers, or sympathizers are in the city anymore. We do not know exactly who outside the castle walls is friend and foe so please take care of yourselves and others.

I want to personally thank you all for risking yourselves. For many of you, this will be your first real battle, and for that, I apologize that you will have to witness this. Even in those societies that celebrate warriors, you must agree that a true battle or blood bath like this changes a person, and not for the best. Many of you will come back with nightmares and guilt and that will not be your fault. The burden of you being here rests on my shoulders and the shoulders of those who have

445

wronged the people of this kingdom." She continues. Murmurs of disagreement ran through the crowd. "Don't argue with me, I know that it is not my fault but part of the burden rests with me because I am the reason you have all gathered. My recompense will be to kick in the teeth of those bigoted bastards as I promised and to relieve the King of his head. I will gift you all a new King for your troubles. I made a promise to those who came before me who never had the reason to showcase the power of being the chosen weapon of the gods that I would make sure that those who forced our hands would regret making me show our claws. I promised all of those who we could not save that I would carry them through this for their justice. Together we will let those we have lost to this corruption rest in peace finally knowing that this will end and that peace and balance will come back to our world. They started this in our blood and we will make them pay with their own." Cheers erupted from the crowd as she finished her speech. "By the end of the night tomorrow Chemerica will have a new King, and I for one am partial to." The wink she threw at Truen earned chuckles. "We will change our world for the better and I thank you all for that."

"You will change it for the better with that I have no doubt." A voice called from the crowd, Xai looked and saw a familiar raven-haired figure by the fire. The firelight illuminated her in a way that could not hide the powerful being that was trapped in a mortal body. A hush fell over the gathering, no one knowing the strange woman beside the daemoness who had been addressing them moments ago.

"Luna," Xai addressed the being causing gasps to come from those gathered. "I didn't know you would be joining us before we won."

"I might be a goddess but I will stand with those I created and those who will protect them. You are my weapon, my

446

child and I will not let any of you go into battle without protection." She smiled at the group. "You are all here to help fix a problem that we did not see in time. We did not want any of this to happen I promise you that. The others and I grew as complacent as everyone else at the peace until we decided to walk among you once more like we like to do every few centuries. Once we were here we were trapped and separated, It wasn't until then that whoever has been corrupting our world acted. I then had to wait for my champion to be born and be ready and that ended with more darkness and more pain and I can not apologize enough. But I am here and now so is Xia. No matter the darkness that surrounds us remember there is always light. The moon and stars will protect you so you may reach the destiny that you were all meant to have. None of you will have to suffer tomorrow even if you fall. I might not be able to stop your destiny but I can protect you all as you approach it." The goddess spoke strongly. "Xai and I will also be working on finding the others and ending those pulling strings that they should not be. Now rest and be calm before the storm that comes tomorrow. You have my Hybrid leading you into battle and even with blood being spilled I will make sure none of you will be truly lost." The crowd cheered again when her words settled over them. They had the blessing of a goddess, they might even have the blessing of all the gods if they felt the same as the woman before them. Xai watched the goddess look over her war party, once their eyes met again the goddess smiled and the daemoness nodded in agreement. There was only going to be one outcome of the next night, as Xai had told them all in the hall of judgment, there was no other option than to win. Within a heartbeat, the goddess was gone, though no one else seemed to notice.

"Tomorrow we follow our destiny and a new reign begins." Truen cried out enjoying the answering cheers. The pride through the bond only served to make the daemoness

447

smile as she put through her own determination in the response. His smile grew knowing that tomorrow they would change lives. Truen had seen more death and blood on this journey than ever in his life but he knew he didn't have to hold on to that alone. And for tonight they all breathed in the last bit of peace they had in the sanctuary of the daemon village hidden in the forest.

Xai took the time to hold her children. This would be hard for them, not knowing where their parents were again and if they would return. Once the children were asleep, too exhausted from the party she handed them to Dremira who along with Crazden promised to keep them safe while the rest were fighting. The human smiled at her promising that they would be fine until she returned. Nodding without a word she walked off to find her mate. She knew they would be fine but tonight she wanted to feel his skin, his heart, and remember for now they were both alive. Tomorrow would not change that she reminded herself but she could not stop the small seed of fear. She needed him to remind her why they were doing this and not just for everyone else. He knew through the bond what she wanted from him. He just smiled as he reached to hug her.

Whatever you want tonight you can have. Just remember we have a big day tomorrow and I rather not be too sore before we embark on our warpath. His words earned a much-needed smile from his daemoness.

The morning started with clouds and a thick cover of fog thanks to the heir apparent and another elemental Mage that had introduced themselves early in the planning, the Princes' distant relation that was close enough to have a similar style of

448

magic to the Queen and Prince. They had warned the remaining Prince that the mark of their arrival would be the clouds clearing in the night, and the storms would rage through the day until they arrived to mask their presence. As they prepared to leave, Mira checked all the armor over one last time, Clarita rushed into the village to say her wishes and help those staying behind. Kato and Hestia could not keep the tears away as they hugged their parents before they left, no matter how many promises were made on their return the two refused to believe it having lost too many parents already. With one final goodbye to those staying behind those who were ready for the siege let out a collective breath before heading out to where the Mages were ready with portals to and from the front lines. The plan had grown more sophisticated with the addition of extra hands and abilities. As they stepped through the magic they looked at the walls of the Royal City, obscured by the trees and the fog. It was the same field that they looked over now that Xai had escaped across all that time ago with the help of Truen. They looked at each other realizing the significance of their journey starting and ending here. But it was also their path to start a war and end a genocide.

They spent the day as quietly as possible setting up stations for basic first aid and planning away from the frontline. They had the time before the sun set so they used it to their advantage in the shroud of the storms and fog. It seemed too soon that Truen and his cousin whose name Xai could not remember brought the storms to a drizzle, but kept the fog through the trees and the fields. It was almost time, and as much as Xai was itching to run into the city before the full moon rose she knew that they had to give Krutz time to move the Queen and her mother to safety. If they were lucky he would have been able to get her younger siblings out of the way as well even if it was not their choice but his. The more time he had the more chance of surprise they had as he made it seem like some nightly comfort instead of an abrupt sanctuary.

Each of the squads gathered together to prepare. Dante stood with his team of ten, each ready for orders and looking as tense as Xai felt. Mi'Kal stood with his brother and Lui's small pack. The two had determined it would be better for them not to fight together so they would not be distracted with worry even if they knew how strong the other was. Razden stood with Asher adjusting his armor that Mira took care to have wings sewn into with magic, the wings themselves made of pure magic. They were not the same as feathers but the last few days practicing and flying with his brother were full of happiness and tears. The elves were checking over their bows once more as the non-combative Mages enchanted quivers and arrows.

The humans and the vampires thought it was smarter for them to mix their forces and divide them between two different squads allowing more adaptability to the vampire forces and more strength for the humans. Magic users who would be fighting were spread into each of the squads to help with the cover, each flexing their magic, Truen had told her it was very much like stretching a muscle before the fight. Xai's squad stood beside her ready to simply walk in. Lux was going over things once more with her mate as he had chosen to stay behind with the others to help strategize on a moment's notice. They had thought they would have to convince Jackdaw to stay behind, not wanting to worry about his disability causing a lapse of judgment in the middle of the battle for any of them. Jackdaw though had informed them he would be staying with the information-gathering team to coordinate changes in the plan and how to retrieve those injured. They didn't want him to have to sit out but he knew his strengths were better used with the information than in the middle of the fight, and that Lux would use anything from him she needed. He also trusted

Xai to bring her back to him. Truen had let the other Mage take over the cover and joined his mate as they waited on Lux to rejoin them. Krutz would be the last member of their squad but he was still inside preparing.

Through the thinning clouds, they watched the moon's light begin to shine, the Mage released the clouds and let the light cover them all in comfort and purpose. Through the fog, each one of the soldiers relaxed remembering the words of the goddess the night before. The light was the cue, Xai sighed and began to walk, she could feel the power surging through her as they walked closer, the moon giving her more than it had ever before. They stood no chance against her or her army. Truen to her left and Lux to her right and both instep. Her breath was even as they reached the main road to the city, she knew the rest of the squads would be taking their positions around the city walls waiting on the signal. The others would not be taking the road into the city but she was determined to walk right in and to the castle without much resistance once the signal was given. The cobblestone road brought back memories of every time she had run from this city and yet here she was, coming straight for the castle, straight for the throne.

"Halt." A voice called as she reached the entrance to the city. Guards swarmed swords drawn and pointed at the daemoness and Prince.

"Now gentlemen, is this truly what you wish to do? Standing between the Prince and me and the castle?" Xai asked tail swishing back and forth, head tilted and sharp eyes seeing easily through the fog.

"Prince Truen has been listed as a traitor to the crown and is not allowed in the city unless he is in chains. He is to be taken to sentencing immediately." The guard spoke like he was unsure of his words. The others looked back and forth between each other not knowing what to do. They had not been expecting Xai to be at the forefront. More so they were not expecting the change in the air around her, the raw power.

"And how may I ask, are you going to take him?" She asked, tilting her head the other way. "Or the better question that you didn't mention, how are you going to stop me from getting to the castle?" Truen and Lux took the steps to no longer stand behind their leader but to stand beside her.

"I don't think they have the plan in place to stop someone like you," Lux answered instead with a quirked brow. She looked the guards over with judgment.

"I don't think they have the plan to stop any of us," Truen added with a smirk.

"I don't think I have been away from the castle long enough for the Royal Guards to think they can stop me." Xai sighed. "How time changes though I guess, it has been years since I walked these streets. Though someone who knows what they are capable of should truly watch how they speak to a Royal Daemon."

"I don't think they have forgotten Xai, I think you became a myth and legend through the guard last I heard," Truen added watching the guards become more uncomfortable with who they were standing in front of. She was a legend, a child who could take an entire squadron of adult guards in the arena and come out the victor.

"I will not say it again." The guard in front spoke again, this time the daemons could smell the fear pouring off him, hearing the tremble in his voice. "Prince Truen is to be taken to the castle in chains, and you will comply. It is the law your father has set in motion."

452

"Now not to sound like a rebellious teenager but I don't think I wish to listen to my father at the moment." Truen sighed. "I feel as though at the moment he has no idea what he could possibly be talking about since he is more of a traitor to his people than I am to him. I just wish him to be held accountable for his actions as any good ruler should be."

"I agree my love, I think it is time we had a conversation with your father and these petty men will not stop us," Xai answered. She turned back to look at each of the other guards with eyes alight with fury and determination. "Choose to move from my path and live or be the first blood to be shed tonight. You have no way to stop me without the full moon, you stand no chance even in your wildest dreams to stop me now." She lifted her hand in front of her and examined her claws elongating as if she were admiring a piece of jewelry. The men could not look away from the dangerous appendages.

"We fight for the King." The guard shouted, trying to find their own determination.

"And I fight for the new King." Xai hissed, her eyes began to glow in the darkness. Truen watched with a shameful amount of lust at the ethereal sight of his heart in the fog looking almost like a spector. Her hair swayed in the breeze, her tail swishing back and forth. He couldn't even follow her movement as she dispatched the guards. In one heartbeat she was standing there and the next the men were missing pieces of their throats and her hands were covered in their blood. "Such a shame to have such a distraction so early in the night." She sighed licking the blood off her finger. The image caught the Prince's breath, but not in fear of what his mate had become.

"That is disgusting." Lux said as she watched her friend clean her claws, "Though your speed is something to be truly admired."

"Thank you." Xai smiled wiping the rest of the blood from her lips. "Though the blood thing might be the vampire blood in my veins now. It definitely tastes more alluring than it used to whenever I had to lick a wound. Though I think you are the only one who thinks it is disgusting if my bond with Truen here has anything to say." She smiled at him, he could feel every part of her predator aura but he was not afraid.

"It wasn't hard to figure out he liked people more powerful than him, those who can handle him if it were." Lux teased. Truen just shrugged, there was no use denying such an obvious fact. "Though it begs the question of who is handling you." She shot Xai a look.

"Who knows." She smiled back looking absolutely feral. "Truen dear I believe it is time for the signal so we can invite the others to the party don't you think?" She asked sweetly looking back at him. He nodded without a thought to him except the need to please her. Squaring his shoulders he pulled at the pool of magic within him. Stepping to the castle walls made of stone he pulled. He pulled hard enough that each interlocking stone brick would cave and crumble. Section by section the wall fell, leaving no barrier to the squads that were waiting for just this cue. This would be a loud enough alarm to wake everyone, to call out all the guards to the city.

"I thought you said you had a subtle plan to cue everyone into the city." Lux sighed as she watched the destruction.

"Where is the fun in subtly," Xai answered, sharing her strength with the Spell Caster. Pushing pride and awe through the bond at the display of power that he showed. Truen's breathing was heavy by the time he was done. They had known that would be his limit of magic without an emergency after the storms. He would have to rely on Xai or his sword for the rest. Such concentrated usage was nothing like his storms which fed into the nature of the weather. "You did well my Prince. Let us do the rest of the heavy lifting." She reassured him.

The change in the night was almost instantaneous. The daemons could hear the commotion through the streets as they stepped into the city, over the bodies they already created. As they heard guards rushing through the city and towards the walls they heard the roar of dragons overhead. It had begun. The sounds of battle cries and weapons clashing broke the silence of the night. None of that deterred Xai though, she kept walking straight for the castle. The city had been locked tight from the perceived threat but they had no chance to know the real threat until now. She could envision the old man on the throne as she walked with her two most trusted souls by her side. A thousand images of what he would say when they got to him enraged her as they continued their march. Occasionally a guard would try to stop them on their mission but they would be quickly dispatched by whichever team was closest.

The guards had not stood a chance against their small army. She was aware that the same wouldn't be the case if the Royal Daemons were part of the fight but that was her part of the fight, not theirs. Her father would most likely be the only one she faced this evening as she killed his Handler. Even if he stood down he would die and she had no remorse for the man who turned his back on his family and his people. He always screamed about loyalty but had been as much of a traitor as his Handler had been all these years. She could feel the pull towards the castle as they made their way over the cobblestone. These streets that used to be home were nothing but a blood-smeared nightmare now. The sounds of fighting and people

455

dying would forever be etched into the stone surrounding them. Stepping over the dead was just one more log onto the fire, her anger being fueled by the pointlessness of this all. If there wasn't an entitled man who thought he was above all others, about consequences then this would never have had to happen. If not for some deranged lunatic who was trying to push a narrative for his own sick vision of the world they would never have gotten to the point where this kind of violence was the answer to the problems that were created out of selfishness.

The three of them did not have to spill another drop of blood as they reached the steps of the castle. Xai remembered it looking more grand and intimidating as a child, now the stone structure was just a building. It had been more of a prison than the cells below to all those who inhabited it.

"Are you ready for this Xai?" Truen asked quietly beside her, feeling her apprehension and determination.

"We have nothing else to do but end this," Xai responded by squaring her shoulders.

"Then let us go make you our Queen." Lux smiled.

Chapter Twenty Four: No More Tyrants

She felt strangely calm as she climbed the stairs into the castle. It might have been a bit dramatic for her to place her hands on each of the large wooden doors and force them open with enough strength to have them fly apart but she had always wanted to do that. Just like in the story books she used to read when the hero storms in to save the day.

"Was that necessary?" A voice called from a safe difference. Krutz stood there watching with a smirk that seemed to be shared between all of the brothers. "You two are looking good, more dangerous than the last time I saw you." He nodded to the daemoness. "Brother you look like shit but that isn't horribly different than normal." There was the snark that the youngest Prince was known for. His mind was finally his own again and it stayed that way. He even looked healthier than the last time they had seen him in person. His green eyes were bright and his red hair was full of healthy curls. The same curls they all had as a child, Jackdaw still did if he let his hair remain short like his brothers.

"Behave brother or you won't get the surprise we have for you." Truen sighed finally having his breath back under control.

"Be nice boys we have things to do, you can squabble when this is over." Xai smiled in the middle of the door frame watching them act as they should always have. This is what she had expected their adult relationship to be like without the patricide. "I need to have a conversation with your father."

"Then let me lead the way." Krutz bowed dramatically. "My Queen." The shit-eating smirk on the little shit's face earned a bark of laughter from the daemoness who was leaning against the frame and an eye roll from the woman he was addressing.

"Then let us go Princling." She responded, stepping further into the castle. Her pack stepped with her as they follow the remaining brother further through the stone halls.

"He and your father are hiding in their war room. We might have to deal with a few guards but I was able to secure our mothers and your siblings in safety."

"Good, where are they?" Xai asked remembering the way through the maze she was raised in, she figured quickly that they were avoiding the easiest route to get to the main door of the chambers.

"The Queen and your mother are being protected in the Queen's chambers, your mother is on high alert and does not know you are the one heading the invasion just that the rebellion is here and the Queen is in no danger from the opposition. Your siblings are in the prison since they wanted to fight and I could not be guaranteed which side. Too much trust is needed for this and I couldn't tell either the plans so I left them there until it was over."

"Good thought process." Truen agreed, unsheathing his sword as they got closer to the internal war room.

"Most of the servants that I knew were not corrupted were moved to the tower as well with those I trusted to defend it, they have at least four lower-ranked daemons defending the entrance."

"Even lower-ranking daemons are more than a Solar or human could hope to overcome," Lux added earning nods from the others.

"Does the King know you are also a traitor?" Xai asked trying to adjust the plan with the new information that the innocent were secured and in less danger of her warpath.

"I am not sure, I think that he was suspicious of everyone but your father but didn't know who would betray him."

"How would your mothers not know it was you two coming if the King knows?" Lux asked suddenly.

"My father and the King would not divulge that information to our mothers. Both being Lunar races would more than likely stand with us. Not only that but they are both strong women who love their children. They almost definitely thought that the two of them would revolt the moment they heard their children were in the rebellion let alone leading it. Honestly, if they knew the Queen and my mother would have killed the two of them long before we could have gotten here if they knew we were on our way to free them and everyone else. Our mothers are not weak-willed women, just bound in unfortunate ways. If they thought there was a chance of escaping with all of us safe and sound the King would have been dead years ago." Xai answered.

"That is exactly why they have been almost entirely imprisoned in the Queen's chambers since Truen and Jackdaw left to follow a familiar daemoness. The King knew that this was the turning point." Krutz added.

"Not to mention whoever is pulling magical strings has felt the breaking of the curse for each of us." Truen pointed out. "They took the wrong children when we lost Lui and Jhelum."

"That is the damn truth." Krutz threw his head back. "If they had taken Xai or Jackdaw instead they probably would have won, we would have destroyed ourselves."

"I have the distinct feeling they thought they had chosen the powerful children between us. Think about it Jhelum and Jackdaw both were born with time-related magic but Jhelum was physically strong and Jackdaw was born sickly. Jackdaw, though his body was much weaker and it did attack his muscles, still was the smartest one of us and incredibly observant. He was the one to put together the puzzle of the memory alterations. As much as I miss him Jhelum would have never been able to do that." Xai explained as they continued through the empty halls.

"That is true, Lui was always more even-tempered than you too," Truen added. "If I would have heard about the Hybrid when we were younger I would have thought it would have been her and not you."

"Exactly, and I know she is the one who would have faced the trials if I had been taken but I don't know if she would have passed if Luna was personally believing in me. I think Lui was the reserve in case I fell before becoming the Hybrid."

"So whoever started this set their own ruin by trying to stop the prophecy." Lux scoffed. "What a fucking idiot."

"It was a good plan in theory but they chose the wrong children based on the ideals of Solars not on the ideals of Lunars. That was their downfall. To remove a Lunar you need to think like one and move like one. They never stood a chance." Truen responded with pride.

"I can't wait to explain that to whomever the bastard is when we find him," Xai responded with a scoff. As the words left her the ornate doors to the war room came into view. Guards stood at the ready outside the door. Xai made the conscious choice to unsheath her sword beside the two Princes, these guards would get the chance to flee but they would not get the honor of her claws. "You have one chance to leave with your lives." She spoke out to the small group gaining their attention. "Leave now and you will live, if you cross steel with any of us you will not see a sunrise again."

"We stand for our King and not the traitors of the Kingdom." One of them called back without lowering his weapon.

"We are the kingdom," Lux answered in return. Her eyes glowed beautifully in the firelight halls. That was their only warning before the daemoness sprung. The golden-eyed woman had ripped a throat out of the speaker before the other guards knew what was happening. Smiling Xai joined running her sword through another, she had no mercy as she ripped her blade back out and let them fall to the stone below. Once the second body dropped the other guards jumped to action, finally out of their stupor. Xai felt as though it was a childhood spar as she played with two of the remaining, leaving Lux to toy with the other two. The Princes stood back, one in pride as he watched and the other in the horror of the death the two left in their wake. It had not taken long for the daemoness' to leave no survivors.

"Can I tell you how glad I am that you brought me back to my senses before trying to challenge her for real? Xai is terrifying." Krutz whistles in awe.

"And never forget it again little brother," Truen spoke in reverence to his now blood-covered mate.

"The look on your face is disgusting brother, how can you be aroused by this?" The younger asked in shock looking between his brother and his mate.

"You will know how when you see it for yourself. There is nothing more beautiful than a daemoness in their power. Doing what they are meant to. Protection and loyalty through blood and sacrifice. Having the love and devotion of one of those powerful creatures changes your view on beauty and true power." Truen responded watching as Xai and Lux smiled at each other. One putting away her blade, the other wiping blood from her face. Both were surrounded by those who opposed them but never stood a chance.

"I will have to take your word for it brother, I lost my chance when my love was stolen from me," Krutz spoke, not bothering to keep the sadness and bitterness from his voice.

"I think you could also experience it for yourself." A voice of bells interjected.

"Finally joining us sister? I thought we would have the fun alone." Xai called down the hall. Krutz spun in shock, the ghost he had not been expecting only steps away. Lui looked like a war specter in her white armor and white hair splattered in blood.

"I do apologize big sister but I needed to help the anigels get the injured out of the battlefield that those streets became. I never thought the guards would stop coming. I don't remember ever having so many guards." She smiled, strutting straight to the red-haired Prince who was standing in shock with his mouth slack. "You grew handsome my Prince, have you missed me?"

"Lui?" He whispered. Krutz looked like he wanted to reach out and touch her but was equally terrified that she would be a hallucination.

"I am here darling." Blood-covered or not Lui through her arms around the youngest Prince, and with no hesitation she caught his lips with her own for a brief but passionate kiss. "I am sorry love but we will have to continue this after the crown is on your brother's head. Then we will have plenty of time to learn about each other in safety." She cooed as she pulled back causing the spitfire Prince to whimper.

"I told you we had a surprise for you little brother," Truen smirked walking past them both and to the war room doors. "Xai would you like the honor?"

"To break open another door? Of course. But remember everyone my father will be protecting the King. There will most likely be other daemons and guards in there. Most in there will not want to be saved and those who do unfortunately can not be saved at this point. Hold nothing back and let us finish this." She reiterated as she walked next to her own Prince. Each had a hand on the doors ready to do this together.

"The next time you come out of this room you will be Queen." Truen smiled.

"No, you will be King." She corrected.

"No love, you love you will leave this room the true ruler of Chemerica." The raven-haired magic user winked. "I will only kneel for you."

"You say that as if it is a hardship for you." She smirked. "Though knowing you as I do I am aware of those fantasies about the throne. Once it has been cleaned of his blood we can discuss those in a private setting. I don't think your brothers will let you live those down if you scare them with the knowledge or sight." With the groan from the group behind them, all in hearing distance of their words, they pushed open the heavy wooden doors. The group was met with weapons of guards and snarling of daemons. Xai could quickly count four sets of Handlers outside of the King who sat on the throne set above and apart from the rest of the room. Her father watched carefully, sharp eyes never leaving his daughter. The larger feline daemon though did not hold the Hybrid's attention, and neither did those who had their weapons drawn at her. It was the man on the throne, he was not what she remembered him being at all, much more pitiful than her nightmares recalled. The King sat there afraid and alone in a room full of people. She could smell his fear, see his paranoia, this was no longer a righteous killing but a mercy to the sorry state of a man whose thoughts were poisoned and his body used as a puppet. This man, no longer a King, knew he would not make it from this room alive or with that crown still upon his head. She was his death coming to claim him.

"You have come to challenge me? Just as predicted." He called through the room as if no one would notice the tremble in his voice due to the volume.

"You have betrayed your people, you will be held accountable for your crimes," Xai spoke back with authority and presence,

"And what crimes could I have committed? I was born to be King, chosen from birth and all of my actions thereby are ordained and righteous. Shouldn't one such as yourself know your place? You were put beneath your betters, to hide in the shadows and the night." He laughed sounding deranged.

"And who was the one who told you that? Because from what I know I was ordained and chosen by the gods themselves to stop you. You are no ones better. You were supposed to bring peace and protection to your people not enslave, violate, and murder those who were born different than yourself. Lunars pull their power from the night that is true but that is because that is when everyone else is most vulnerable. We were made to protect, to be powerful, and to bow to no one. Even daemons with Handlers have a voice and a choice. You have taken choices away from those who are innocent and frankly much more than you could ever hope to be." Xai growled trying not to lose her patience with his drivel.

"I was chosen by the one true god. He told me I was to follow my destiny to subjugate those beneath me the way nature intended. This is his world, his story and you are not supposed to win here." The words made those who stood before him tense. Who would call themselves the one true god? All Xai could think of was the similar sounds of the shadow man's words.

"I can guarantee you that I will win and your head will roll. Your false god and his lies will not stop destiny. You will die by my hand before the sun rises tonight. I don't care who you have beside you in your delusion." Xai answered by starting to retrieve her sword again but thinking better of it. This she would do with her own claws like intended. She was a daemon before she was a Hybrid and she will end this like one. "Do you think you three can handle the guards while Truen and I handle the piss stain in Truen's seat?" She kept her eyes on the man while waiting for affirmatives from those beside her.

"Should be easy enough," Lux responded. "I can handle these over here if you two can handle yours."

"Don't worry about us puppy, let us show you how a feline hands an annoyance." Lui shot back with a hiss. The response was a growl as Lux lunged at the closest set in front of Xai to show her competition she was no hindrance. Lui matched her with the other effectively clearing the path to the throne. Xai took the opportunity to make her way toward the throne with the speed her counterparts could only wish to have, the speed of a vampire and the power of a daemon. Her speed caught her father off guard as she stood beside him in front of his master within the blink of an eye. Leaning over the

King suddenly earned a high-pitched scream from the man's lips.

"I don't think you know what you are playing with old man. Are you sure you can keep up? I am not the same child you knew all those years ago. Honestly standing against me will not last you long"

"Franzer kill your daughter." The man shouted pulling the attention of the large black feline beside him, finally giving him a reason to stand. The dark blue eyes watched her, analyzing her every movement.

"Xai," Truen called from down the steps. "We do this together." She nodded, stepping back, giving her father the chance, the illusion that he could stand before her.

"I am not the scared daughter on the run any longer. You stand against me and I will not hesitate again. You turned your back on those who needed you but you did teach me something important as a daemon. Any daemon worth their salt should follow this you said. It was a universally known law of daemons you preached. And now you are the one who will fall to the words you drove into us." Xai growled at the dark beast. "If they stand behind you give them protection and safety. If they stand beside you give them respect and loyalty. If they stand against you give them no mercy."

"The kingdom stands behind her, We stand next to her, and you stand against her," Truen added. " You will get no mercy from any of us."

"Make your move." She hissed at the man who had been her father. Her words are the push for his action. Once upon a time, she would have hard a time sparring against her father but now it was child's play. If it was the power of the bond and Truen's focus or if it was the power she gained accepting her

466

destiny as the Hybrid she didn't know but it made tracking his movements too easy. It was as if she was watching an inexperienced child instead of a hardened soldier. She could see every swipe of his claws, every twitch before pouncing. It felt too easy to slice him open with her own claws, small but many. Truen could tell she was playing with him through the bond, immobilizing him without his notice. One misstep on his part was due to the rapid and almost unnoticeable blood loss and his body collapsed on itself. "Mother taught me how to make small cuts around the joints and muscle groups that could render an opponent useless under their own weight. You screamed at her that it was dishonest and cheating in a true fight to use such underhanded tactics. And yet here you are succumbing to such trickery so easily. Leaving your master so vulnerable." She pushed crouching beside his paralyzed body.

"And it looks as though your associates could not stand very long against our pack," Truen spoke looking around at the bodies. Lui and Lux had both shifted in their fight. "So fast, I wonder if there was an issue in the training, maybe some corners cut in the haste of paranoia." Shaking her fur loose Lux walked beside the raven-haired Prince, Lui sauntering to the other side. Both watched their sister, Krutz standing by the wall still in shock and awe at the carnage the two daemoness caused once more. He had never been the fighter of the brothers though his mouthy nature would suggest otherwise. Truen knew that look on his brother's face, it was the same awe and confusion both she and Jackdaw felt when they first saw their mates fight. Xai looked back at him in confusion at the amusement in the bond. She was about to kill his father and he was amused. The Prince shook his head and nodded back to the wall. A smile threatened to appear when she saw what had caused his amusement.

"It looks like some of us have more pressing matters to attend to so let us finish this shall we?" She stood back at her full height looking once more back at the man whose eyes had gone wide in fear at the easy defeat of his strongest defender.

"Wait." He shouted. "What if I give you the throne and set down?" He begged, panic clear on his face.

"Disgusting." Xai spat. "Your daemon is defeated and you can not fight like your own man? Did you forget you were a King? A Spell Castor? You disgust me."

"You do not get to abdicate the throne," Truen spoke up once more. "That would not bring justice to the lives you took. All the blood before tonight is on your hands and you will have to settle that score father. We have come as the speakers of the kingdom. We have come as your consequences and as their retribution."

"You have not even once claimed that you think your actions were justified father, only that you were entitled to them." Krutz finally spoke making his way carefully over the blood and bodies."You can do nothing but give excuses for the wrongs you have committed, why you should be allowed and face no repercussions."

"And we stood idle by for too long. It was my daemoness who knocked sense into me, it was the son you gave up on who made me see reason beyond the manipulation." Truen continued.

"There is no saving or redeeming you father, you are a vile puppet to something that wants nothing but suffering and you allowed it because you were drunk on the power," Krutz added standing next to his brother.

"Normally I am not one to agree with judge, jury, and executioner," Lux spoke as she shifted back, adjusting the armor that Mira made for her. "But justice needs to be served."

"We have come to collect your debts." Xai finished stepping back in front of the miserable excuse of a ruler. She placed herself between his legs as he pushed himself as far away from her as he could. "You are pathetic." She hissed quietly as she leaned down towards his face. "You caused this and now you are sniveling and pleading with me like a coward. You have no reasoning for your actions and you thought you would never be pinned down for punishment." She leaned back, standing straight again. Reaching towards him caused the powerless man to flinch as she removed the crown that he wore from his head. Without another word, she stepped back and turned her back to him. Down the steps, she walked calmly and up to her mate. Gently she placed the crown on his head and then dropped into a kneel before him. Following her lead, the others knelt before their new King beside her.

"Rise my Queen. You are the one who shall never kneel before me." Truen bent to reach for his mate, guiding her to her feet once more.

"Before I am your Queen on the battlefield I am your daemon." She answered knowing that their fathers were watching as the other remained knelt.

"No, you will always be my Queen and my partner at the same time, never one more than the other my love," Truen spoke softly, wiping the blood from her face.

"My King, what would you have me do with your predecessor?" She asked carefully.

"Do your duty my dearest champion. Deal with them as you see fit. I know you were told to deliver them to the hall of judgment." He quick his brow at her.

"That is very true. Then I shall follow your recommendation. Watch me if you can." She smiled feeling

469

peace wash over her, this was almost over. She couldn't tell anyone where the moon was in the sky but she knew the nightmare was almost over.

"I could never take my eyes off you even if I wanted to." He promised, the bond staying stead with love and pride. Even faced with killing and war this man never saw her as a monster or a weapon only the woman he was meant to stand beside through it all. Pushing away from the new King once more she faced the man on the throne. The daemoness stalked silently towards the steps, feeling and looking every bit of the predator she was; tail still, fangs bared, eyes alight. He didn't even have a chance to utter a scream as lunged at his terrified form. Before he could even register the pain her claws has already sliced through his skin, rending his traitorous tongue missing from his skull. He would never be able to spew his hateful rhetoric again. Blood rushed from his mouth but that did not stop her from reaching for his throat. One hand around it, and a flick of her wrist snapped the connections in his neck taking his life in a pitiful manner, one that would fit such a pitiful man. His face was forever frozen in shock and horror. With barely an ounce of strength, she tossed the corpse from the chair to land with the body of his daemon. Normally there would be a sense of honor to witness her father die with his Handler, but none of them felt anything but mild disgust at their actions. Not even as the others stood to look at the damage around them.

"It is over." Lui sighed, clutching onto Krutz.

"For now." Xai nodded looking over at her sister. "Pass the message on, the old King is dead, and the new King reigns. We have won."

Once they had a moment to catch their breath they split up once more. Lux went to spread the message and make it back to her own mate. This time it was Lui who stayed with them, unable to let go of Krutz. The red-haired Prince walked as though he was in a daze, not that they weren't all in shock that it was over. The old King was dead finally. One of Xai's tasks as the Hybrid was completed. Three more to go, find the gods, save the gods, and stop the shadow man. They ran into a few strangling guards through the hallways but the daemoness sisters quickly dispatched each aggressor without a second thought. Krutz led them to a door they each recognized, the women looked at each other with more hesitation than they had fighting through to the end of the prophecy. Somehow this was more terrifying than facing a King and his army.

"It is Krutz, I am coming in." The Prince announced. With a call of affirmation, he opened the door stepping through first. Leaving the door open for the others. Truen followed his brother but waited for the daemoness.

"They will want to see you," Truen spoke calmly.

"Who do we want to see?" A woman called back from inside the room. Truen nodded them in. Instead of fighting for their lives only moments ago the two bloodied daemons felt like scared children waiting for rejection as they stepped into the simple room.

"My babies?" Another voice choked. Looking up the two purple eyes women looked into similar lilac eyes full of tears. White hair was genetic in their family, passed down from their mother, and so were their eyes and lean builds. There she was in her glory, a beautiful gown gracing her figure.

"Moletra please tell me I am not seeing things." The other woman asked in a voice thick with emotion. She was older than they remembered but Truen looked so much like her still.

Dark hair yet her eyes were now much paler than they had been. Memories of their childhood getting in trouble flood Xai's mind, remembering eavesdropping on a conversation the Queen had with her mother, the King's spell was taking her eyes little by little every time she fought back against him. Queen Luara never gave up the fight then, it was clear to see in her clouded eyes.

"No, my dearest friend, you are not seeing things. Our daughters have been returned to us." Tears spilled from the elder daemoness' eyes. "You brought them back to us."

"No ma'am they brought us back to you before we were too far lost." Truen smiled, stepping away from Xai to hug his mother close to him. "They found their way here themselves."

"You always told us to never underestimate our mates." Krutz breathed. "Never underestimate Lurra women, it will be your undoing."

"Lurra women are all of our undoing boys." The Queen smiled letting go of her sons. "Now give your mother a hug so I can hold you two as well. You have quite the story to tell us."

"But for now we just want to know for ourselves that you are safe and together the way you are meant to be." Their mother finished. Both younger women looked at each other before they rushed to their mother. Some things even age can not take away from you, including the comfort of a mother's touch.

The sunrise came too soon. Hours of finishing putting to rest any resistance and helping those still fighting their rebellions took the rest of the night. Soon enough though the new King stood in front of his people. He was met with cheers and cries of joy.

"I personally wish to thank you all for fighting with us for this change. I know we lost people along the way and there is no way to make those losses easier but through the grief, we found our strength again. Growing up as the heir apparent I apologize for how long it took the other Princes and me to act but we needed the strength of our own. Even we needed a reason to fight. I found mine and she stands beside me. She fought for all of you because she needed to with no need for recognition long before we left to bring the champion from myth to reality. I would like to introduce you to your Queen and my partner in war and life Xai, the Hybrid."

"Truen." She called into the darkness, she knew her mate was awake. She could feel his sated relaxation had not yet led to sleep as he curled around her.

"Yes, my love." He mumbled into her bare skin.

"What do we do next?" Her life had been non-stop fighting, and now they were on the other side of the journey they didn't think they would survive. Her words made the new King tighten around her.

"Well, we can start simple or we can go head first into the next part of the plans the gods laid out for us."

"What would be simple?" She whispered.

"Well, our mothers want a proper wedding for us all. We also need to get our children fitted for royal clothing once we get them out of our mother's clutches." Xai chuckled at the imagery of trying to get Kato and Hestia away from their grandmothers.

"I would rather fight another army than try and get our children away from our mothers honestly."

"I was thinking the same thing. We also need to free all of those enslaved in the hidden camps. That seems on the easier side." She groaned as he laughed, knowing that would be an incredibly annoying but necessary task. "Let us not forget getting the kingdom back in order; courts, laws, and diplomacy."

"That is your list love, not mine."

"That is true you have to find two other gods and figure out how to free them from the mortal bodies along with stopping someone who claims themselves to be a god. I will take my list, thank you." He groaned, stretching further around her.

"All I can think of is what your grandmother said. 'This will be a war against the silence. A war to redeem those who walked the path with no disregard for those harmed. And most importantly remember what has happened so it shall not happen again. Not all of these will be fought with blood and steel.'"

"We will figure it out together, we will not lose each other again." He promised. "We will fight every war that comes our way."

"I hope we can, we have too much to lose now that we have made it this far." She sighed rolling over in his arms to bury her face under his chin. "We have worked so hard to get here, to get peace, and I want it to stay."

"We will make sure the peace will stay. As they told you Xai, you will see us through this to actual peace and prosperity. You will see this through to the end."

"Hopefully we won't lose everything in the process." She answered.

"We will talk more about this in the morning. We have a long day ahead and we need some rest, my love." Truen smiled, kissing her forehead, trying to calm her racing thoughts. But as she finally succumbed to sleep all she could think about was that the time of peace was to begin, peace and prosperity. Though clouds of foreboding future were upon casting a shadow, a shadow in the silhouette of a man.

Thank you all for sticking through the first installment of the Wars of Chemirica Trilogy.

Hopefully we will see you next time in…

War of Redemption

Made in the USA
Middletown, DE
04 June 2023

31812750R00265